DOKi! Nowadays™

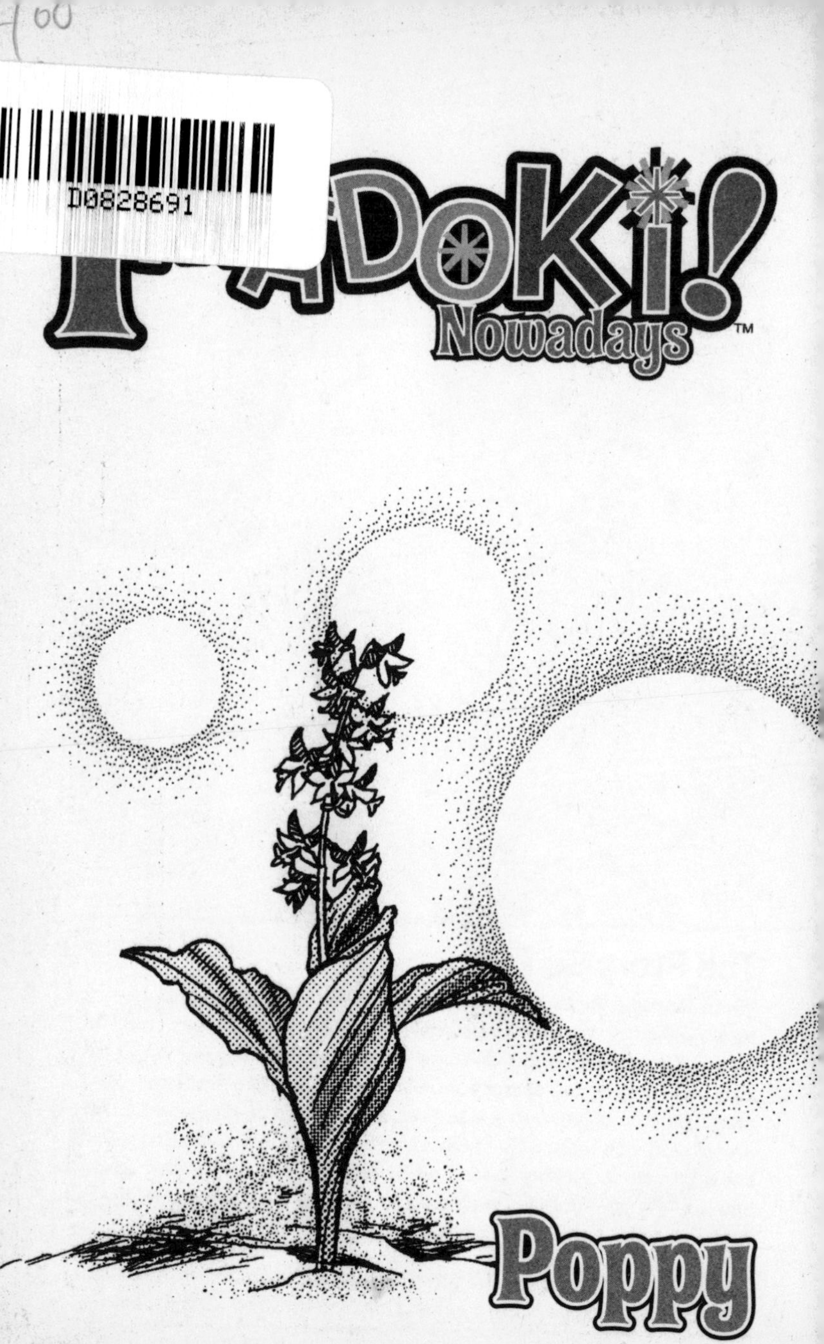

Poppy

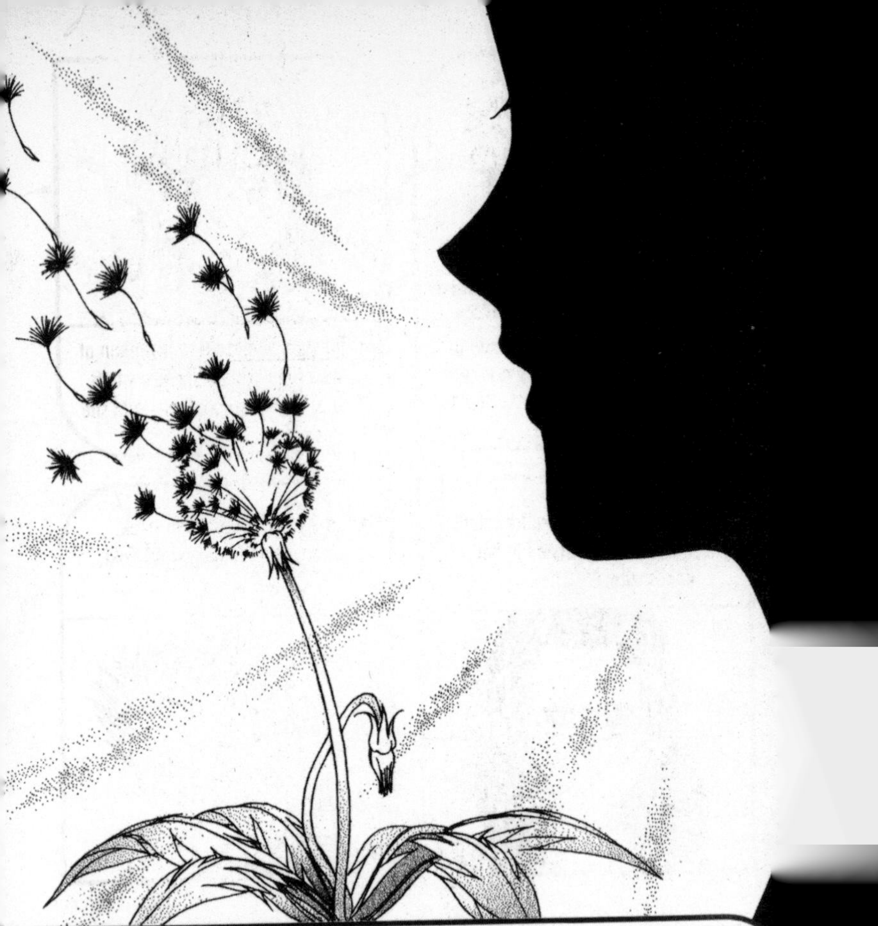

The Story So Far:

When Tanpopo Yamazaki first comes to elite Meio High School from rural Hokkaido, she feels hopelessly out of place among her snobbish classmates. But Tanpopo isn't one to let anything keep her down for long. Koki Kugyo, son of the school's founder and the first boy she meets at school, seems nice at first, only to turn cold whenever others are around, but Tanpopo's charm eventually wins him over. Soon, even the aristocratic Tsukiko Saionji, who once secretly tormented Tanpopo, and Aoi "Flippy" Kyogoku, who used to despise the powerful Kugyo family, come to be her close friends.

On a visit to Koki's house, Tanpopo learns that his older brother, Yoji, disappeared two years before, and that Yoji's former fiancée, Erika

♥ Tanpopo Yamazaki, a freshman at Meio High School. She just wants to enjoy her school life—until she meets Koki.

♥ Koki Kugyo, also a freshman at Meio. Koki comes from a very wealthy family.

♥ Aoi Kyogoku, computer geek, classmate of Tanpopo and Koki.

♥ Tsukiko Saionji, wealthy vixen. Was once determined to become Koki's wife.

Yanahara, is now engaged to Koki and living with him. Even so, Tanpopo and Koki gradually grow closer when they form the Planting Club together. Then Yoji suddenly shows up in Hokkaido, but—to Tanpopo and Koki's disappointment—Erika decides to remain engaged to Koki. With Koki seemingly forever out of reach, Tanpopo decides to date Yoji. But when Yoji realizes that Tanpopo can't forget his brother, he bows out.

Now Koki has decided to take control of his own life, and has broken his engagement to Erika. But before he and Tanpopo can have their long-awaited moment, word comes that Erika has tried to kill herself! On top of that, Tanpopo's grandmother has just left an urgent message on Tanpopo's answering machine...

IMADOKI! NOWADAYS
5

CONTENTS

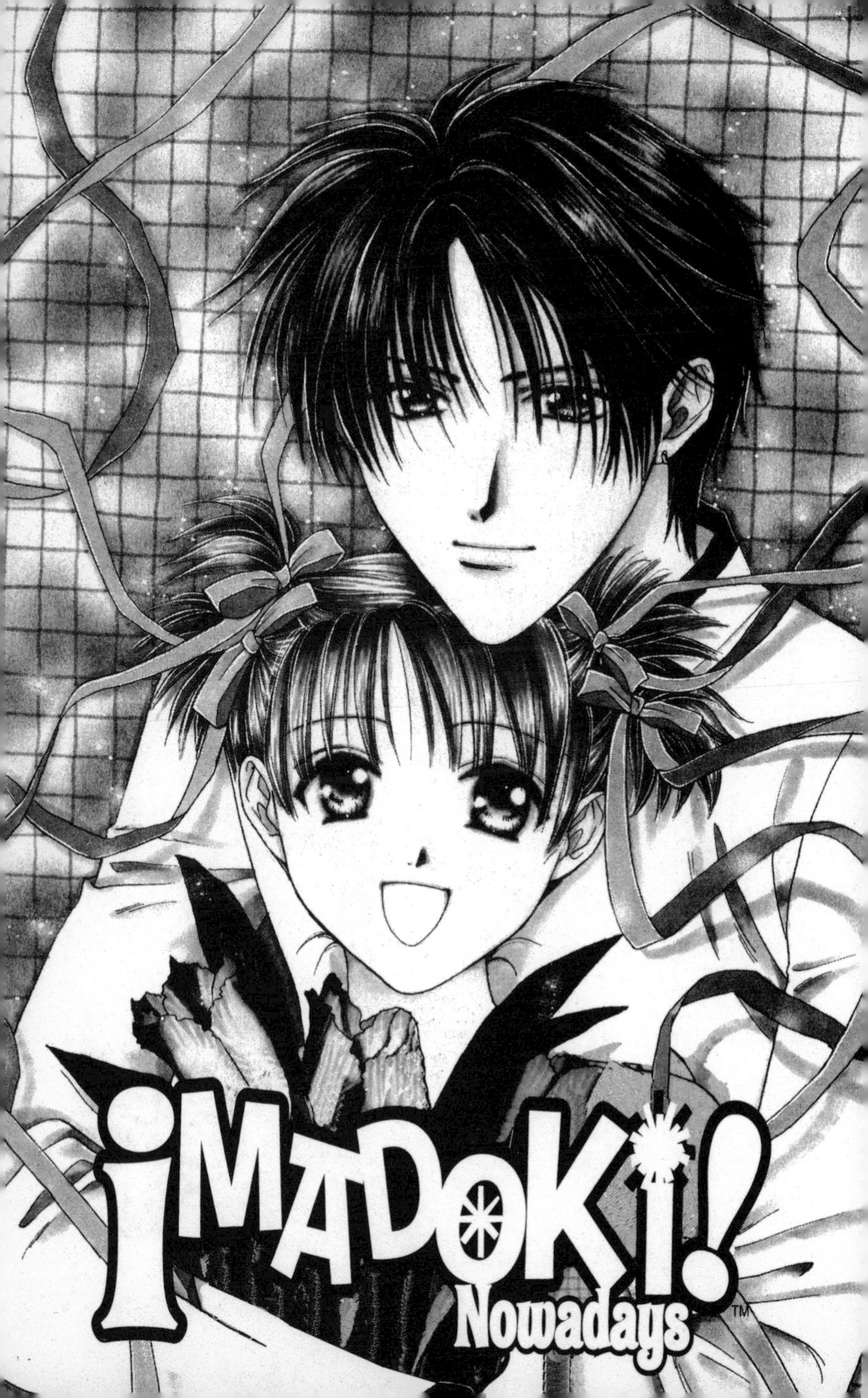
iMADOKI!
Nowadays™

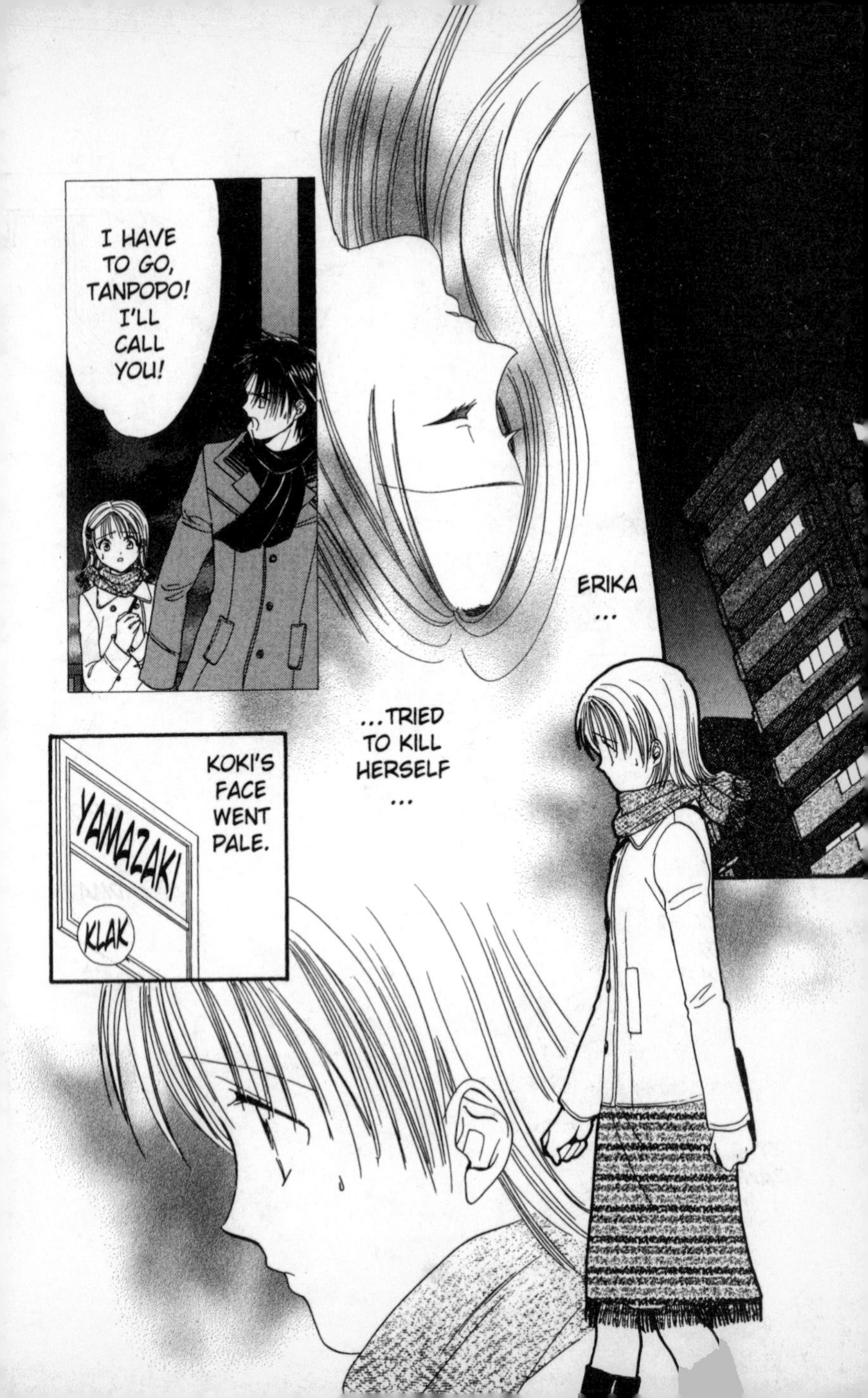
ERIKA ...
...TRIED TO KILL HERSELF ...
I HAVE TO GO, TANPOPO! I'LL CALL YOU!
KOKI'S FACE WENT PALE.
YAMAZAKI
KLAK

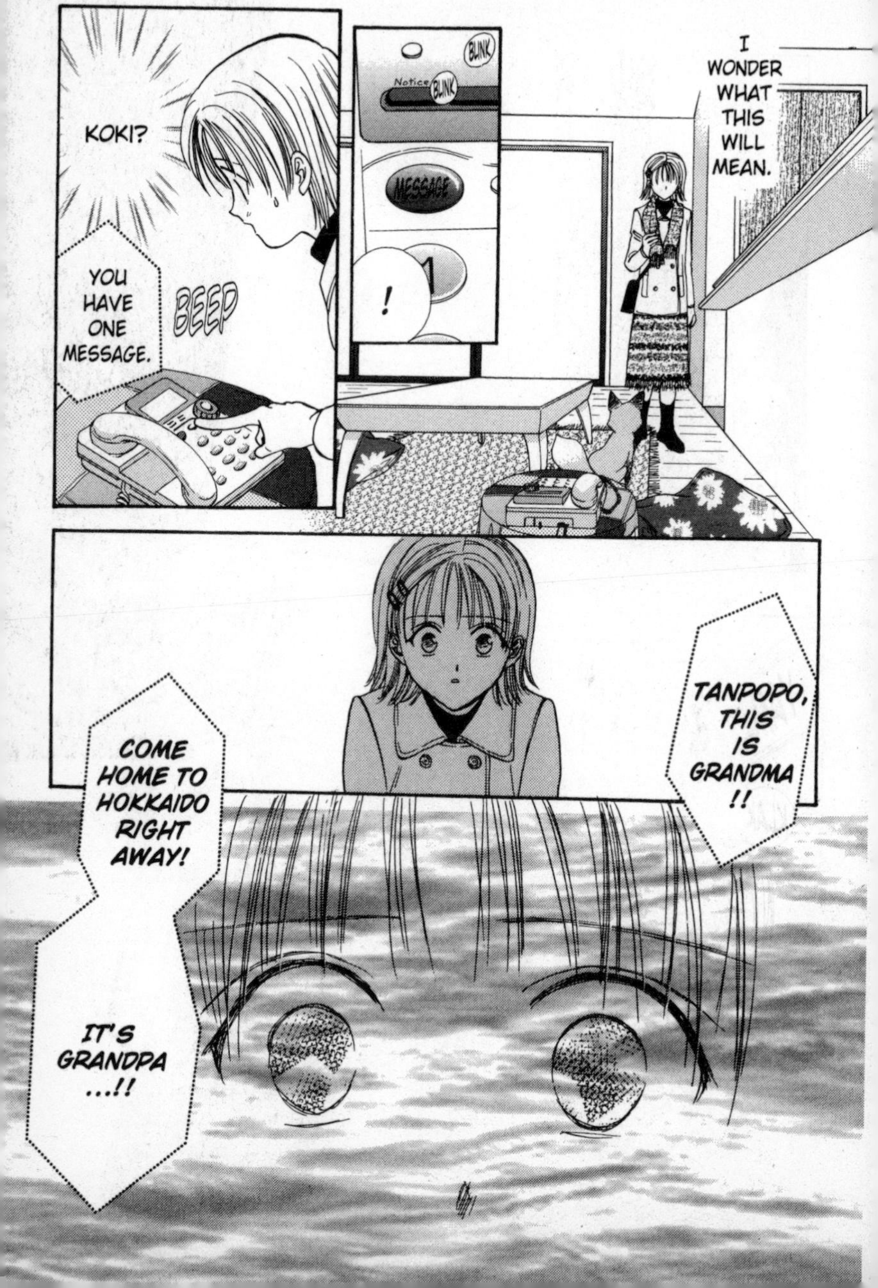
I WONDER WHAT THIS WILL MEAN.
BLINK
Notice
BLINK
MESSAGE
!
KOKI?
BEEP
YOU HAVE ONE MESSAGE.
TANPOPO, THIS IS GRANDMA !!
COME HOME TO HOKKAIDO RIGHT AWAY!
IT'S GRANDPA ...!!

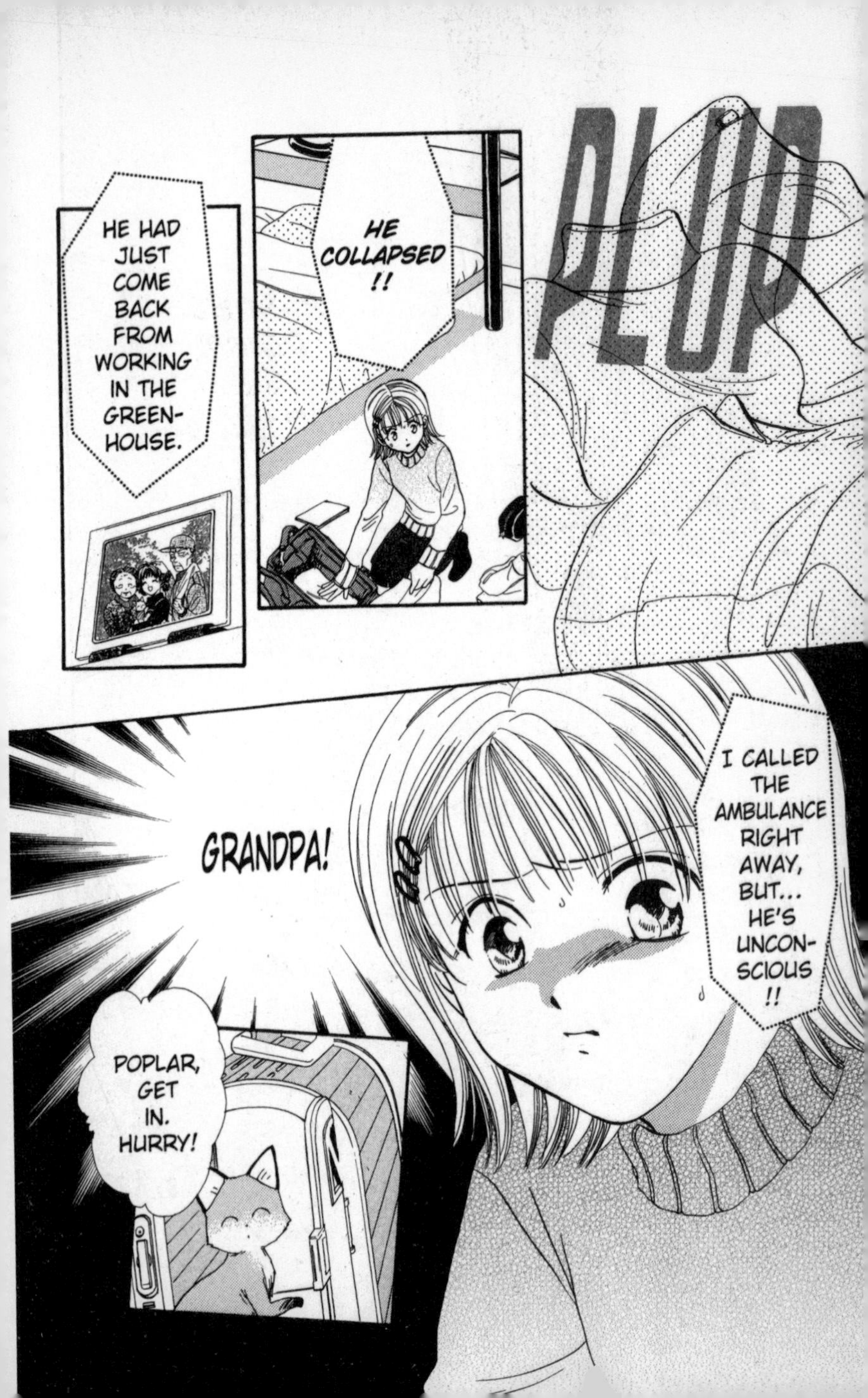
PLOP
HE COLLAPSED!!
HE HAD JUST COME BACK FROM WORKING IN THE GREEN-HOUSE.
I CALLED THE AMBULANCE RIGHT AWAY, BUT... HE'S UNCON-SCIOUS!!
GRANDPA!
POPLAR, GET IN. HURRY!

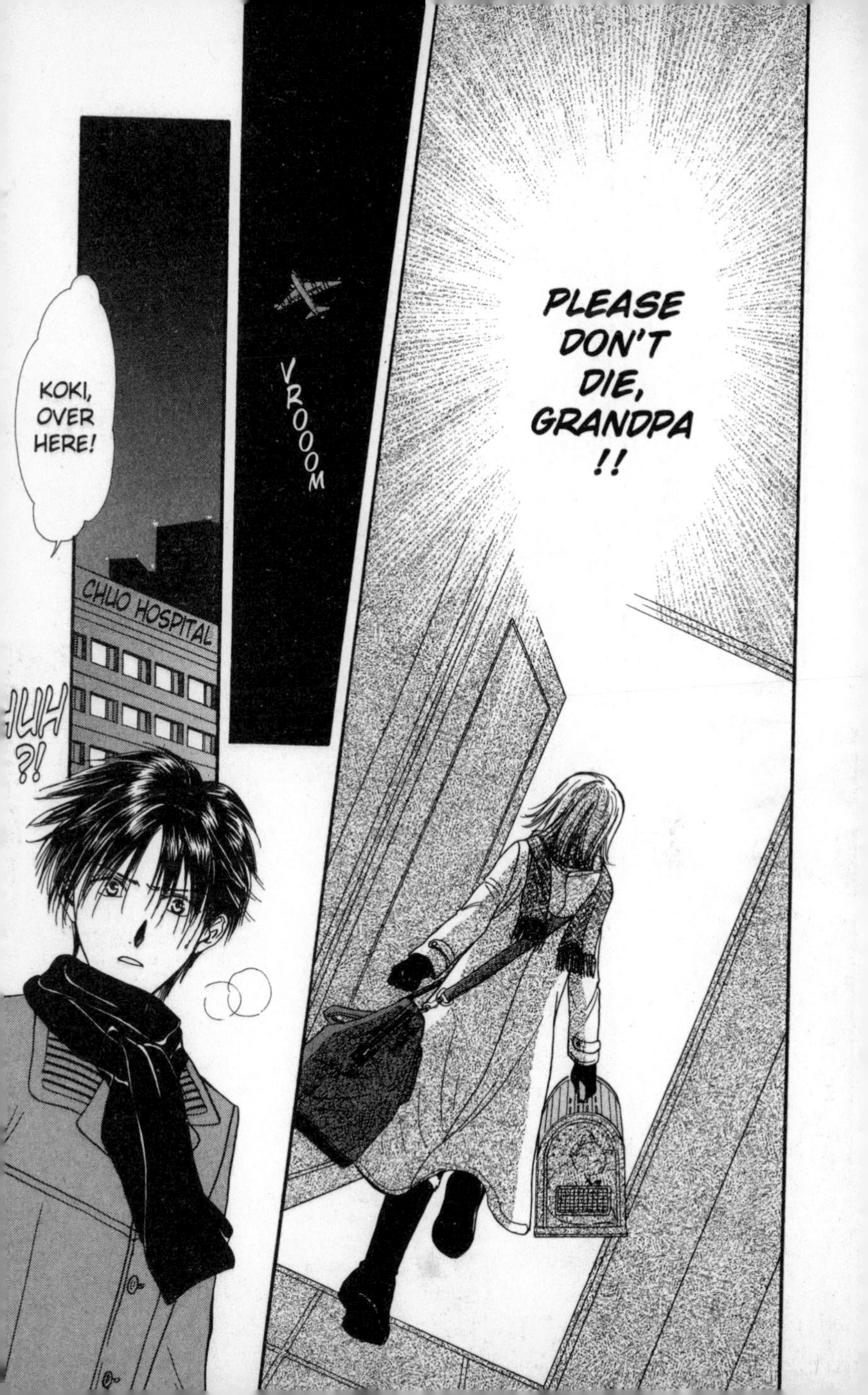
PLEASE DON'T DIE, GRANDPA!!
VROOOOM
KOKI, OVER HERE!
CHUO HOSPITAL
HUH?!

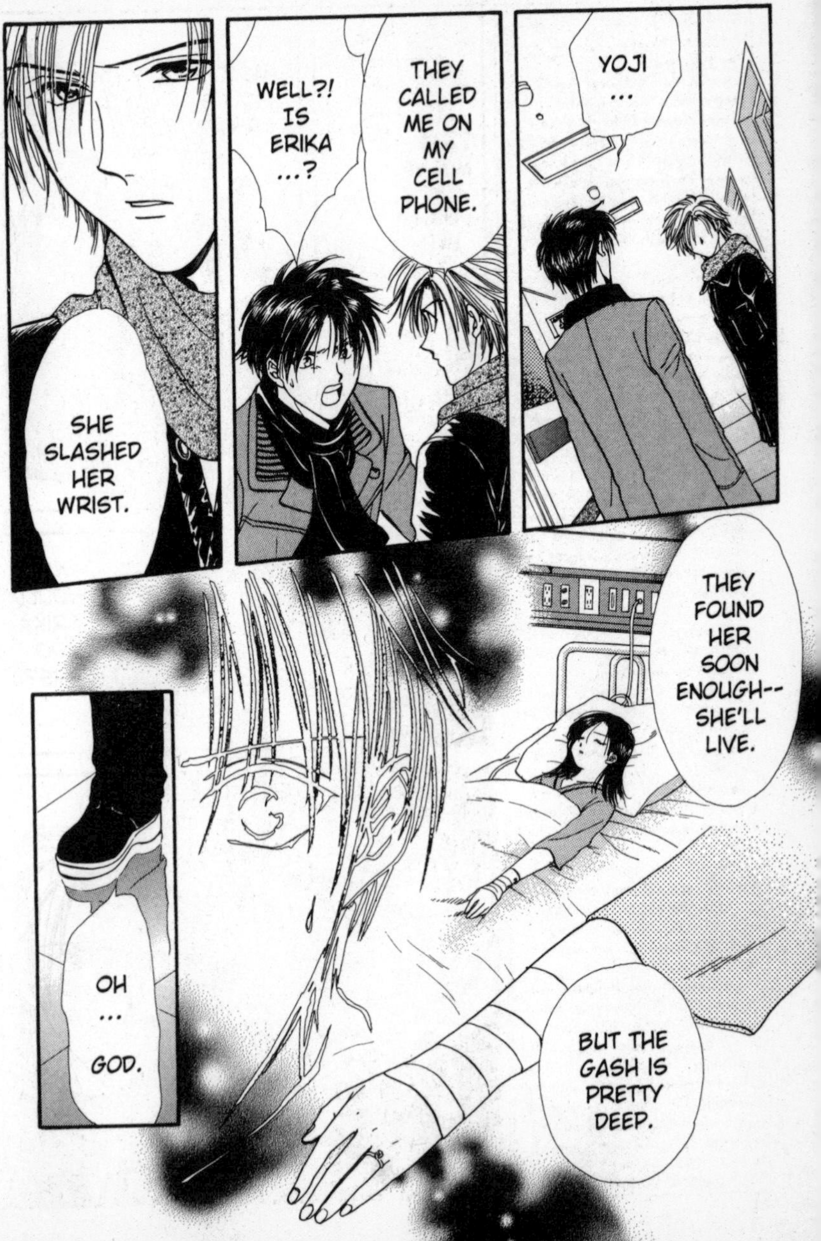
YOJI ...
THEY CALLED ME ON MY CELL PHONE.
WELL?! IS ERIKA ...?
SHE SLASHED HER WRIST.
THEY FOUND HER SOON ENOUGH-- SHE'LL LIVE.
BUT THE GASH IS PRETTY DEEP.
OH ... GOD.

KLIK
GASP
MOM?! HOW'S ERIKA?
SHE'S STABLE AND SLEEPING NOW.
HER MOTHER IS WITH HER.
505
YANAHARA
WHY WOULD ERIKA DO THIS?!
SHE SEEMED SO HAPPY WITH YOU, KOKI...
...

Hey! (What?)
Watase, here! Uhhh...
I'm pooped!!
I haven't had a decent night's sleep in more than a month!! I worked close to 12 hours almost every day, and I still couldn't finish!! My work and schedule seemed neverending! And in the middle of all this, I attended an anime fan event in the U.S.! On the plane, I seriously thought, "I'm gonna die."

Working myself to death?! I don't want that! ☆ But it's got me worried. Secretly, I broke into a cold sweat at the thought. One time, I took to my bed 'cause my whole body felt like lead! I couldn't get up, so I had to have my mother bring me food. How can a daughter be flat on her back in front of her mother?! They said the color had drained from my face.

Just the other day, my assistants kept saying, "What are those dark circles under your eyes?! Did somebody punch you? It looks like it." (smile) And I'd even put on extra makeup to hide it!! (sob) They said, "You look so pitiful. Boss, you're going to die."

It's not even funny!! ☆ But my assistants were really worried.

But when "Workaholic Watase" (uh-oh) gets a day off, I get restless and I don't know what to do with myself. (hee) Heh heh heh... hee hee hee... Get a hold of yourself!!

But listen to this!! About three days ago, I slept eight hours for the first time in a month!! I did it, did it, did it...

After all, when I got back to Japan, I was suffering from jet lag too, so I'd wake up after only sleeping five hours and say, "Ow. My head." It's hard when you want to sleep, but can't! And I had a hacking cough that delivered the knockout punch!! When you cough in bed, stuff gets stuck in your throat, and you have trouble breathing.

Right now, my head and back are throbbing. Sometimes danger spots hurt really bad. I'm at the end of my rope... Ow, now my wisdom tooth is starting to hurt.

Get me to a hospital! ☆

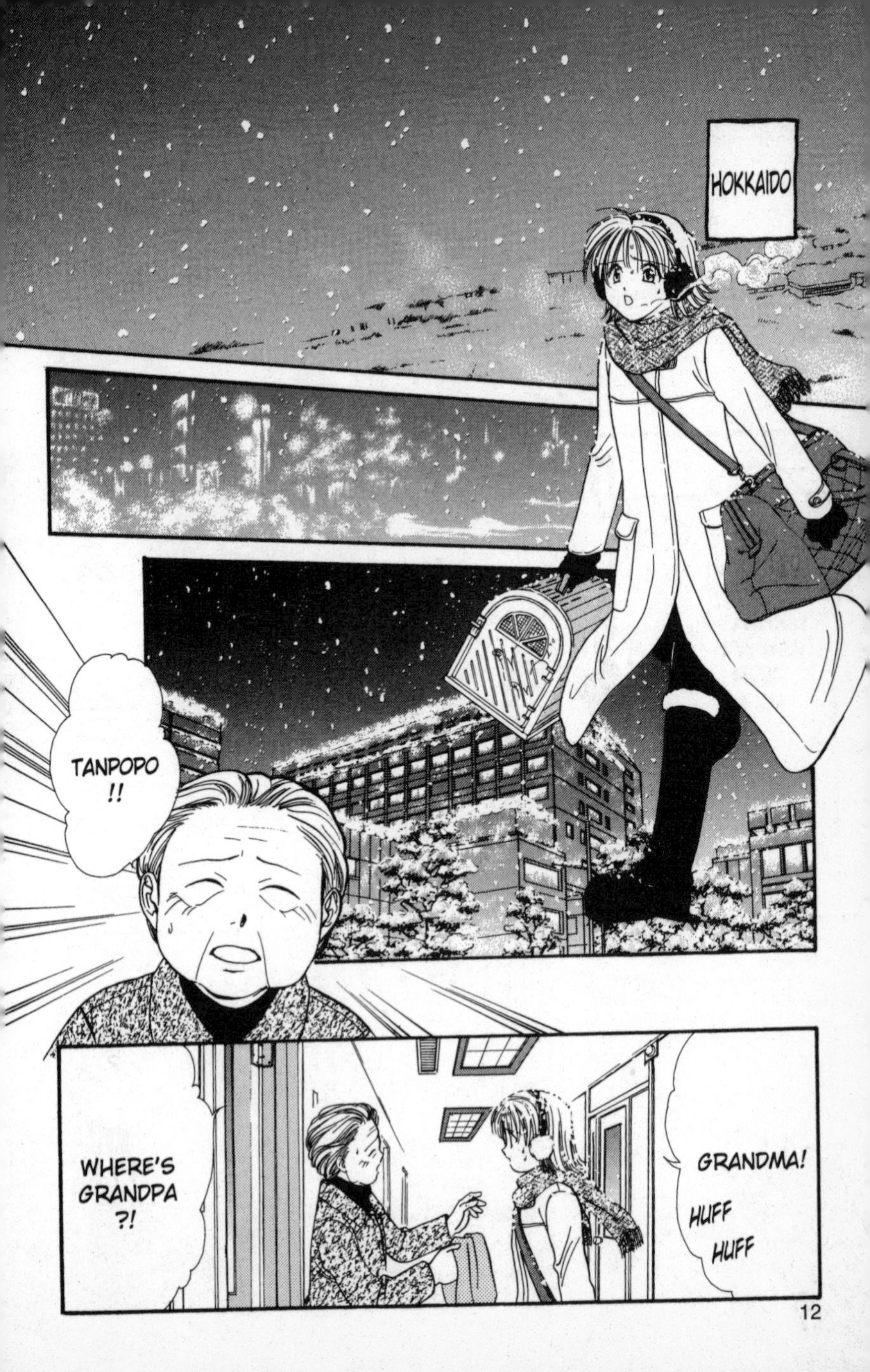
HOKKAIDO
TANPOPO !!
GRANDMA!
HUFF HUFF
WHERE'S GRANDPA ?!

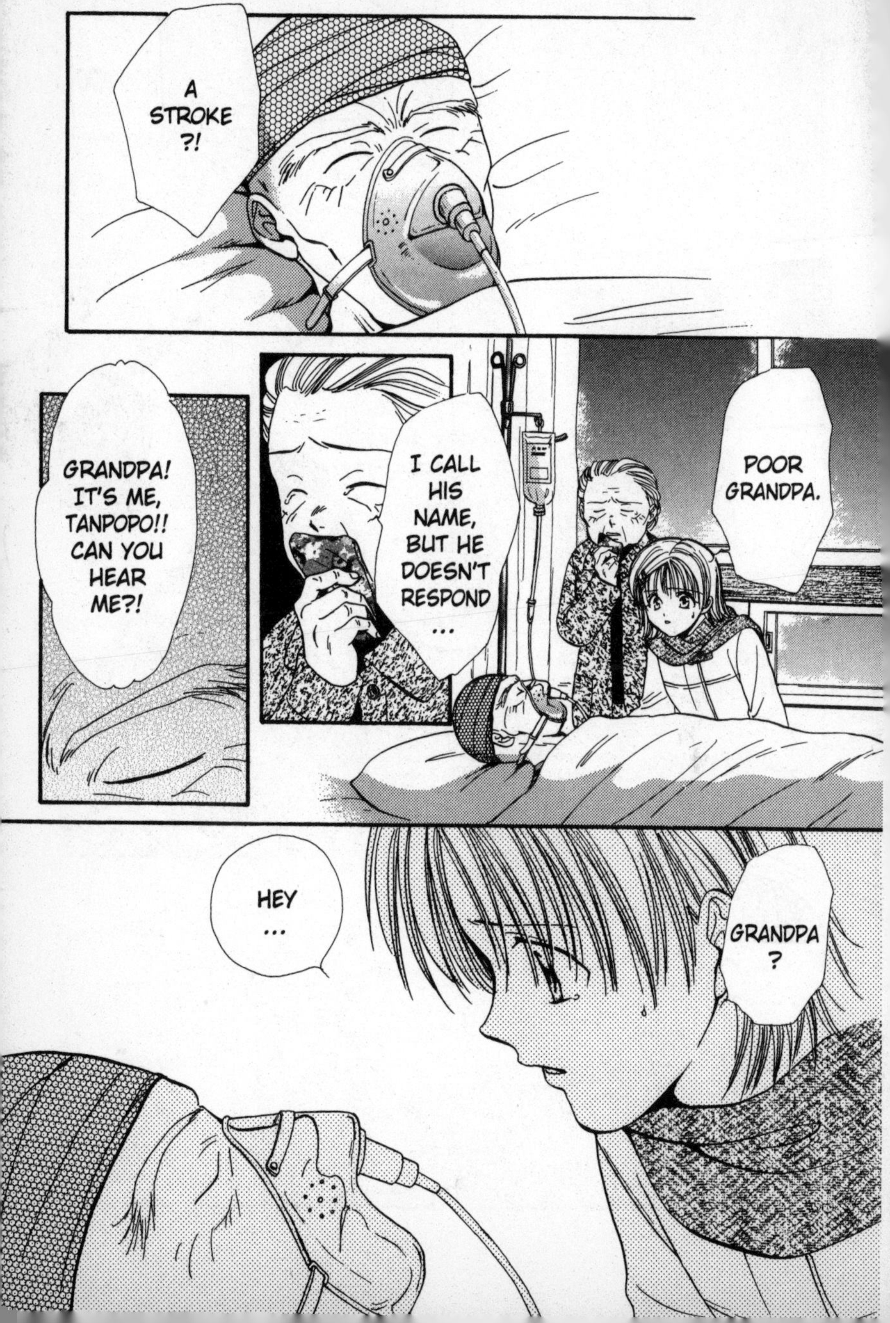
A STROKE ?!
POOR GRANDPA.
I CALL HIS NAME, BUT HE DOESN'T RESPOND ...
GRANDPA! IT'S ME, TANPOPO!! CAN YOU HEAR ME?!
GRANDPA ?
HEY ...

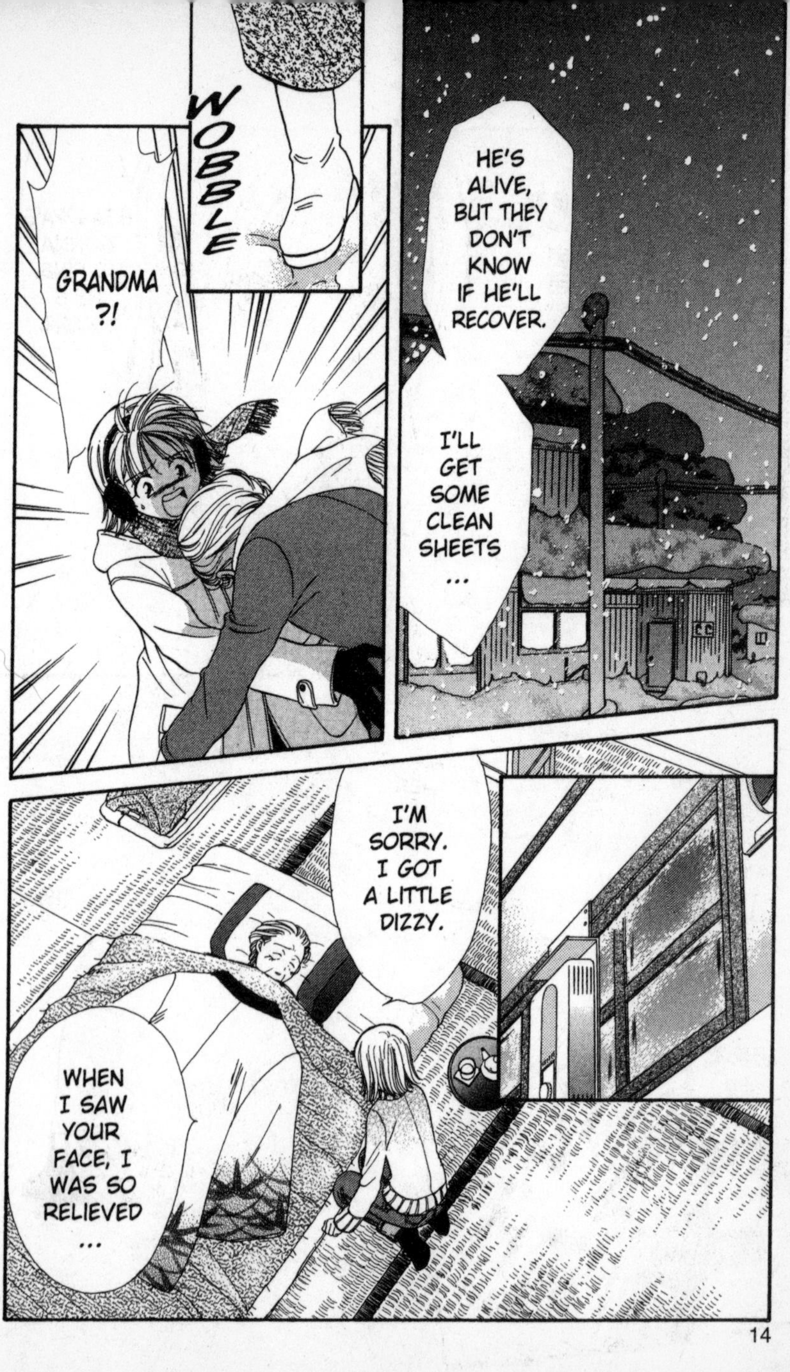
HE'S ALIVE, BUT THEY DON'T KNOW IF HE'LL RECOVER.
I'LL GET SOME CLEAN SHEETS ...
WOBBLE
GRANDMA ?!
I'M SORRY. I GOT A LITTLE DIZZY.
WHEN I SAW YOUR FACE, I WAS SO RELIEVED ...

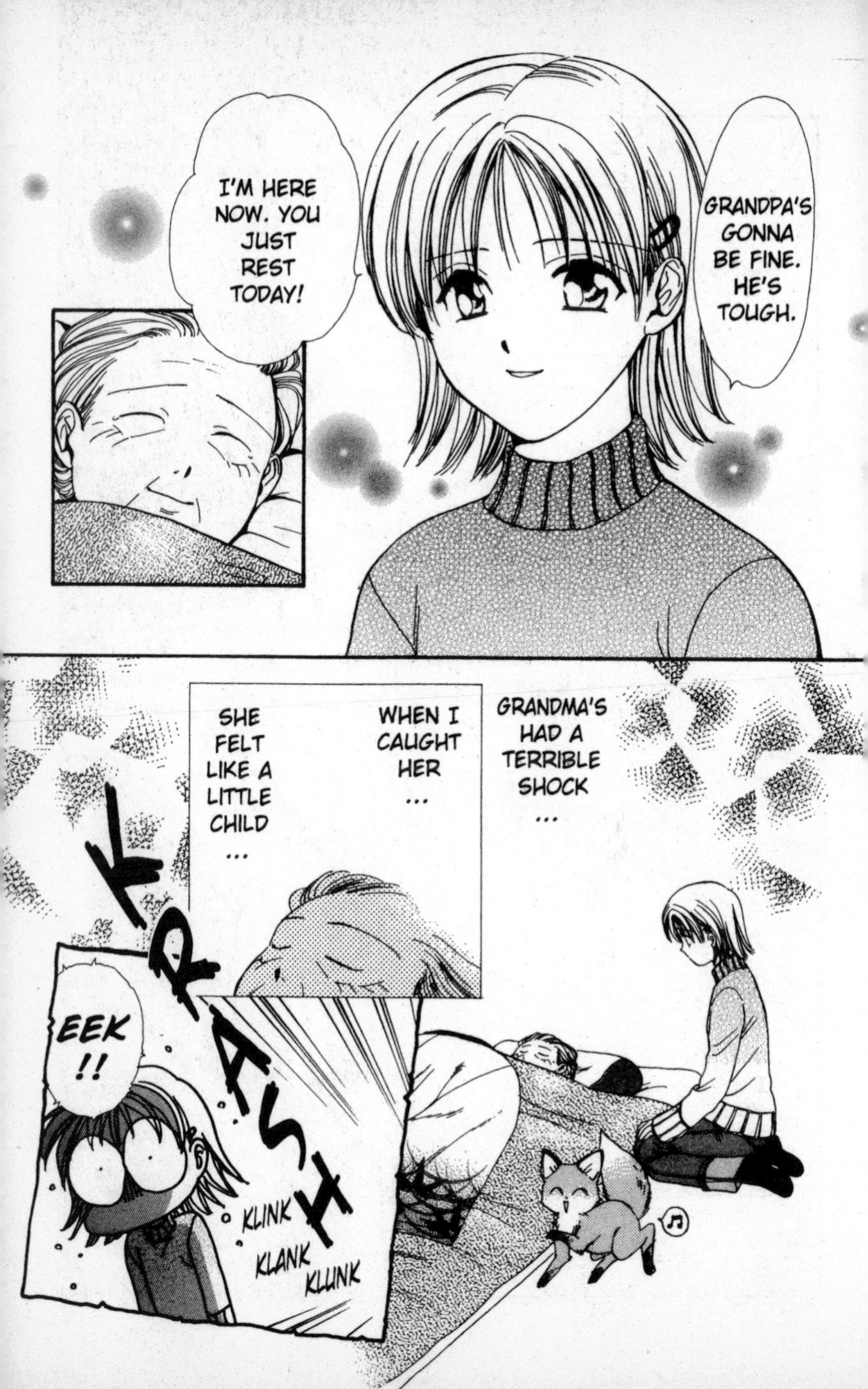
GRANDPA'S GONNA BE FINE. HE'S TOUGH.
I'M HERE NOW. YOU JUST REST TODAY!
GRANDMA'S HAD A TERRIBLE SHOCK ...
WHEN I CAUGHT HER ...
SHE FELT LIKE A LITTLE CHILD ...
KRASH
EEK !!
KLINK
KLANK
KLUNK

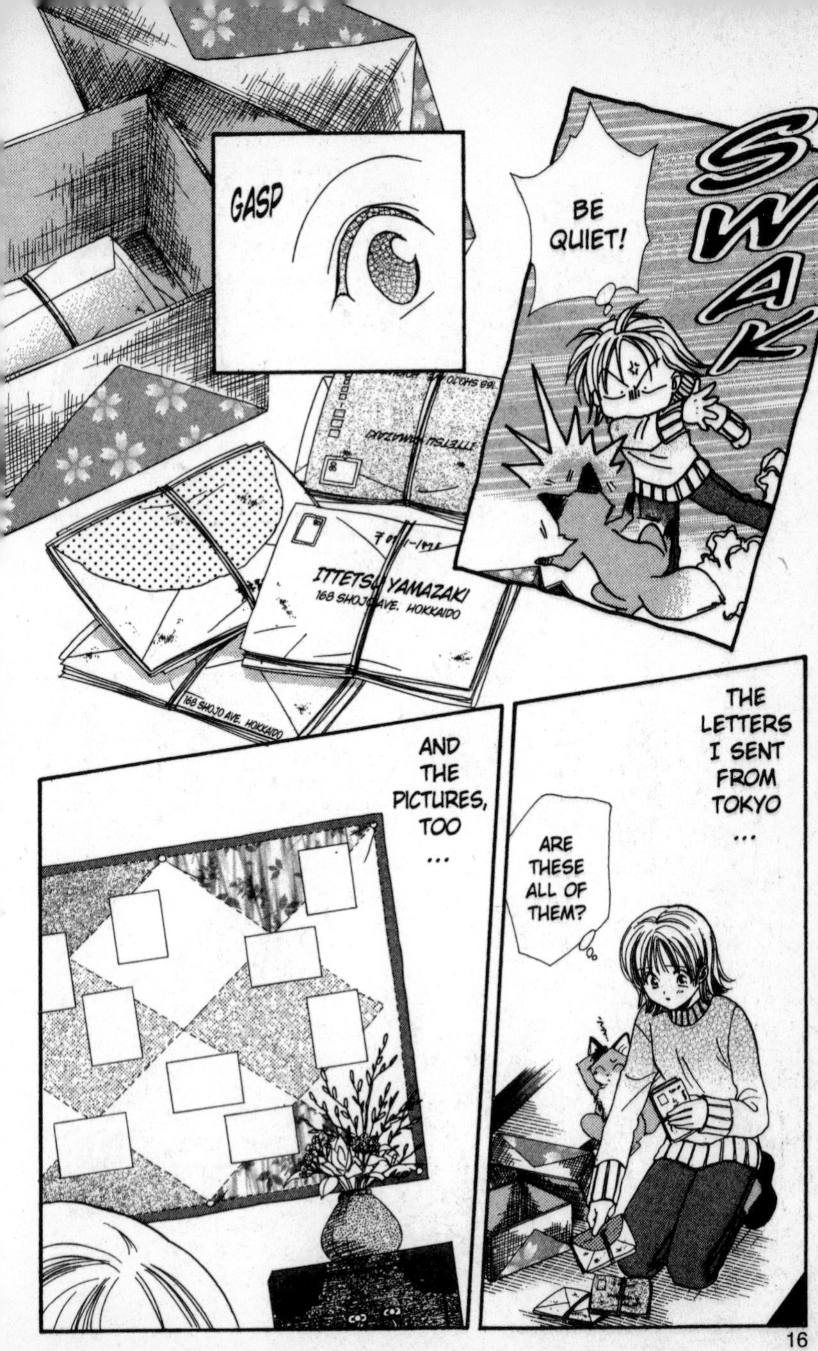
BE QUIET!
SWAK
GASP
ITTETSU YAMAZAKI
168 SHOJO AVE. HOKKAIDO
THE LETTERS I SENT FROM TOKYO ...
ARE THESE ALL OF THEM?
AND THE PICTURES, TOO ...

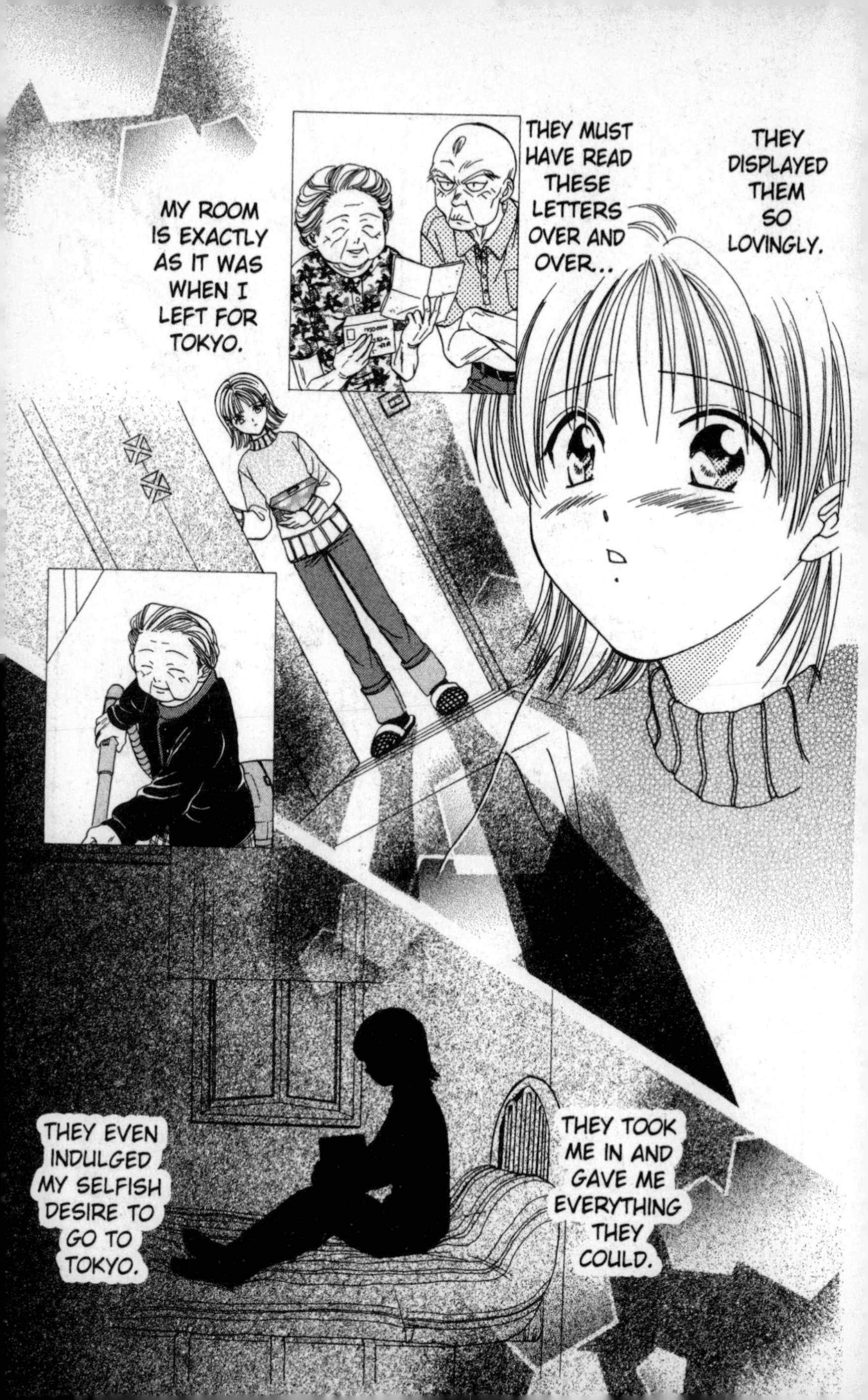
THEY DISPLAYED THEM SO LOVINGLY.
THEY MUST HAVE READ THESE LETTERS OVER AND OVER...
MY ROOM IS EXACTLY AS IT WAS WHEN I LEFT FOR TOKYO.
THEY TOOK ME IN AND GAVE ME EVERYTHING THEY COULD.
THEY EVEN INDULGED MY SELFISH DESIRE TO GO TO TOKYO.

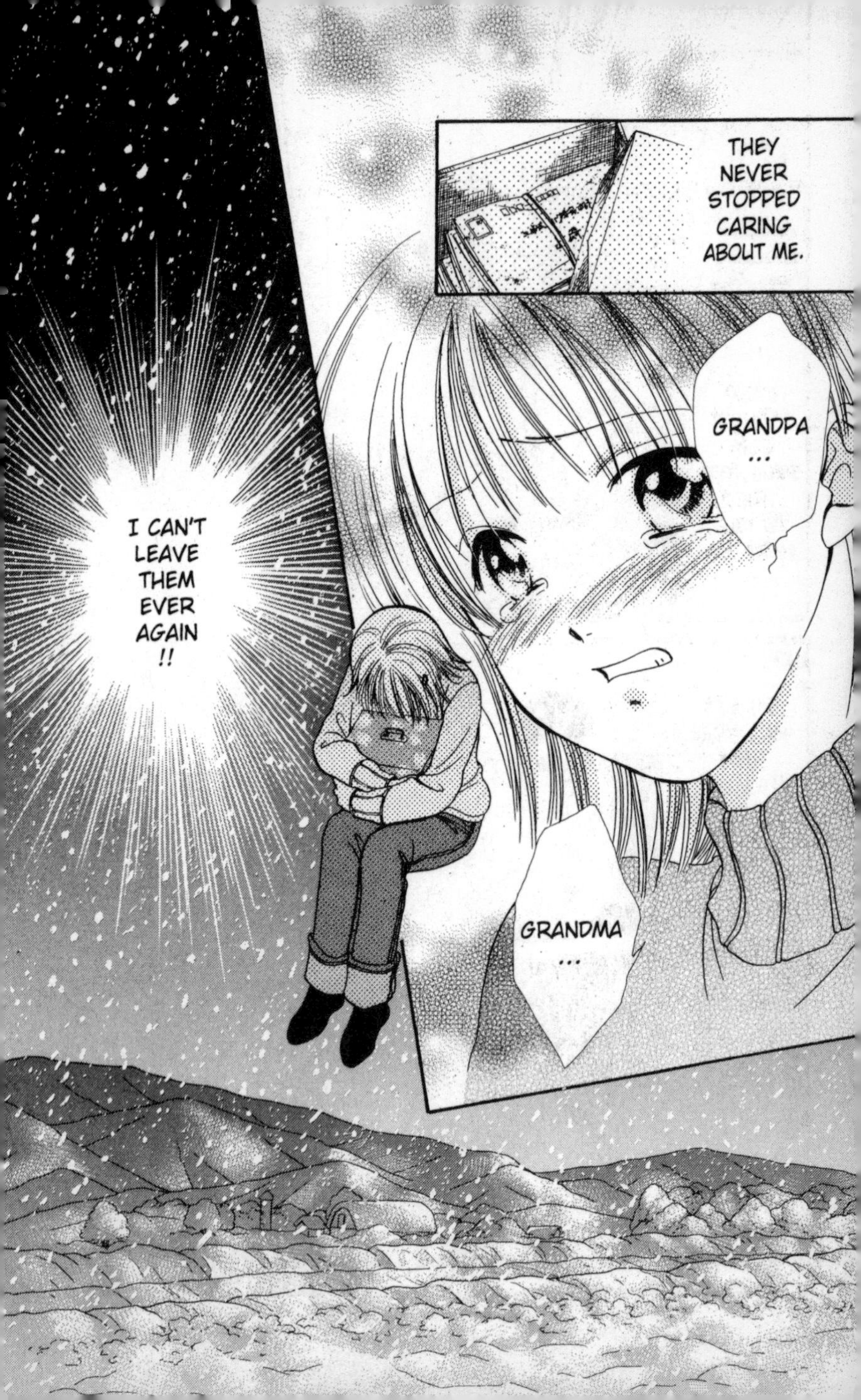
THEY NEVER STOPPED CARING ABOUT ME.
GRANDPA ...
GRANDMA ...
I CAN'T LEAVE THEM EVER AGAIN !!

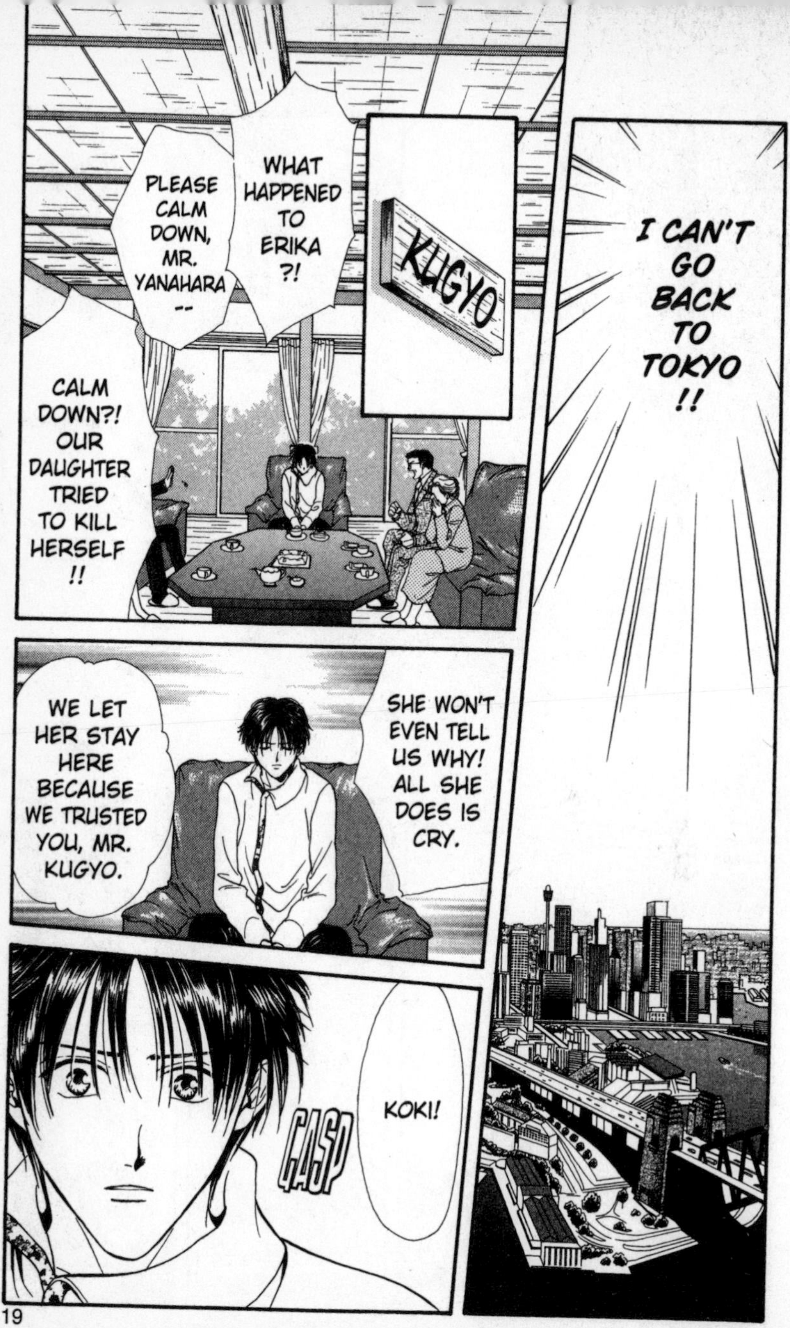
I CAN'T GO BACK TO TOKYO!!
KUGYO
WHAT HAPPENED TO ERIKA?!
PLEASE CALM DOWN, MR. YANAHARA--
CALM DOWN?! OUR DAUGHTER TRIED TO KILL HERSELF!!
SHE WON'T EVEN TELL US WHY! ALL SHE DOES IS CRY.
WE LET HER STAY HERE BECAUSE WE TRUSTED YOU, MR. KUGYO.
KOKI!
GASP

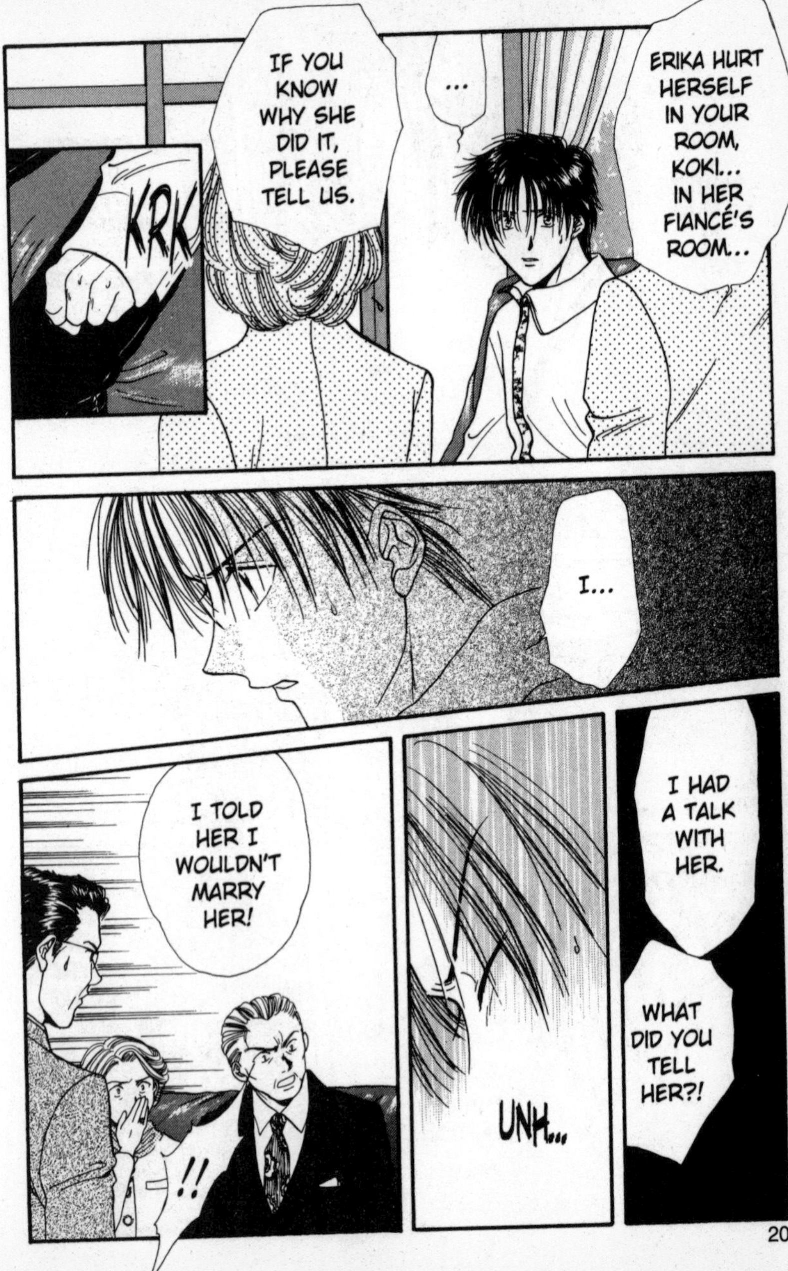
ERIKA HURT HERSELF IN YOUR ROOM, KOKI... IN HER FIANCÉ'S ROOM...
...
IF YOU KNOW WHY SHE DID IT, PLEASE TELL US.
KRK
I...
I HAD A TALK WITH HER.
WHAT DID YOU TELL HER?!
UNH...
I TOLD HER I WOULDN'T MARRY HER!
!!

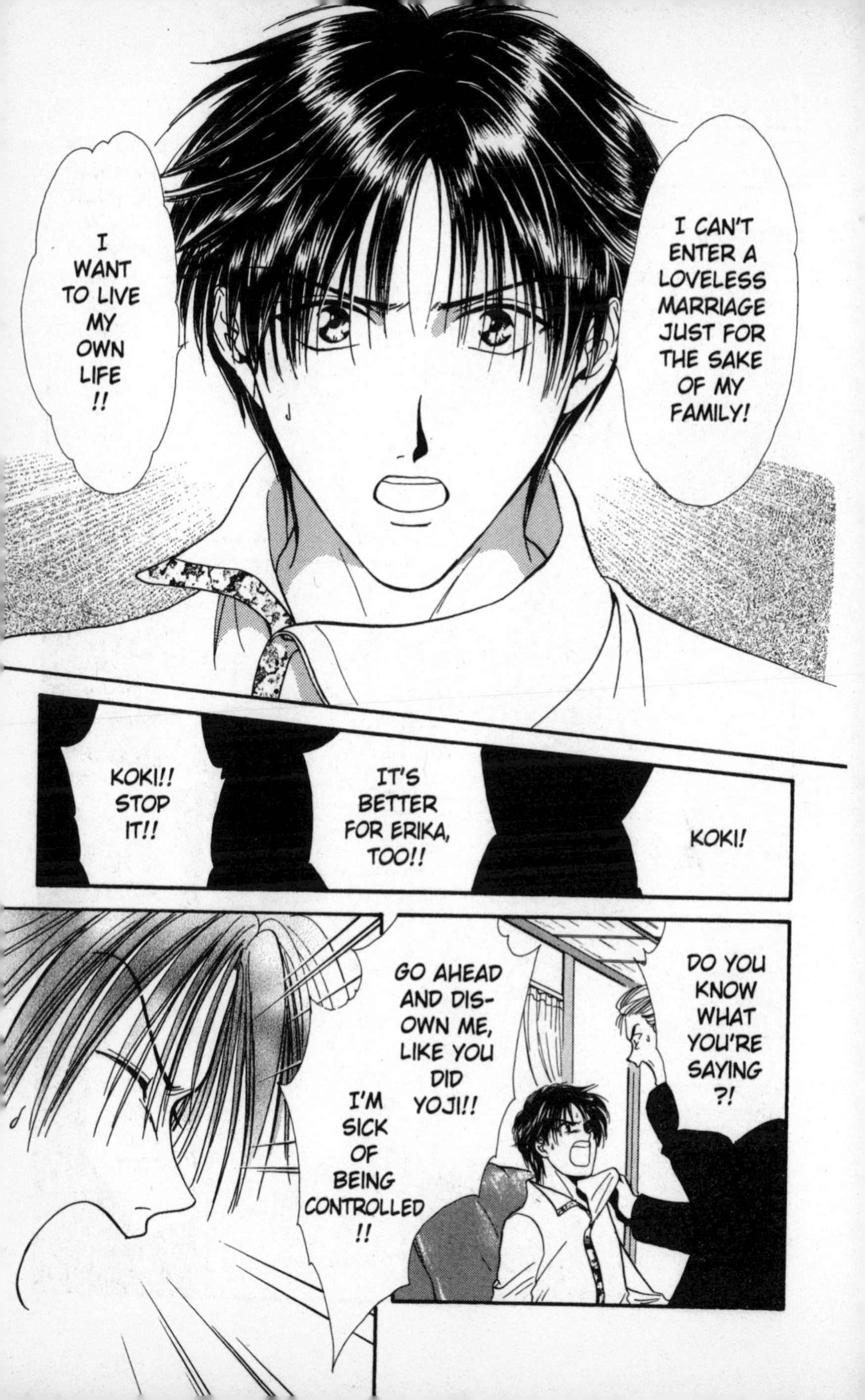
I CAN'T ENTER A LOVELESS MARRIAGE JUST FOR THE SAKE OF MY FAMILY!
I WANT TO LIVE MY OWN LIFE!!
KOKI!
IT'S BETTER FOR ERIKA, TOO!!
KOKI!! STOP IT!!
DO YOU KNOW WHAT YOU'RE SAYING?!
GO AHEAD AND DISOWN ME, LIKE YOU DID YOJI!!
I'M SICK OF BEING CONTROLLED!!

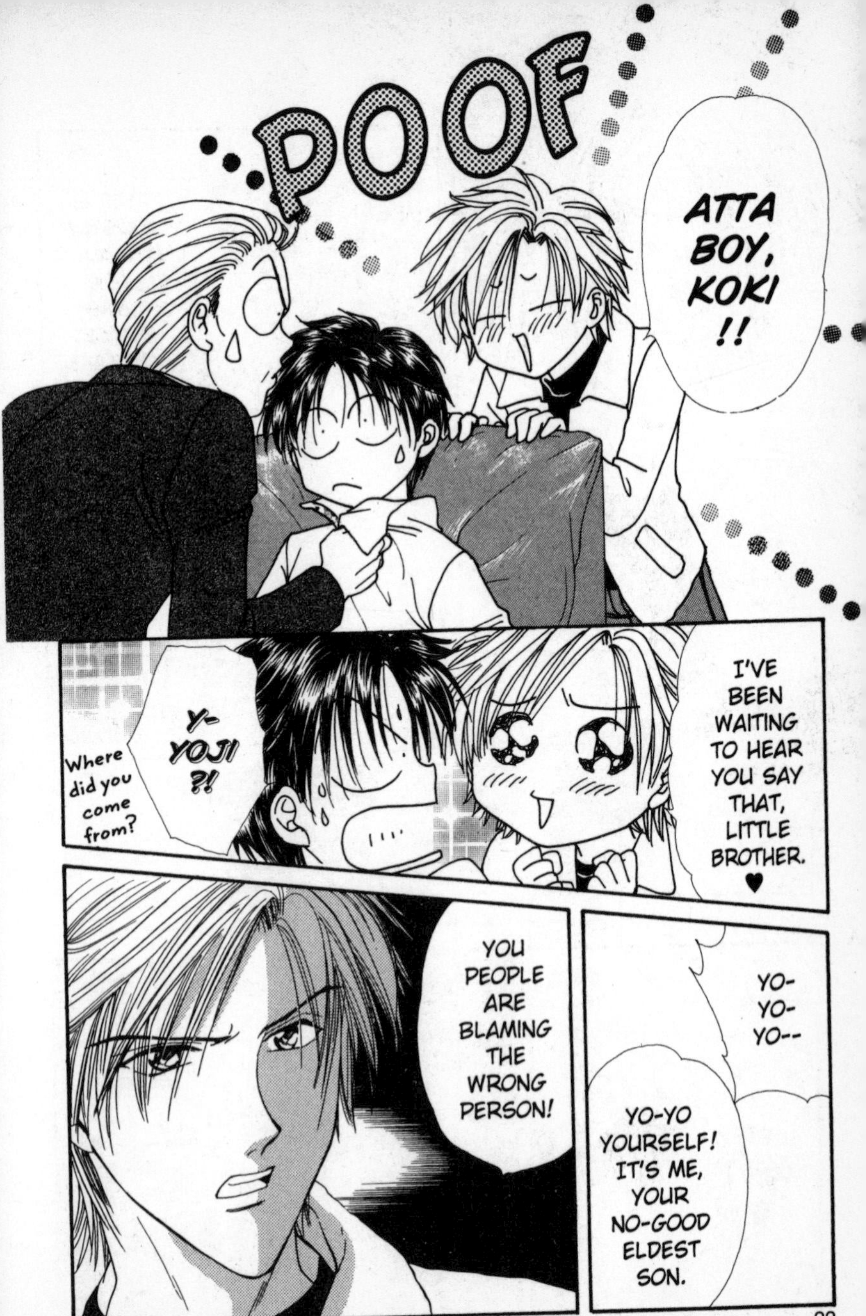
ATTA BOY, KOKI!!
POOF
I'VE BEEN WAITING TO HEAR YOU SAY THAT, LITTLE BROTHER. ♥
Y-YOJI?!
Where did you come from?
YO-YO-YO--
YO-YO YOURSELF! IT'S ME, YOUR NO-GOOD ELDEST SON.
YOU PEOPLE ARE BLAMING THE WRONG PERSON!

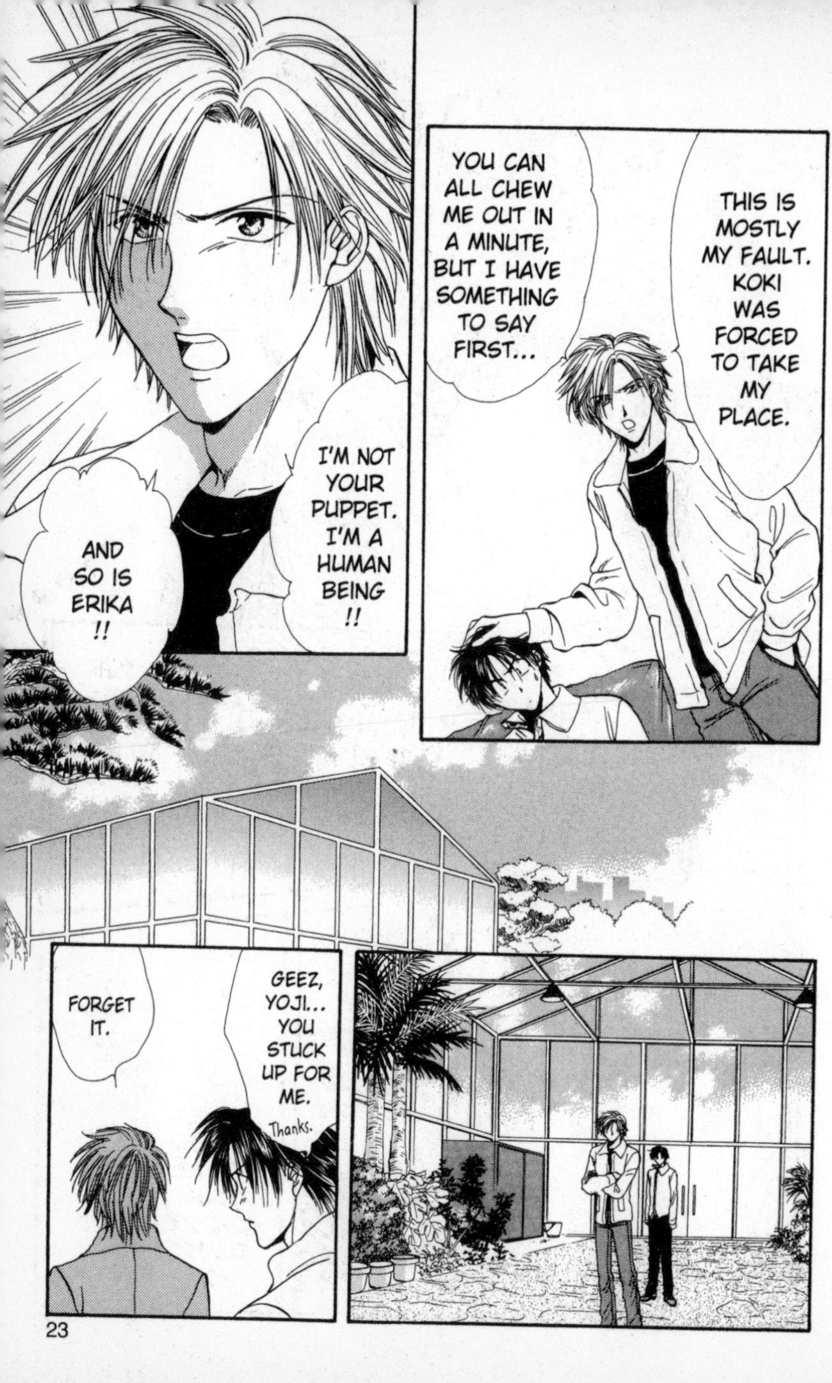
THIS IS MOSTLY MY FAULT. KOKI WAS FORCED TO TAKE MY PLACE.
YOU CAN ALL CHEW ME OUT IN A MINUTE, BUT I HAVE SOMETHING TO SAY FIRST...
I'M NOT YOUR PUPPET. I'M A HUMAN BEING!!
AND SO IS ERIKA!!
GEEZ, YOJI... YOU STUCK UP FOR ME.
Thanks.
FORGET IT.

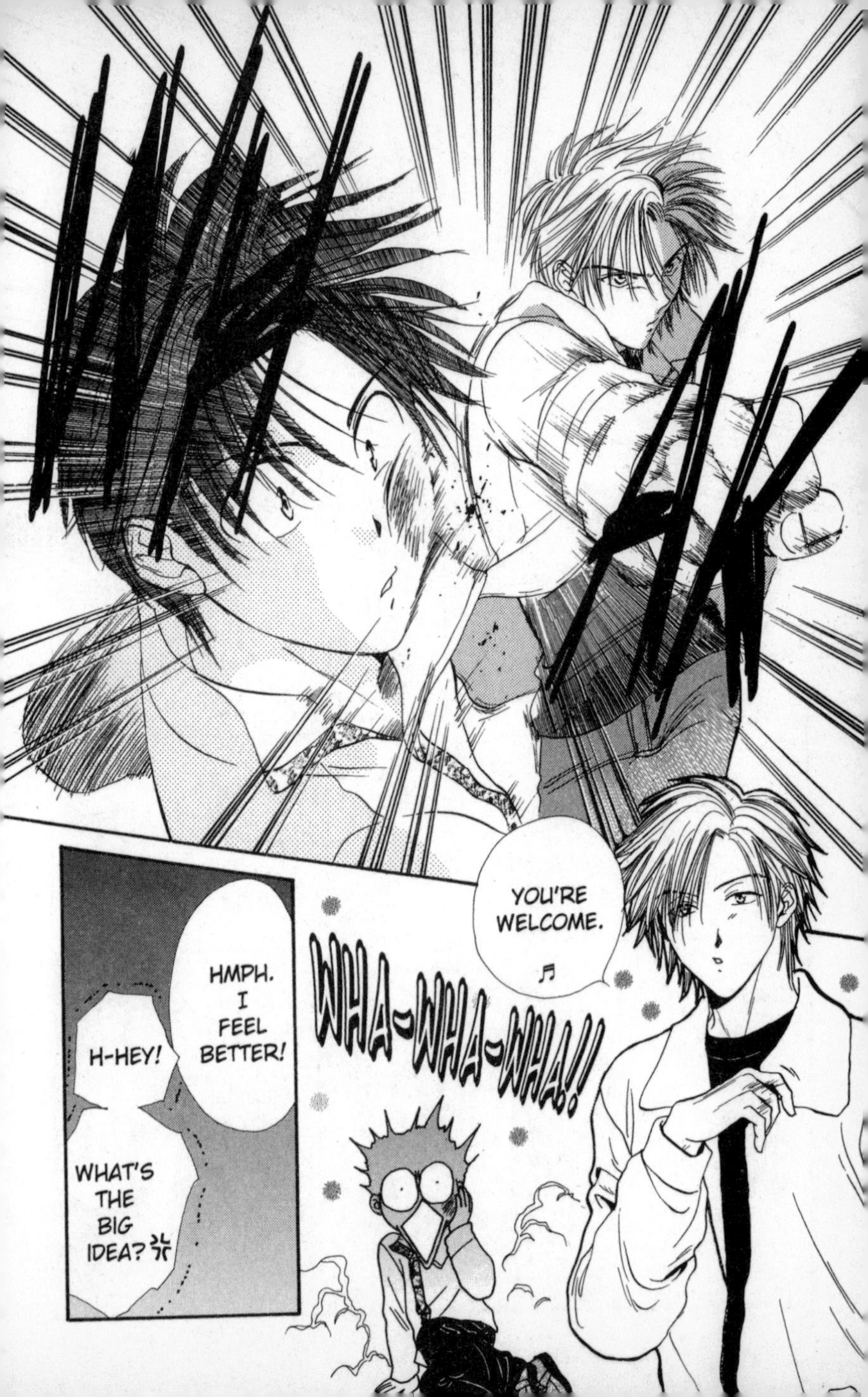
YOU'RE WELCOME. ♬
WHA-WHA-WHA!!
HMPH. I FEEL BETTER!
H-HEY!
WHAT'S THE BIG IDEA?

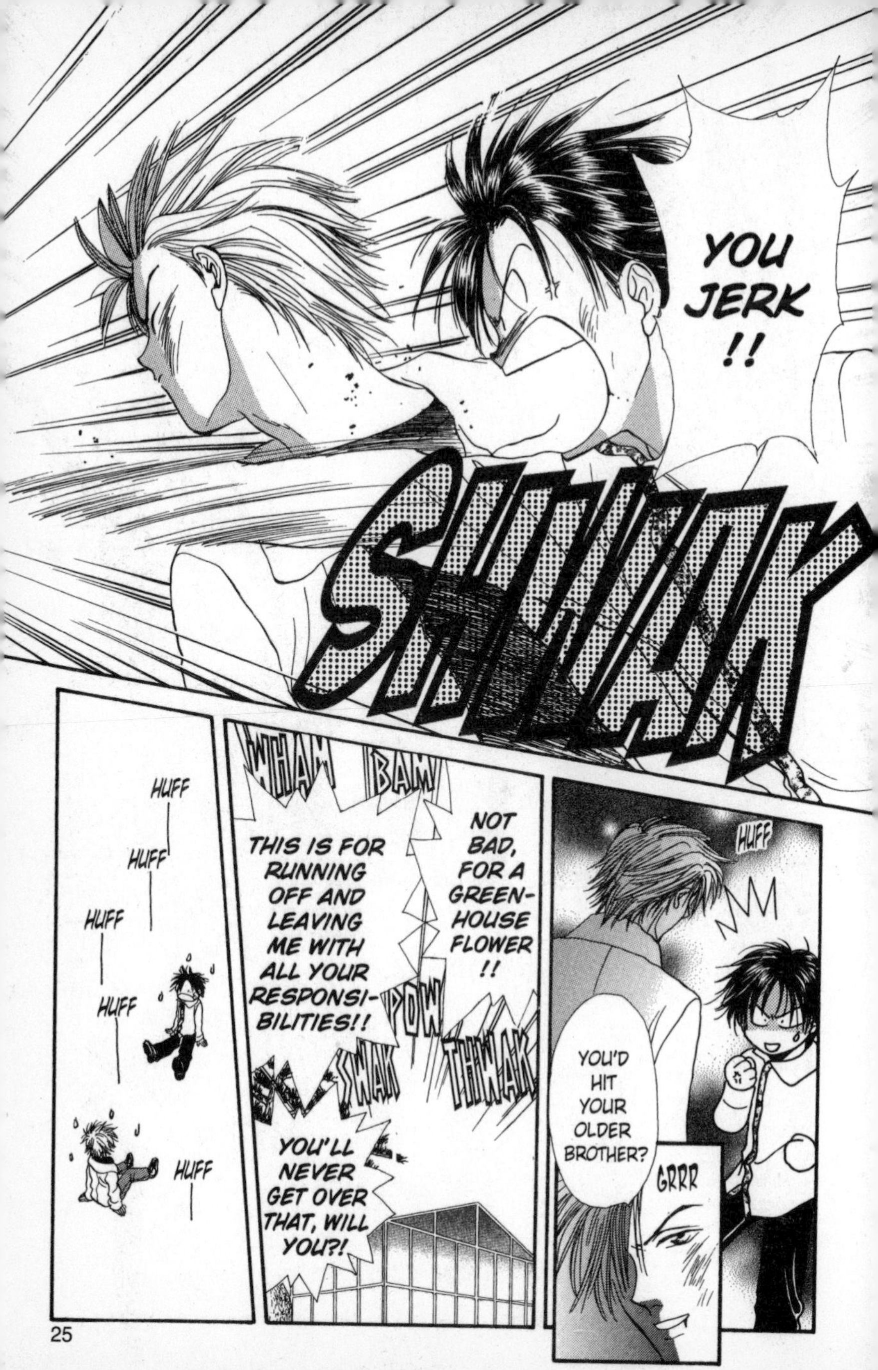
YOU JERK!!
HUFF
YOU'D HIT YOUR OLDER BROTHER?
GRRR
WHAM
BAM
NOT BAD, FOR A GREEN-HOUSE FLOWER!!
THIS IS FOR RUNNING OFF AND LEAVING ME WITH ALL YOUR RESPONSI-BILITIES!!
POW
THWAK
SWAK
YOU'LL NEVER GET OVER THAT, WILL YOU?!
HUFF
HUFF
HUFF
HUFF
HUFF

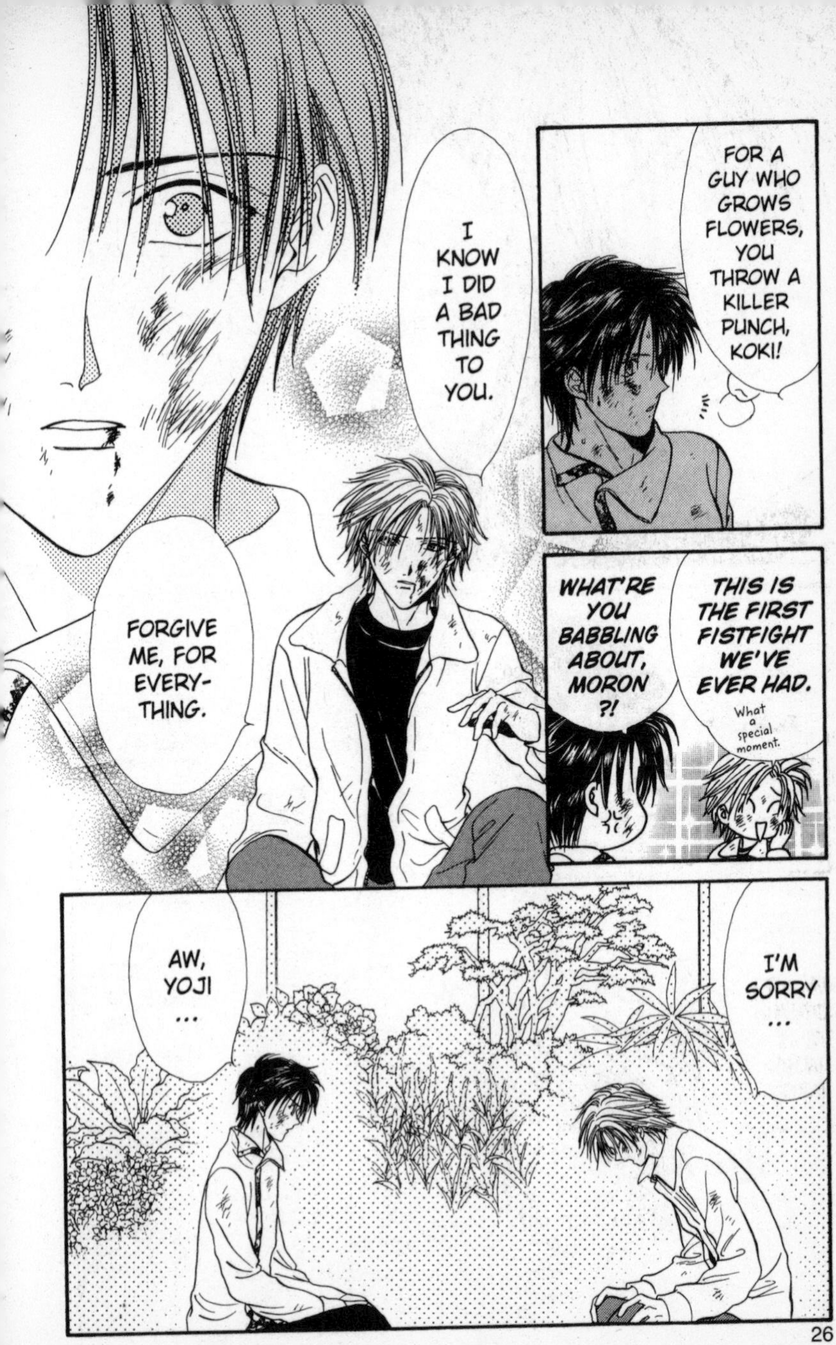

FOR A GUY WHO GROWS FLOWERS, YOU THROW A KILLER PUNCH, KOKI!
THIS IS THE FIRST FISTFIGHT WE'VE EVER HAD.
What a special moment.
WHAT'RE YOU BABBLING ABOUT, MORON ?!
I KNOW I DID A BAD THING TO YOU.
FORGIVE ME, FOR EVERY-THING.
I'M SORRY ...
AW, YOJI ...

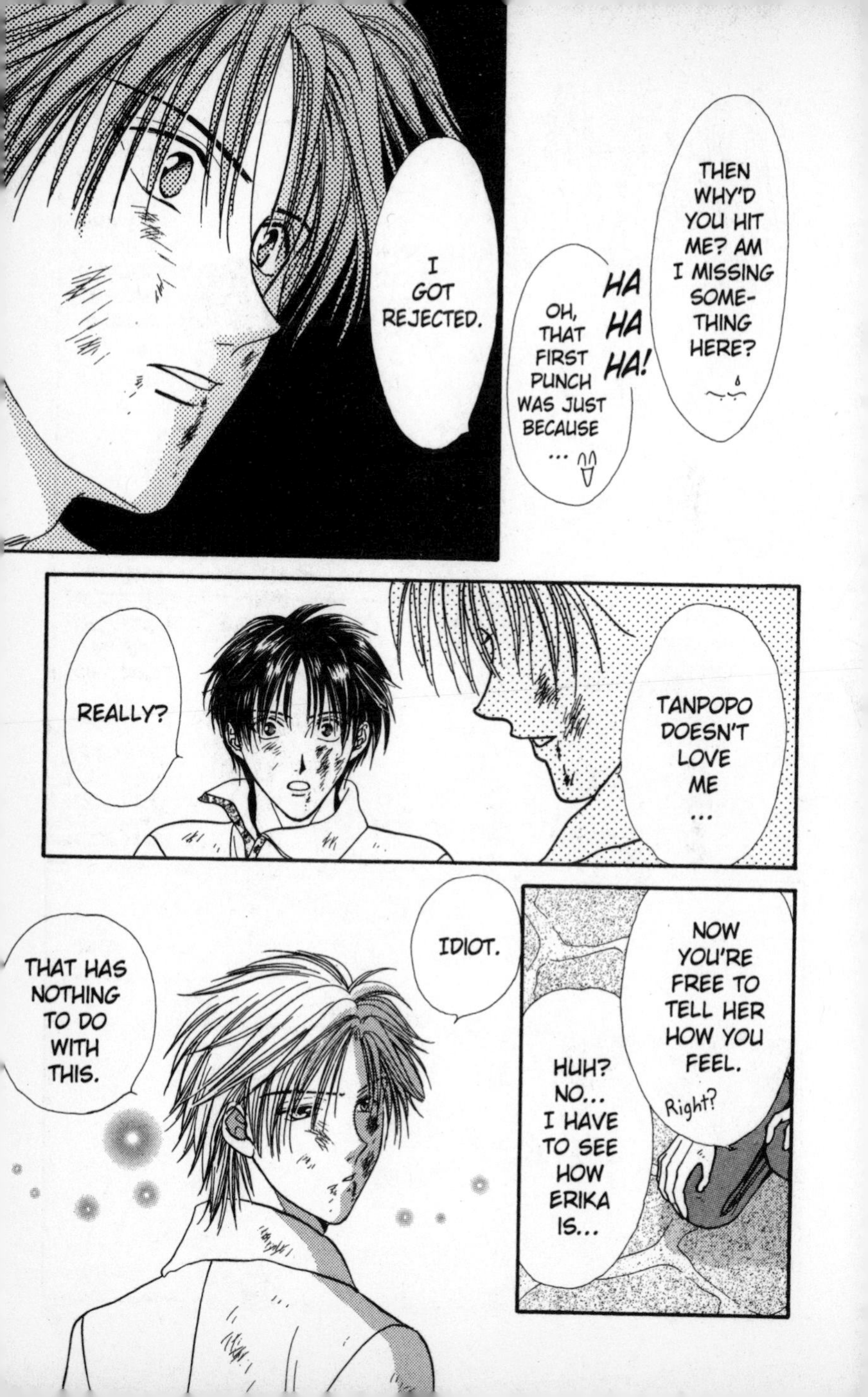
THEN WHY'D YOU HIT ME? AM I MISSING SOME- THING HERE?
HA HA HA!
OH, THAT FIRST PUNCH WAS JUST BECAUSE ...
I GOT REJECTED.
TANPOPO DOESN'T LOVE ME ...
REALLY?
NOW YOU'RE FREE TO TELL HER HOW YOU FEEL.
Right?
HUH? NO... I HAVE TO SEE HOW ERIKA IS...
IDIOT.
THAT HAS NOTHING TO DO WITH THIS.

ISN'T IT ABOUT TIME YOU WERE HONEST WITH YOURSELF?

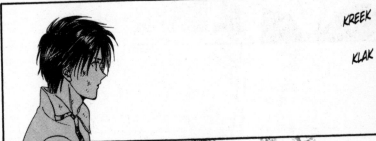

KREEK

KLAK

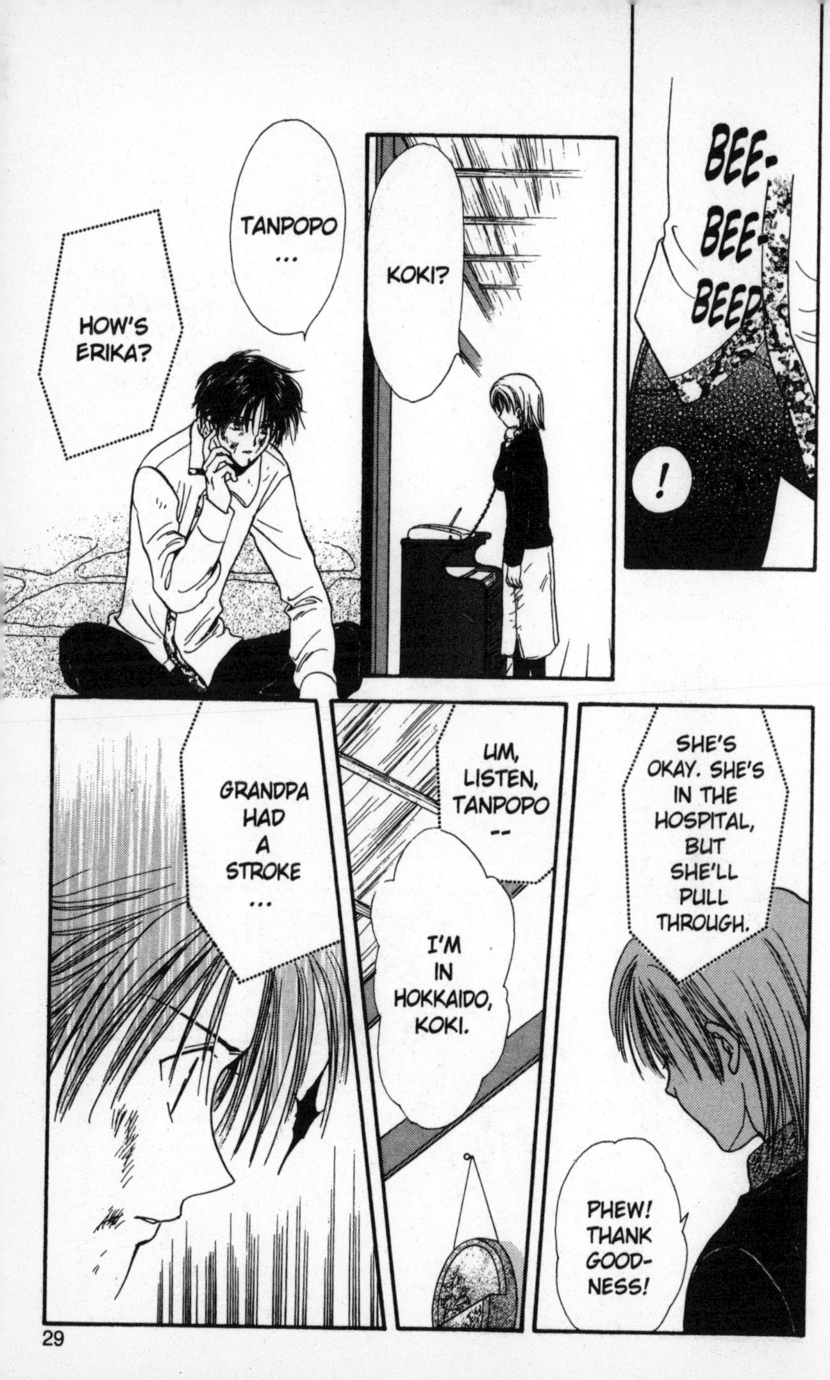
BEE-BEE-BEED
!
KOKI?
TANPOPO ...
HOW'S ERIKA?
SHE'S OKAY. SHE'S IN THE HOSPITAL, BUT SHE'LL PULL THROUGH.
PHEW! THANK GOOD-NESS!
UM, LISTEN, TANPOPO --
I'M IN HOKKAIDO, KOKI.
GRANDPA HAD A STROKE ...

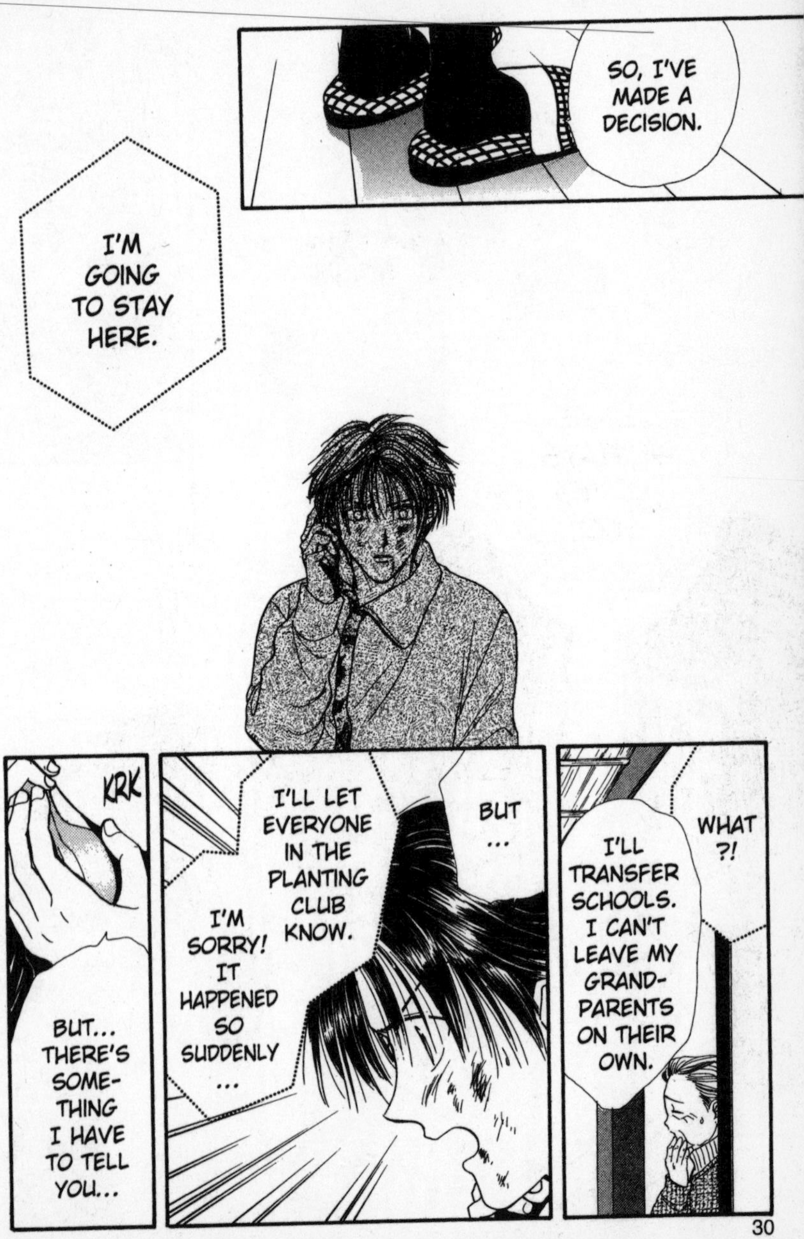
SO, I'VE MADE A DECISION.
I'M GOING TO STAY HERE.
WHAT?!
I'LL TRANSFER SCHOOLS. I CAN'T LEAVE MY GRAND-PARENTS ON THEIR OWN.
BUT...
I'LL LET EVERYONE IN THE PLANTING CLUB KNOW.
I'M SORRY! IT HAPPENED SO SUDDENLY...
KRK
BUT... THERE'S SOME-THING I HAVE TO TELL YOU...

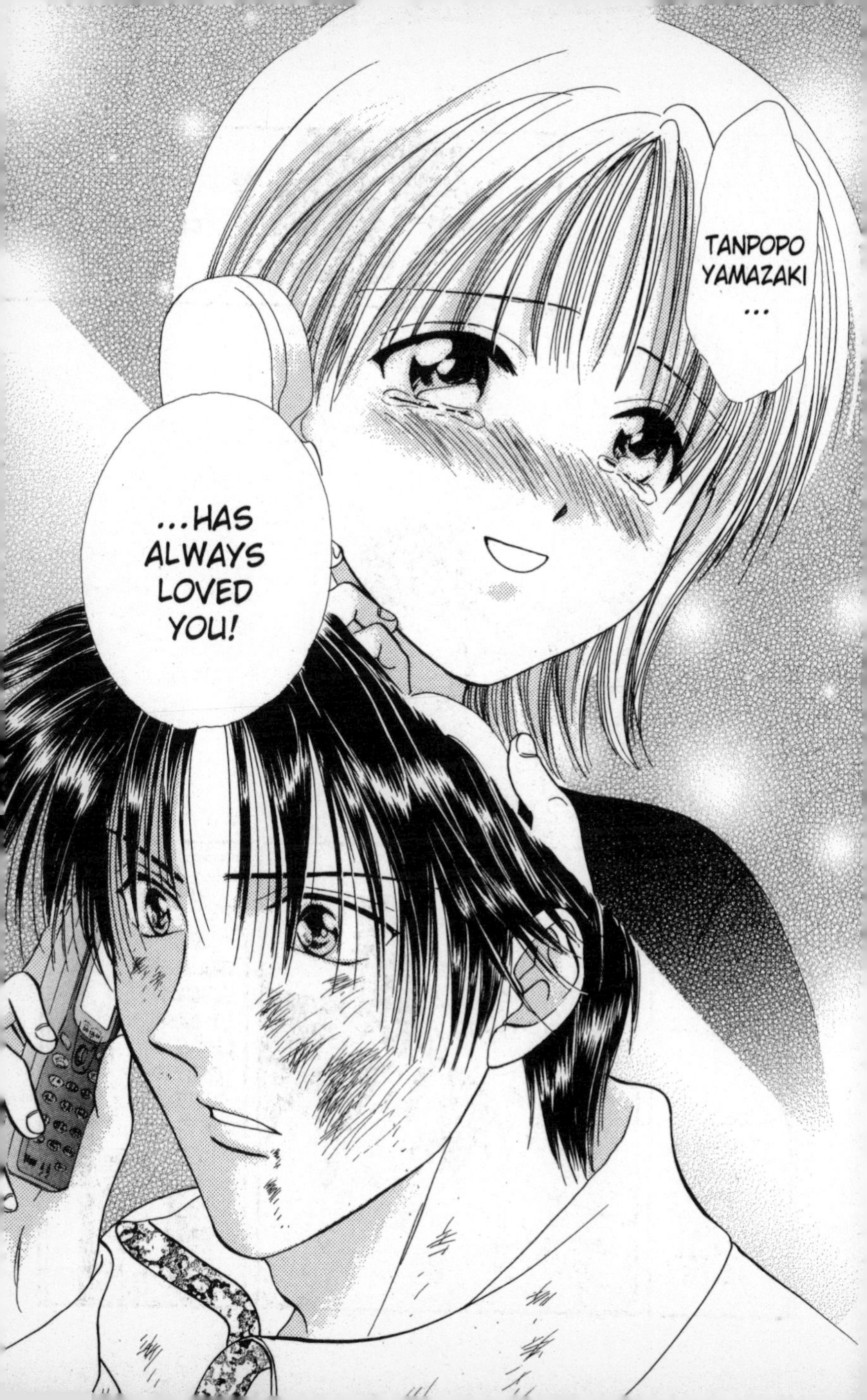
TANPOPO YAMAZAKI ...
...HAS ALWAYS LOVED YOU!

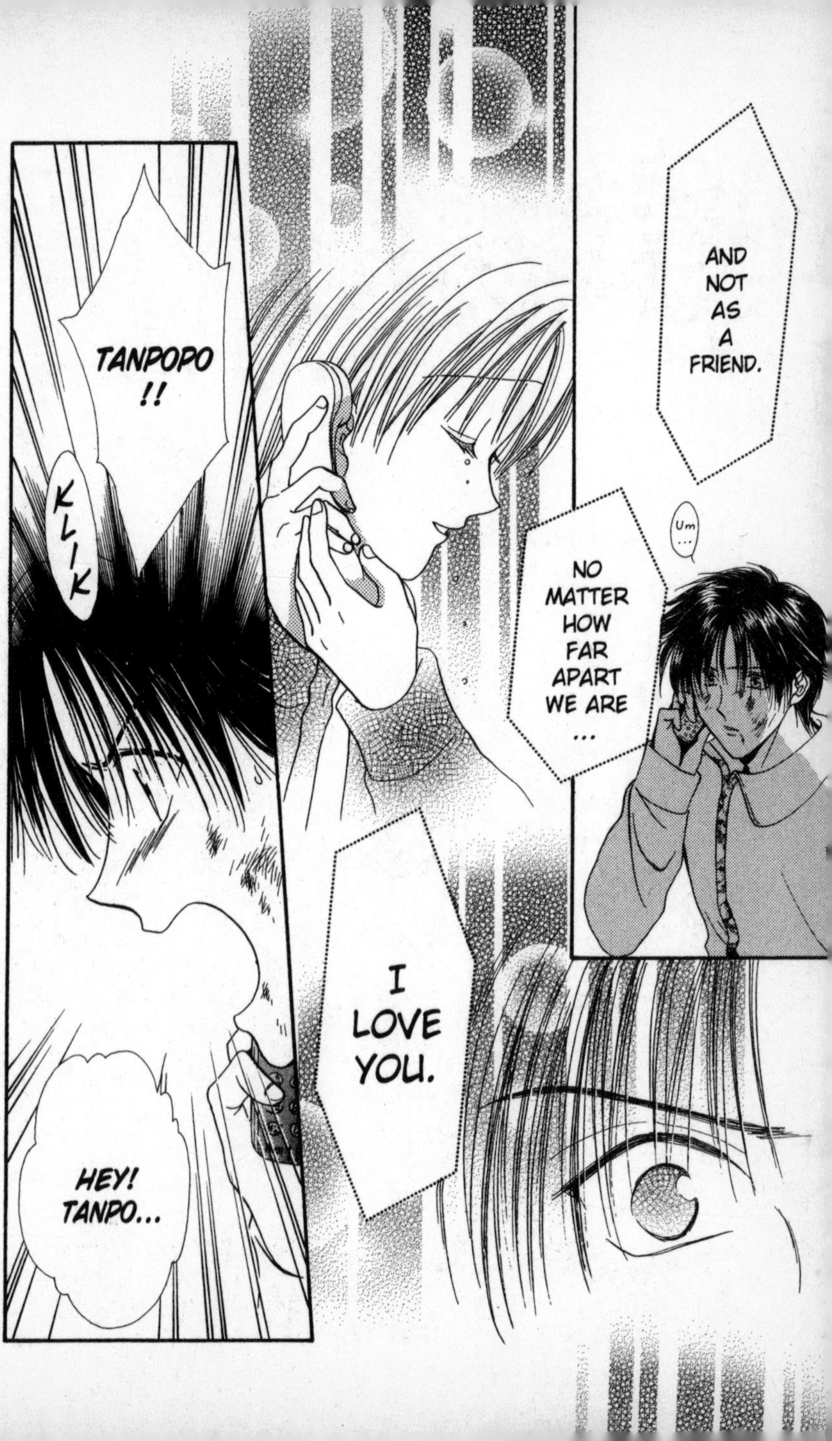
AND NOT AS A FRIEND.
NO MATTER HOW FAR APART WE ARE ...
Um ...
I LOVE YOU.
TANPOPO !!
KLIK
HEY! TANPO...

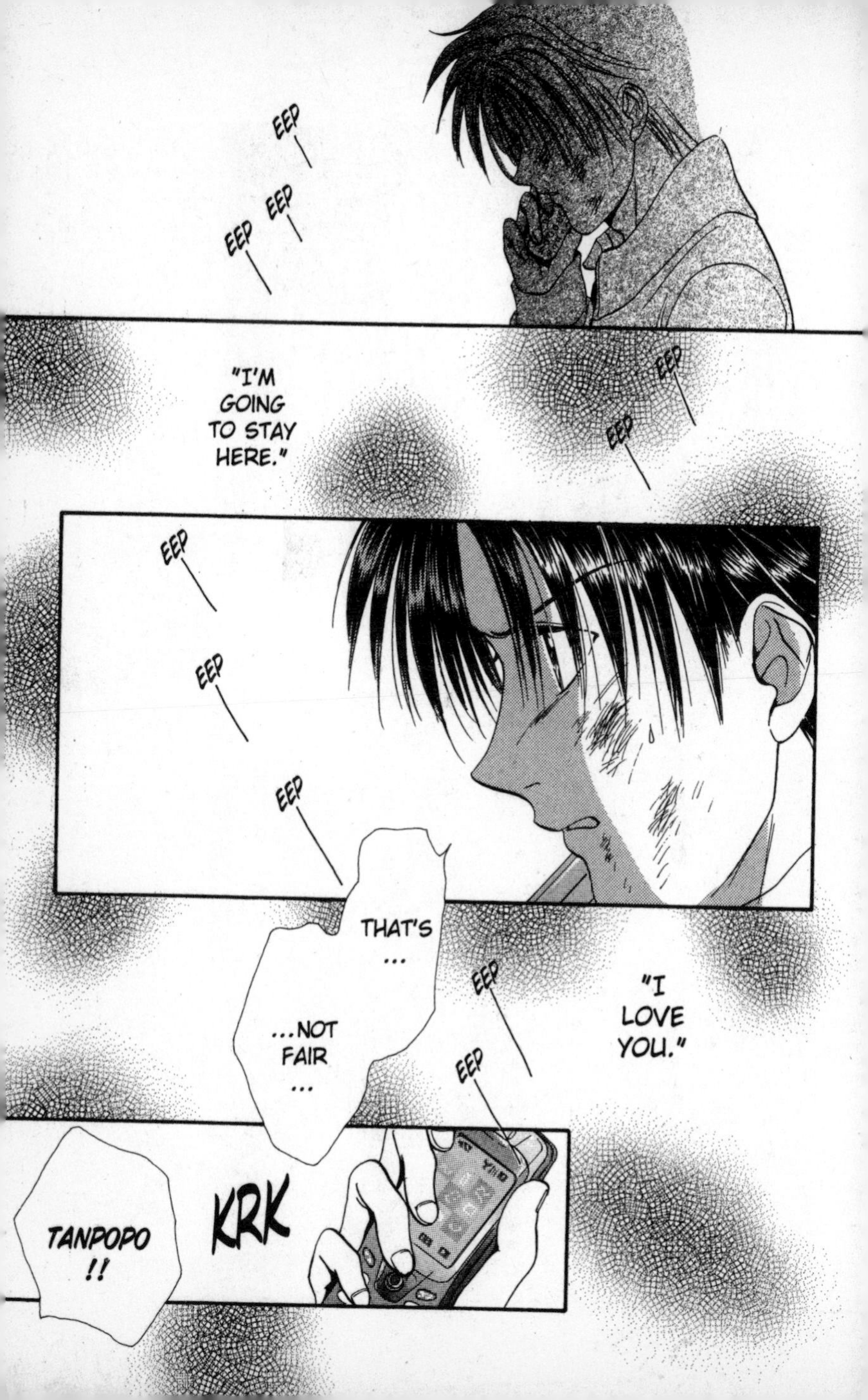
EEP
EEP
EEP
EEP
EEP
"I'M GOING TO STAY HERE."
EEP
EEP
EEP
THAT'S ...
...NOT FAIR ...
"I LOVE YOU."
EEP
EEP
KRK
TANPOPO !!

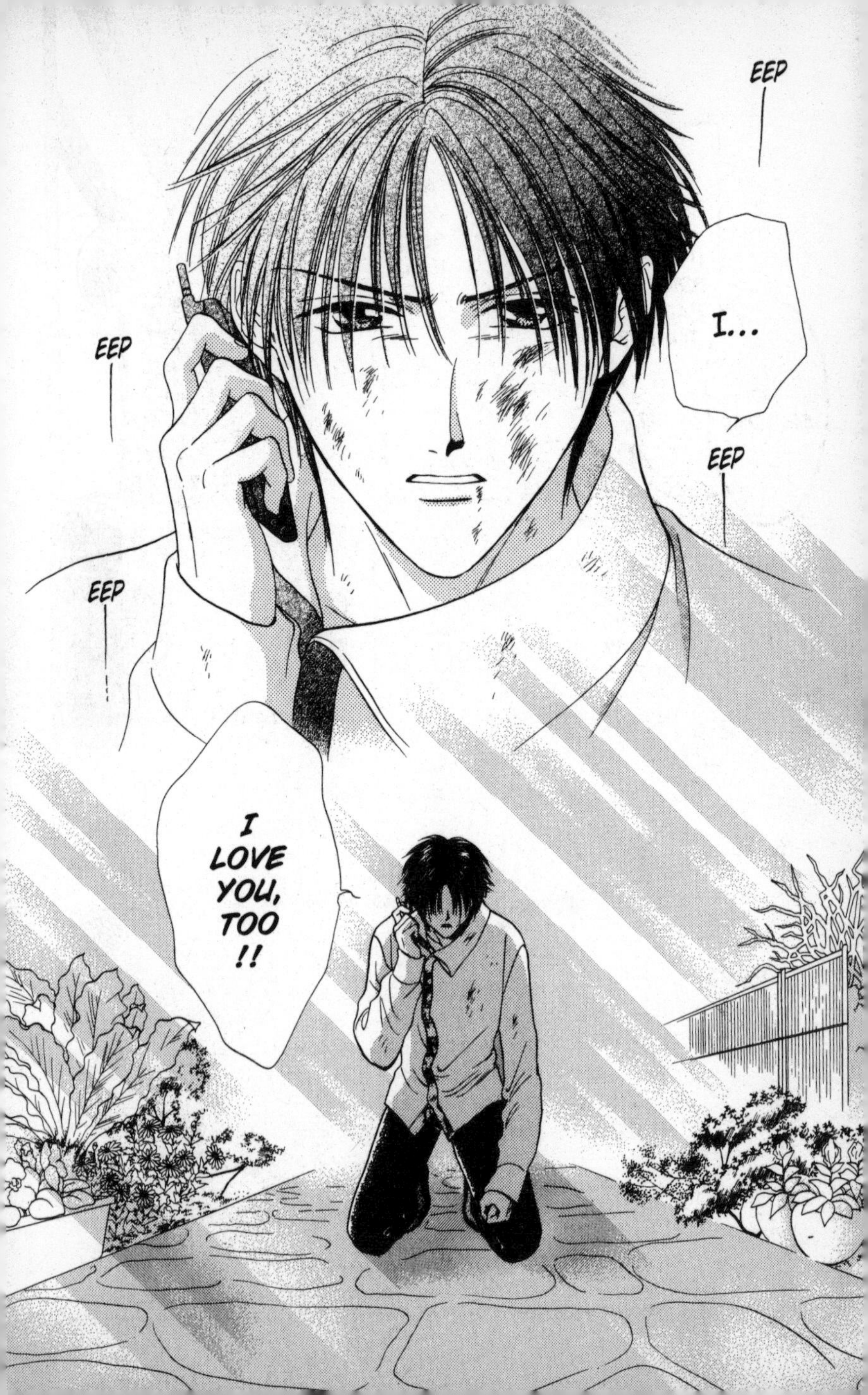
EEP
I...
EEP
EEP
EEP
I LOVE YOU, TOO!!

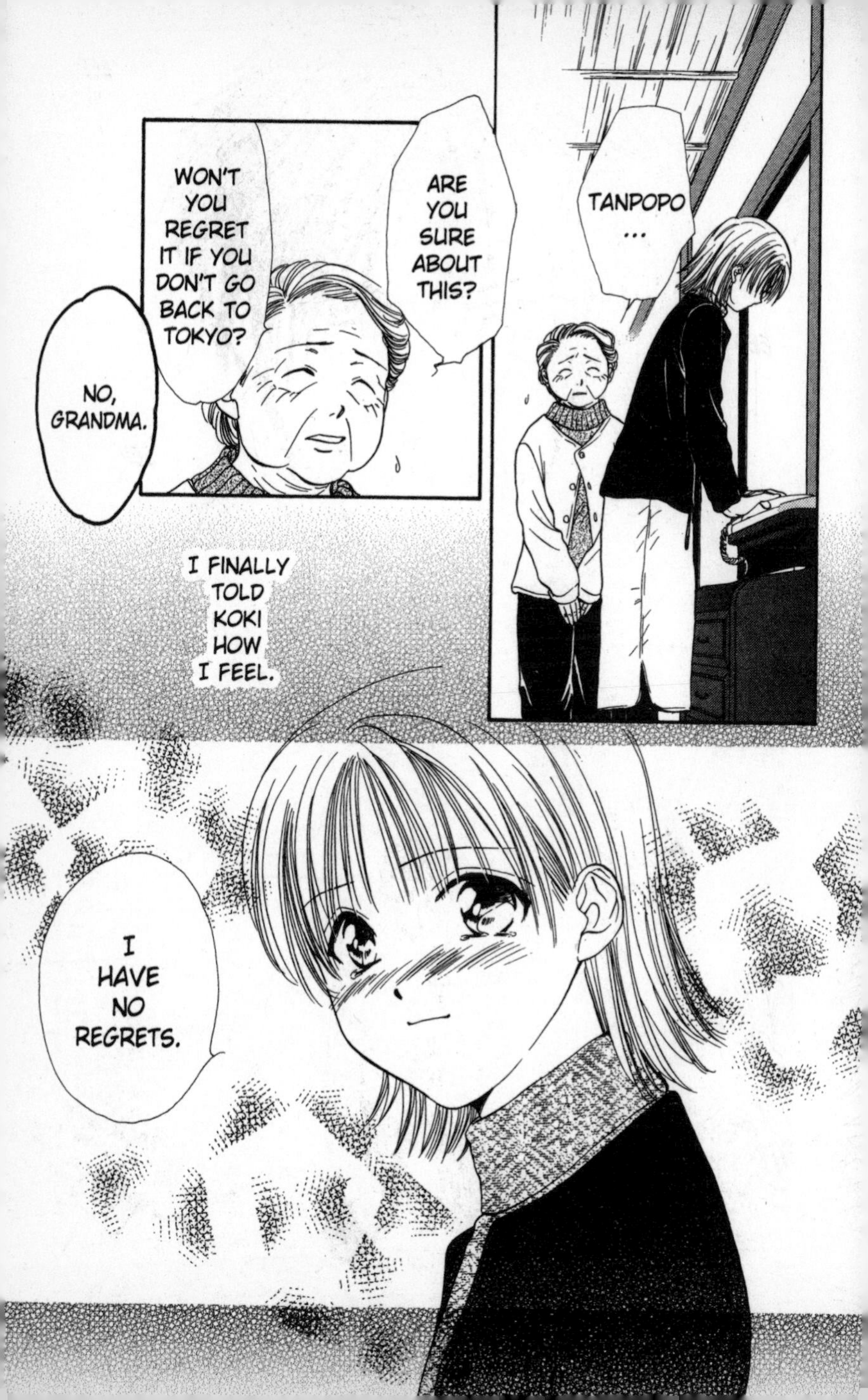

TANPOPO ...
ARE YOU SURE ABOUT THIS?
WON'T YOU REGRET IT IF YOU DON'T GO BACK TO TOKYO?
NO, GRANDMA.
I FINALLY TOLD KOKI HOW I FEEL.
I HAVE NO REGRETS.

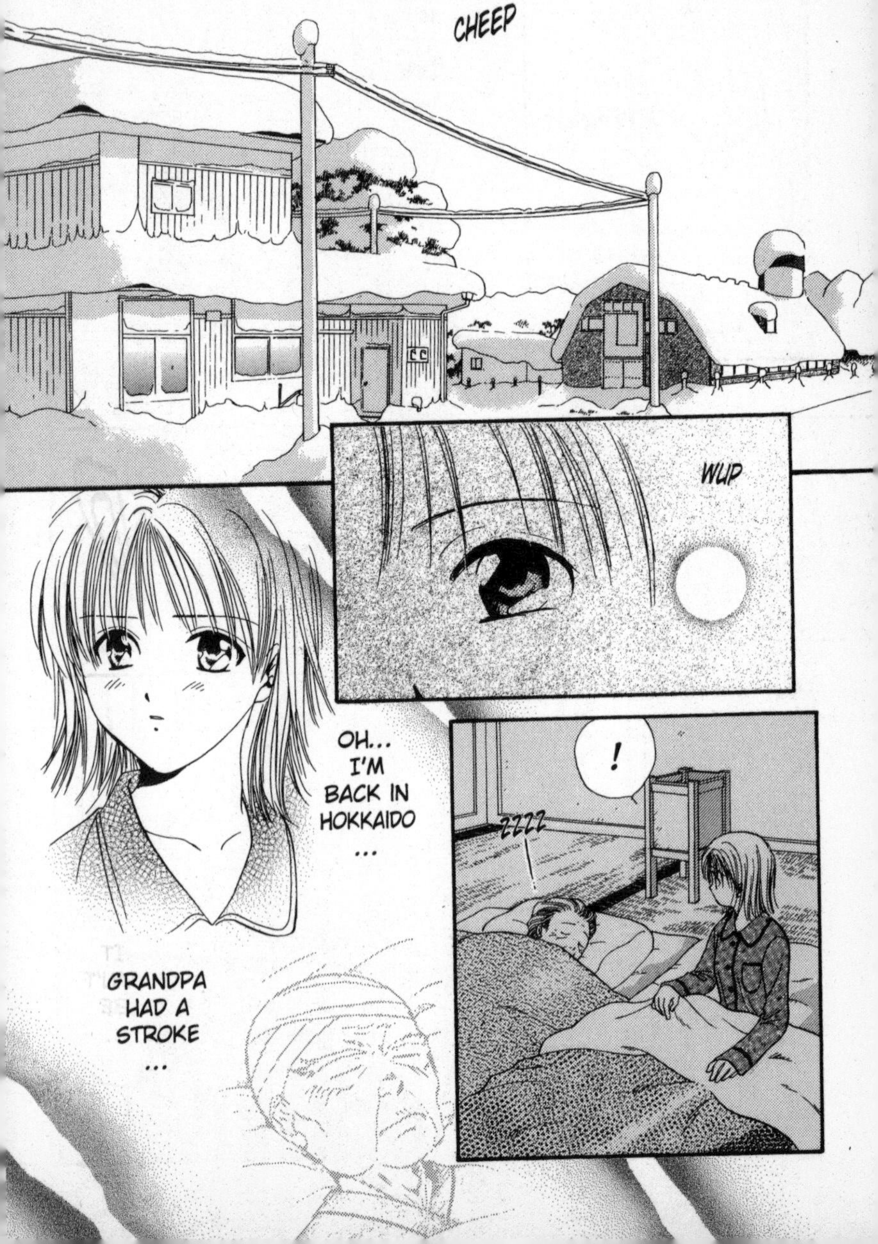
CHEEP
WUP
!
ZZZZ
OH... I'M BACK IN HOKKAIDO ...
GRANDPA HAD A STROKE ...

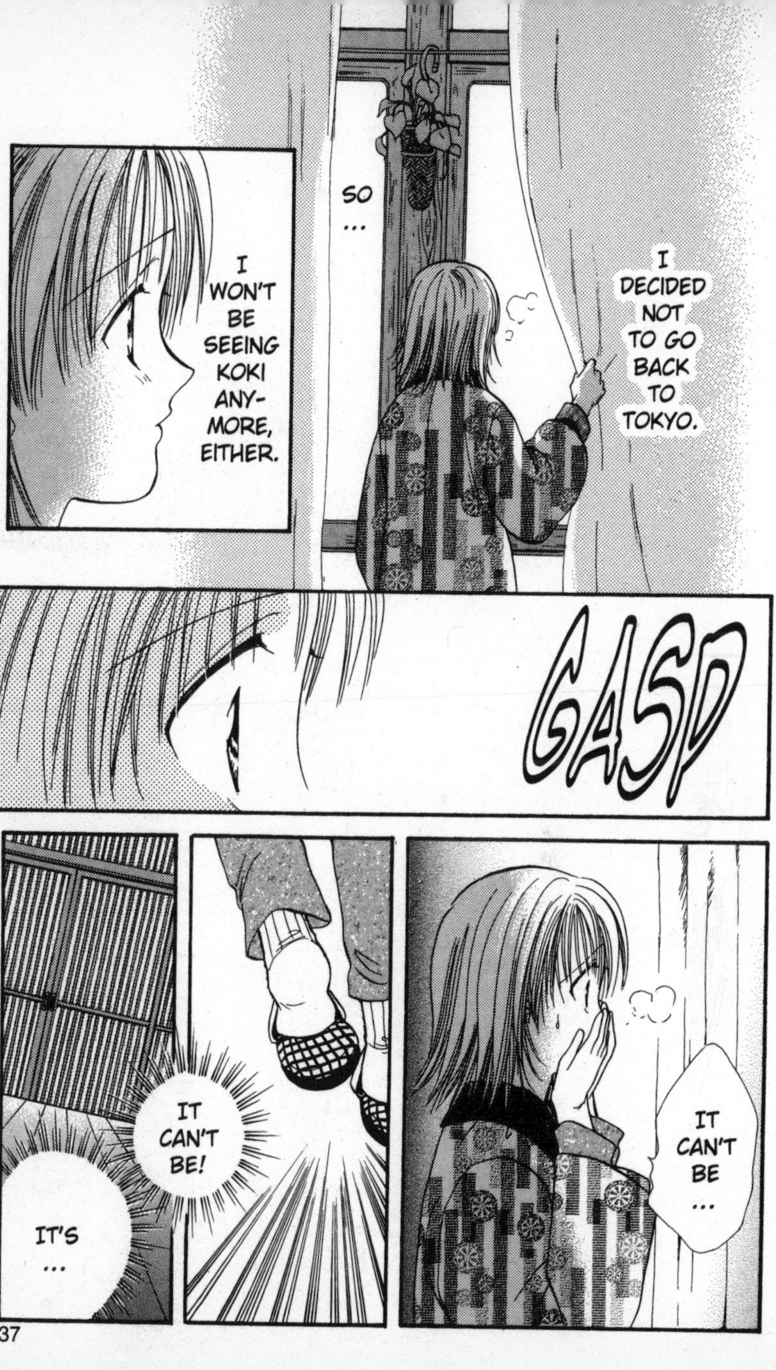
I DECIDED NOT TO GO BACK TO TOKYO.
SO ...
I WON'T BE SEEING KOKI ANY-MORE, EITHER.
GASP
IT CAN'T BE ...
IT CAN'T BE!
IT'S ...

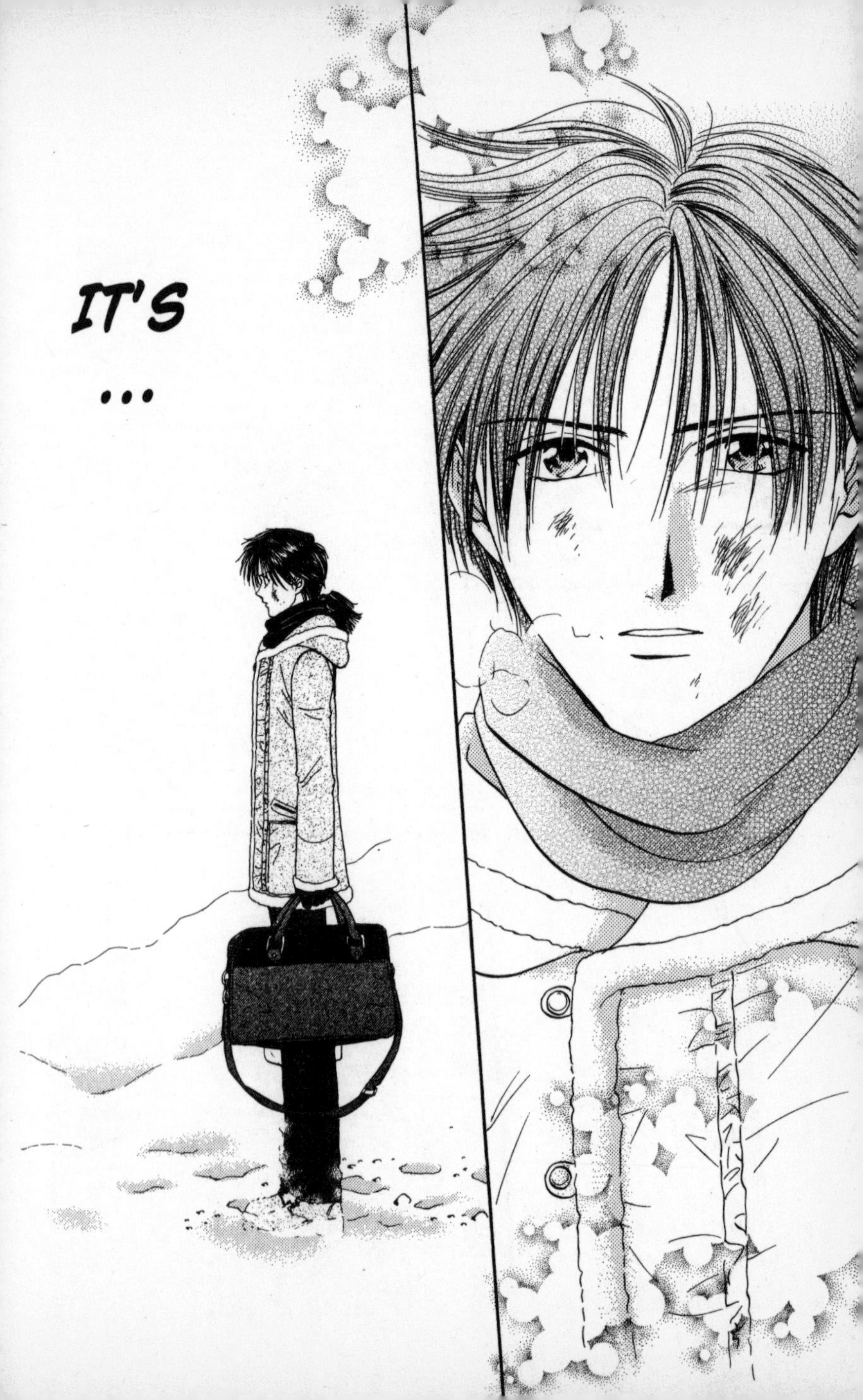
IT'S ...

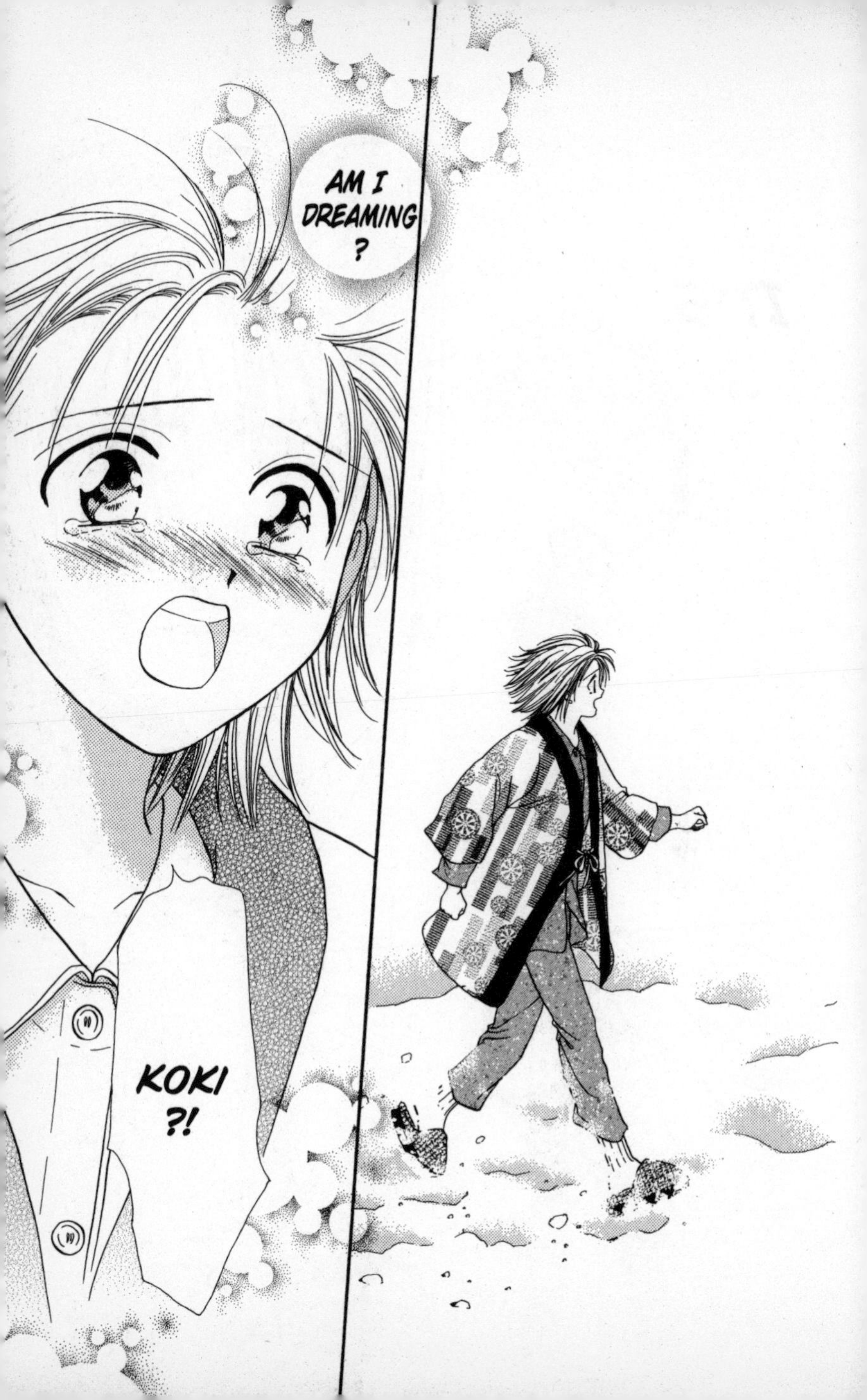
AM I DREAMING ?
KOKI ?!

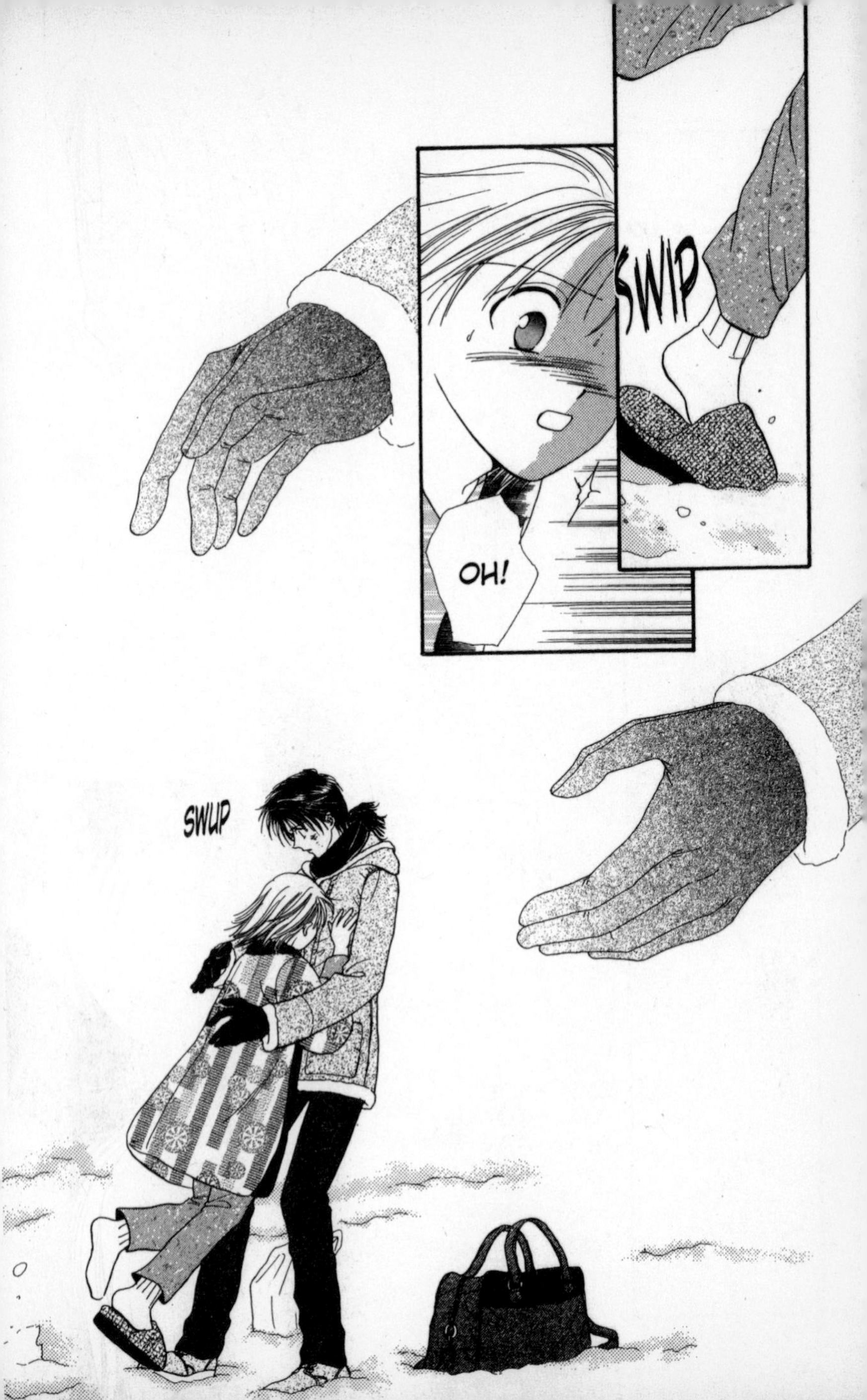
SWIP
OH!
SWUP

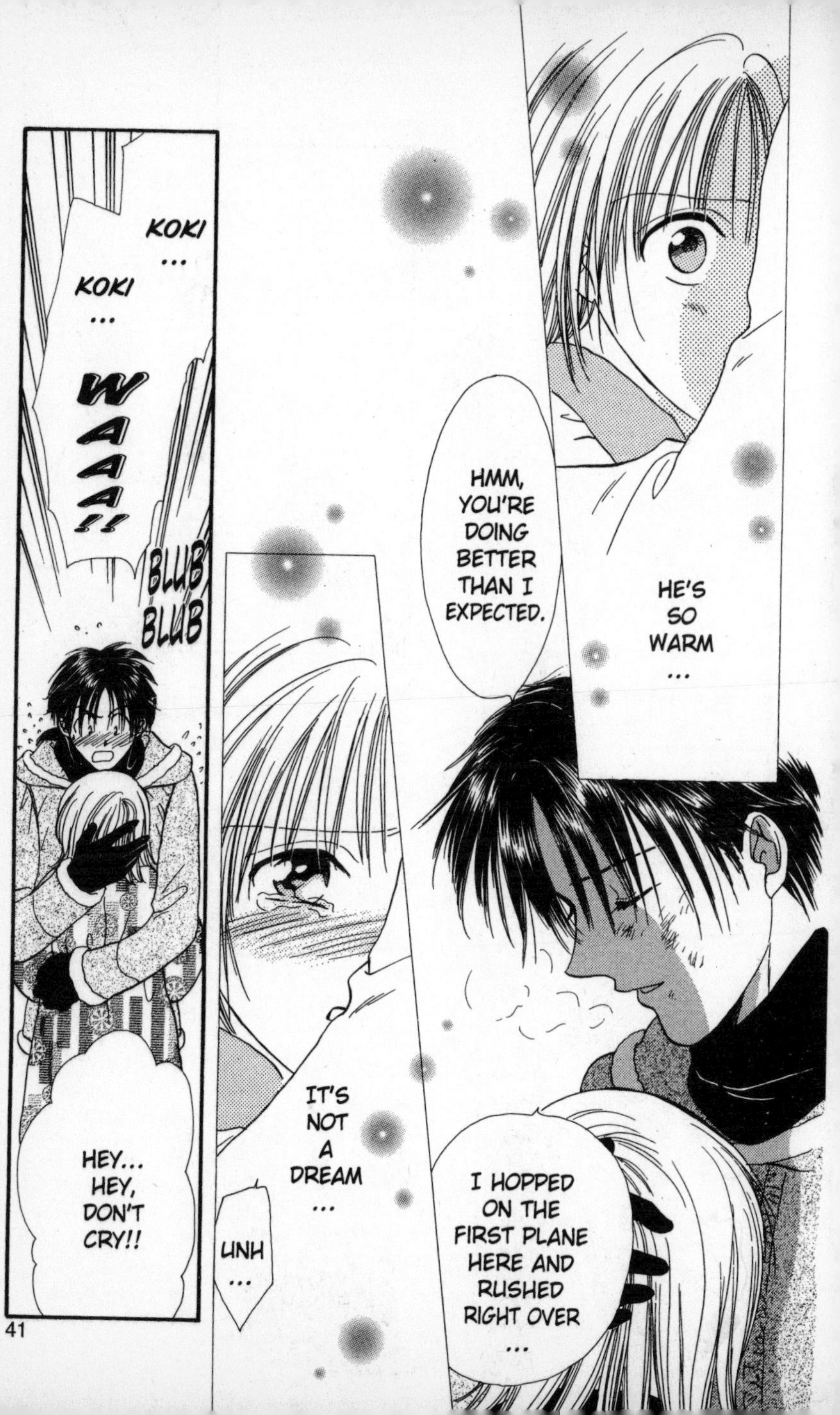

HMM, YOU'RE DOING BETTER THAN I EXPECTED.
HE'S SO WARM ...
I HOPPED ON THE FIRST PLANE HERE AND RUSHED RIGHT OVER ...
IT'S NOT A DREAM ...
UNH ...
KOKI ... KOKI ...
WAAAA!!
BLUB BLUB
HEY... HEY, DON'T CRY!!

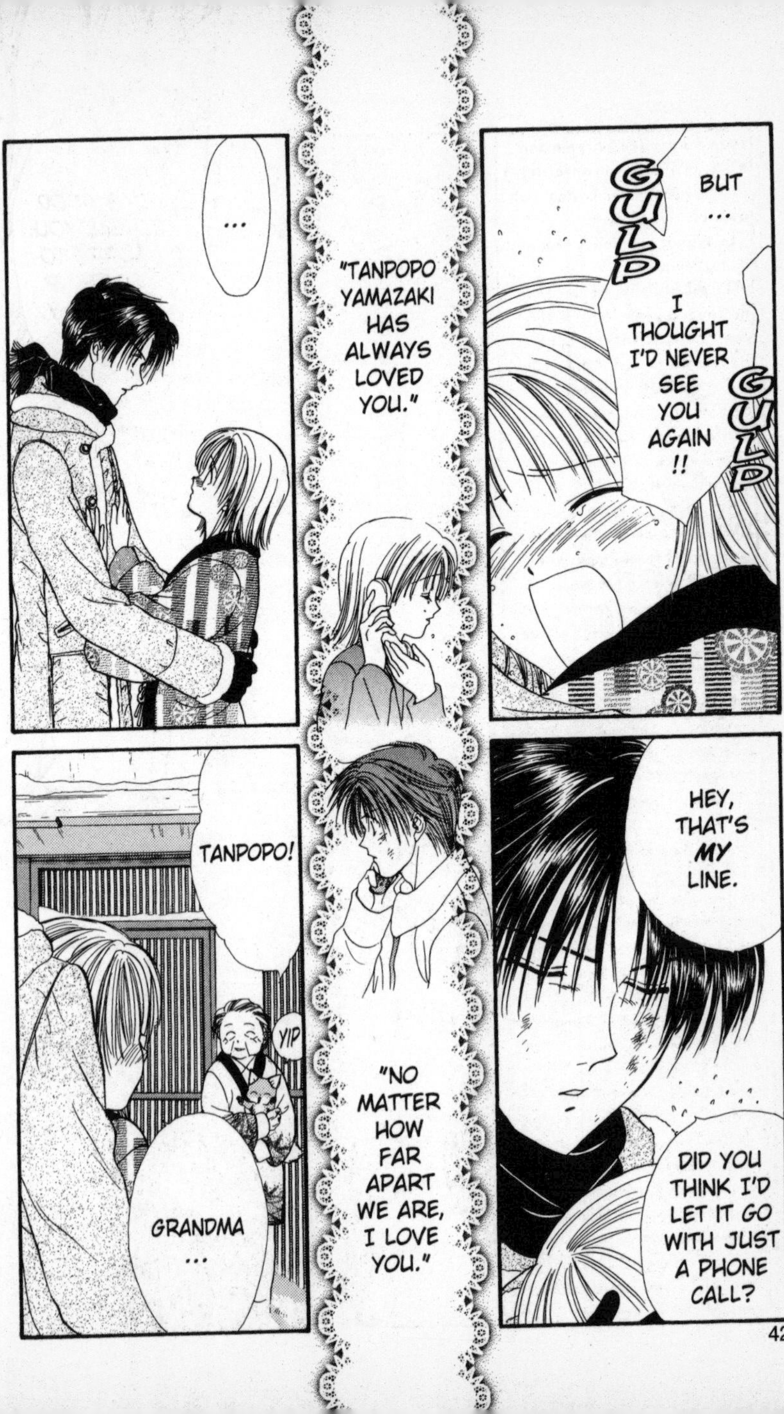
BUT ...
GULP
I THOUGHT I'D NEVER SEE YOU AGAIN !!
GULP
"TANPOPO YAMAZAKI HAS ALWAYS LOVED YOU."
...
HEY, THAT'S *MY* LINE.
DID YOU THINK I'D LET IT GO WITH JUST A PHONE CALL?
"NO MATTER HOW FAR APART WE ARE, I LOVE YOU."
TANPOPO!
YIP
GRANDMA ...

IT'S GOOD TO SEE YOU. SORRY TO SHOW UP SO EARLY.
HOW'S MR. YAMAZAKI?
CHUO HOSPITAL

Even if I am deathly pale and dizzy, I still have an appetite, so I'll live--somehow. Eating is an absolute necessity.

Imadoki! has finally reached its last episode.

The series has been going for just over a year. That's pretty short for a Watase story, isn't it? Thanks to you, it did well in **Shōjo Comics**, and Tanpopo and her friends were loved by readers more than I expected.

For me, it was kind of an unusual work...

As I write this today (June 17, 2001), I've already started the manuscript for my new series, **Alice 19th** (and the same thing is happening to me again). **Imadoki!** was finished at the end of February, so I took about two months off until the new series started... but I ended up doing all kinds of other work. I suppose I got some rest. I wonder...

In **Shōjo Comic's** view, I got two issues' worth of vacation time. If I actually took it, I'd really collapse from overwork and land in the hospital. So for me, I finished pretty far in advance but was still working like crazy, so I'm not sure what to say about that. (^^;)

On the other hand, I received lots of mail from readers. Most of the letters were like, "It made me think about my friends."

Is that how Tanpopo and Koki's romance is, too? The second half is coming up. I think the theme is "friendship," after all. (What do you mean, "think"?) I'm glad I told it the way I did. I was impressed by some of the letters I got.

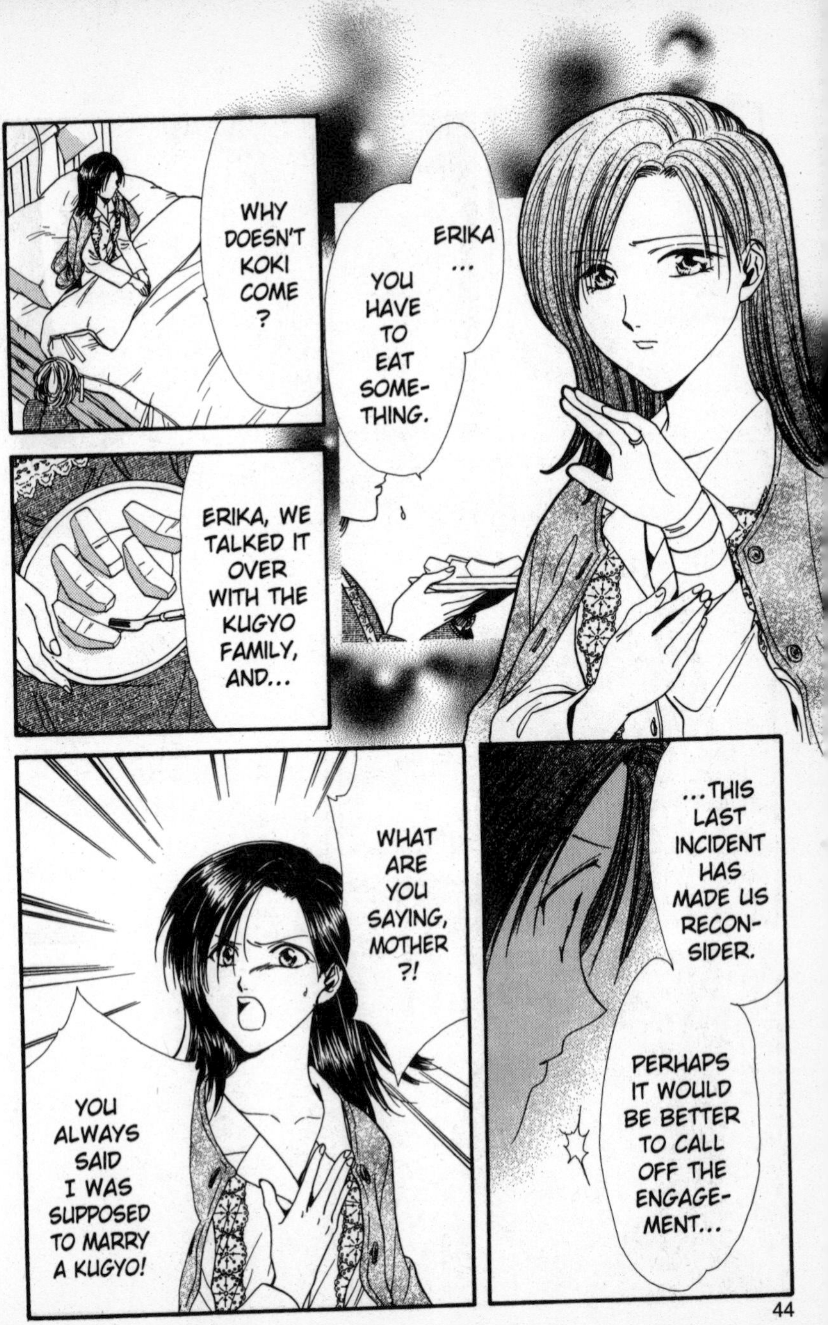
ERIKA ...
YOU HAVE TO EAT SOME-THING.
WHY DOESN'T KOKI COME ?
ERIKA, WE TALKED IT OVER WITH THE KUGYO FAMILY, AND...
...THIS LAST INCIDENT HAS MADE US RECON-SIDER.
PERHAPS IT WOULD BE BETTER TO CALL OFF THE ENGAGE-MENT...
WHAT ARE YOU SAYING, MOTHER ?!
YOU ALWAYS SAID I WAS SUPPOSED TO MARRY A KUGYO!

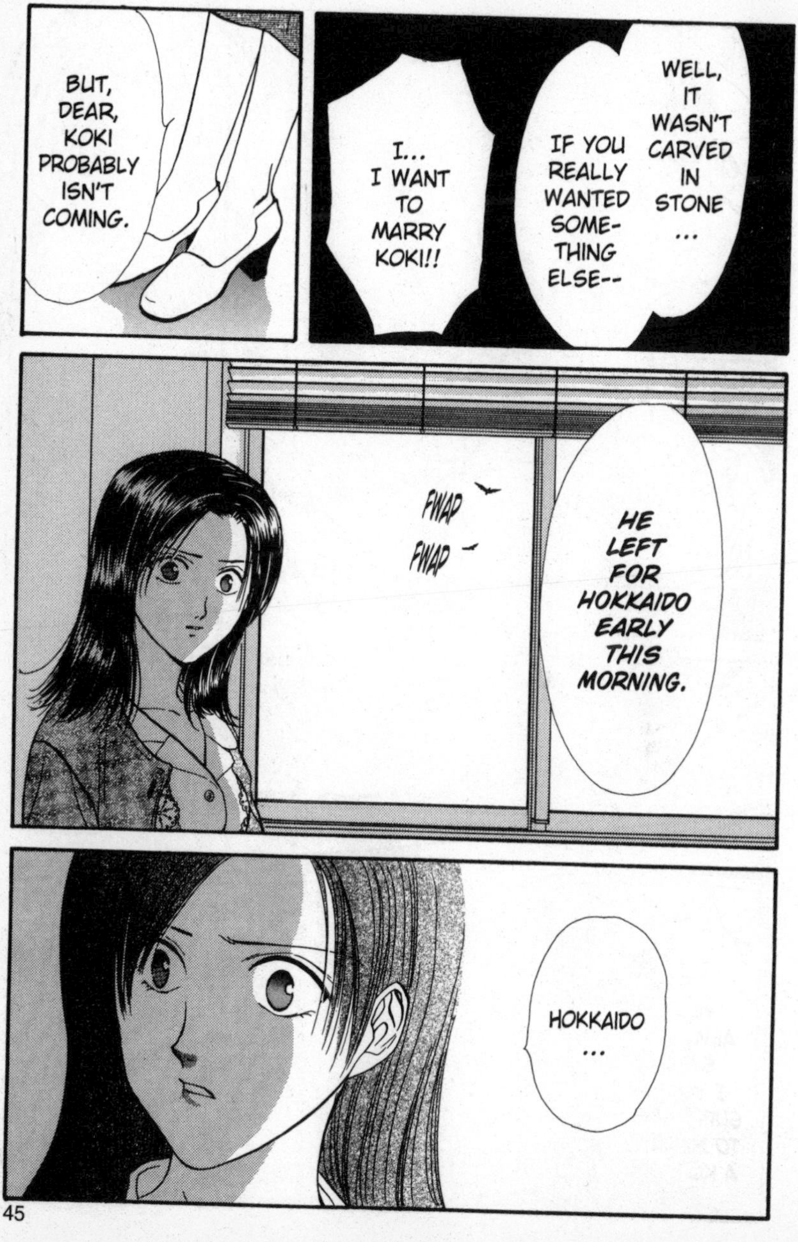
WELL, IT WASN'T CARVED IN STONE...
IF YOU REALLY WANTED SOME-THING ELSE--
I... I WANT TO MARRY KOKI!!
BUT, DEAR, KOKI PROBABLY ISN'T COMING.
HE LEFT FOR HOKKAIDO EARLY THIS MORNING.
FWAP
FWAP
HOKKAIDO...

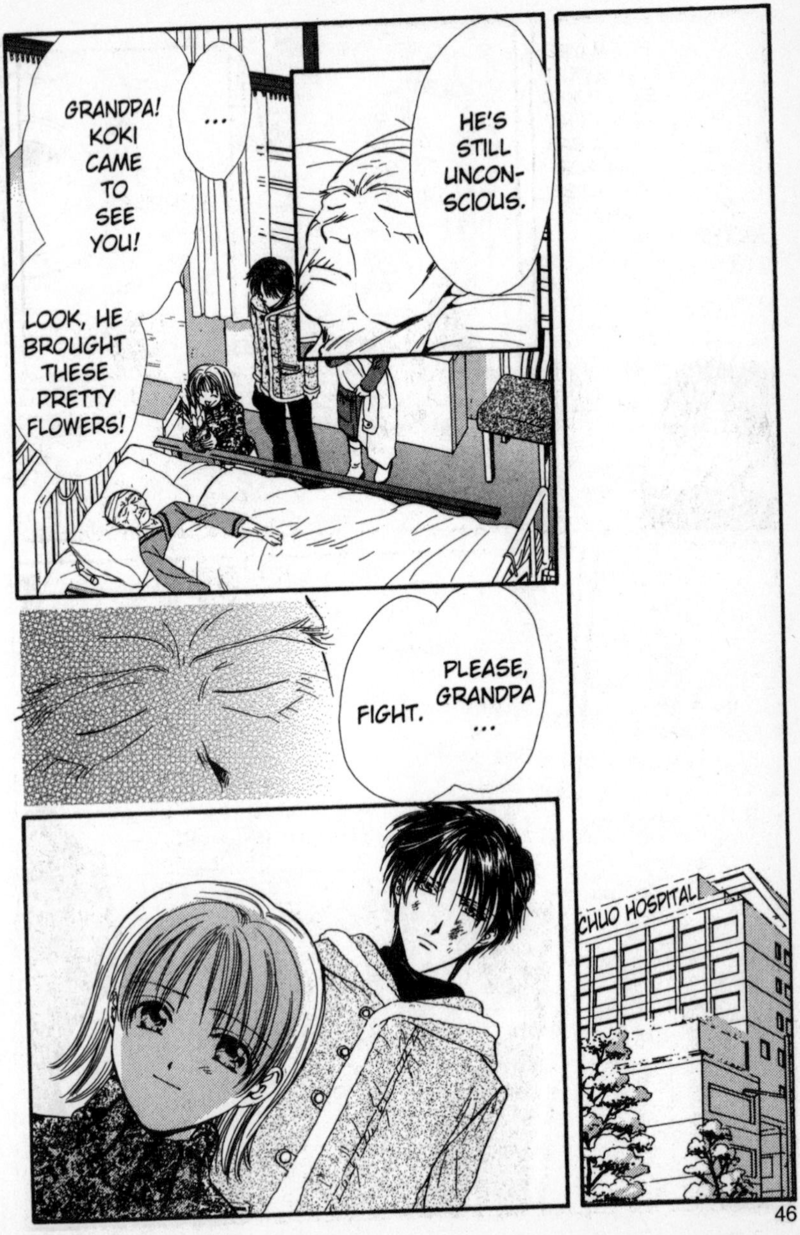

CHUO HOSPITAL
HE'S STILL UNCONSCIOUS.
...
GRANDPA! KOKI CAME TO SEE YOU!
LOOK, HE BROUGHT THESE PRETTY FLOWERS!
PLEASE, GRANDPA ...
FIGHT.

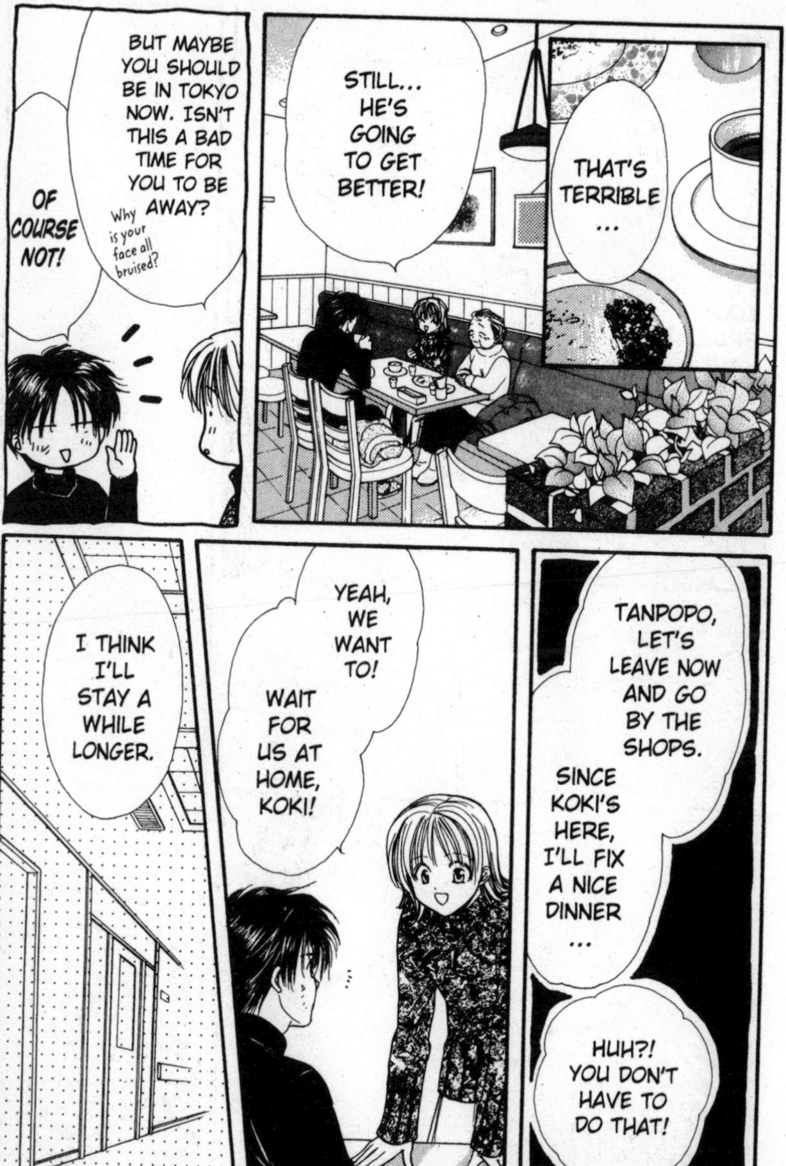
THAT'S TERRIBLE...
STILL... HE'S GOING TO GET BETTER!
BUT MAYBE YOU SHOULD BE IN TOKYO NOW. ISN'T THIS A BAD TIME FOR YOU TO BE AWAY?
Why is your face all bruised?
OF COURSE NOT!
TANPOPO, LET'S LEAVE NOW AND GO BY THE SHOPS.
SINCE KOKI'S HERE, I'LL FIX A NICE DINNER...
HUH?! YOU DON'T HAVE TO DO THAT!
YEAH, WE WANT TO!
WAIT FOR US AT HOME, KOKI!
I THINK I'LL STAY A WHILE LONGER.

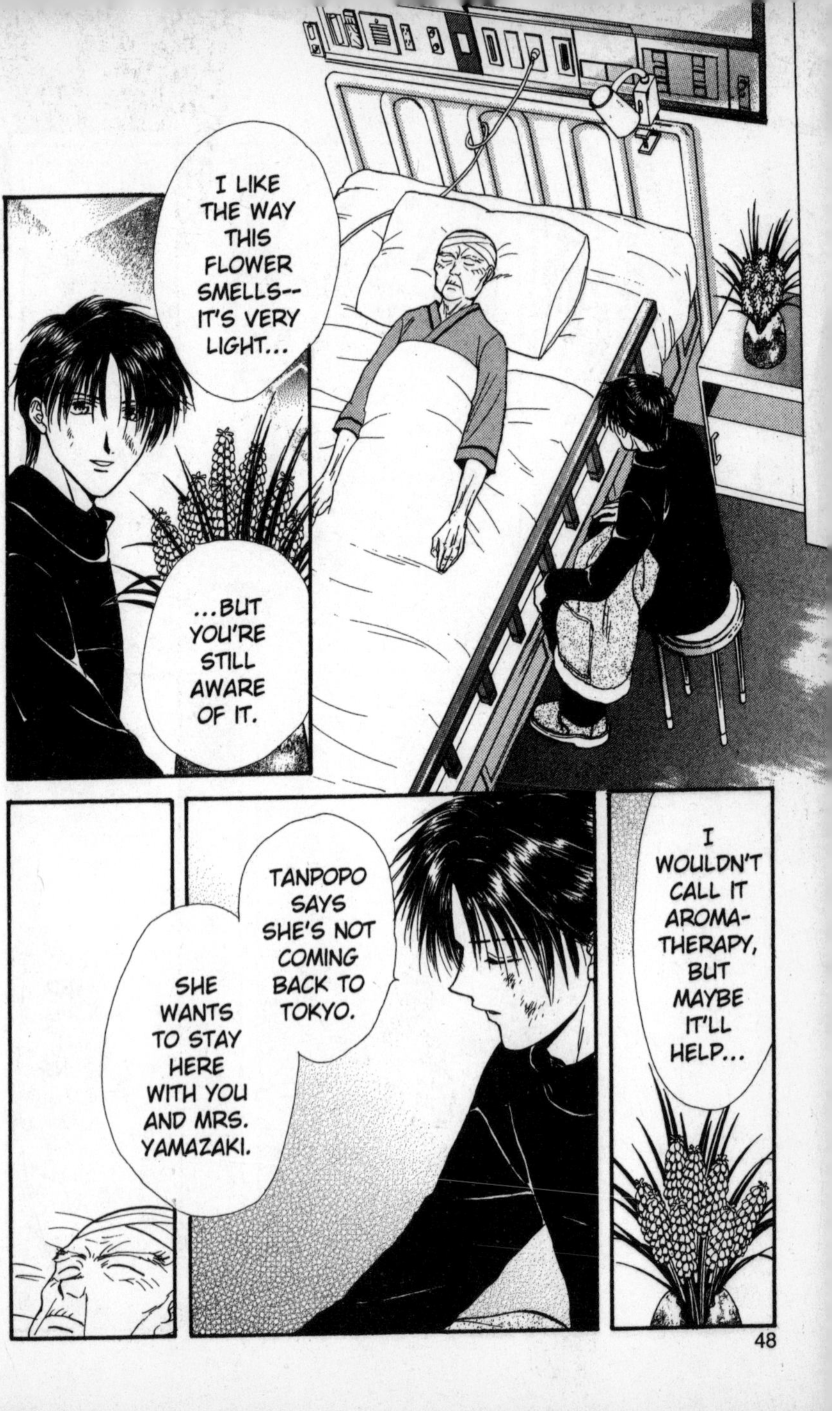
I LIKE THE WAY THIS FLOWER SMELLS--IT'S VERY LIGHT...
...BUT YOU'RE STILL AWARE OF IT.
I WOULDN'T CALL IT AROMA-THERAPY, BUT MAYBE IT'LL HELP...
TANPOPO SAYS SHE'S NOT COMING BACK TO TOKYO.
SHE WANTS TO STAY HERE WITH YOU AND MRS. YAMAZAKI.

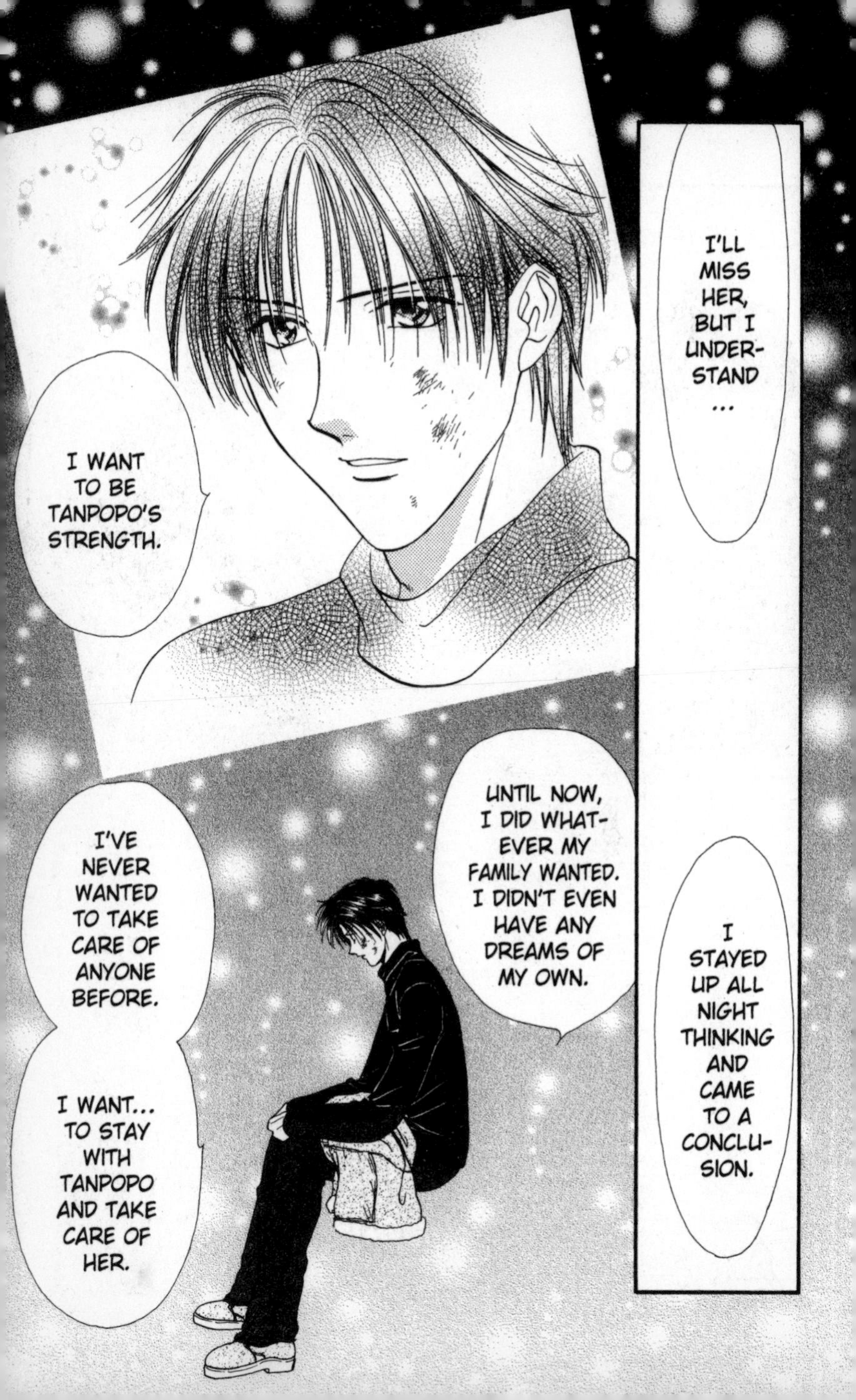
I'LL MISS HER, BUT I UNDERSTAND...
I STAYED UP ALL NIGHT THINKING AND CAME TO A CONCLUSION.
I WANT TO BE TANPOPO'S STRENGTH.
UNTIL NOW, I DID WHATEVER MY FAMILY WANTED. I DIDN'T EVEN HAVE ANY DREAMS OF MY OWN.
I'VE NEVER WANTED TO TAKE CARE OF ANYONE BEFORE.
I WANT... TO STAY WITH TANPOPO AND TAKE CARE OF HER.

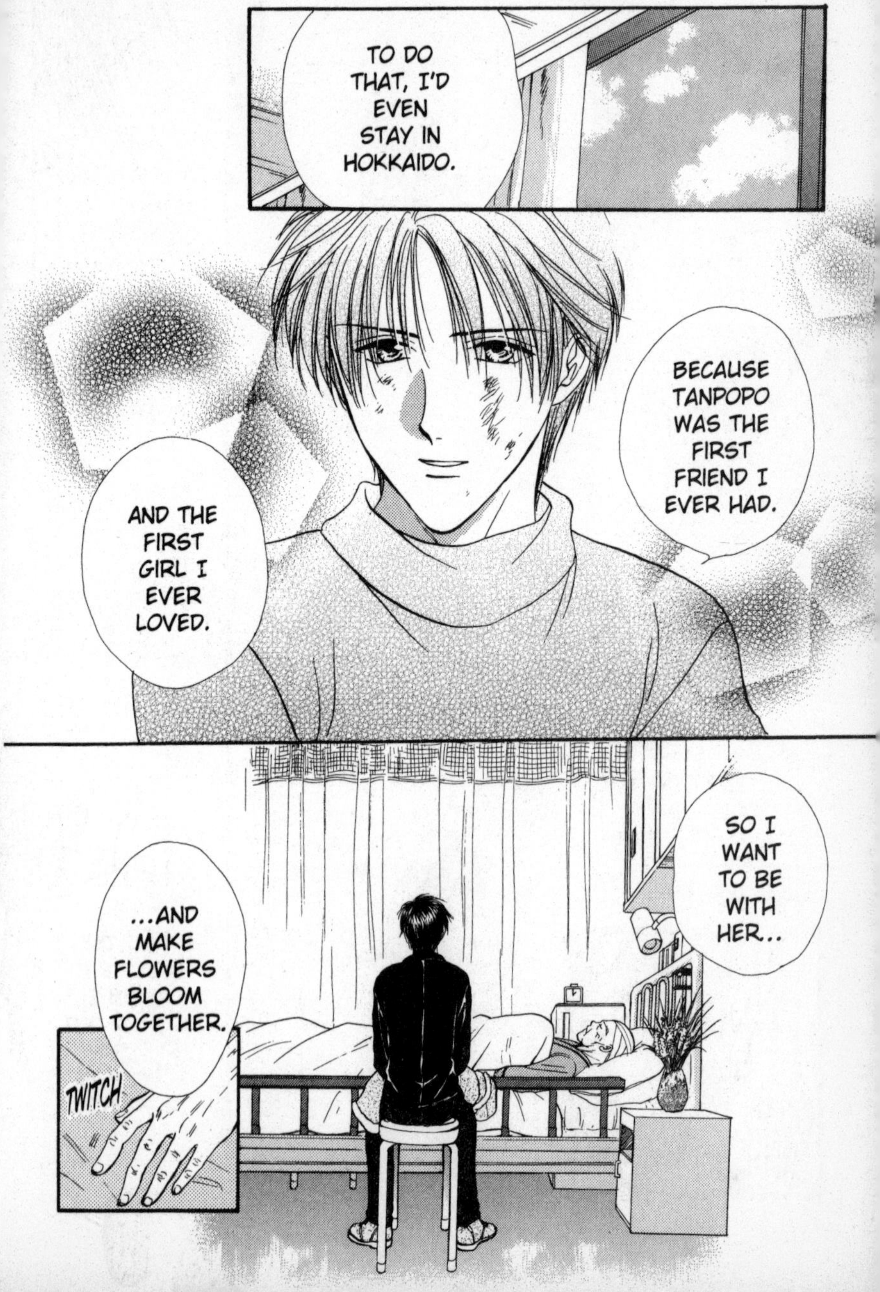
TO DO THAT, I'D EVEN STAY IN HOKKAIDO.
BECAUSE TANPOPO WAS THE FIRST FRIEND I EVER HAD.
AND THE FIRST GIRL I EVER LOVED.
SO I WANT TO BE WITH HER...
...AND MAKE FLOWERS BLOOM TOGETHER.
TWITCH

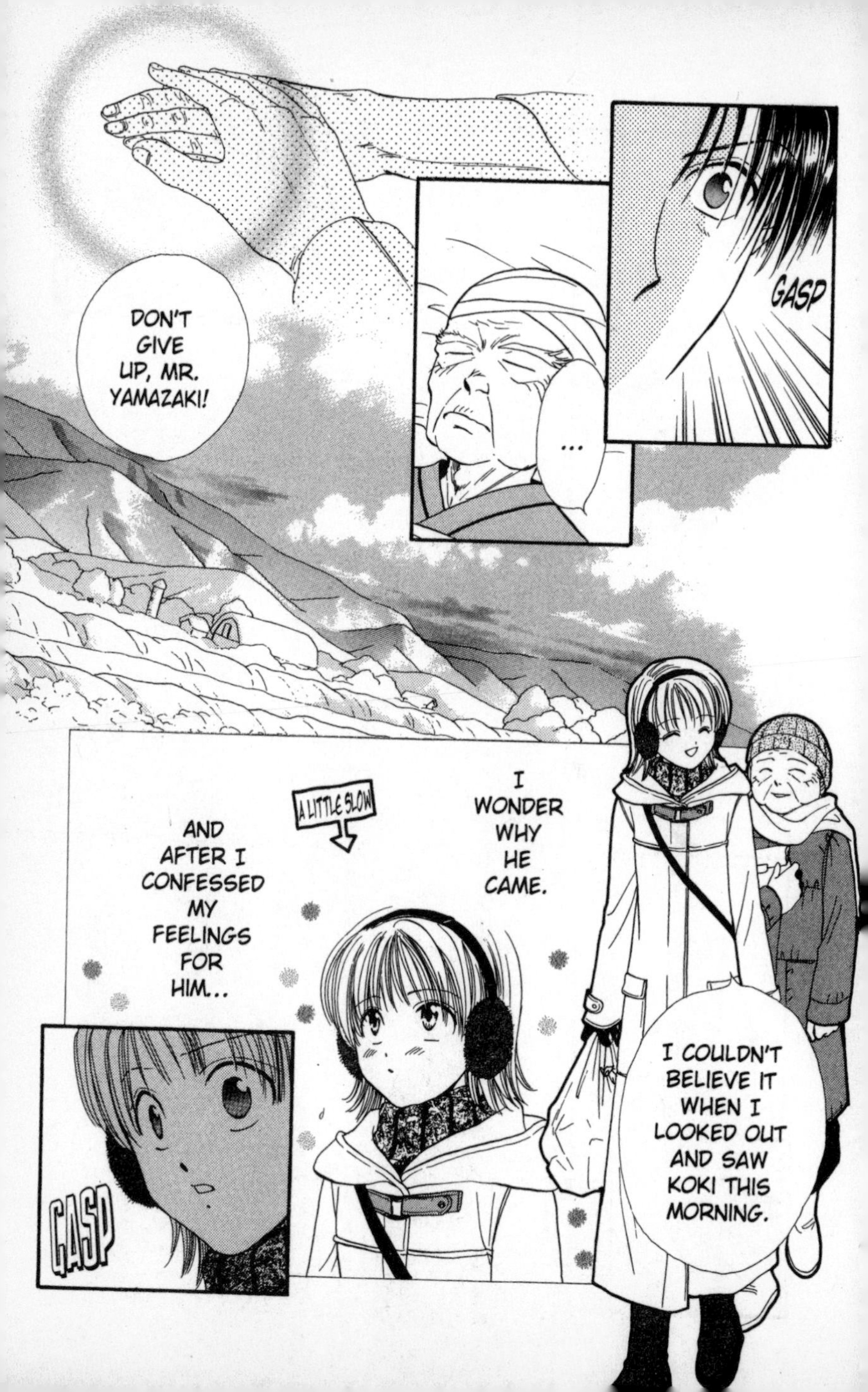
GASP
...
DON'T GIVE UP, MR. YAMAZAKI!
I COULDN'T BELIEVE IT WHEN I LOOKED OUT AND SAW KOKI THIS MORNING.
I WONDER WHY HE CAME.
A LITTLE SLOW
AND AFTER I CONFESSED MY FEELINGS FOR HIM...
GASP

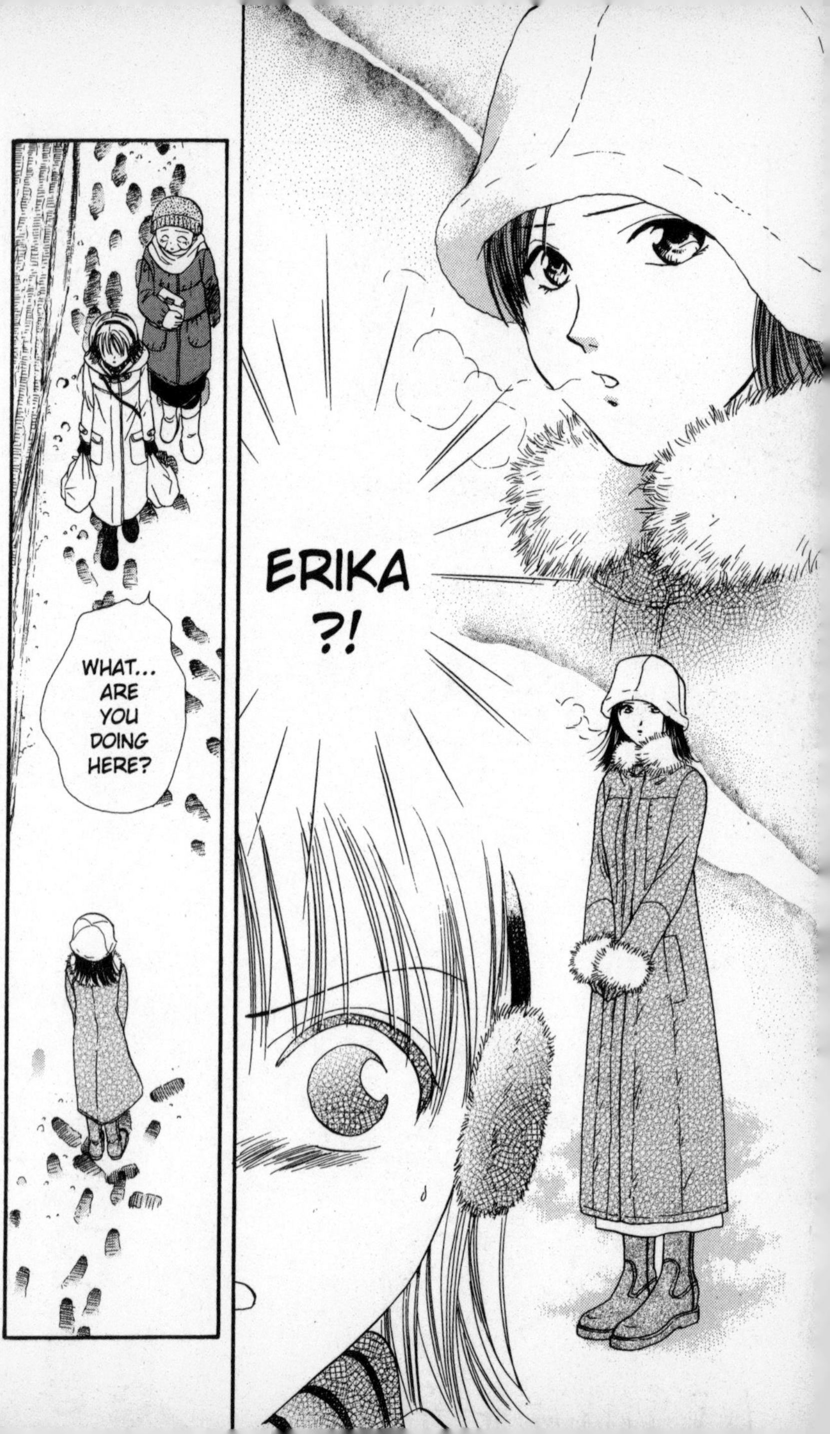
ERIKA ?!
WHAT... ARE YOU DOING HERE?

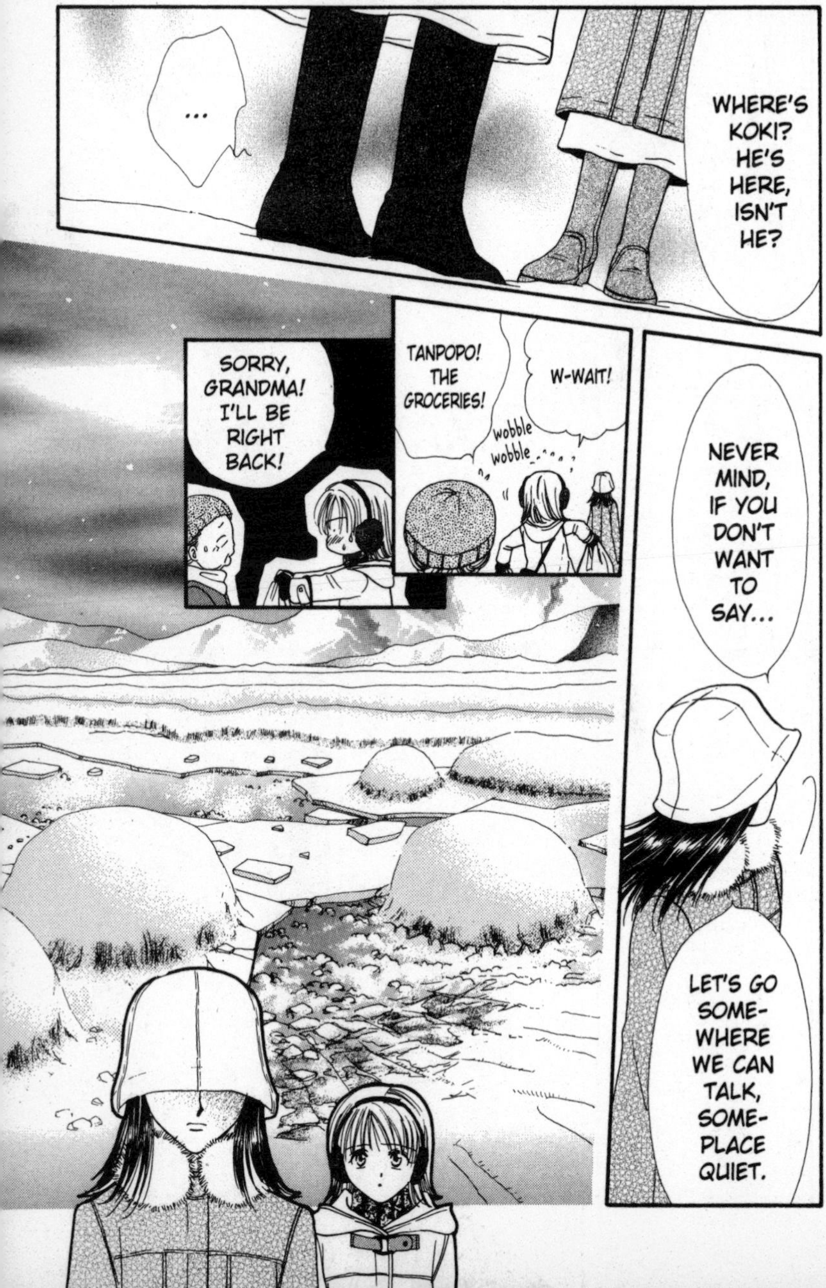
WHERE'S KOKI? HE'S HERE, ISN'T HE?
...
NEVER MIND, IF YOU DON'T WANT TO SAY...
LET'S GO SOME-WHERE WE CAN TALK, SOME-PLACE QUIET.
W-WAIT!
TANPOPO! THE GROCERIES!
wobble wobble
SORRY, GRANDMA! I'LL BE RIGHT BACK!

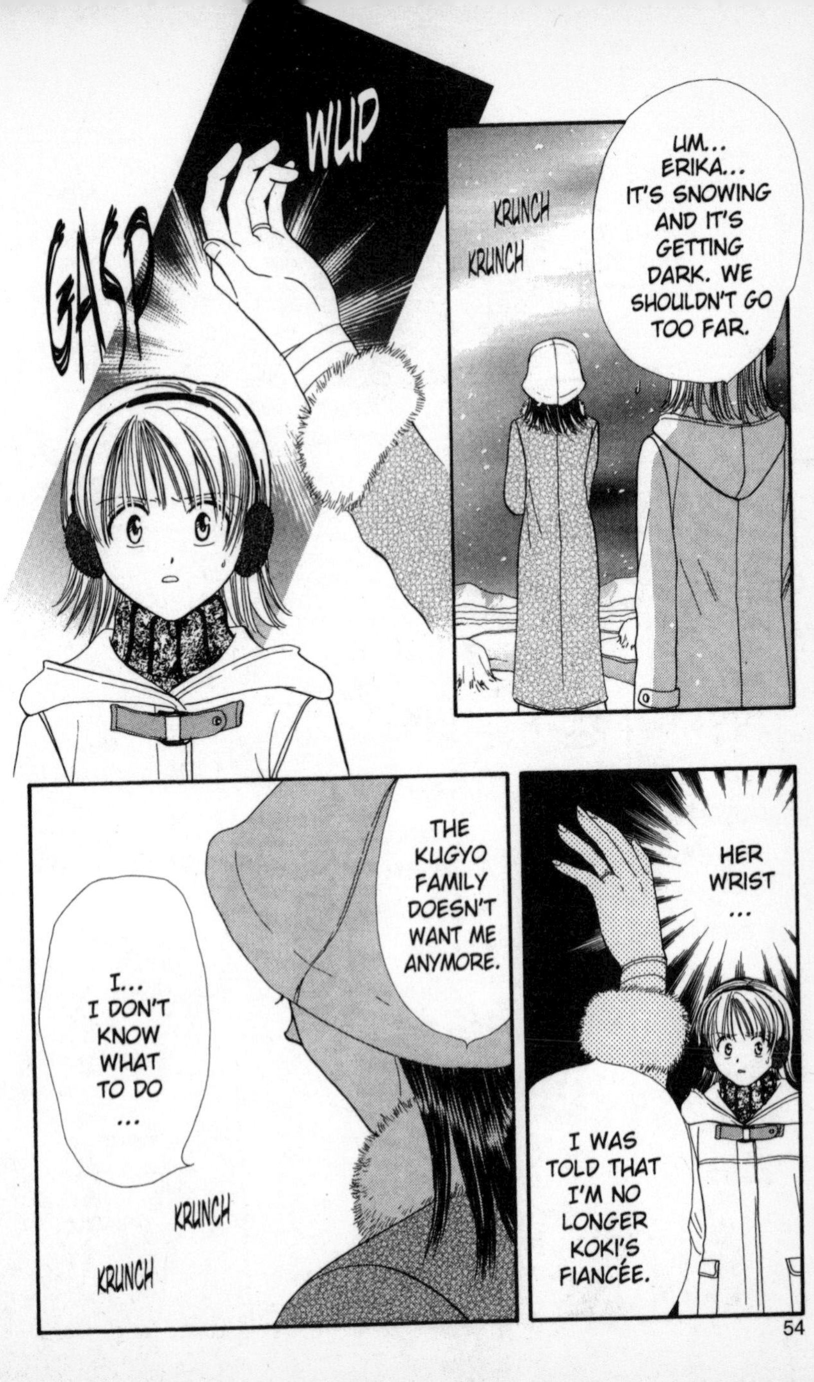
UM... ERIKA... IT'S SNOWING AND IT'S GETTING DARK. WE SHOULDN'T GO TOO FAR.
KRUNCH
KRUNCH
WUP
GASP
HER WRIST ...
I WAS TOLD THAT I'M NO LONGER KOKI'S FIANCÉE.
THE KUGYO FAMILY DOESN'T WANT ME ANYMORE.
I... I DON'T KNOW WHAT TO DO ...
KRUNCH
KRUNCH

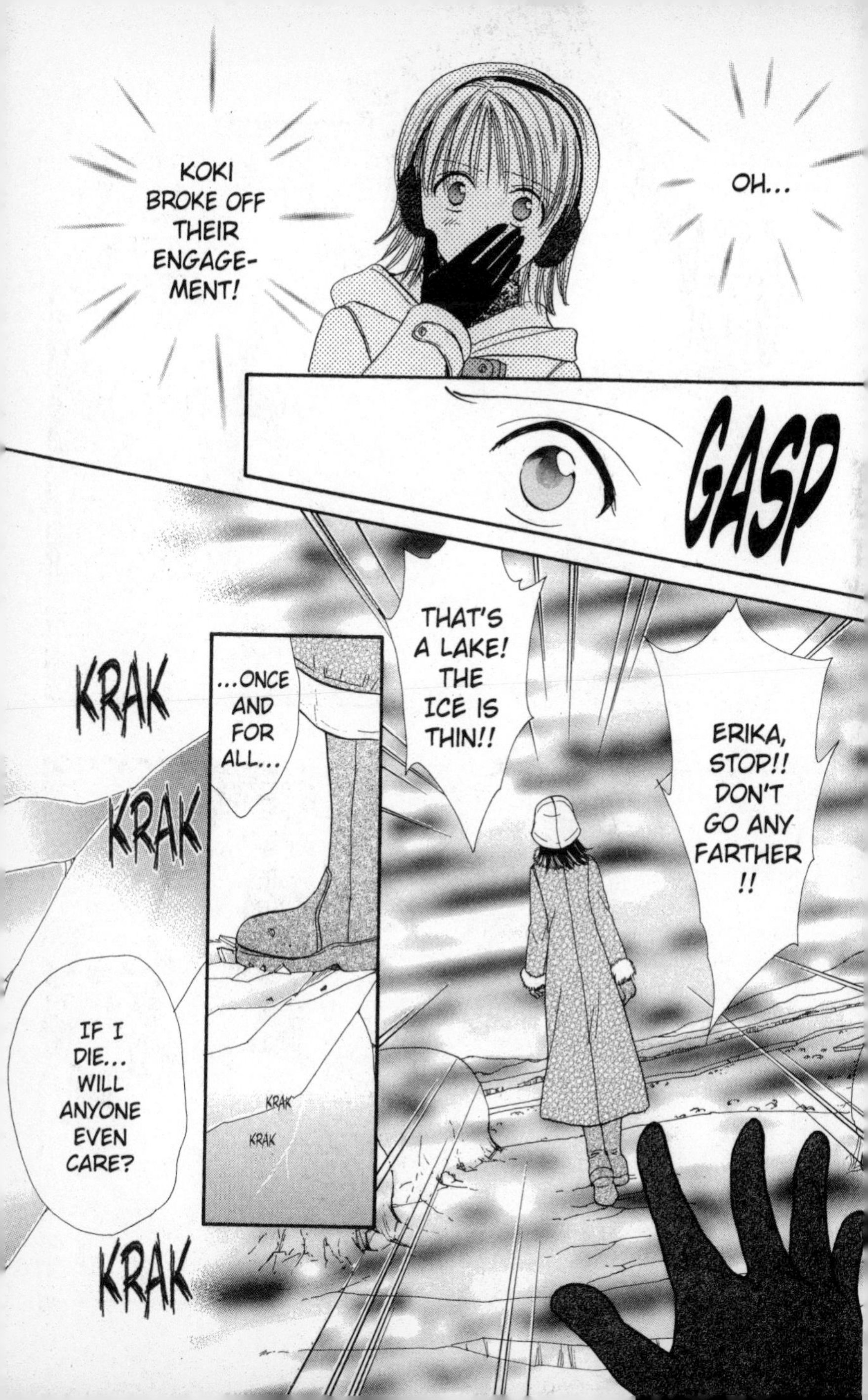
OH...
KOKI BROKE OFF THEIR ENGAGE-MENT!
GASP
ERIKA, STOP!! DON'T GO ANY FARTHER !!
THAT'S A LAKE! THE ICE IS THIN!!
...ONCE AND FOR ALL...
KRAK
KRAK
KRAK
KRAK
IF I DIE... WILL ANYONE EVEN CARE?
KRAK

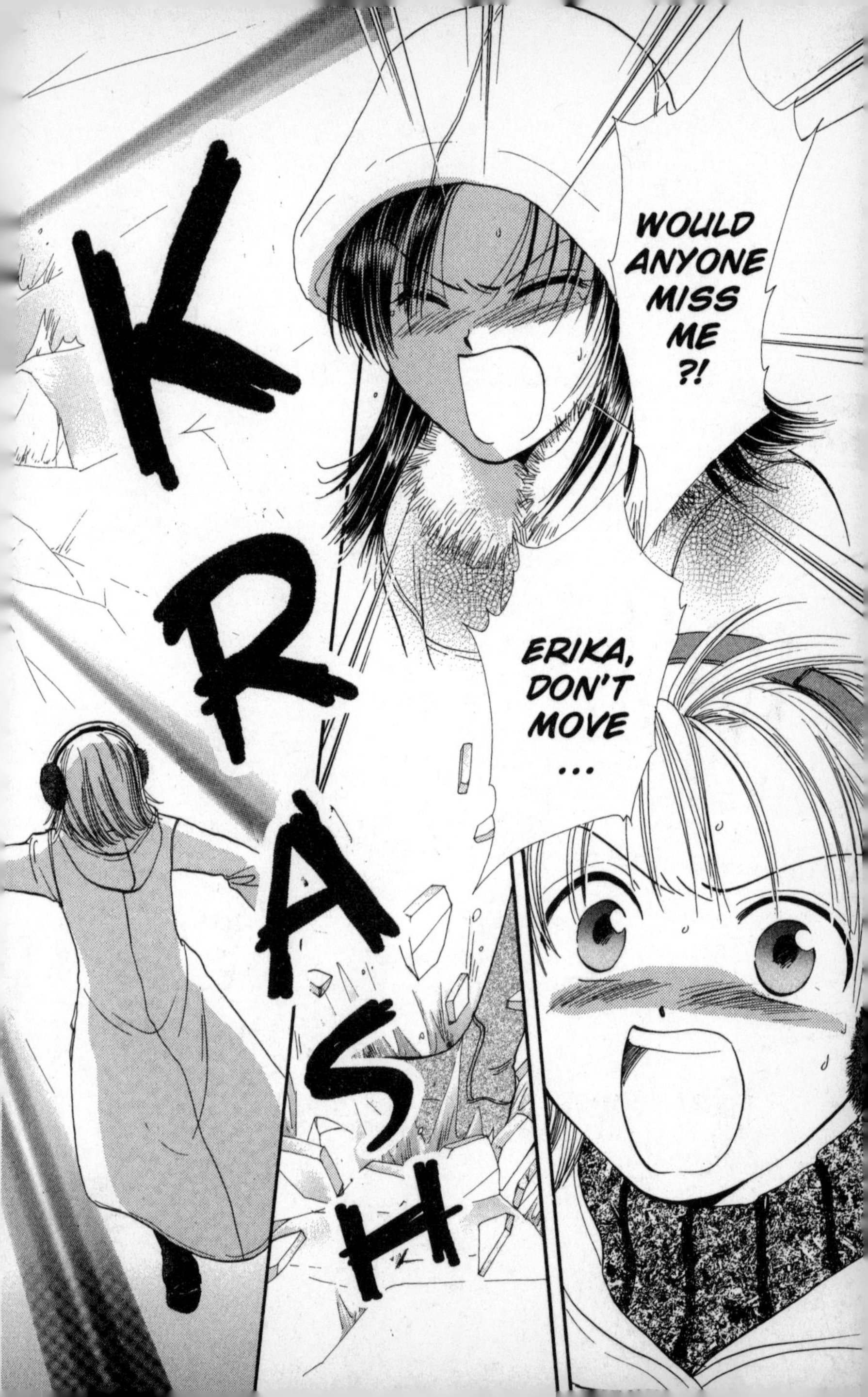
WOULD ANYONE MISS ME ?!
ERIKA, DON'T MOVE ...
KRASH

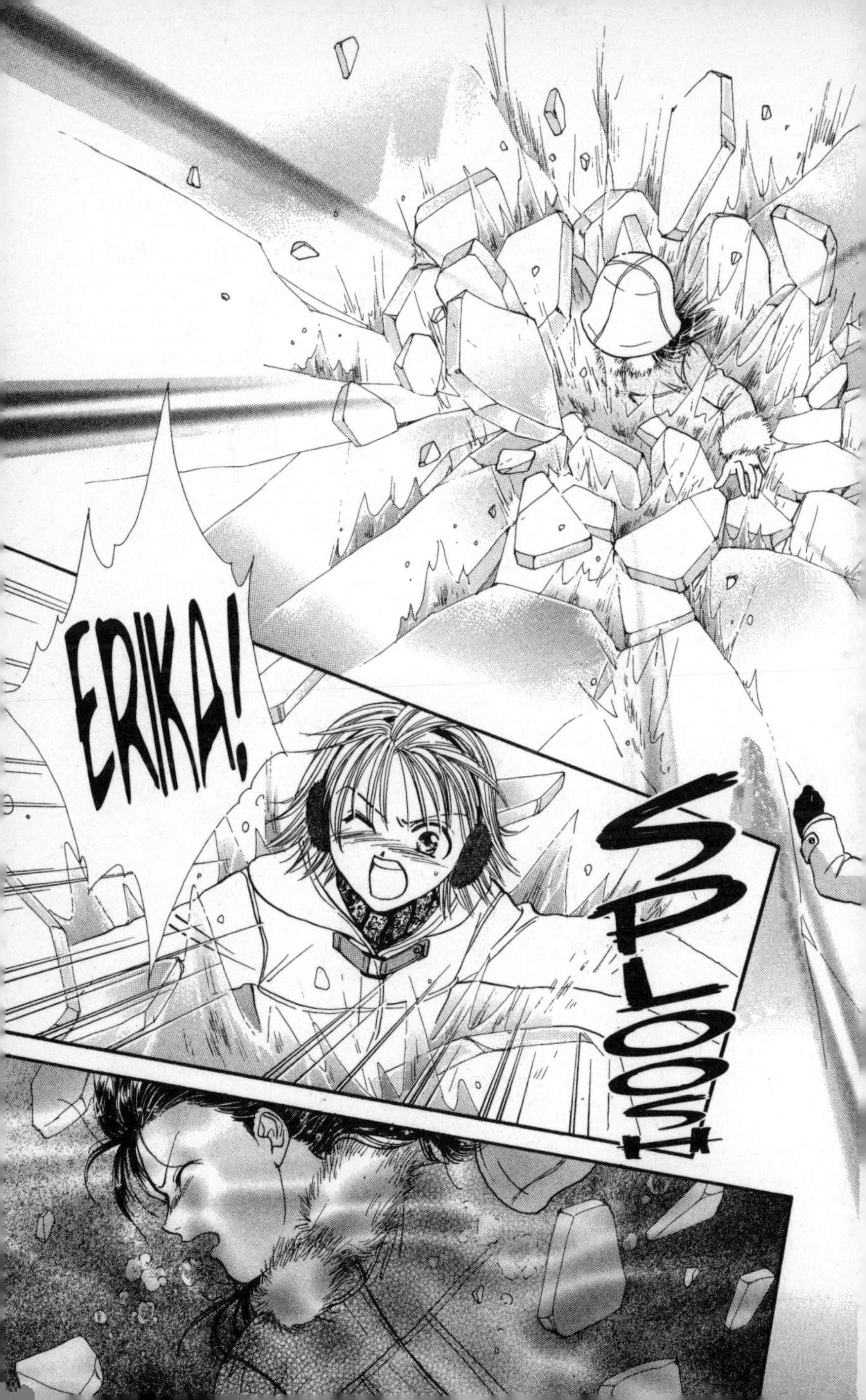
ERIKA!
SPLOOSH!!

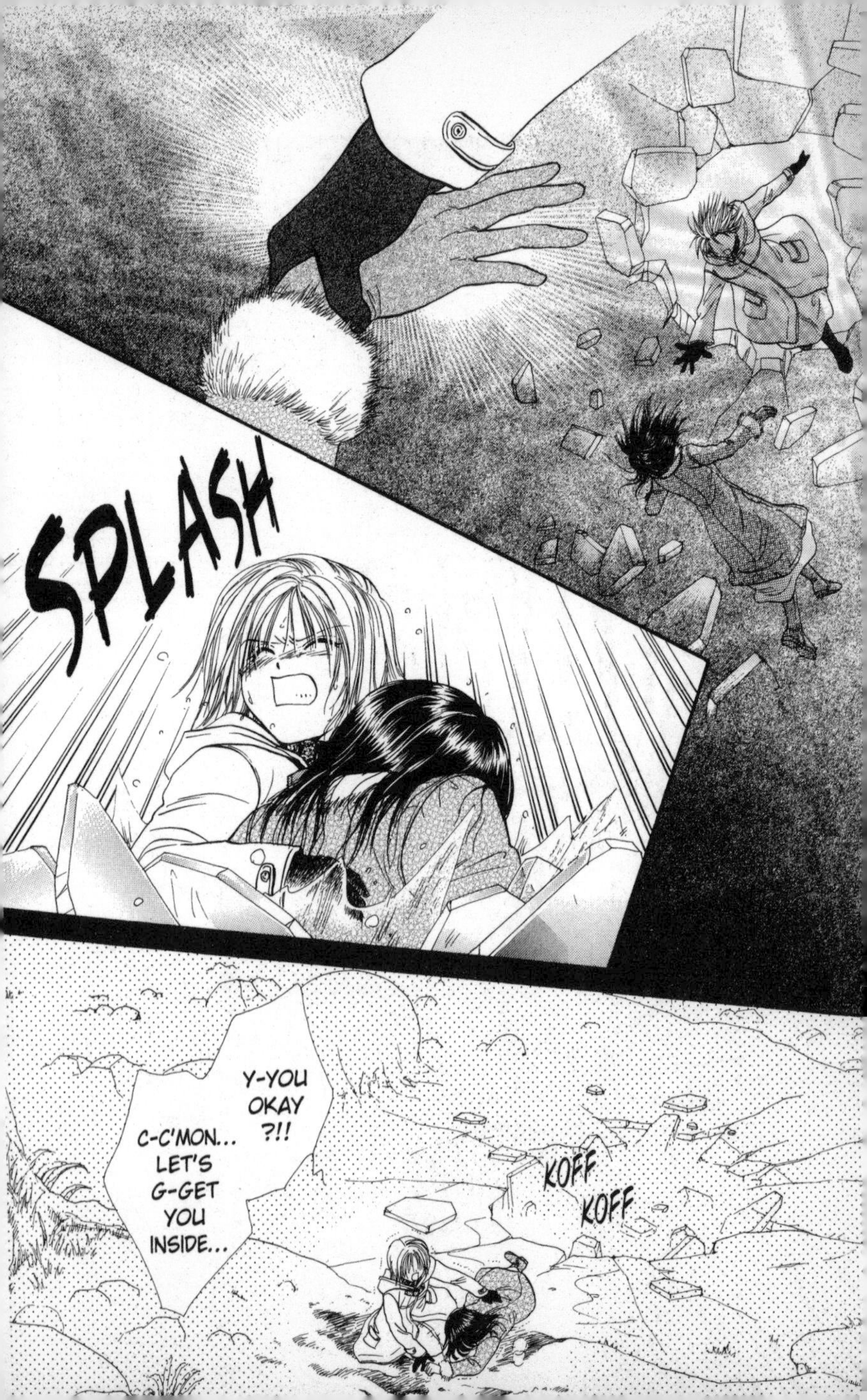
SPLASH
Y-YOU OKAY ?!!
C-C'MON... LET'S G-GET YOU INSIDE...
KOFF KOFF

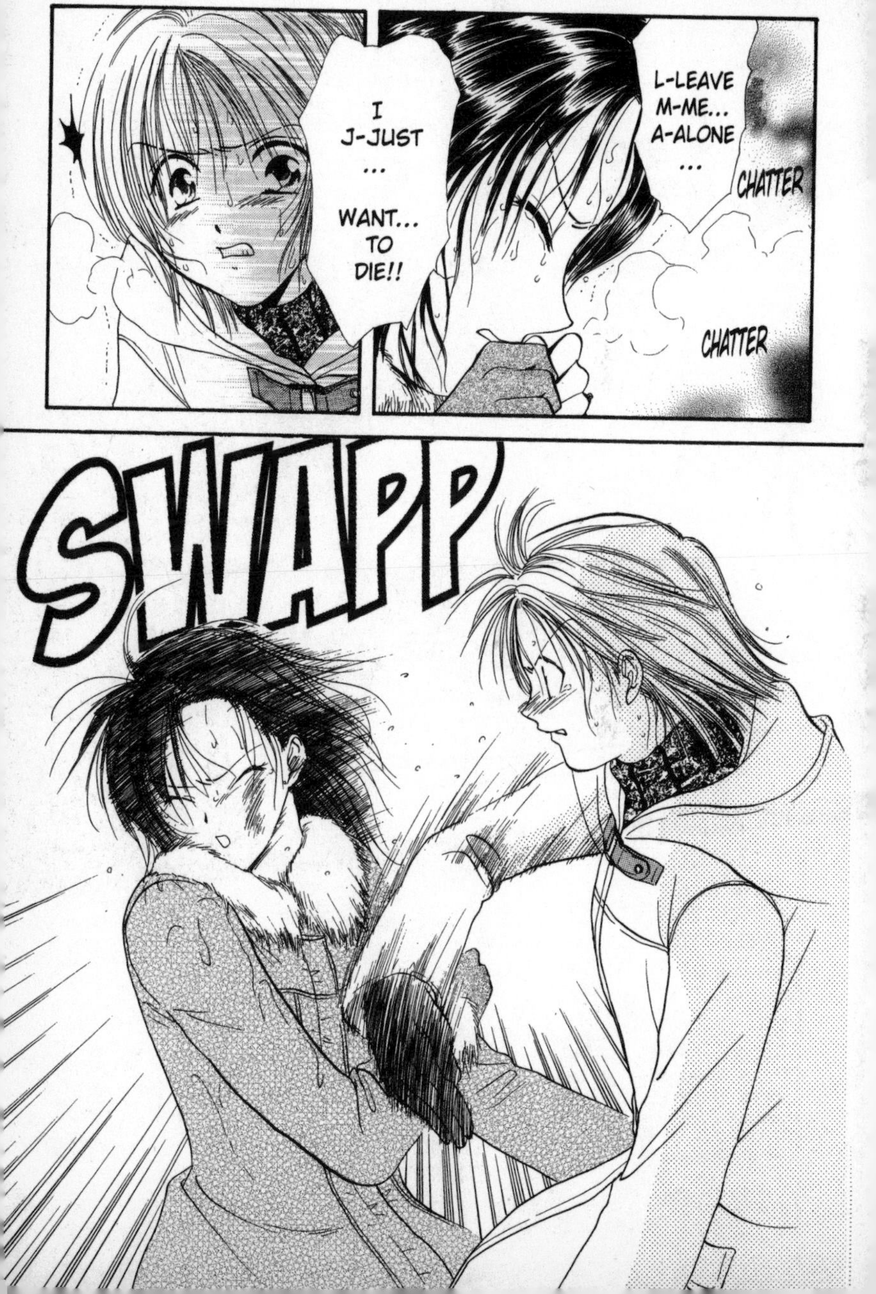
L-LEAVE M-ME... A-ALONE ...
CHATTER
CHATTER
I J-JUST ... WANT... TO DIE!!
SWAPP

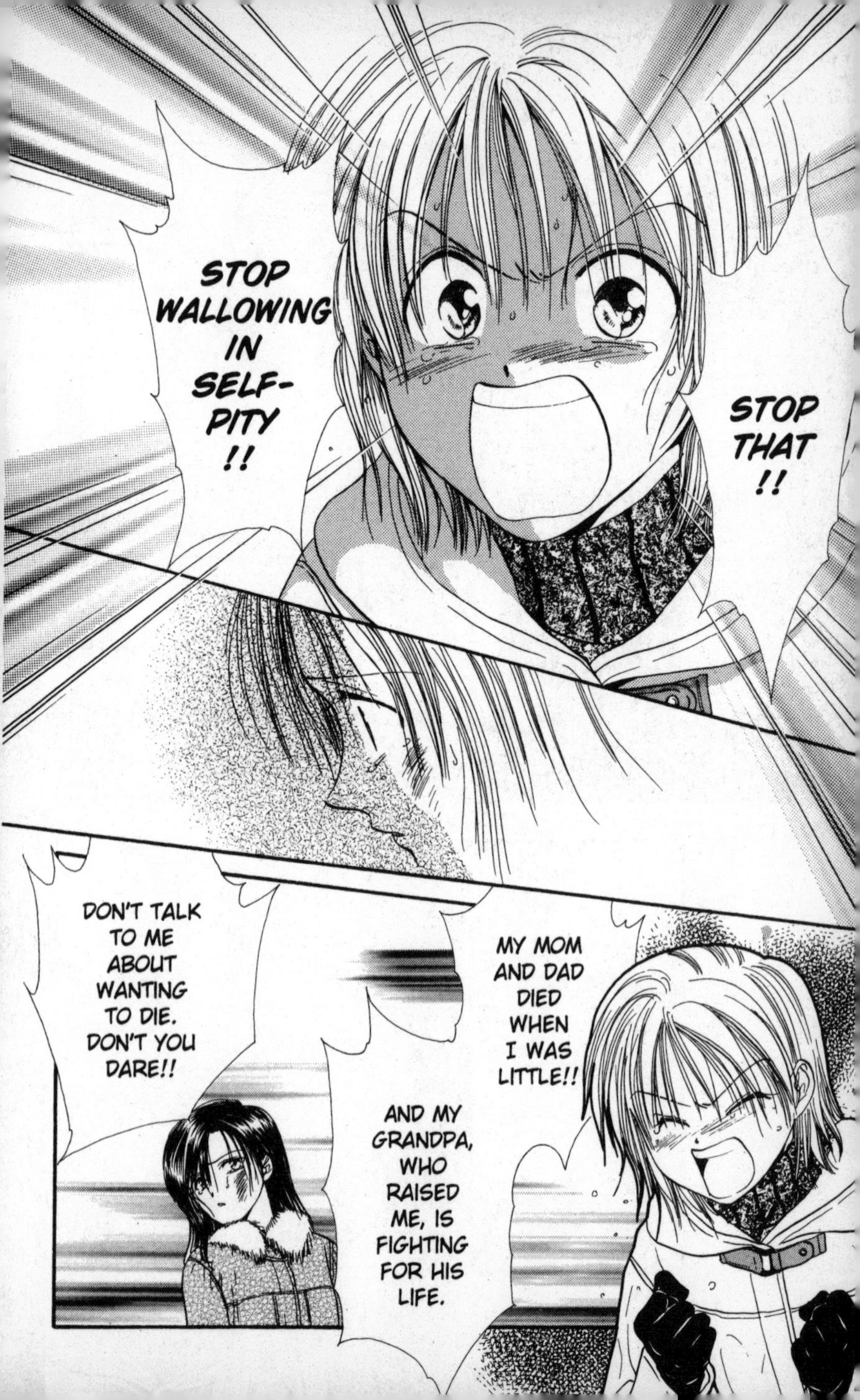
STOP THAT!!
STOP WALLOWING IN SELF-PITY!!
MY MOM AND DAD DIED WHEN I WAS LITTLE!!
AND MY GRANDPA, WHO RAISED ME, IS FIGHTING FOR HIS LIFE.
DON'T TALK TO ME ABOUT WANTING TO DIE. DON'T YOU DARE!!

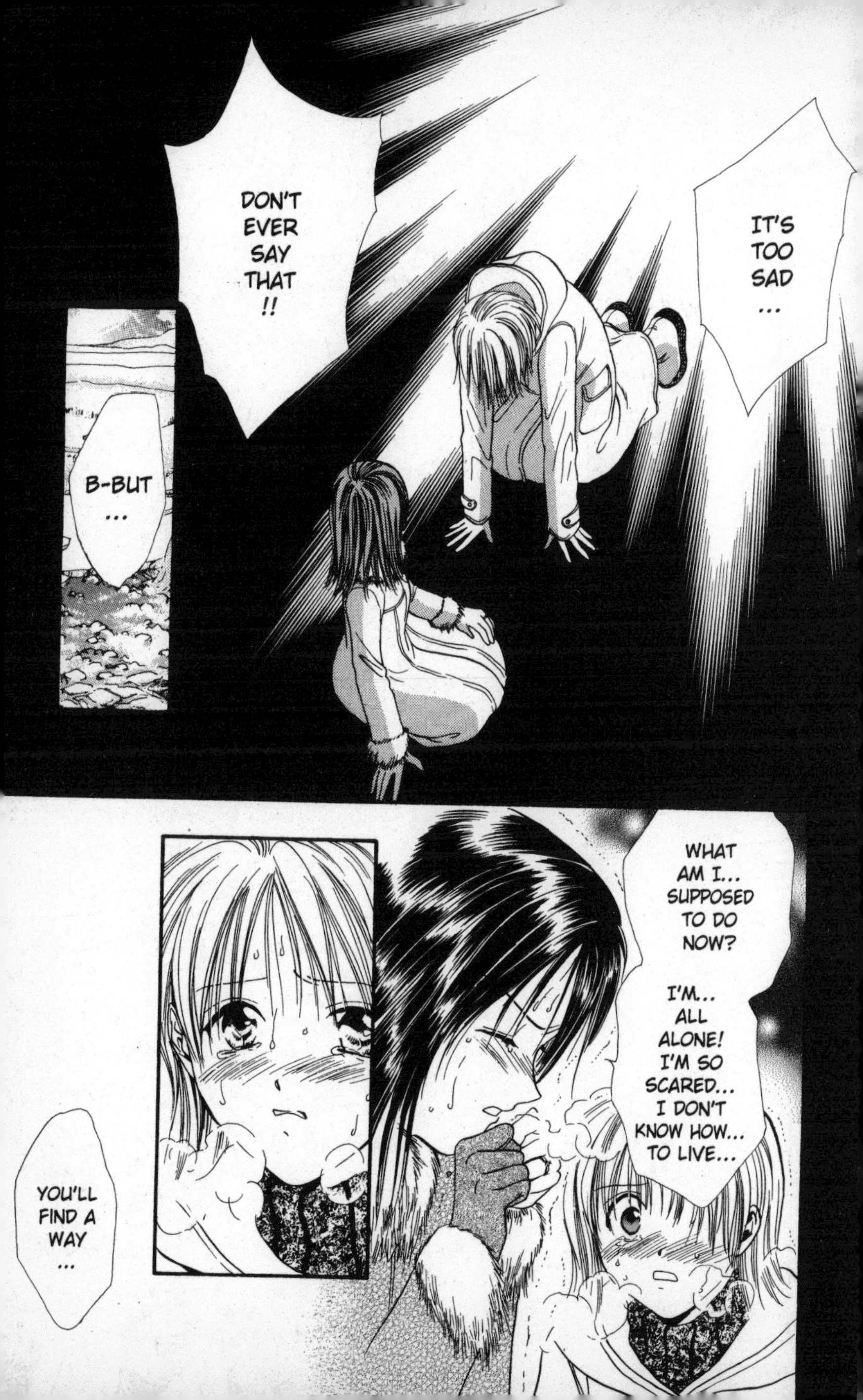
IT'S TOO SAD ...
DON'T EVER SAY THAT !!
B-BUT ...
WHAT AM I... SUPPOSED TO DO NOW?
I'M... ALL ALONE! I'M SO SCARED... I DON'T KNOW HOW... TO LIVE...
YOU'LL FIND A WAY ...

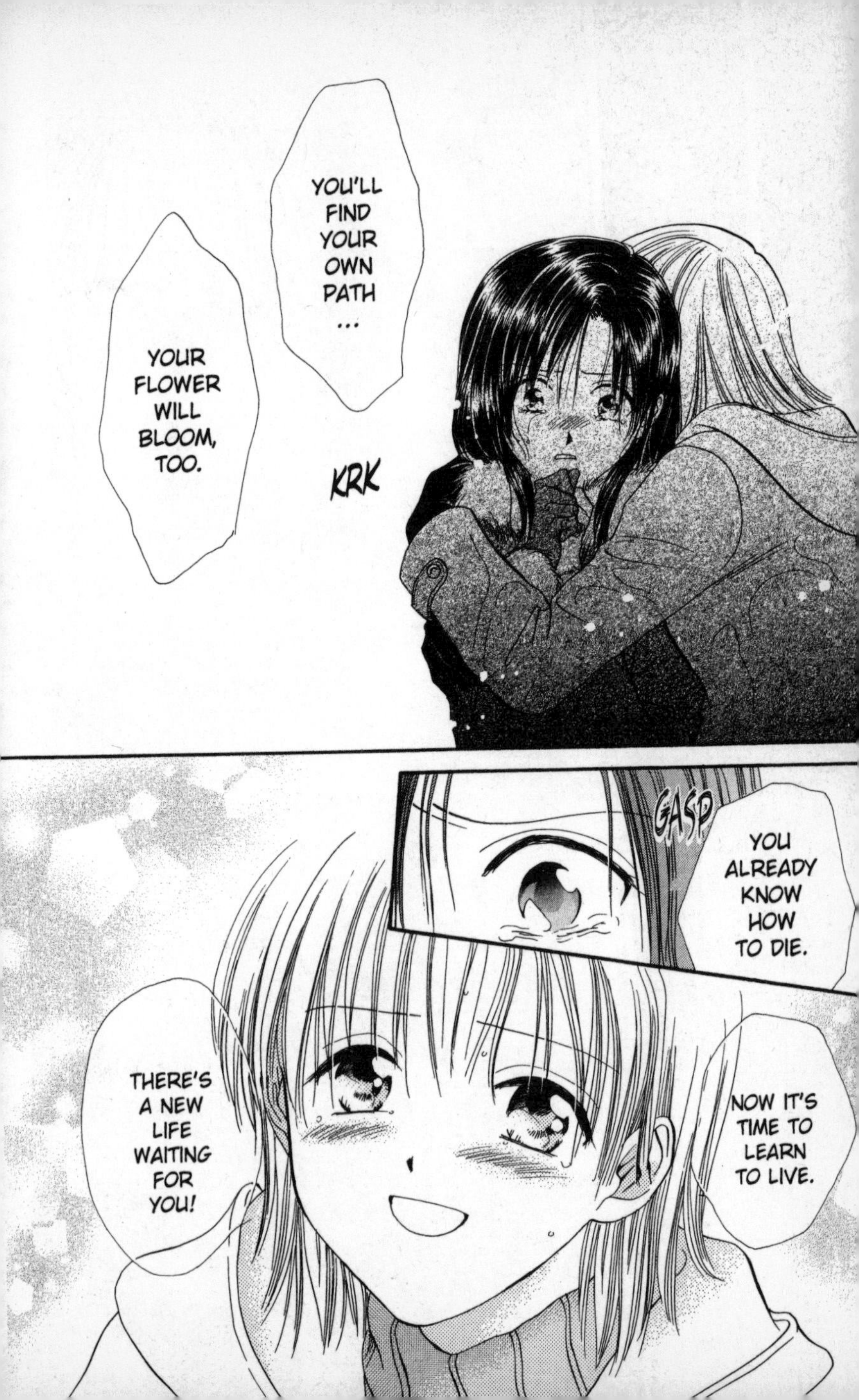
YOU'LL FIND YOUR OWN PATH ...
YOUR FLOWER WILL BLOOM, TOO.
KRK
GASP
YOU ALREADY KNOW HOW TO DIE.
NOW IT'S TIME TO LEARN TO LIVE.
THERE'S A NEW LIFE WAITING FOR YOU!

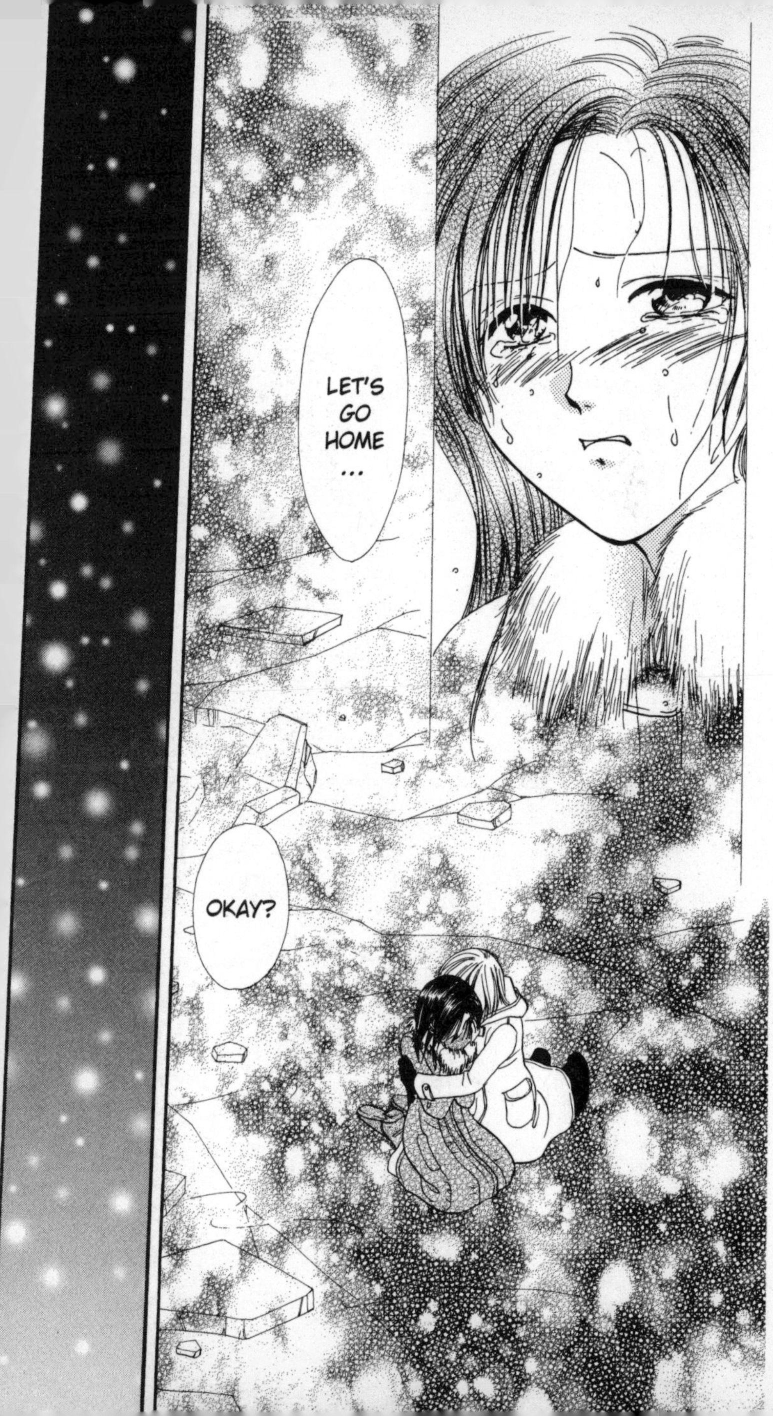
LET'S GO HOME ...
OKAY?

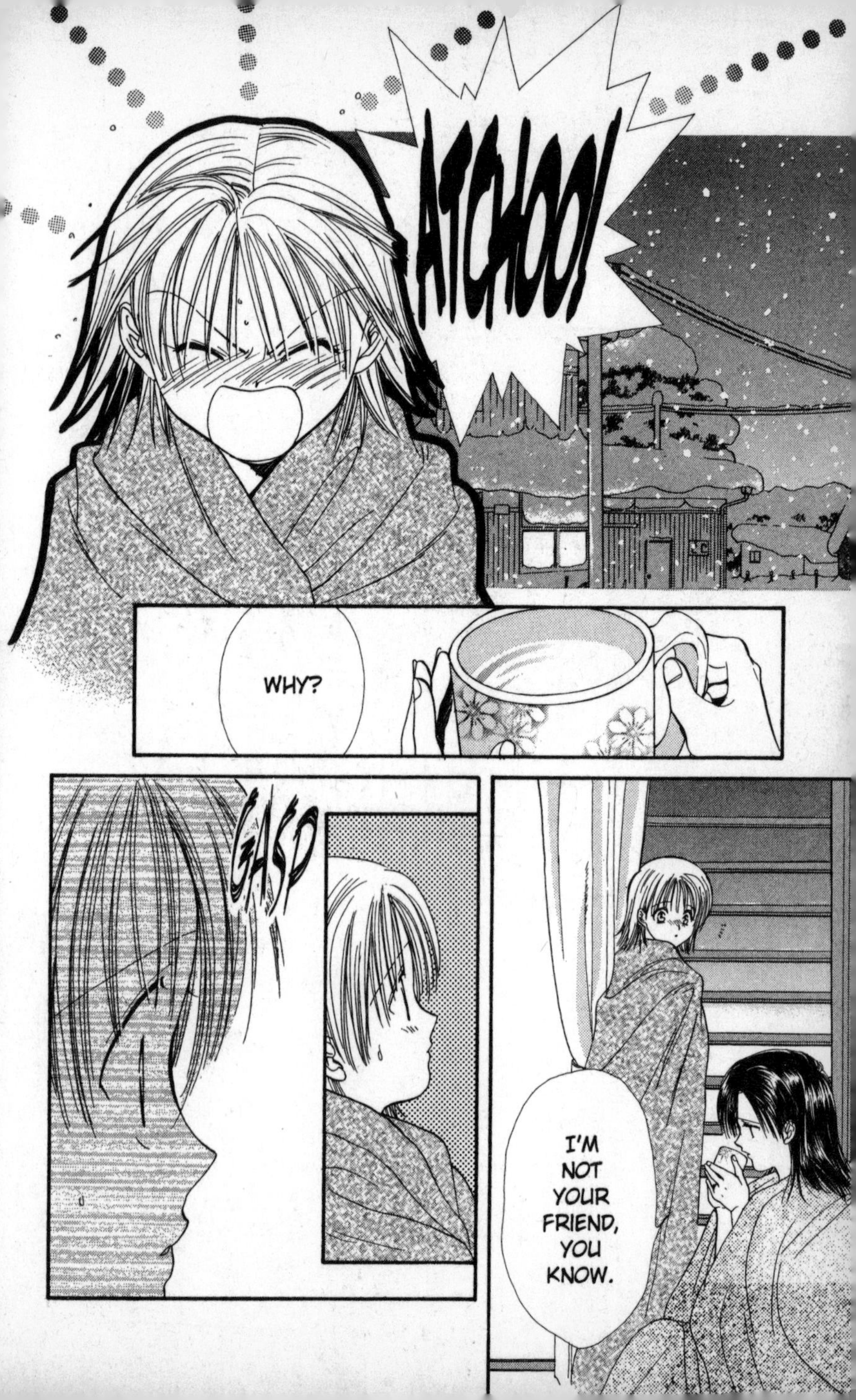
ATCHOO!
WHY?
I'M NOT YOUR FRIEND, YOU KNOW.
GASP

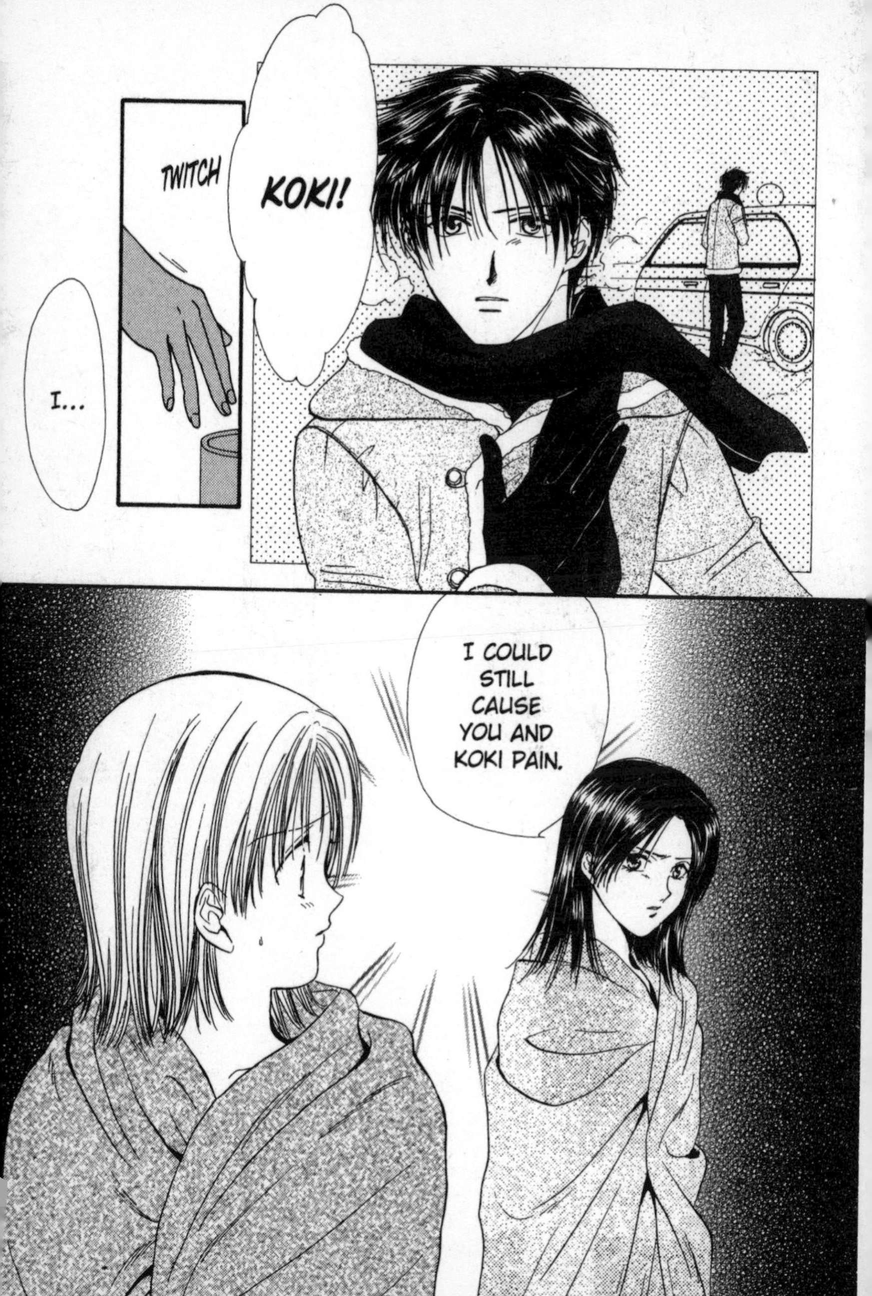
KOKI!
TWITCH
I...
I COULD STILL CAUSE YOU AND KOKI PAIN.

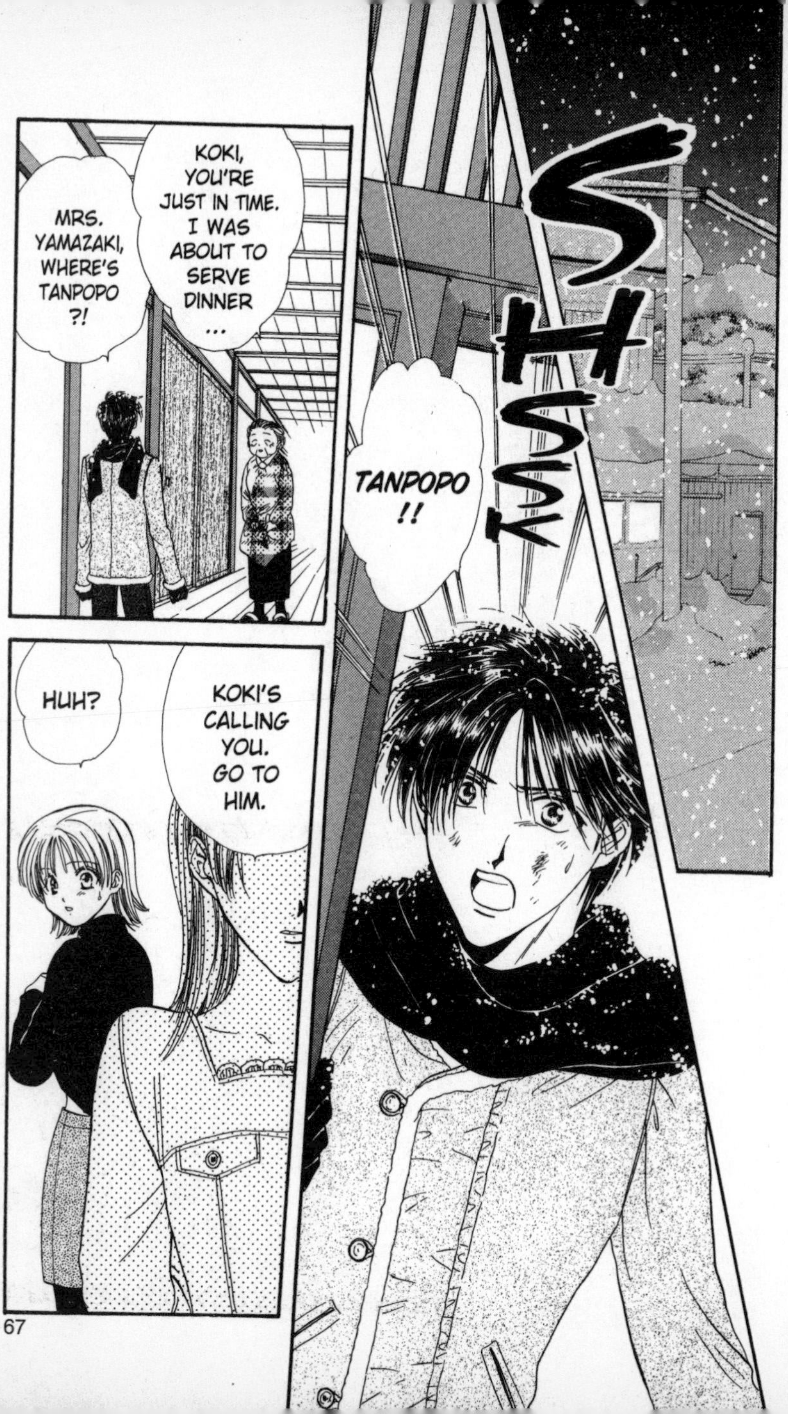
SHHSSK
TANPOPO !!
KOKI, YOU'RE JUST IN TIME. I WAS ABOUT TO SERVE DINNER ...
MRS. YAMAZAKI, WHERE'S TANPOPO ?!
KOKI'S CALLING YOU. GO TO HIM.
HUH?

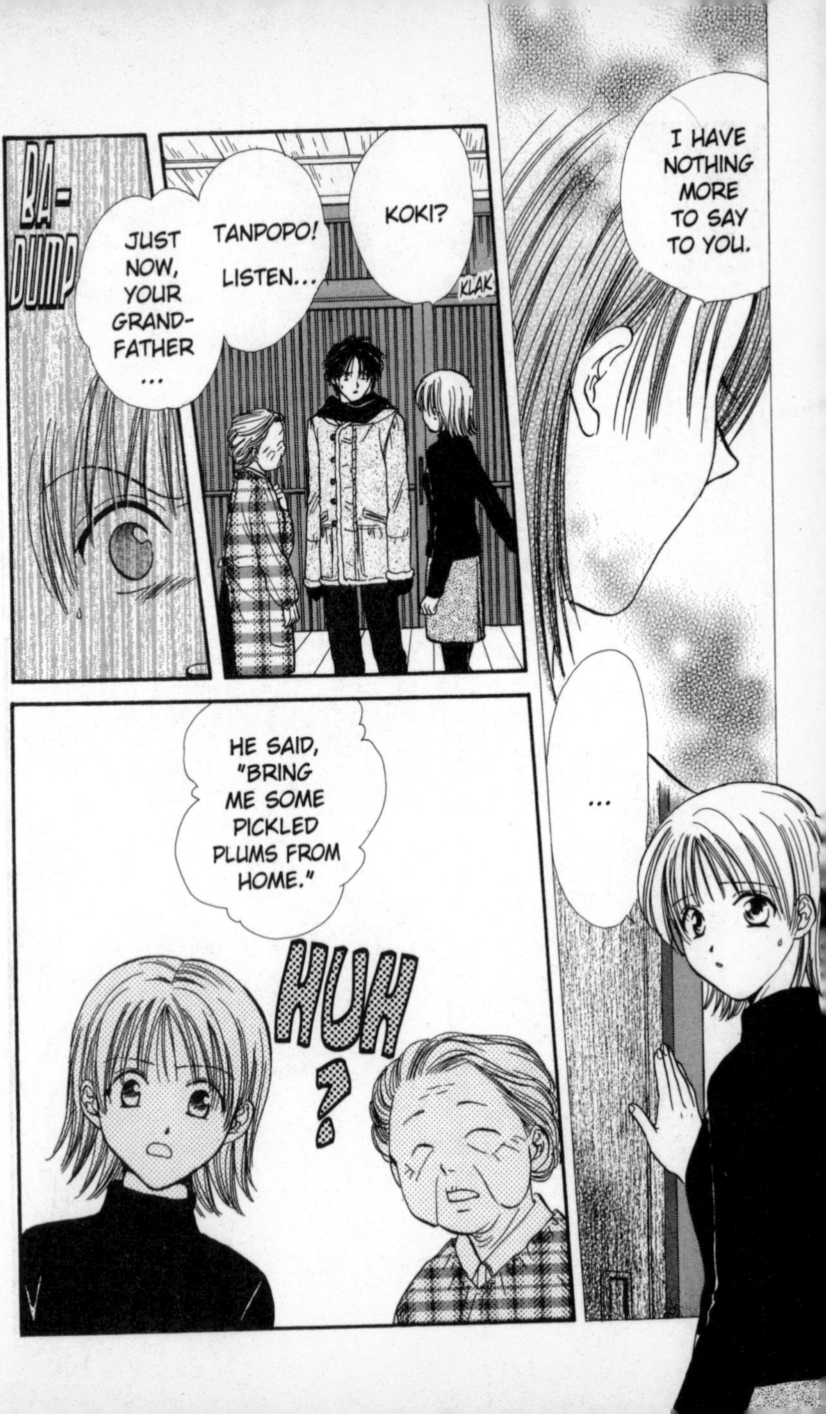
I HAVE NOTHING MORE TO SAY TO YOU.
...
KOKI?
KLAK
TANPOPO! LISTEN...
BA-DUMP
JUST NOW, YOUR GRANDFATHER ...
HE SAID, "BRING ME SOME PICKLED PLUMS FROM HOME."
HUH ?

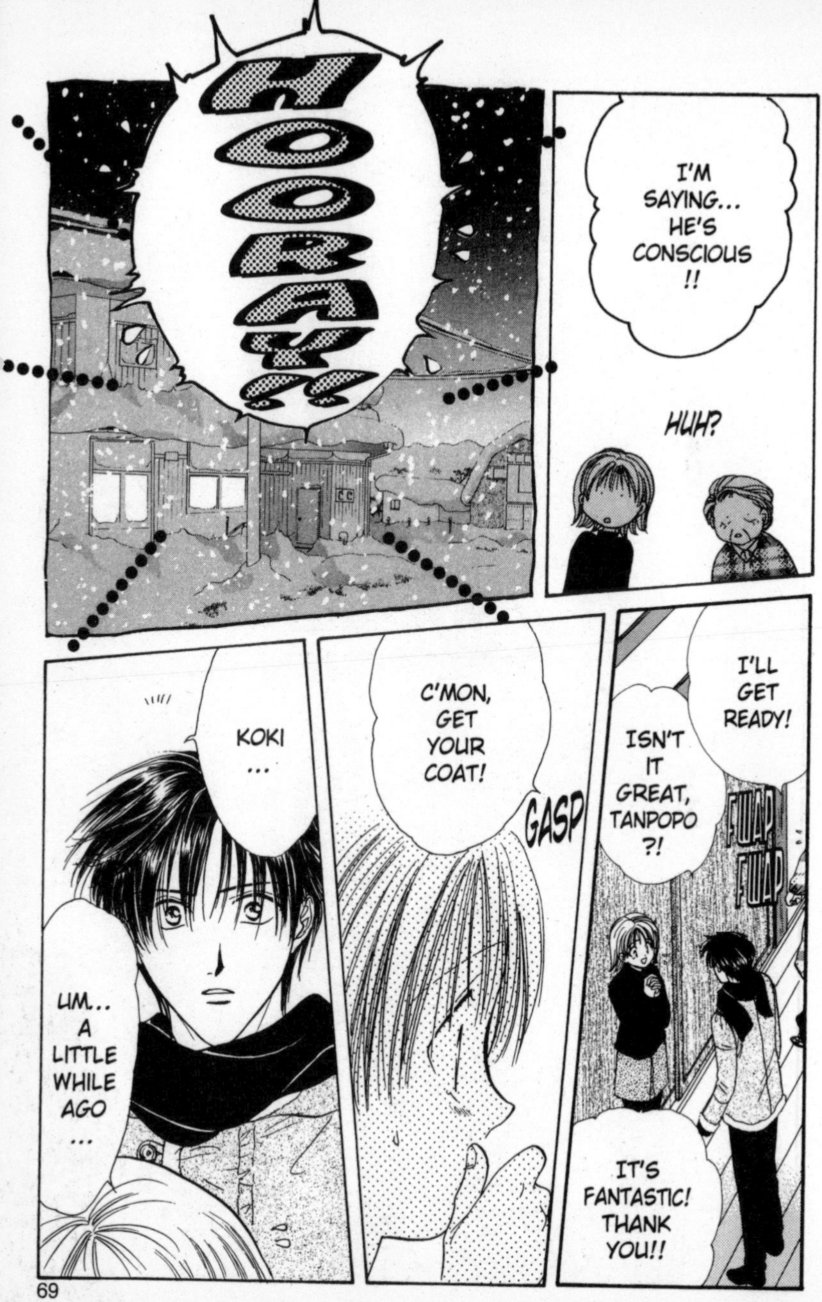
I'M SAYING... HE'S CONSCIOUS!!
HUH?
HOORAY!!
I'LL GET READY!
ISN'T IT GREAT, TANPOPO?!
FWAP FWAP
IT'S FANTASTIC! THANK YOU!!
C'MON, GET YOUR COAT!
GASP
KOKI...
UM... A LITTLE WHILE AGO...

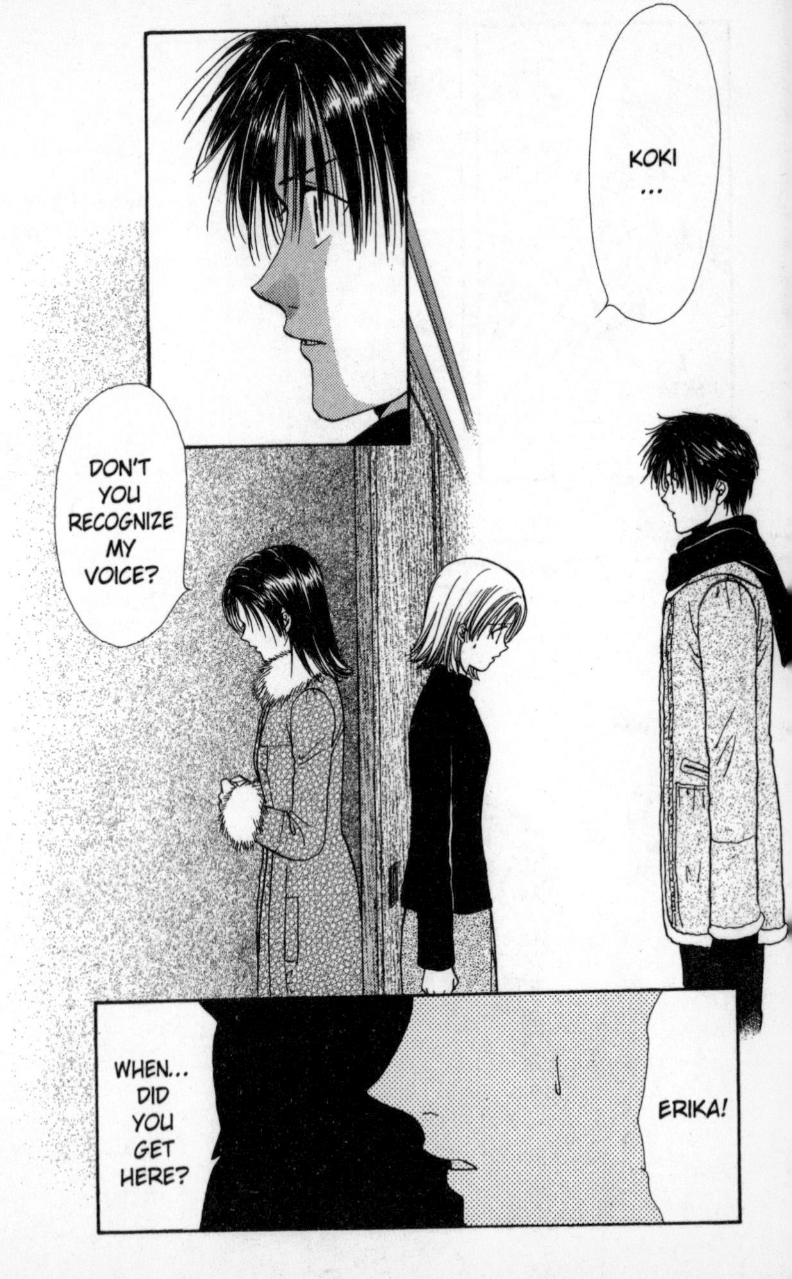
KOKI ...
DON'T YOU RECOGNIZE MY VOICE?
ERIKA!
WHEN... DID YOU GET HERE?

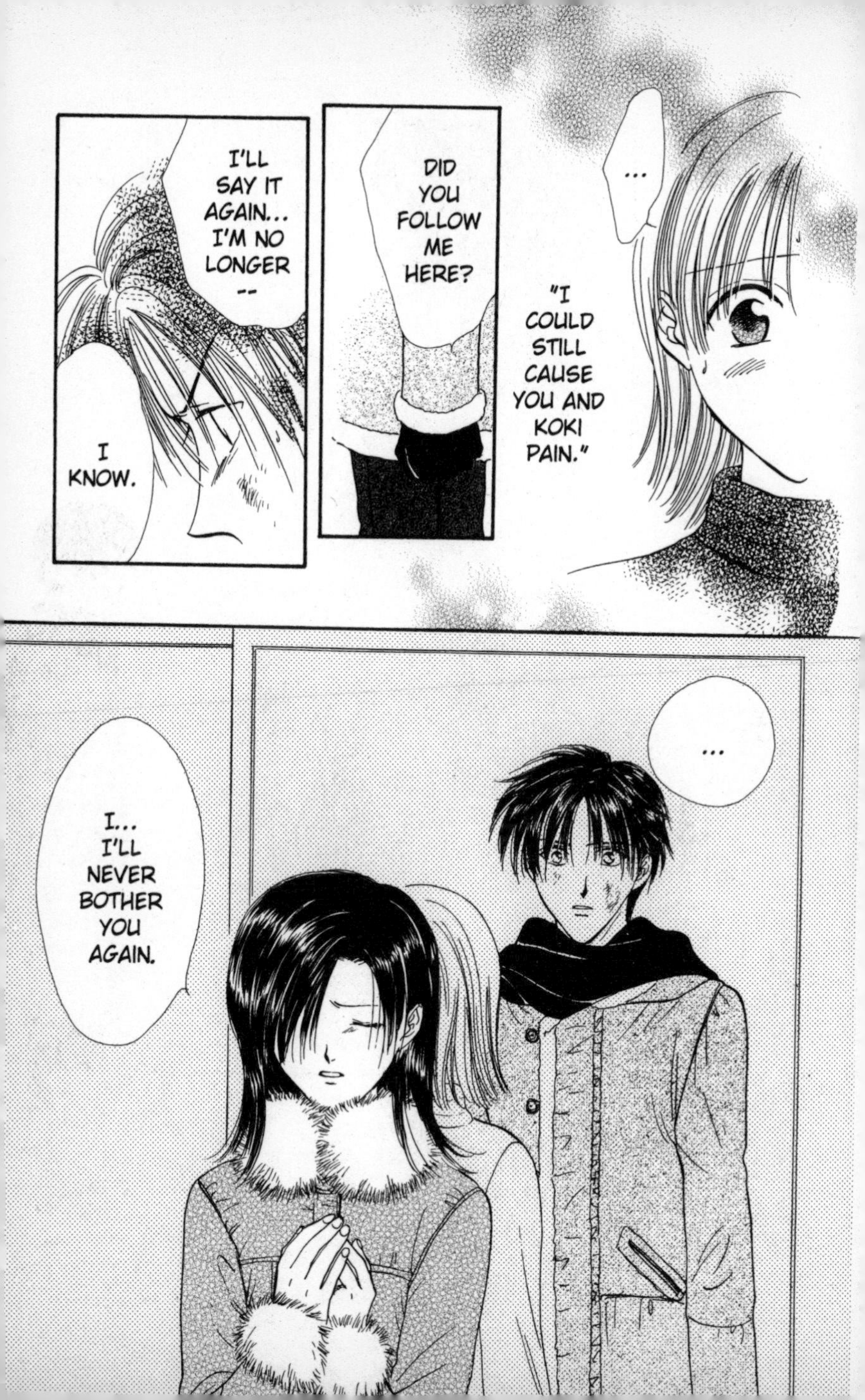
...
"I COULD STILL CAUSE YOU AND KOKI PAIN."
DID YOU FOLLOW ME HERE?
I'LL SAY IT AGAIN... I'M NO LONGER --
I KNOW.
...
I... I'LL NEVER BOTHER YOU AGAIN.

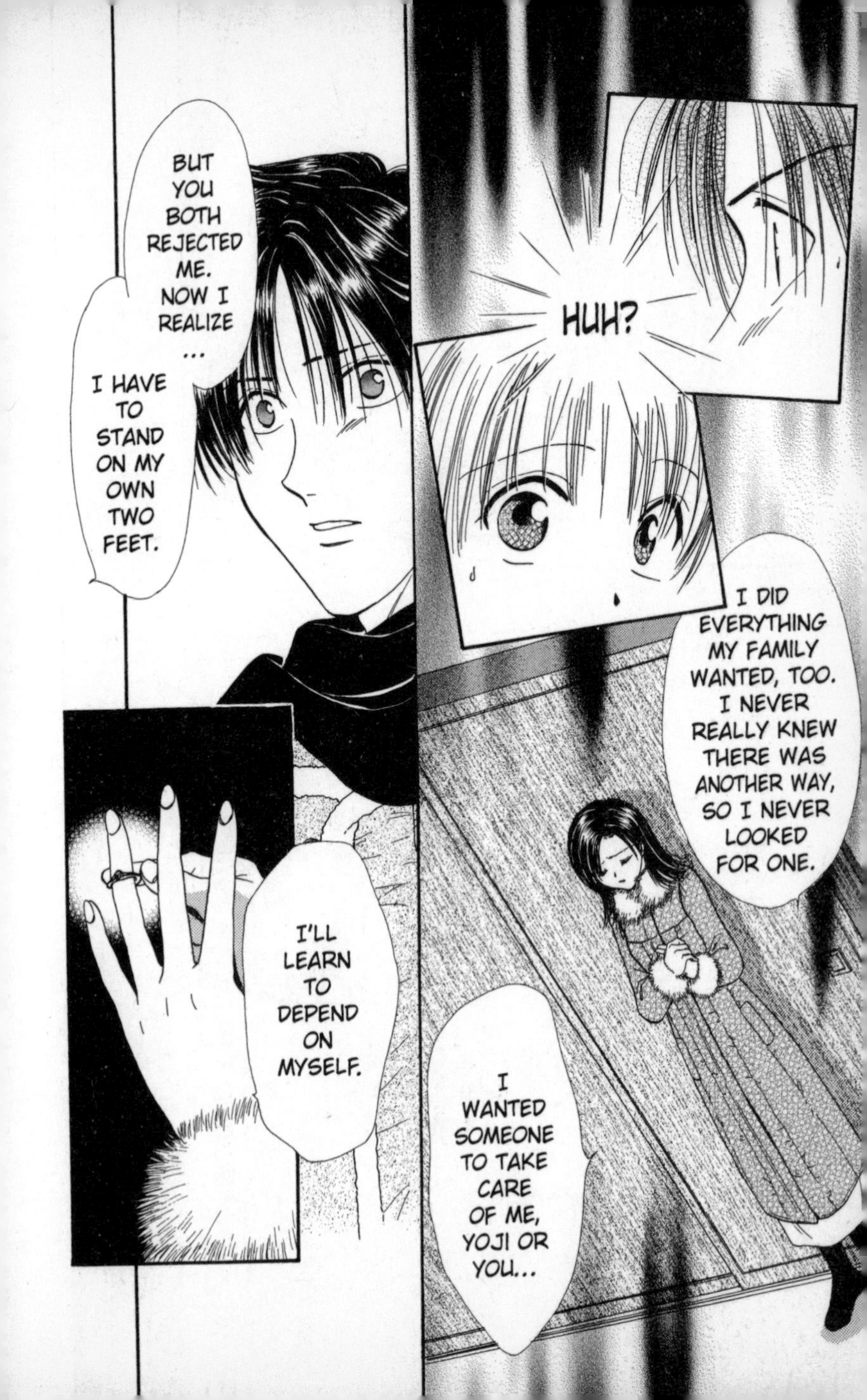
HUH?
I DID EVERYTHING MY FAMILY WANTED, TOO. I NEVER REALLY KNEW THERE WAS ANOTHER WAY, SO I NEVER LOOKED FOR ONE.
I WANTED SOMEONE TO TAKE CARE OF ME, YOJI OR YOU...
BUT YOU BOTH REJECTED ME. NOW I REALIZE...
I HAVE TO STAND ON MY OWN TWO FEET.
I'LL LEARN TO DEPEND ON MYSELF.

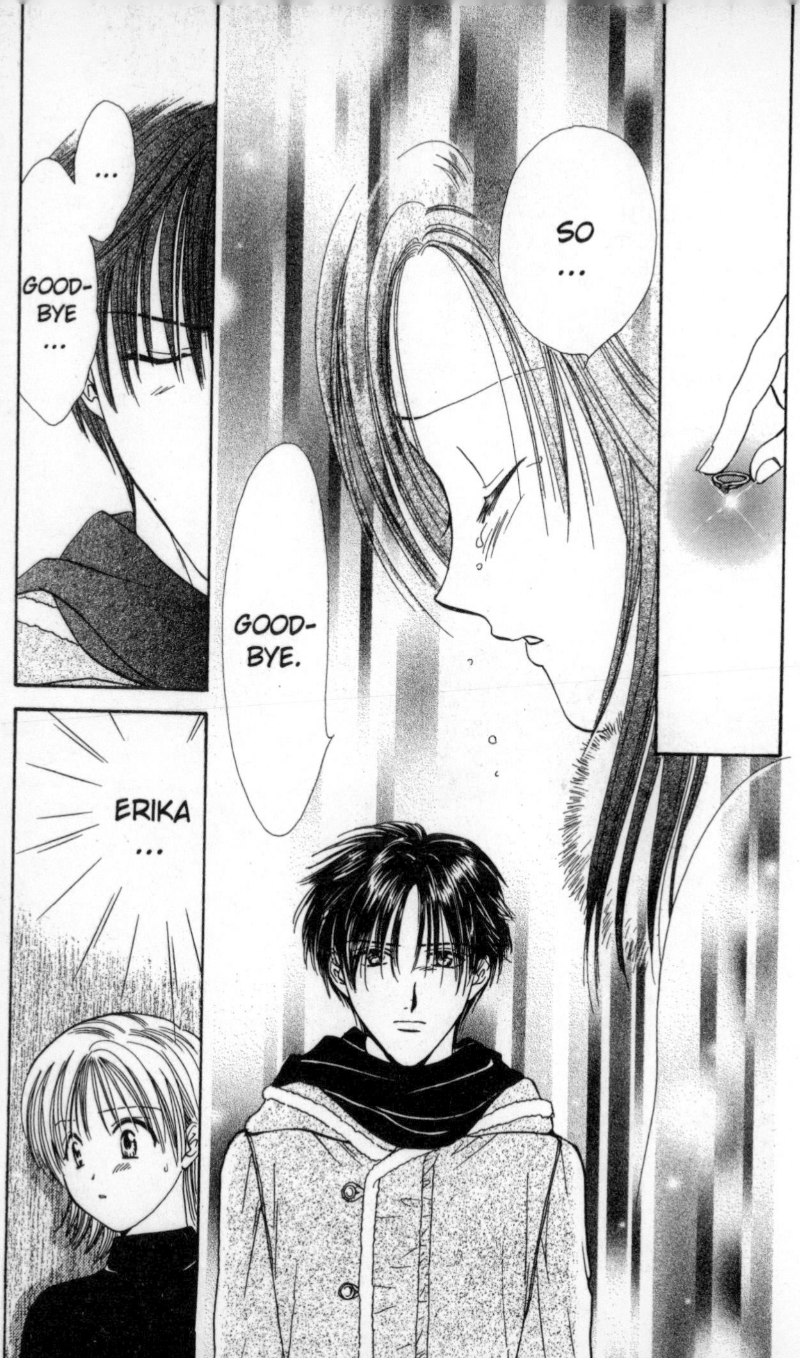
SO ...
GOOD-BYE.
...
GOOD-BYE ...
ERIKA ...

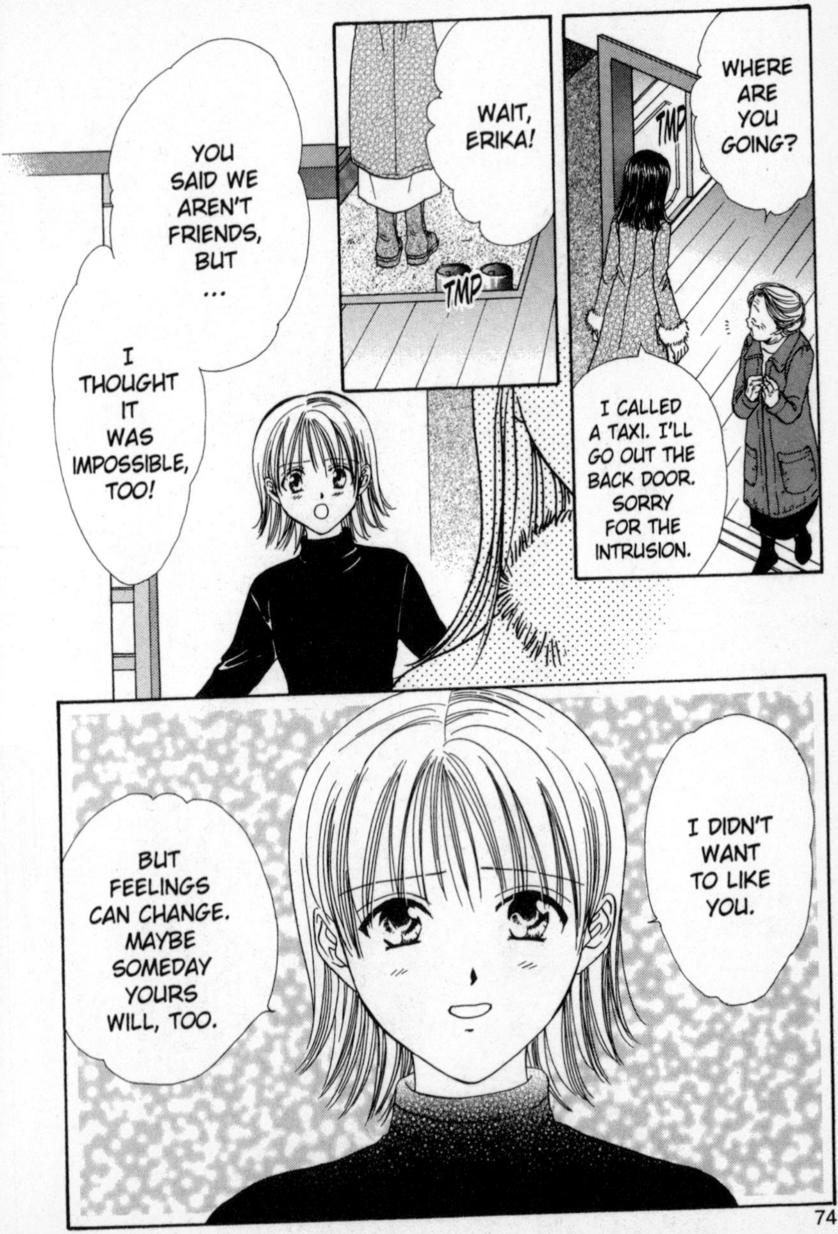
WHERE ARE YOU GOING?
TMP
I CALLED A TAXI. I'LL GO OUT THE BACK DOOR. SORRY FOR THE INTRUSION.
WAIT, ERIKA!
TMP
YOU SAID WE AREN'T FRIENDS, BUT ...
I THOUGHT IT WAS IMPOSSIBLE, TOO!
I DIDN'T WANT TO LIKE YOU.
BUT FEELINGS CAN CHANGE. MAYBE SOMEDAY YOURS WILL, TOO.

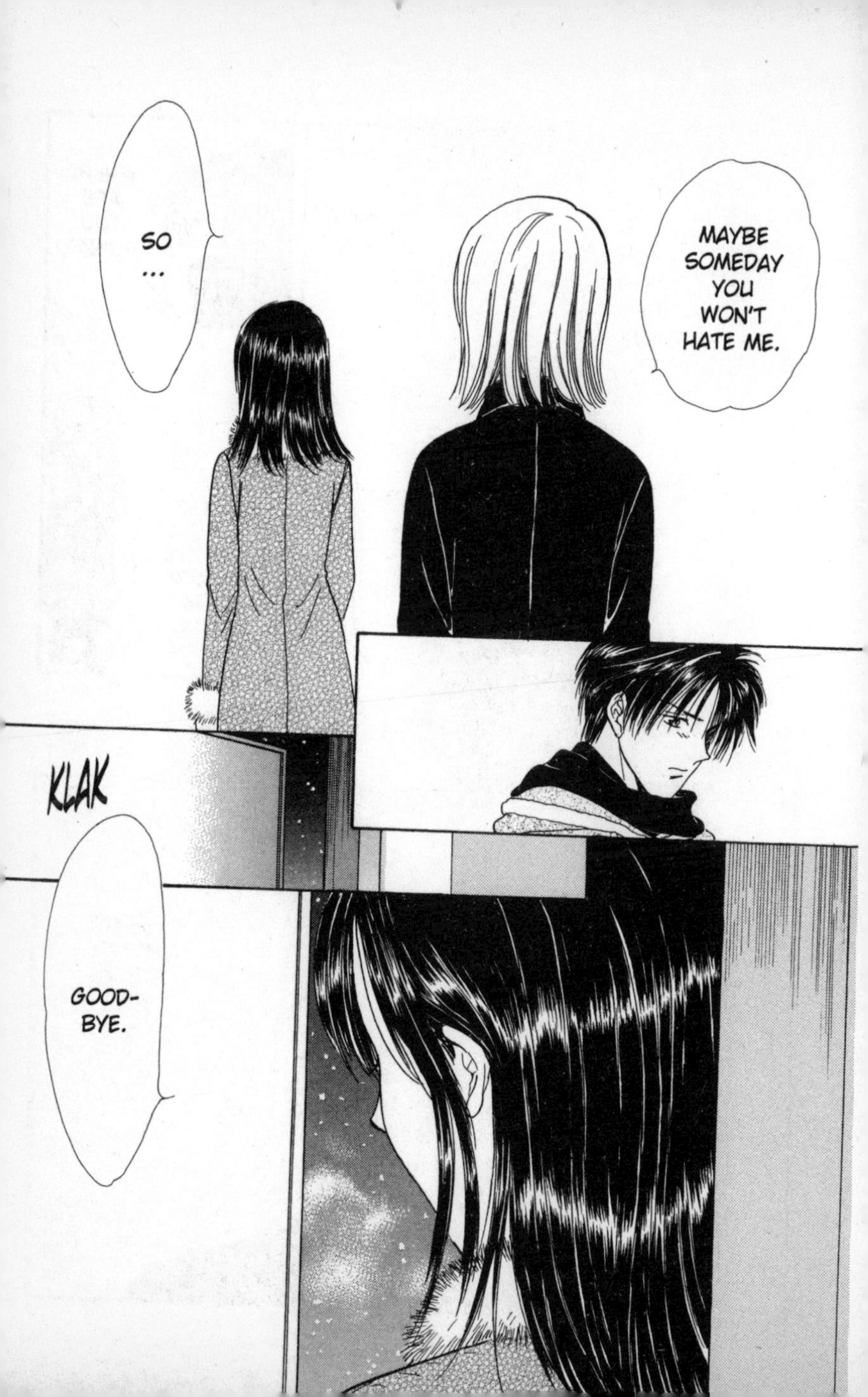
MAYBE SOMEDAY YOU WON'T HATE ME.
SO ...
KLAK
GOOD-BYE.

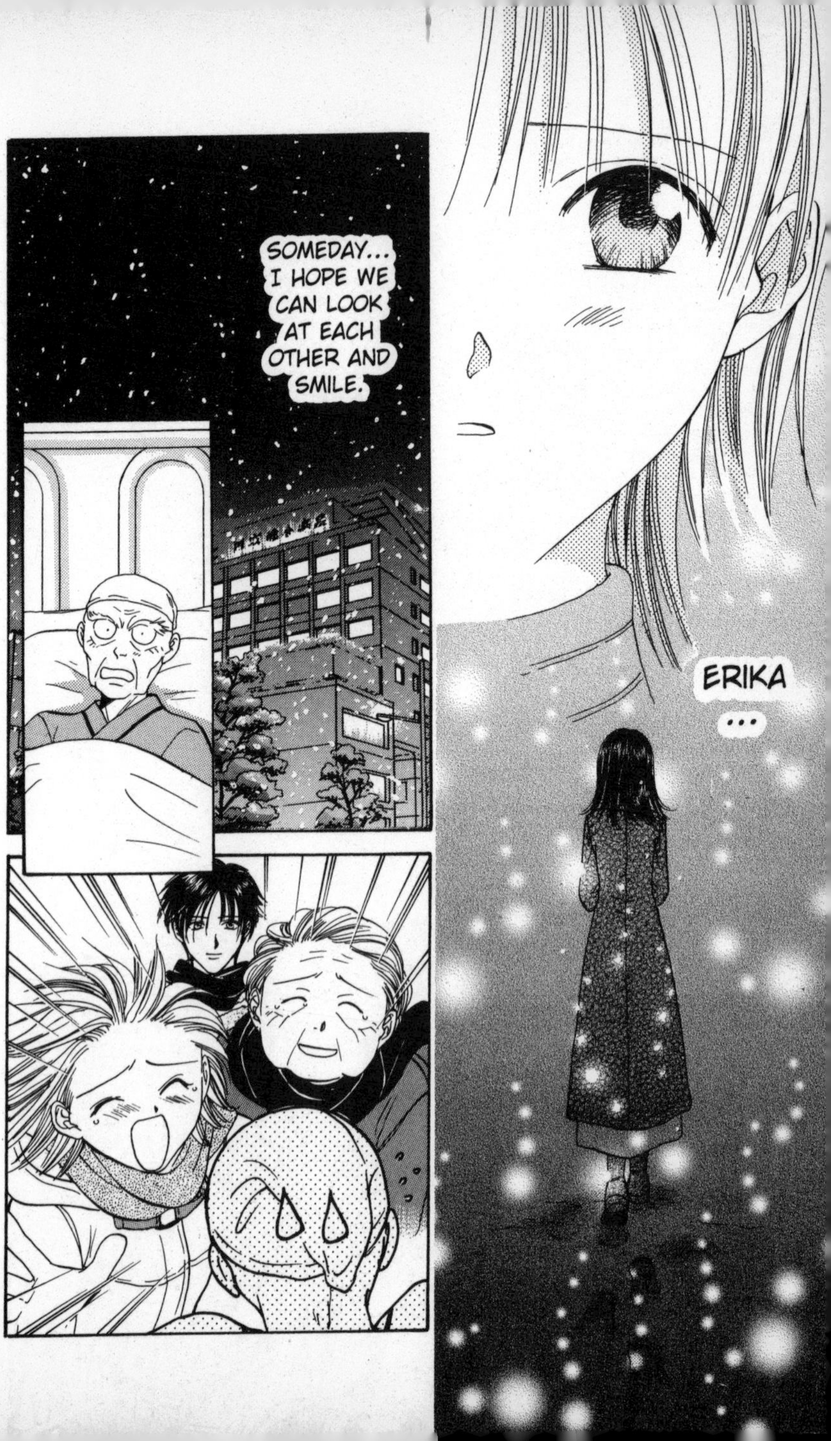
ERIKA ...
SOMEDAY... I HOPE WE CAN LOOK AT EACH OTHER AND SMILE.

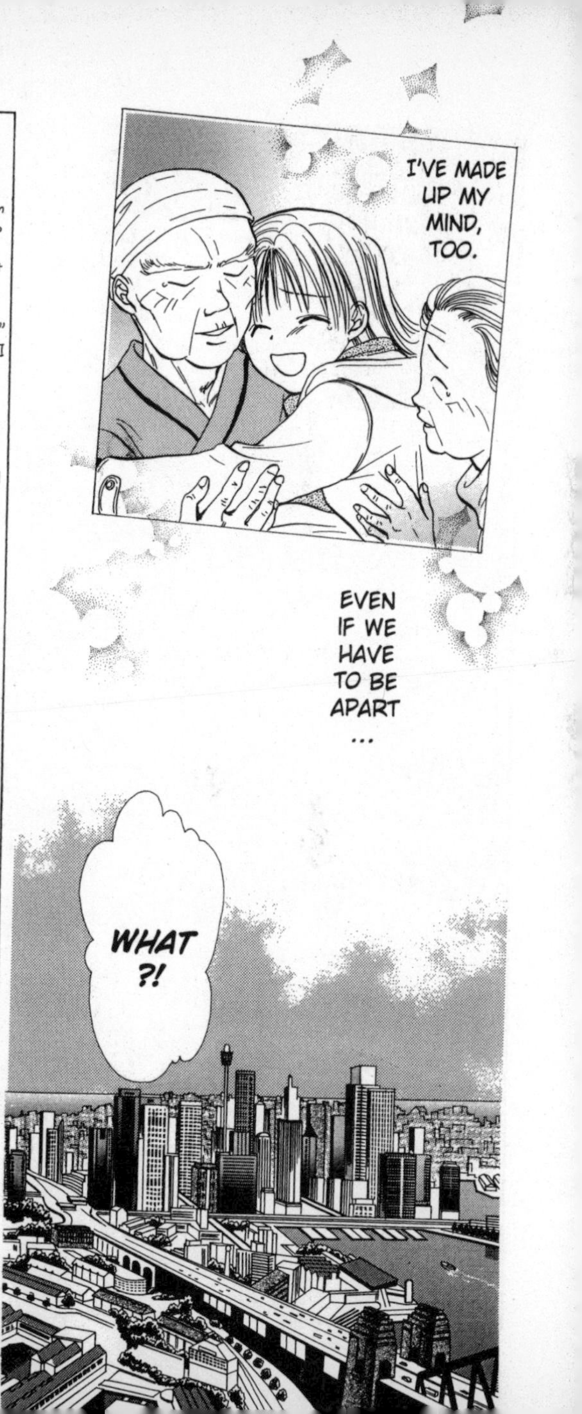
I'VE MADE UP MY MIND, TOO.
EVEN IF WE HAVE TO BE APART...
WHAT ?!

My readers often make me think, too. In any case, the series is over. By the way, about the flower language for the dandelion that everybody liked--I knew that from before, so I was glad that it fit into the story so nicely. By the way, the Planting Club gang planted five seeds, but six flowers bloomed--one was Erika's. Come to think of it, I wrote about the "cherry blossom, plum blossom" idea in this space in volume 3, and I got positive feedback about that.

Make the flowers of your own "new selves" bloom, too. ♥ ☺

Still, a lot of fans were upset.

People were disappointed that the story was so short, but I wanted to let the flower of my own personality bloom, so I started a new kind of series. I hope you'll continue to support me.

What I gained from **Imadoki!** was a new kind of storyline. It might blossom in my new series. By the time this book is out, I will have started it. I'm excited...

Now, then... things were crazy around here, because I had the new series, plus the illustrations for the **Ayashi no Ceres** novel and trading cards! I also set up characters for the new **Fushigi Yûgi** video, so it was really hard to get any vacation time. So...

All three volumes of the **Ayashi no Ceres** "Episode of Miku" books are on sale now. Trading cards are also out together with **Fushigi Yûgi II**...

Prints of the original **Fushigi Yûgi** (about 22,000 yen) + **Fushigi Yûgi** Box (with seven Celestival Warrior items) are also coming out! These will be sold by order only. There will probably be more about this in the new comics... (and **Shôjo Comic.**)

*Available only in summer 2001.

By the way, it seems that sale of the **Fushigi Yûgi** OVA is being pushed back to December...

For some reason, I'm ending with a bunch of information, but I'll say goodbye now. Thank you for your support.

See you again in my new series (around October?).

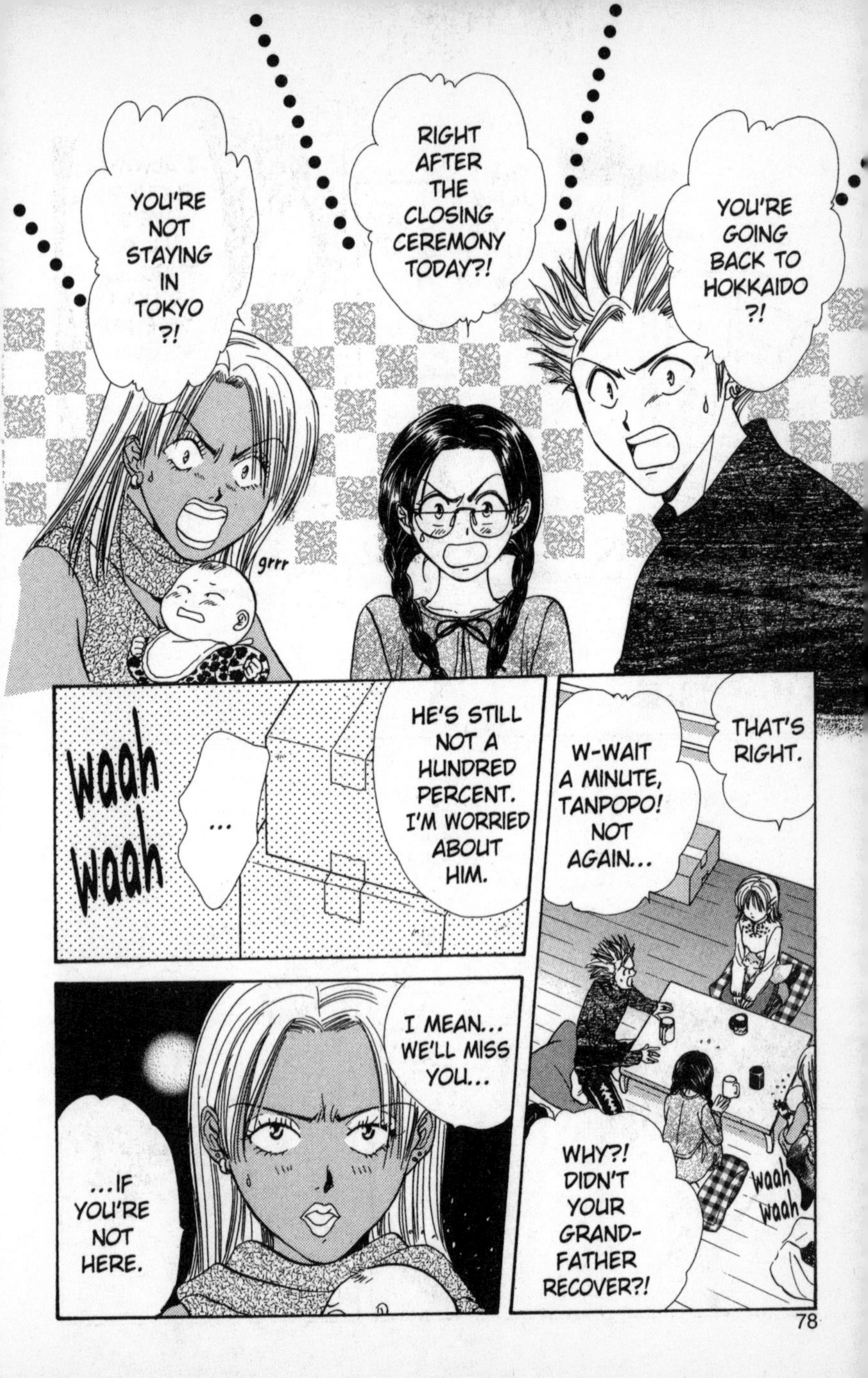
YOU'RE GOING BACK TO HOKKAIDO ?!
RIGHT AFTER THE CLOSING CEREMONY TODAY?!
YOU'RE NOT STAYING IN TOKYO ?!
grrr
THAT'S RIGHT.
W-WAIT A MINUTE, TANPOPO! NOT AGAIN...
WHY?! DIDN'T YOUR GRAND-FATHER RECOVER?!
waah waah
HE'S STILL NOT A HUNDRED PERCENT. I'M WORRIED ABOUT HIM.
...
waah waah
I MEAN... WE'LL MISS YOU...
...IF YOU'RE NOT HERE.

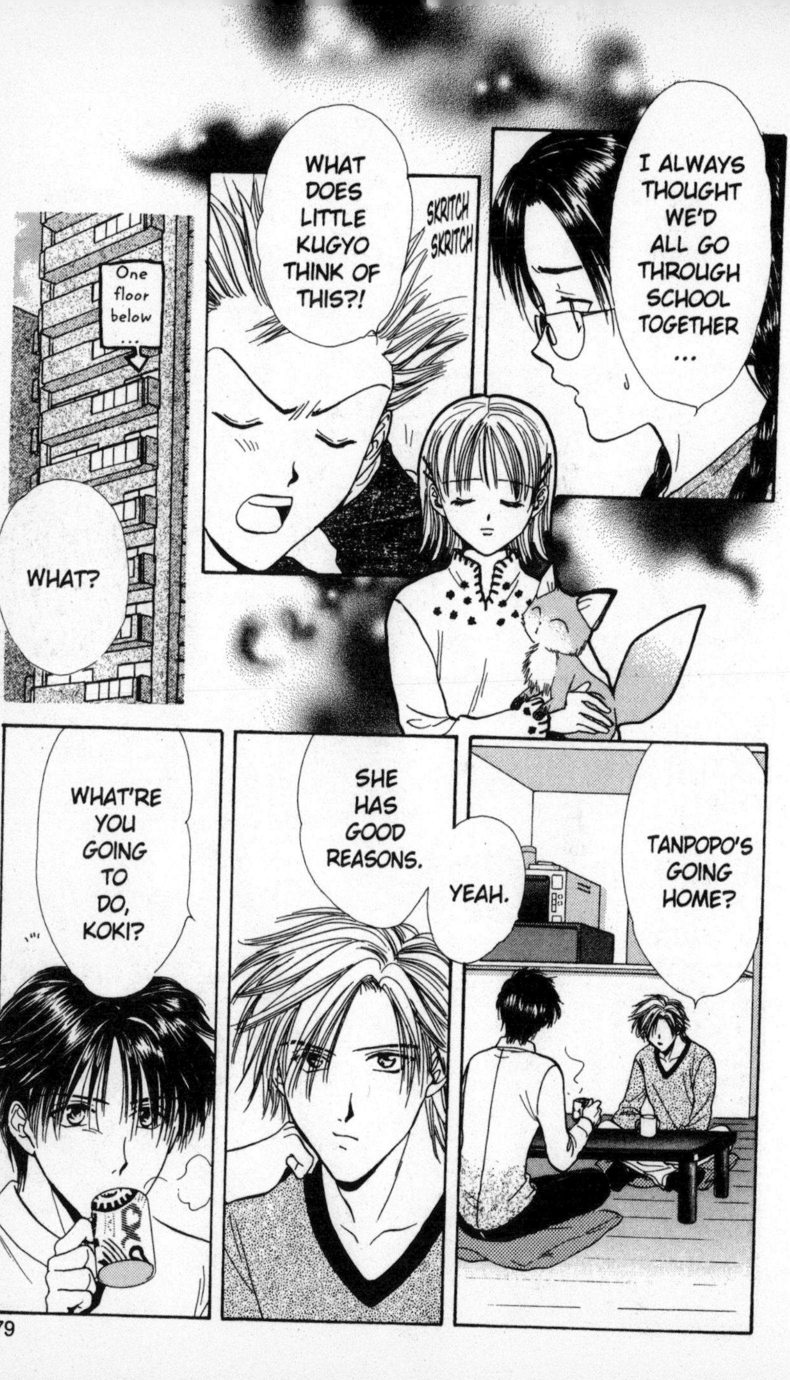
I ALWAYS THOUGHT WE'D ALL GO THROUGH SCHOOL TOGETHER ...
SKRITCH SKRITCH
WHAT DOES LITTLE KUGYO THINK OF THIS?!
One floor below ...
WHAT?
TANPOPO'S GOING HOME?
YEAH.
SHE HAS GOOD REASONS.
WHAT'RE YOU GOING TO DO, KOKI?

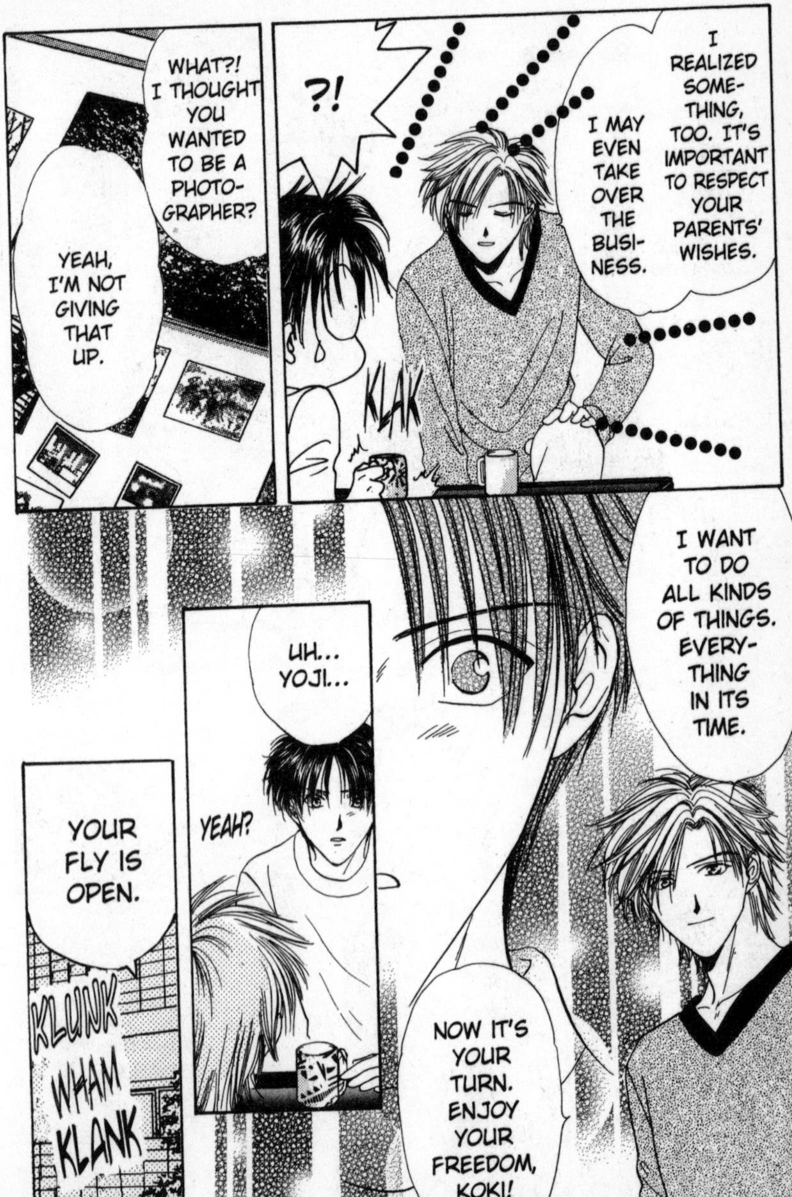
I REALIZED SOME-THING, TOO. IT'S IMPORTANT TO RESPECT YOUR PARENTS' WISHES.
I MAY EVEN TAKE OVER THE BUSI-NESS.
?!
KLAK
WHAT?! I THOUGHT YOU WANTED TO BE A PHOTO-GRAPHER?
YEAH, I'M NOT GIVING THAT UP.
I WANT TO DO ALL KINDS OF THINGS. EVERY-THING IN ITS TIME.
NOW IT'S YOUR TURN. ENJOY YOUR FREEDOM, KOKI!
UH... YOJI...
YEAH?
YOUR FLY IS OPEN.
KLUNK
WHAM
KLANK

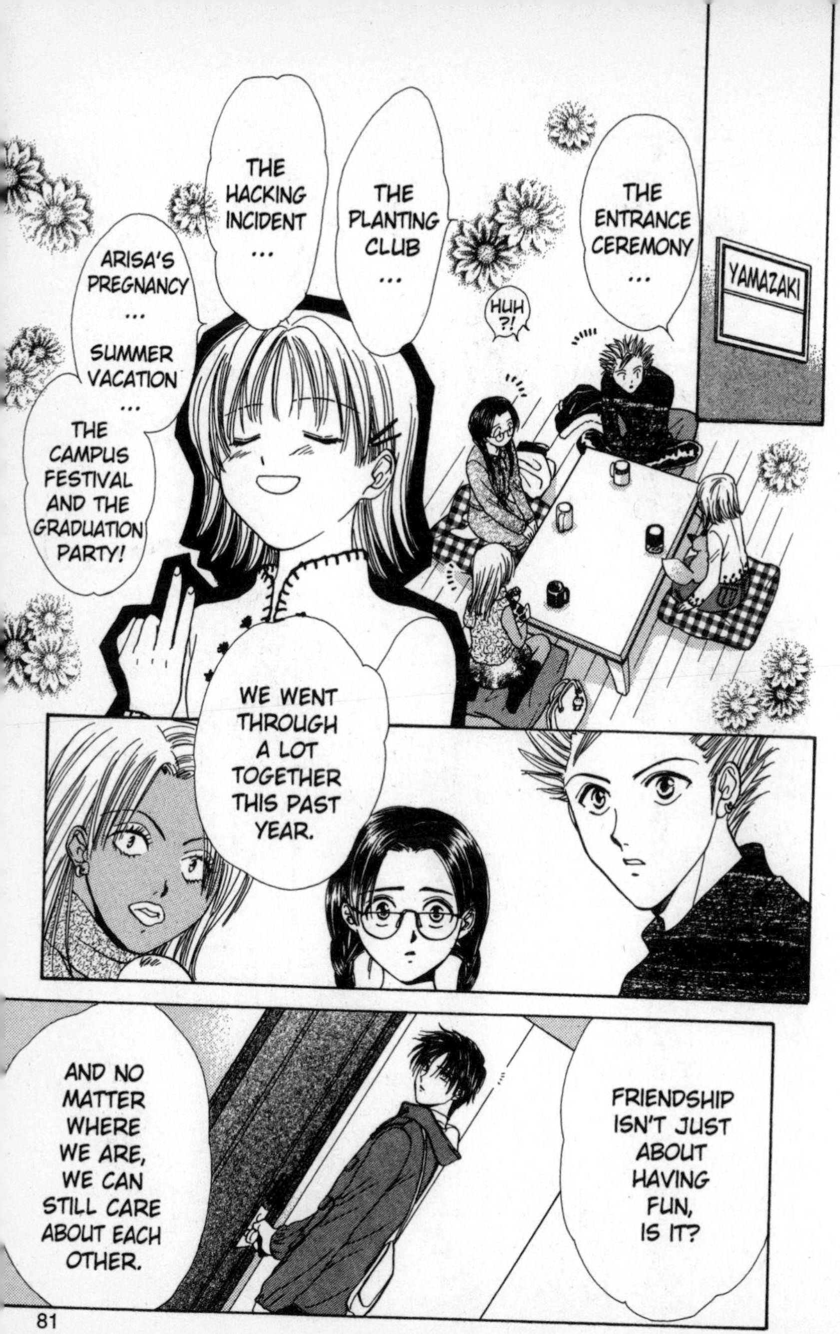
YAMAZAKI
THE ENTRANCE CEREMONY ...
HUH ?!
THE PLANTING CLUB ...
THE HACKING INCIDENT ...
ARISA'S PREGNANCY ...
SUMMER VACATION ...
THE CAMPUS FESTIVAL AND THE GRADUATION PARTY!
WE WENT THROUGH A LOT TOGETHER THIS PAST YEAR.
FRIENDSHIP ISN'T JUST ABOUT HAVING FUN, IS IT?
AND NO MATTER WHERE WE ARE, WE CAN STILL CARE ABOUT EACH OTHER.

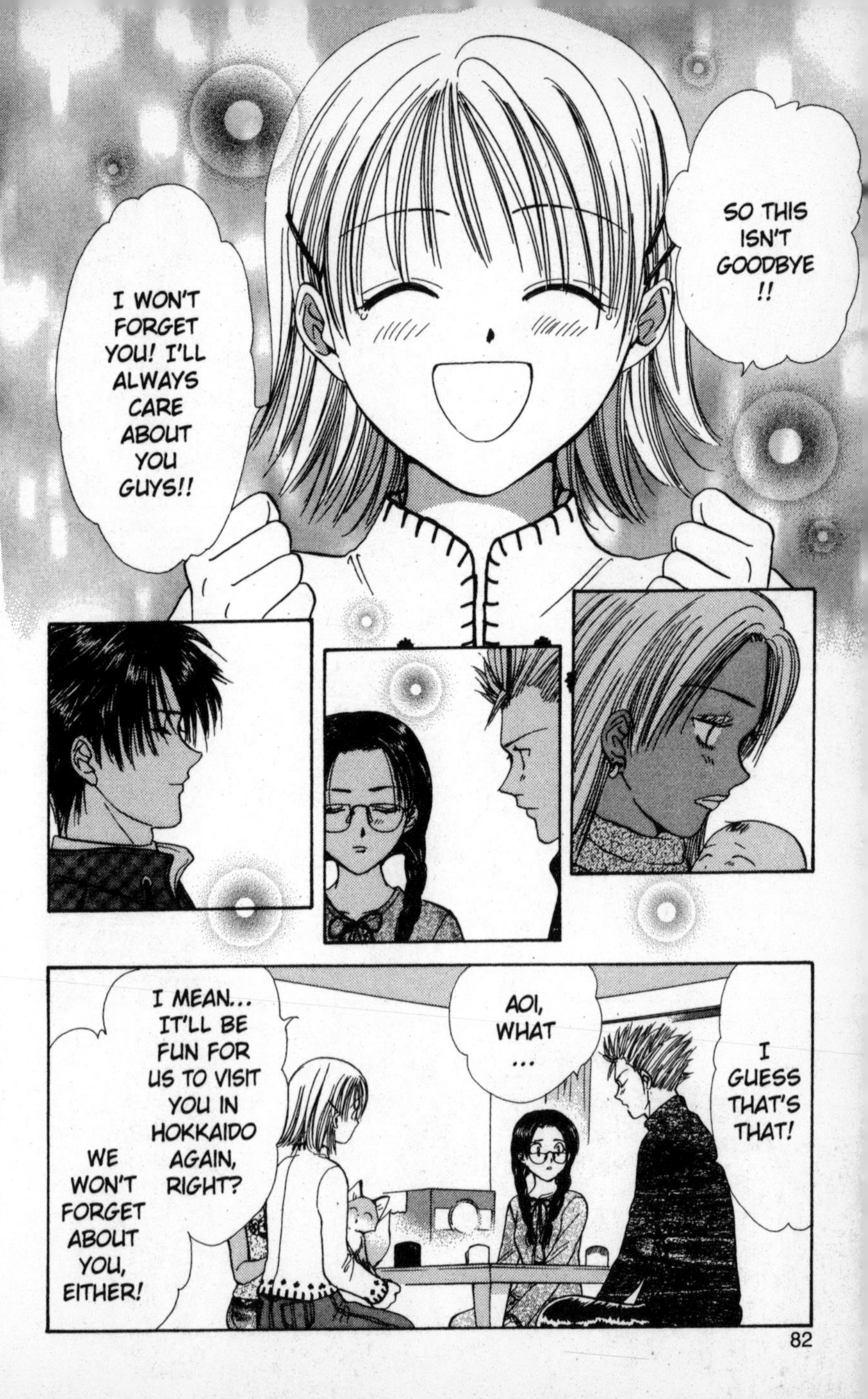
SO THIS ISN'T GOODBYE !!
I WON'T FORGET YOU! I'LL ALWAYS CARE ABOUT YOU GUYS!!
I GUESS THAT'S THAT!
AOI, WHAT ...
I MEAN... IT'LL BE FUN FOR US TO VISIT YOU IN HOKKAIDO AGAIN, RIGHT?
WE WON'T FORGET ABOUT YOU, EITHER!

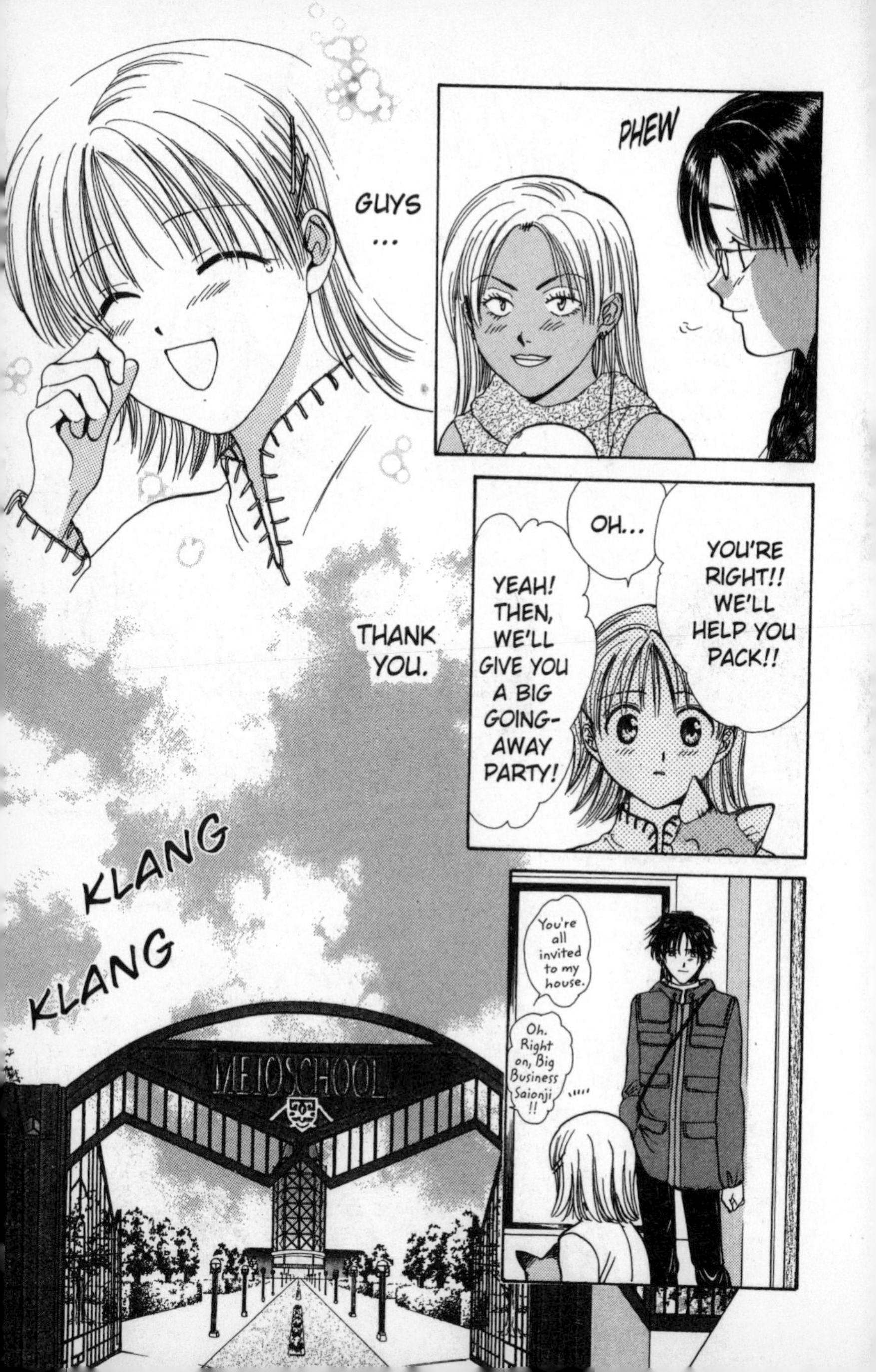
PHEW
OH...
YOU'RE RIGHT!! WE'LL HELP YOU PACK!!
YEAH! THEN, WE'LL GIVE YOU A BIG GOING-AWAY PARTY!
You're all invited to my house.
Oh. Right on, Big Business Saionji!!
GUYS ...
THANK YOU.
KLANG
KLANG

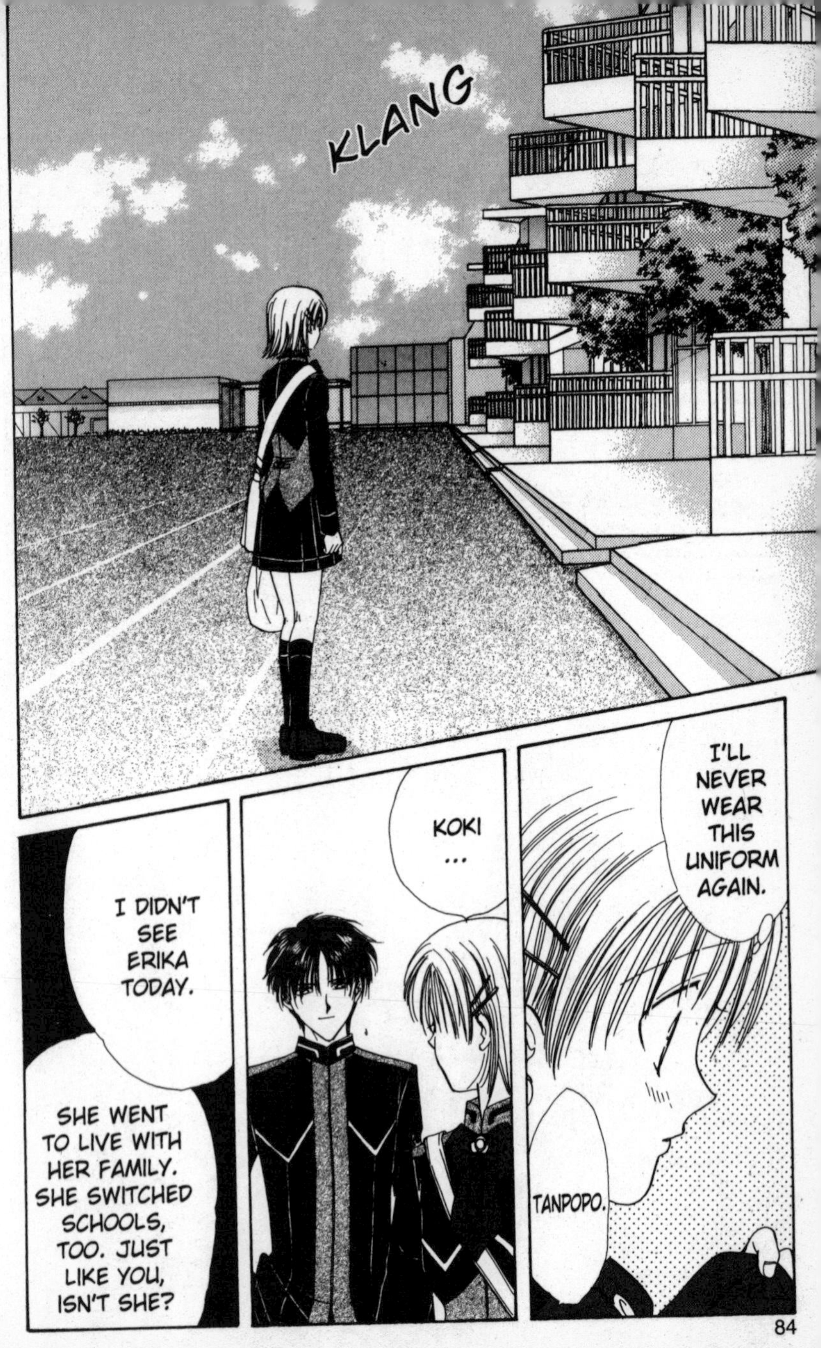
KLANG
I'LL NEVER WEAR THIS UNIFORM AGAIN.
TANPOPO.
KOKI ...
I DIDN'T SEE ERIKA TODAY.
SHE WENT TO LIVE WITH HER FAMILY. SHE SWITCHED SCHOOLS, TOO. JUST LIKE YOU, ISN'T SHE?

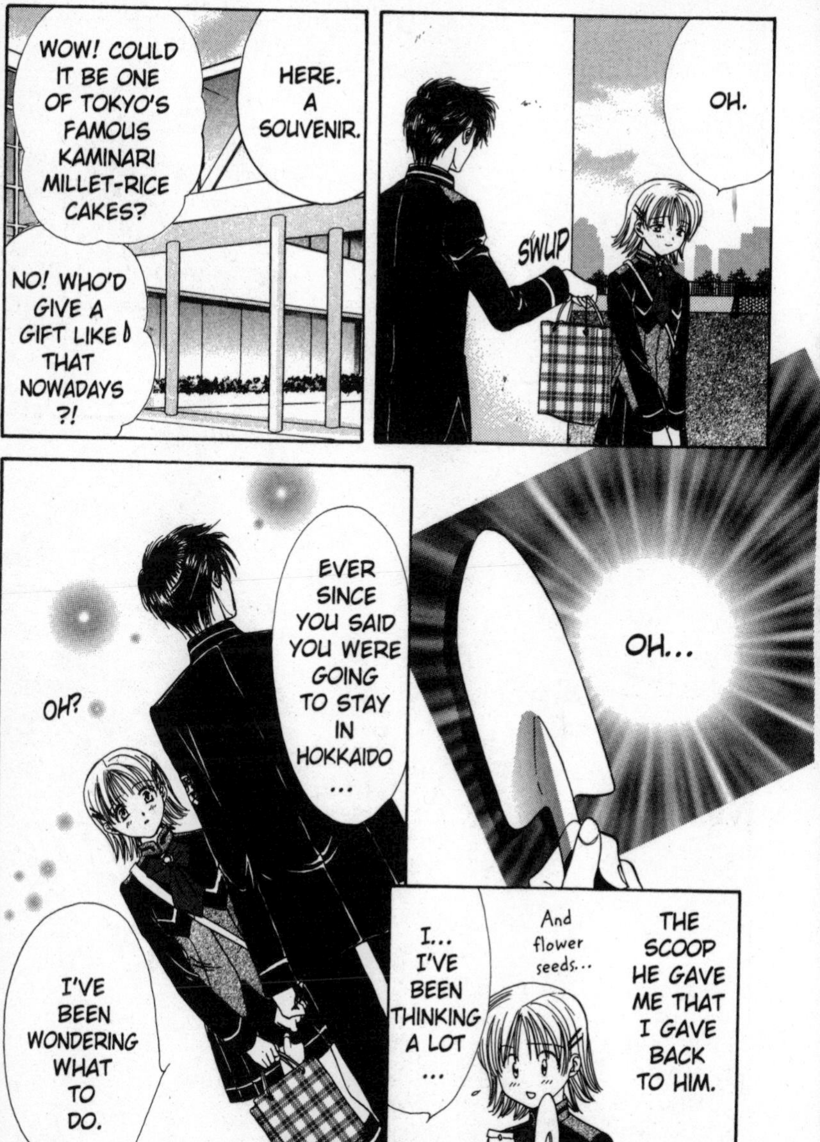
OH.
SWUP
HERE. A SOUVENIR.
WOW! COULD IT BE ONE OF TOKYO'S FAMOUS KAMINARI MILLET-RICE CAKES?
NO! WHO'D GIVE A GIFT LIKE THAT NOWADAYS ?!
OH...
THE SCOOP HE GAVE ME THAT I GAVE BACK TO HIM.
And flower seeds...
I... I'VE BEEN THINKING A LOT ...
EVER SINCE YOU SAID YOU WERE GOING TO STAY IN HOKKAIDO ...
OH?
I'VE BEEN WONDERING WHAT TO DO.

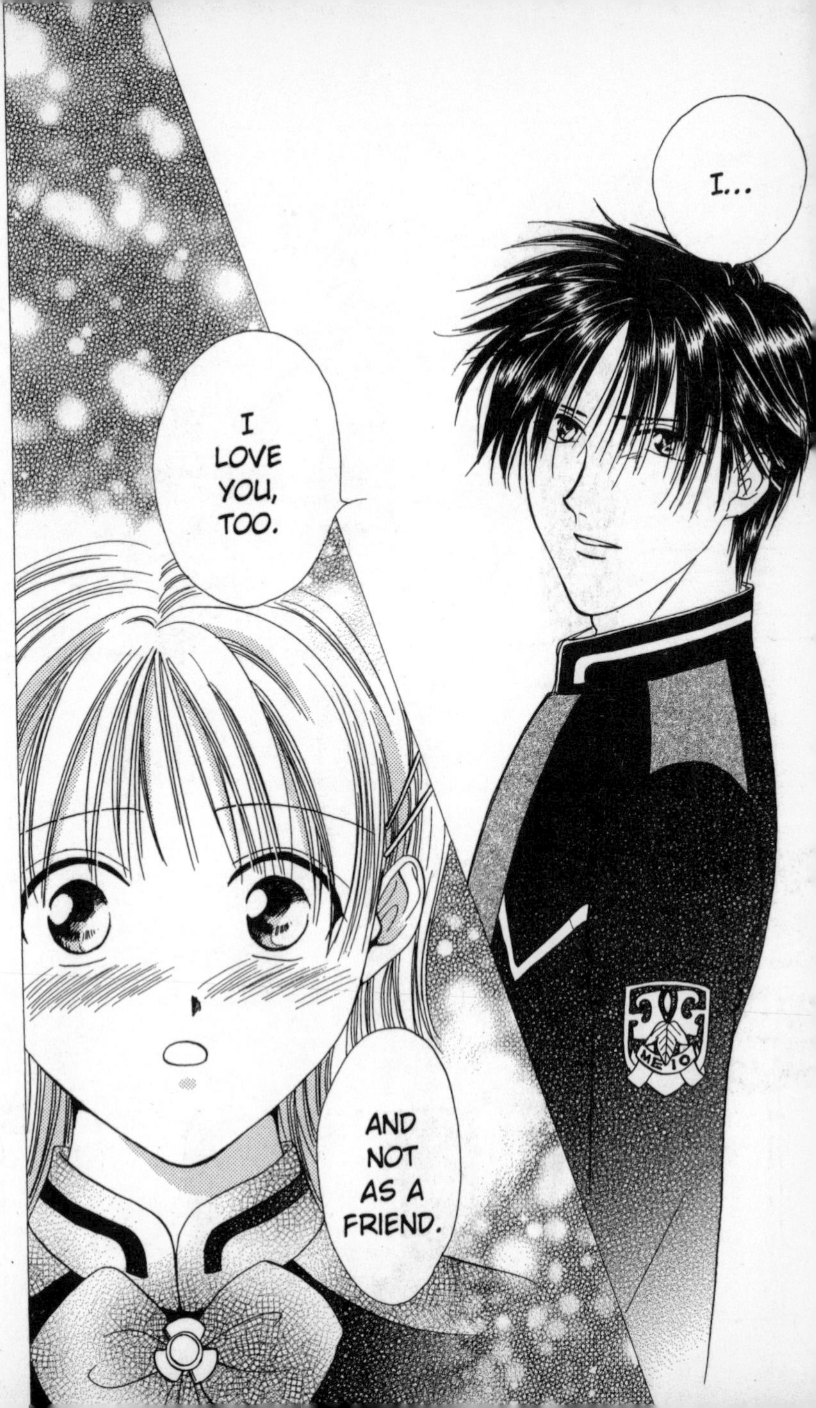
I...
I LOVE YOU, TOO.
AND NOT AS A FRIEND.

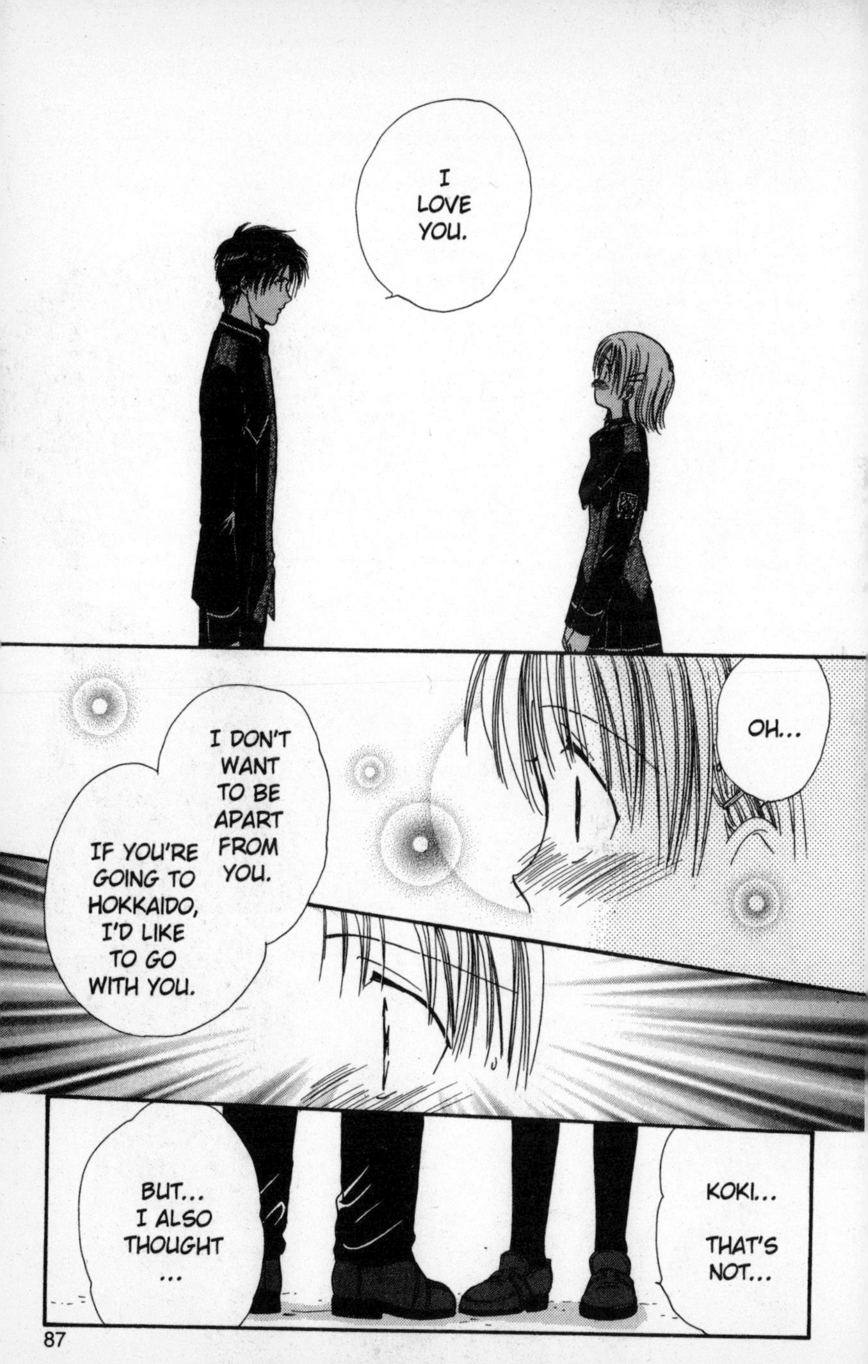
I LOVE YOU.
OH...
I DON'T WANT TO BE APART FROM YOU.
IF YOU'RE GOING TO HOKKAIDO, I'D LIKE TO GO WITH YOU.
KOKI... THAT'S NOT...
BUT... I ALSO THOUGHT ...

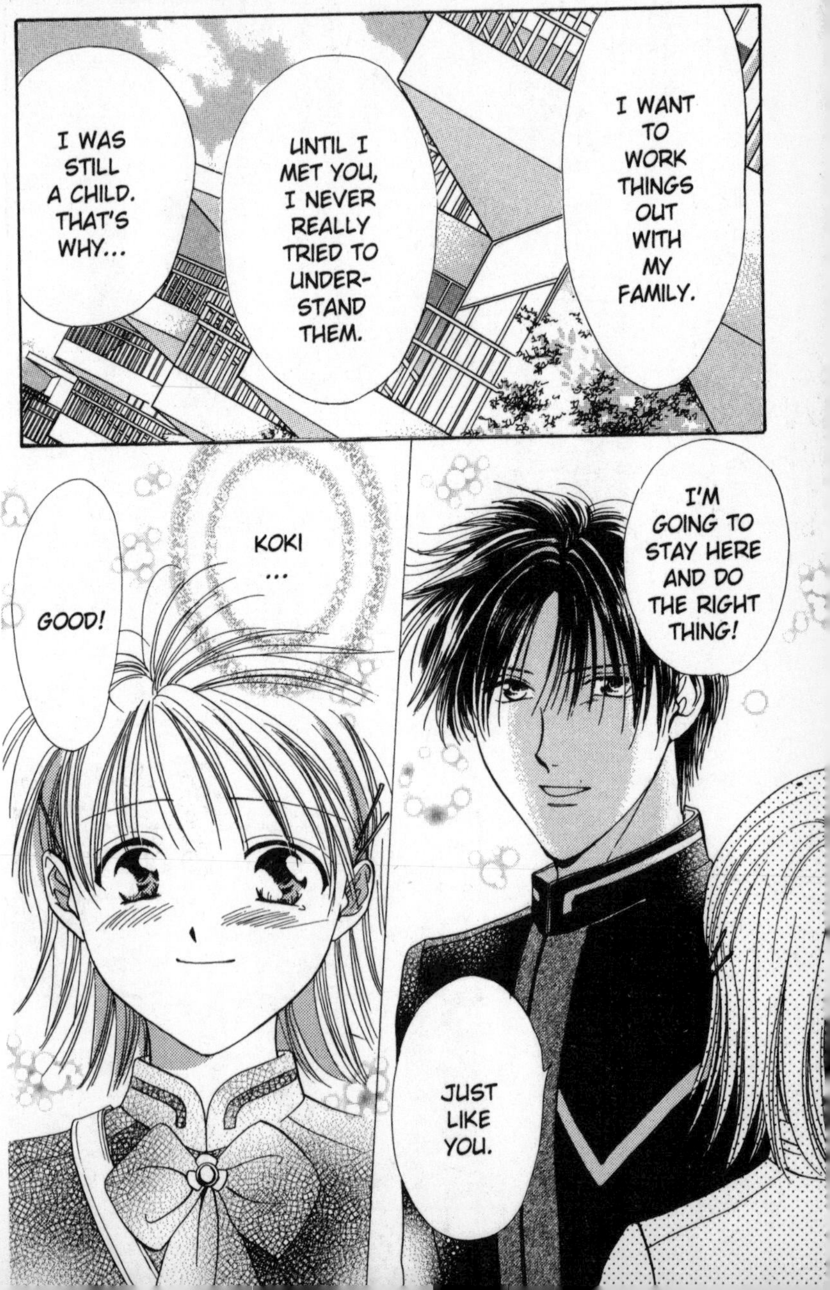
I WANT TO WORK THINGS OUT WITH MY FAMILY.
UNTIL I MET YOU, I NEVER REALLY TRIED TO UNDER-STAND THEM.
I WAS STILL A CHILD. THAT'S WHY...
I'M GOING TO STAY HERE AND DO THE RIGHT THING!
JUST LIKE YOU.
KOKI ...
GOOD!

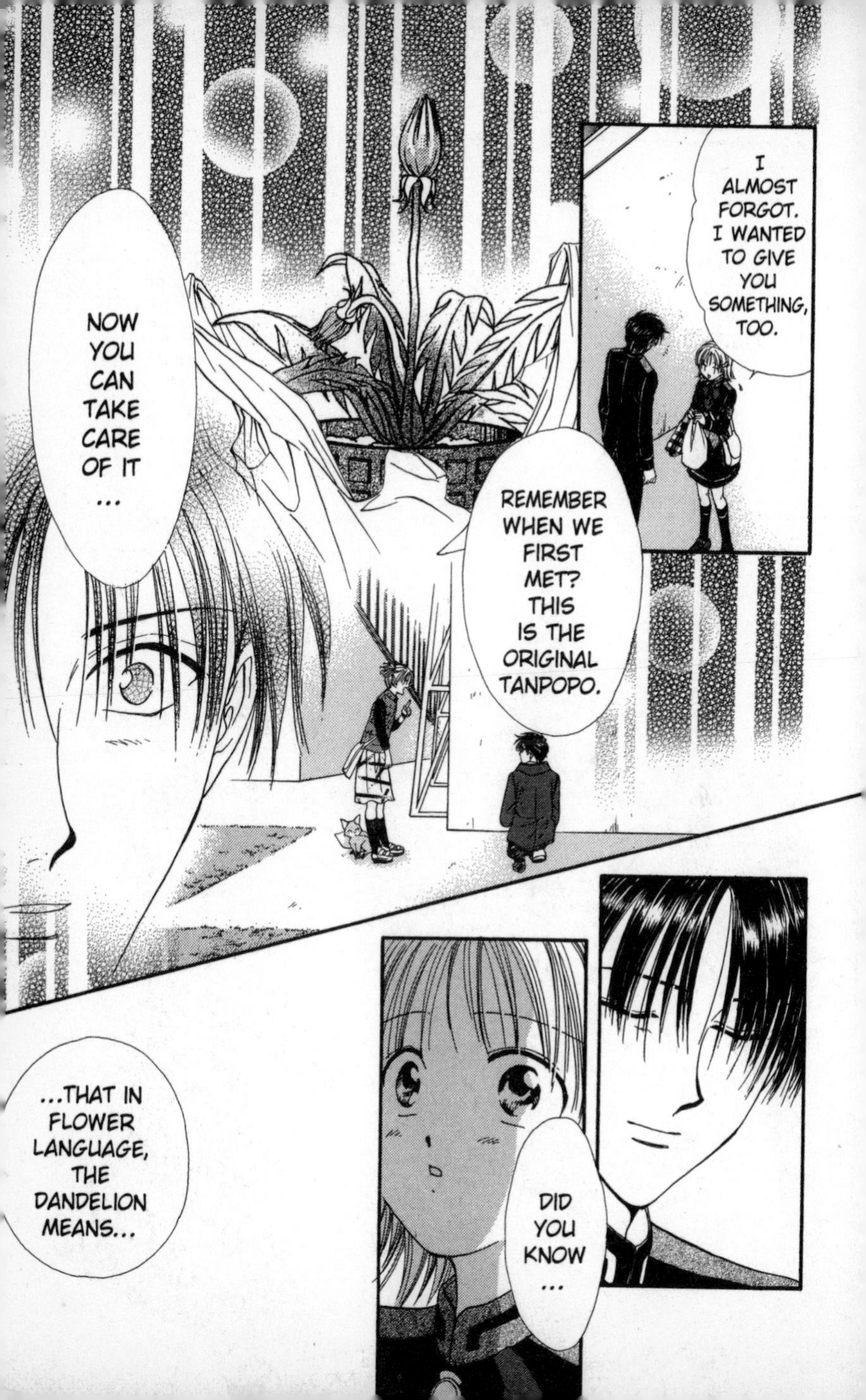
I ALMOST FORGOT. I WANTED TO GIVE YOU SOMETHING, TOO.
REMEMBER WHEN WE FIRST MET? THIS IS THE ORIGINAL TANPOPO.
NOW YOU CAN TAKE CARE OF IT ...
DID YOU KNOW ...
...THAT IN FLOWER LANGUAGE, THE DANDELION MEANS...

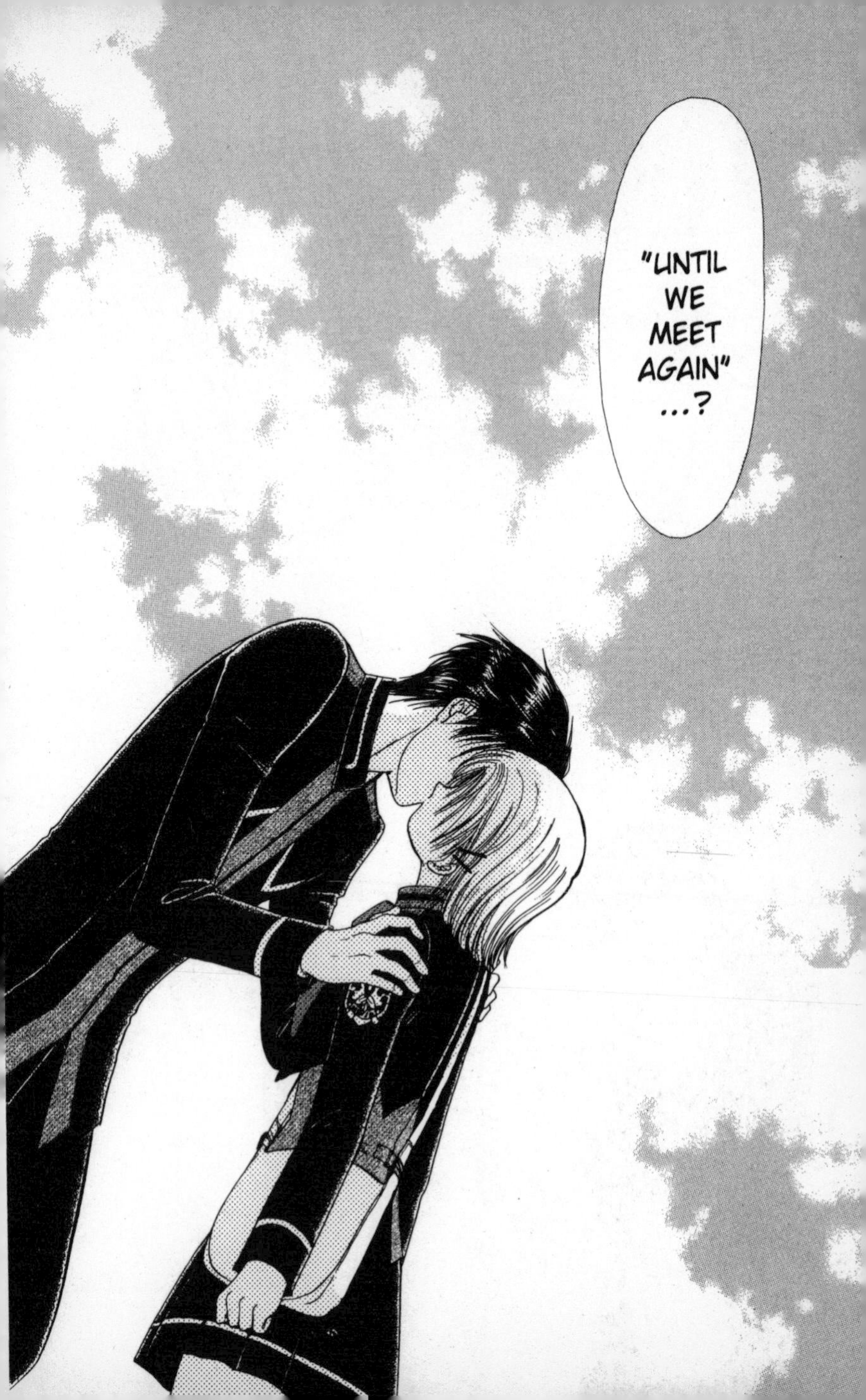
"UNTIL WE MEET AGAIN" ...?

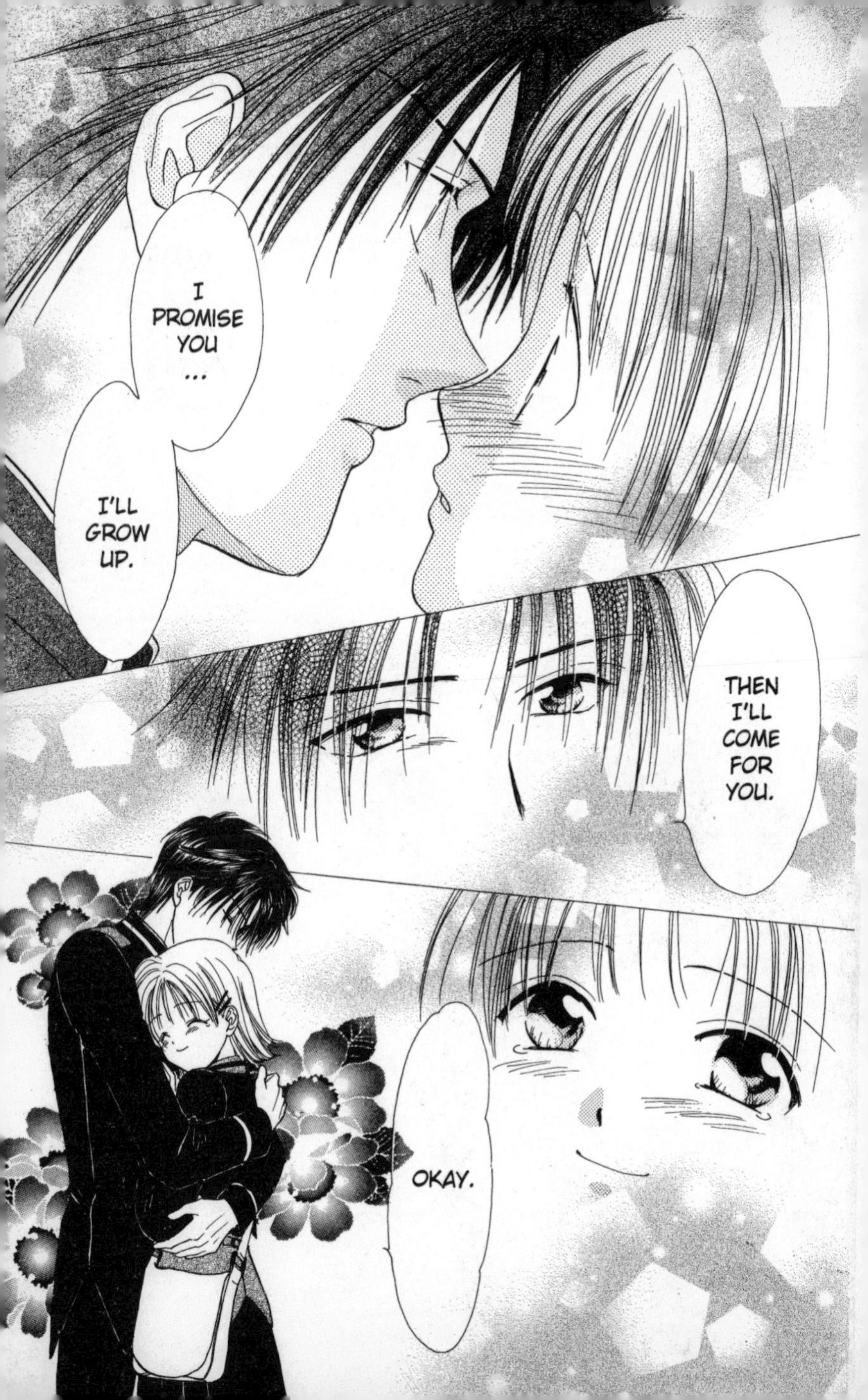
I PROMISE YOU ...
I'LL GROW UP.
THEN I'LL COME FOR YOU.
OKAY.

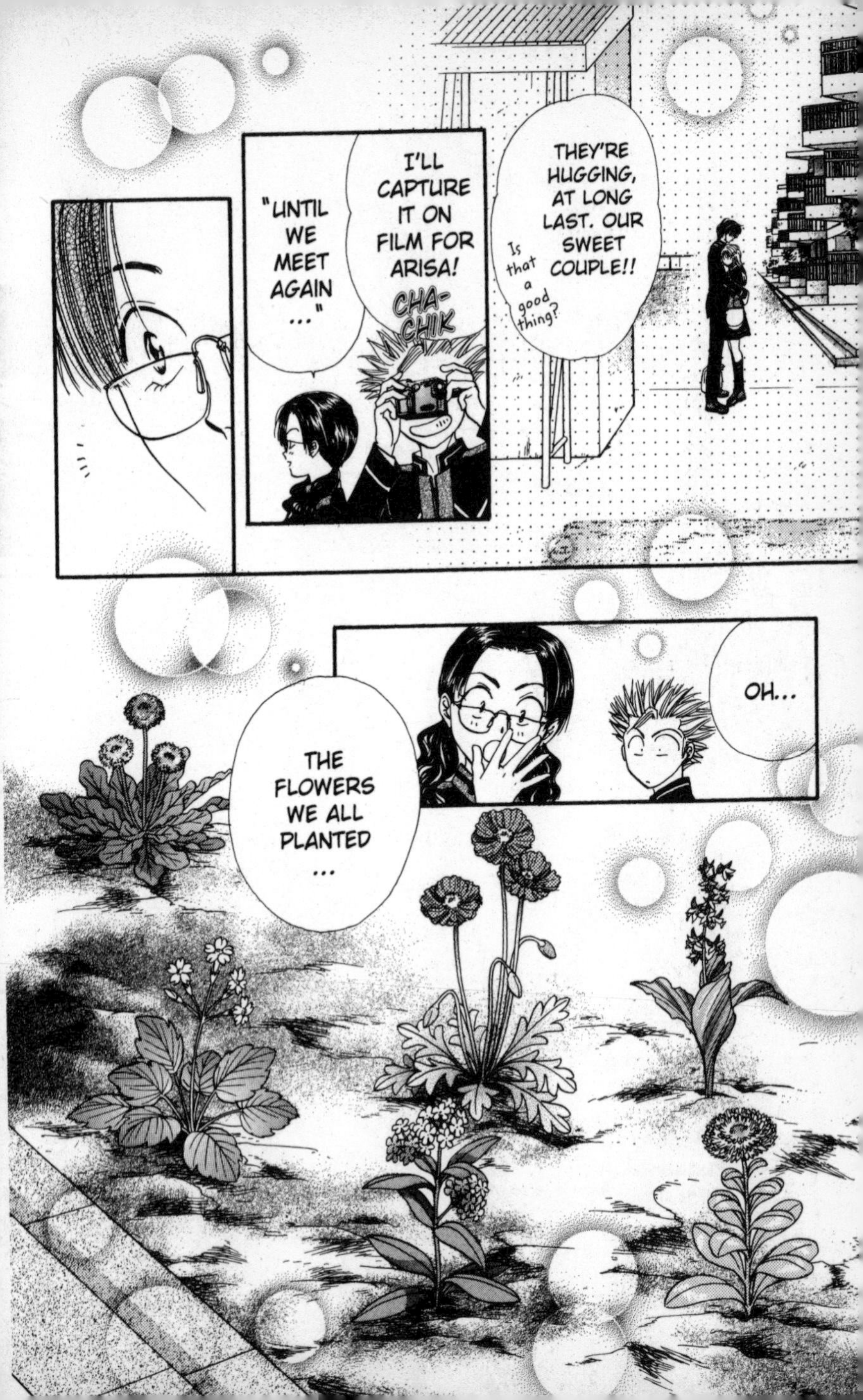
THEY'RE HUGGING, AT LONG LAST. OUR SWEET COUPLE!!
Is that a good thing?
I'LL CAPTURE IT ON FILM FOR ARISA!
CHA-CHIK
"UNTIL WE MEET AGAIN..."
OH...
THE FLOWERS WE ALL PLANTED...

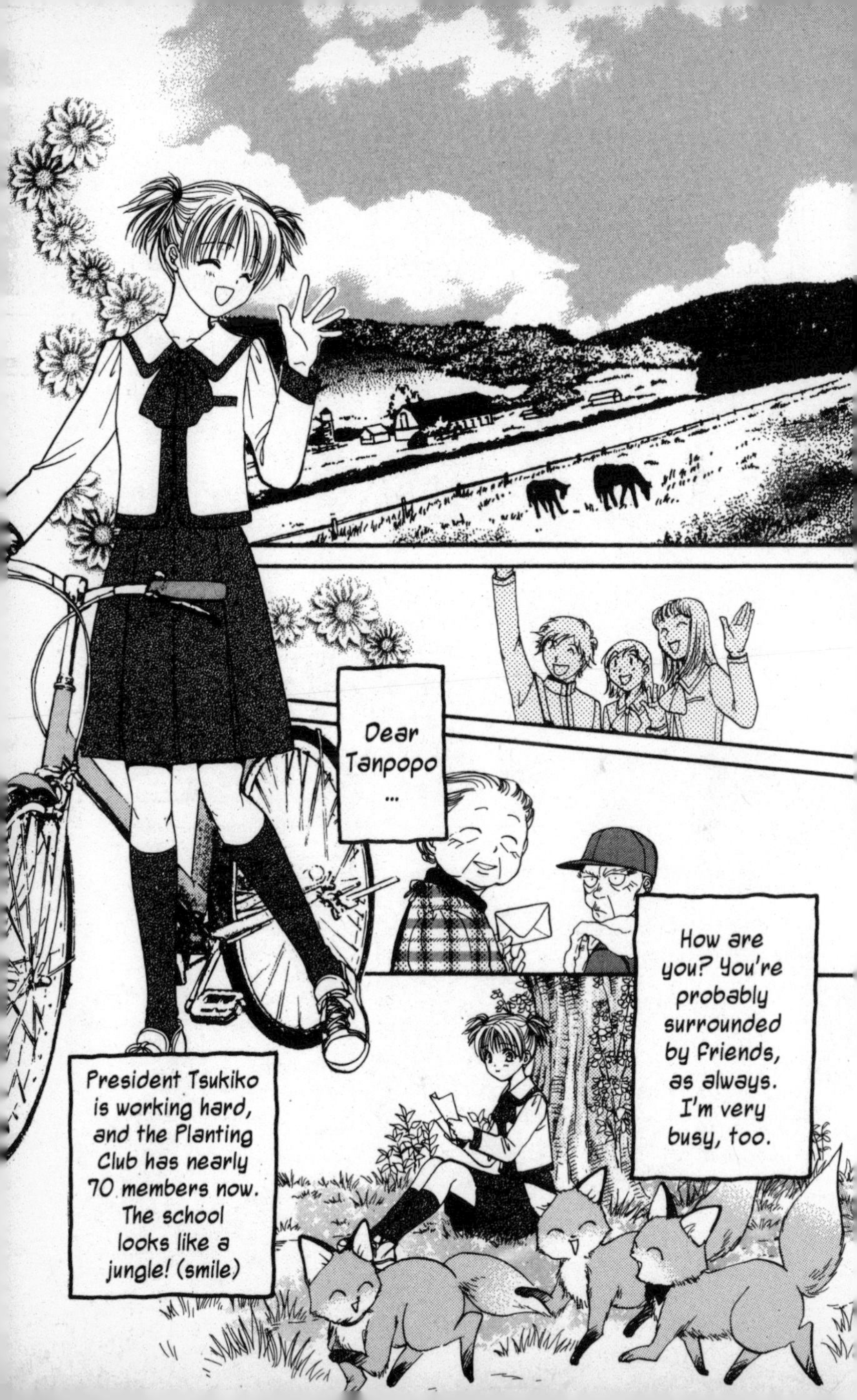
Dear Tanpopo ...
How are you? You're probably surrounded by friends, as always. I'm very busy, too.
President Tsukiko is working hard, and the Planting Club has nearly 70 members now. The school looks like a jungle! (smile)

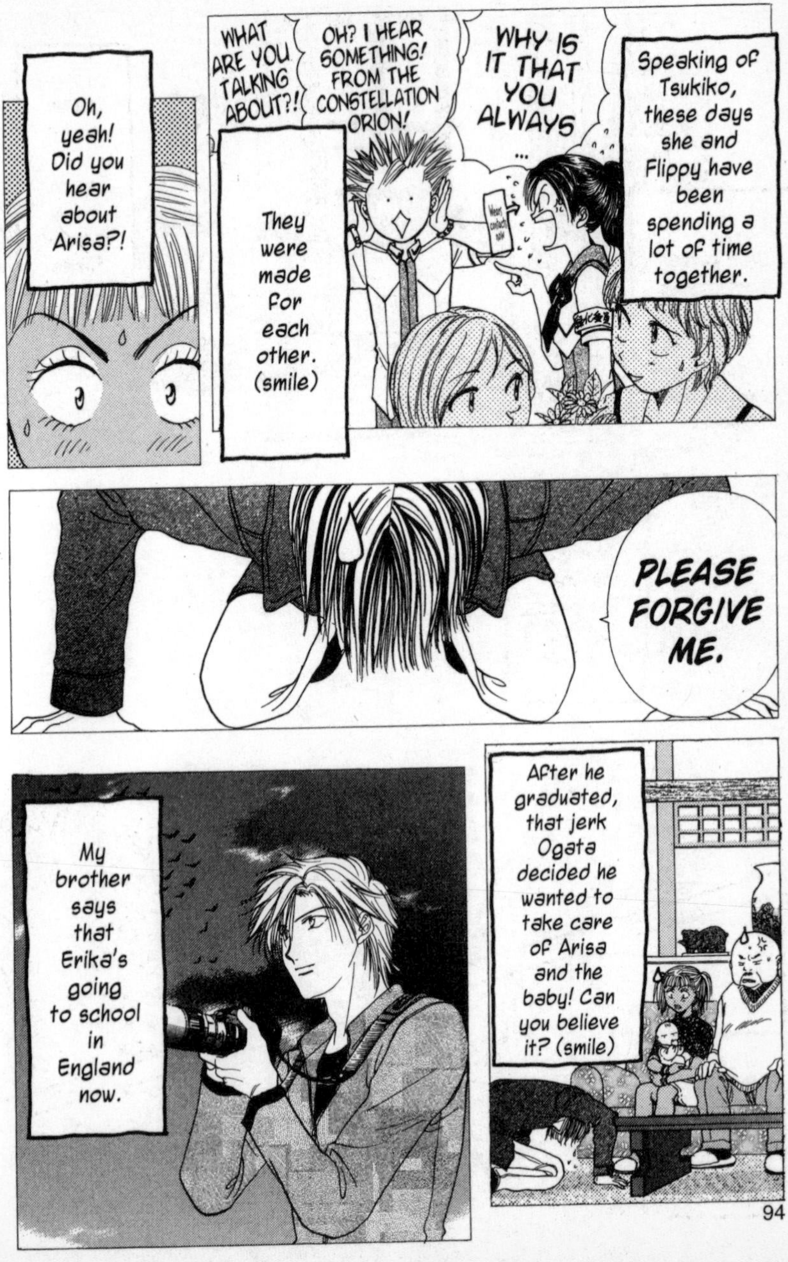
Speaking of Tsukiko, these days she and Flippy have been spending a lot of time together.
WHY IS IT THAT YOU ALWAYS ...
OH? I HEAR SOMETHING! FROM THE CONSTELLATION ORION!
WHAT ARE YOU TALKING ABOUT?!
They were made for each other. (smile)
Oh, yeah! Did you hear about Arisa?!
PLEASE FORGIVE ME.
After he graduated, that jerk Ogata decided he wanted to take care of Arisa and the baby! Can you believe it? (smile)
My brother says that Erika's going to school in England now.

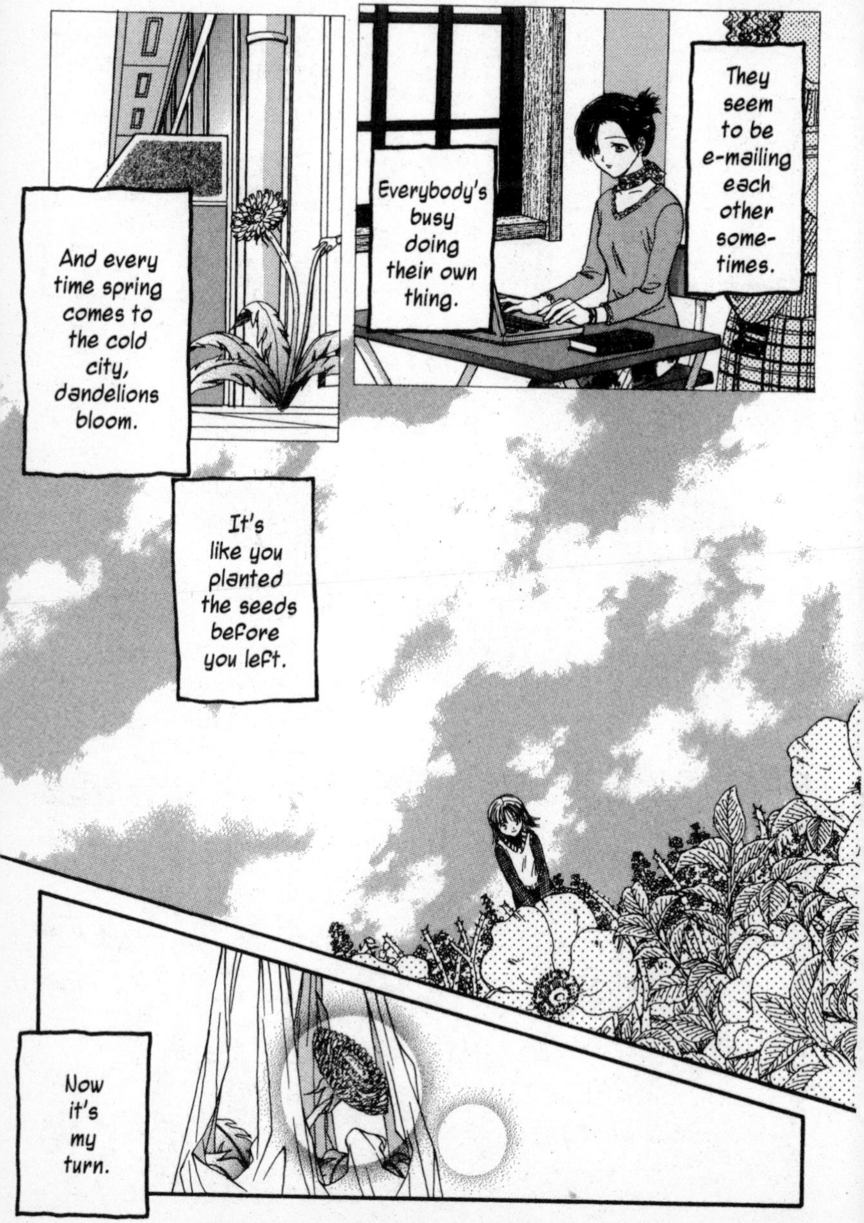
They seem to be e-mailing each other some-times.
Everybody's busy doing their own thing.
And every time spring comes to the cold city, dandelions bloom.
It's like you planted the seeds before you left.
Now it's my turn.

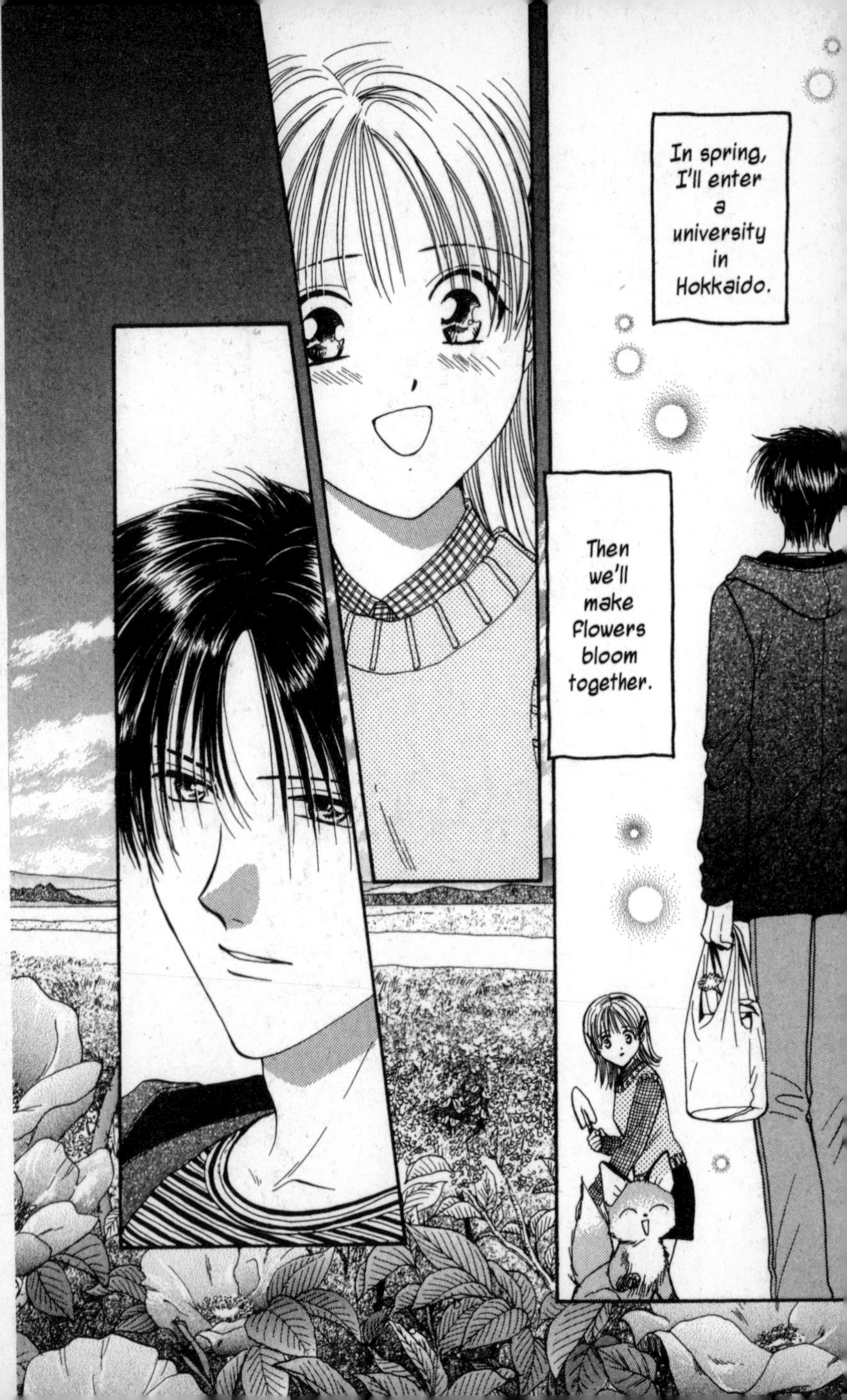
In spring, I'll enter a university in Hokkaido.
Then we'll make flowers bloom together.

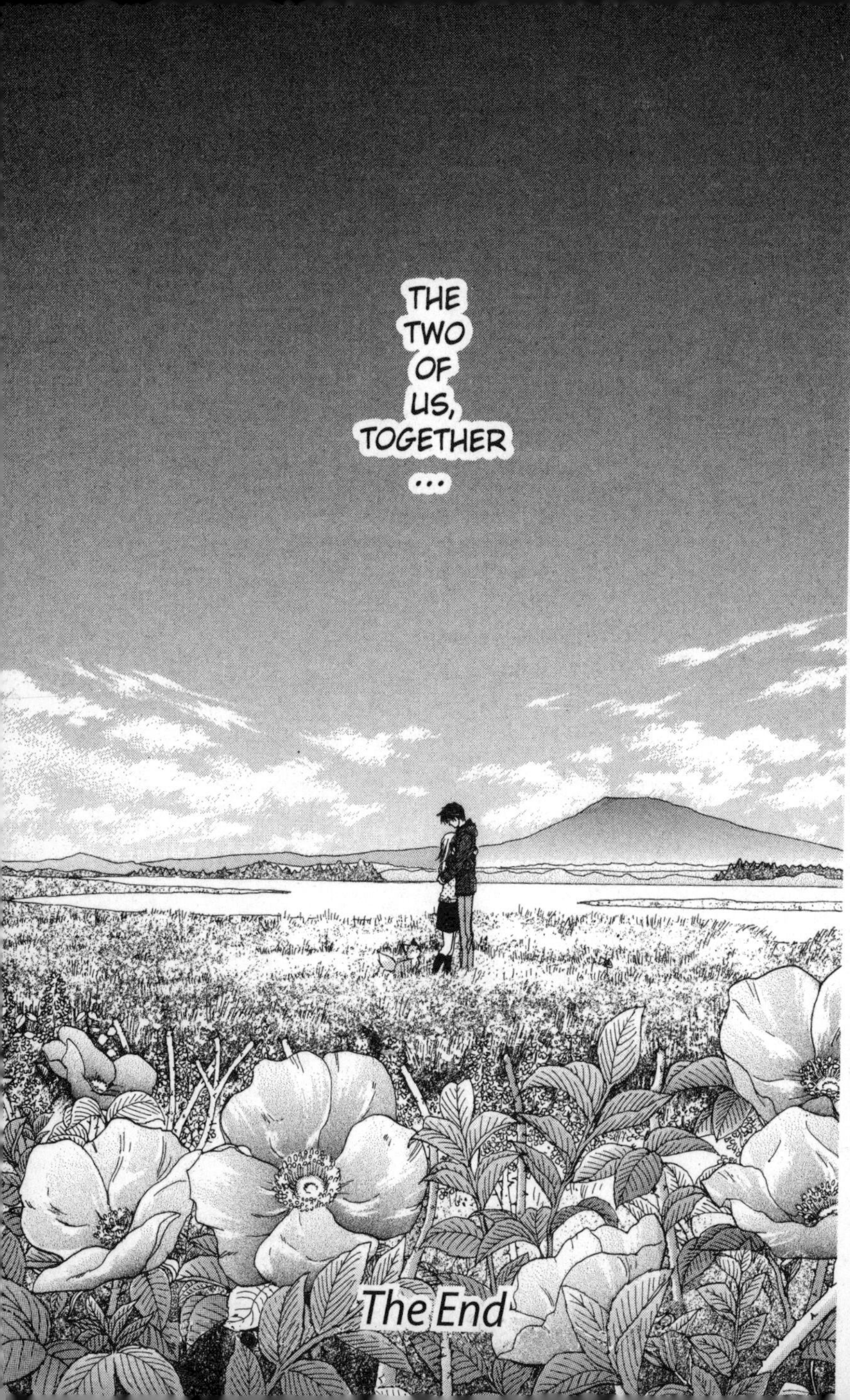
THE TWO OF US, TOGETHER...
The End

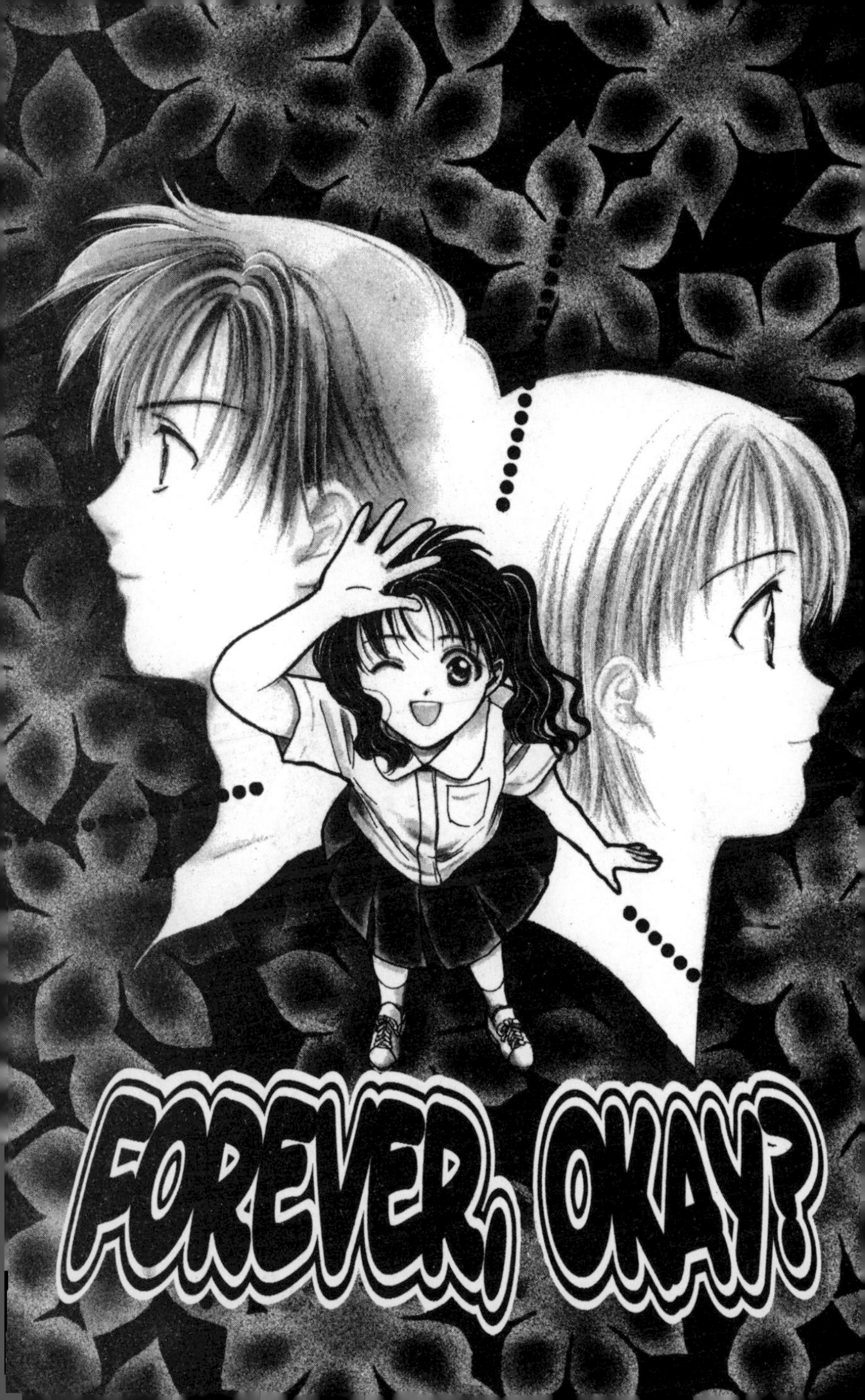
FOREVER, OKAY?

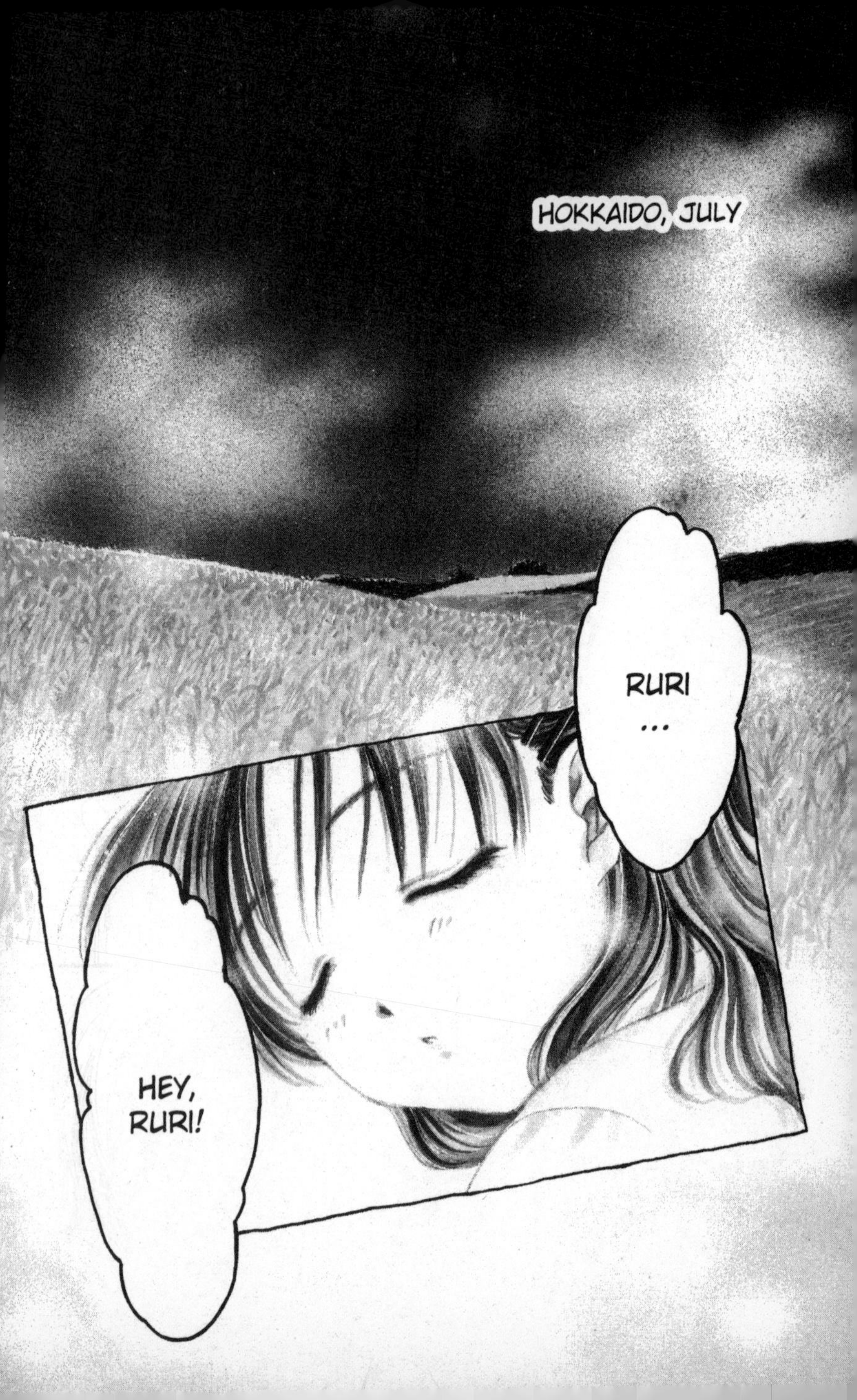
HOKKAIDO, JULY
RURI ...
HEY, RURI!

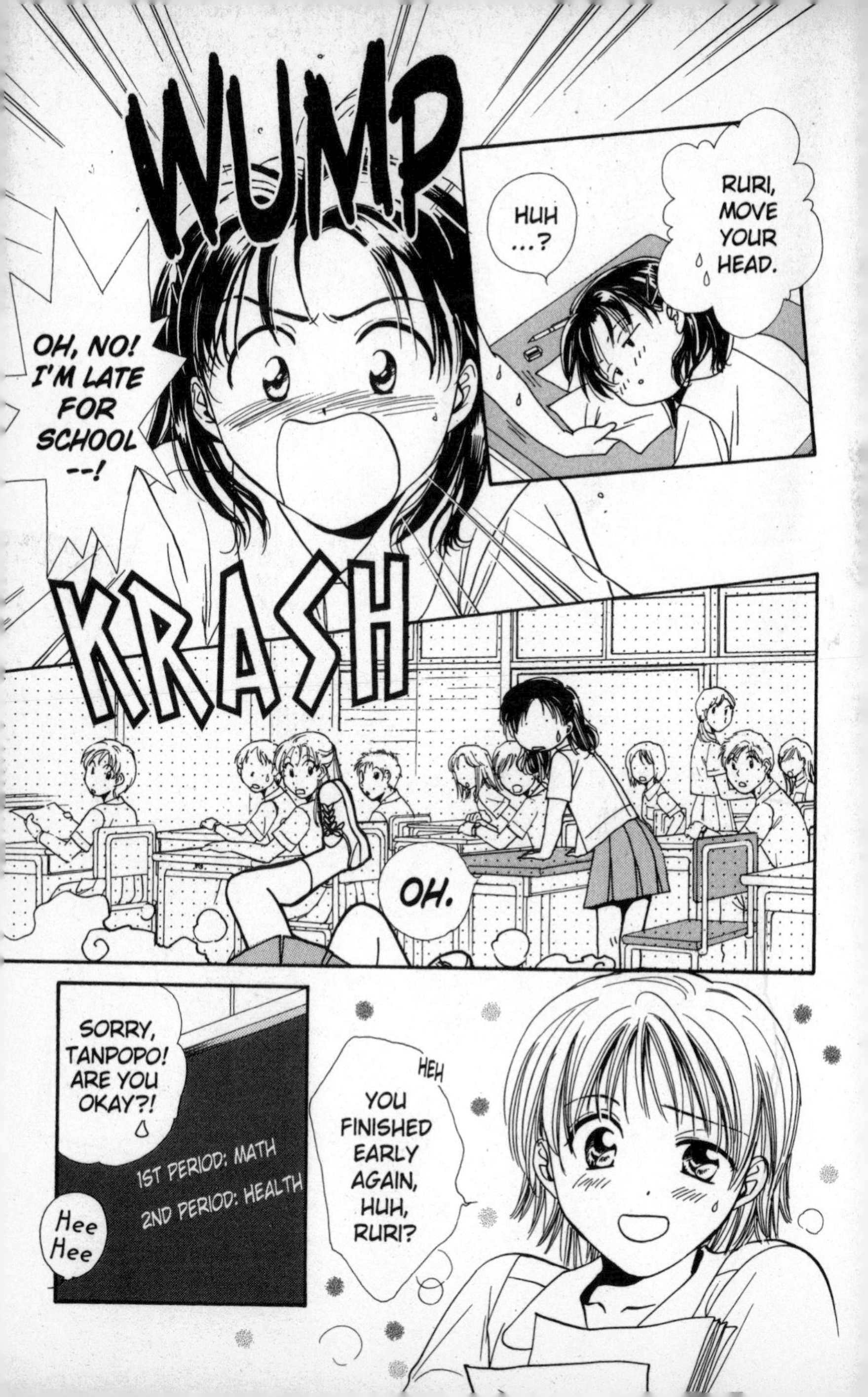
RURI, MOVE YOUR HEAD.
HUH ...?
WUMP
OH, NO! I'M LATE FOR SCHOOL --!
KRASH
OH.
HEH
YOU FINISHED EARLY AGAIN, HUH, RURI?
SORRY, TANPOPO! ARE YOU OKAY?!
1ST PERIOD: MATH
2ND PERIOD: HEALTH
Hee Hee

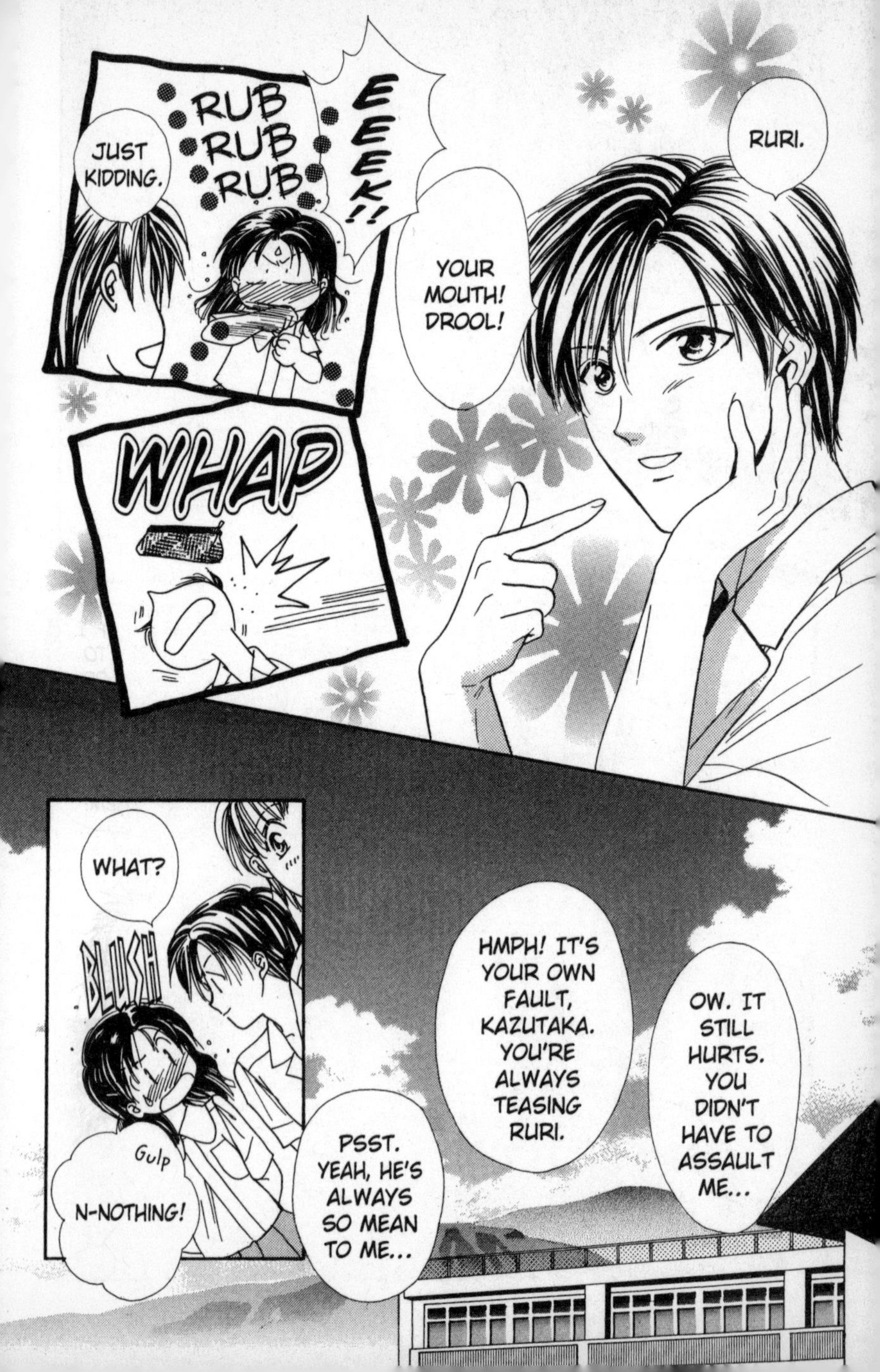
RURI.
YOUR MOUTH! DROOL!
EEEEK!!
RUB RUB RUB
JUST KIDDING.
WHAP
OW. IT STILL HURTS. YOU DIDN'T HAVE TO ASSAULT ME...
HMPH! IT'S YOUR OWN FAULT, KAZUTAKA. YOU'RE ALWAYS TEASING RURI.
PSST. YEAH, HE'S ALWAYS SO MEAN TO ME...
WHAT?
BLUSH
Gulp
N-NOTHING!

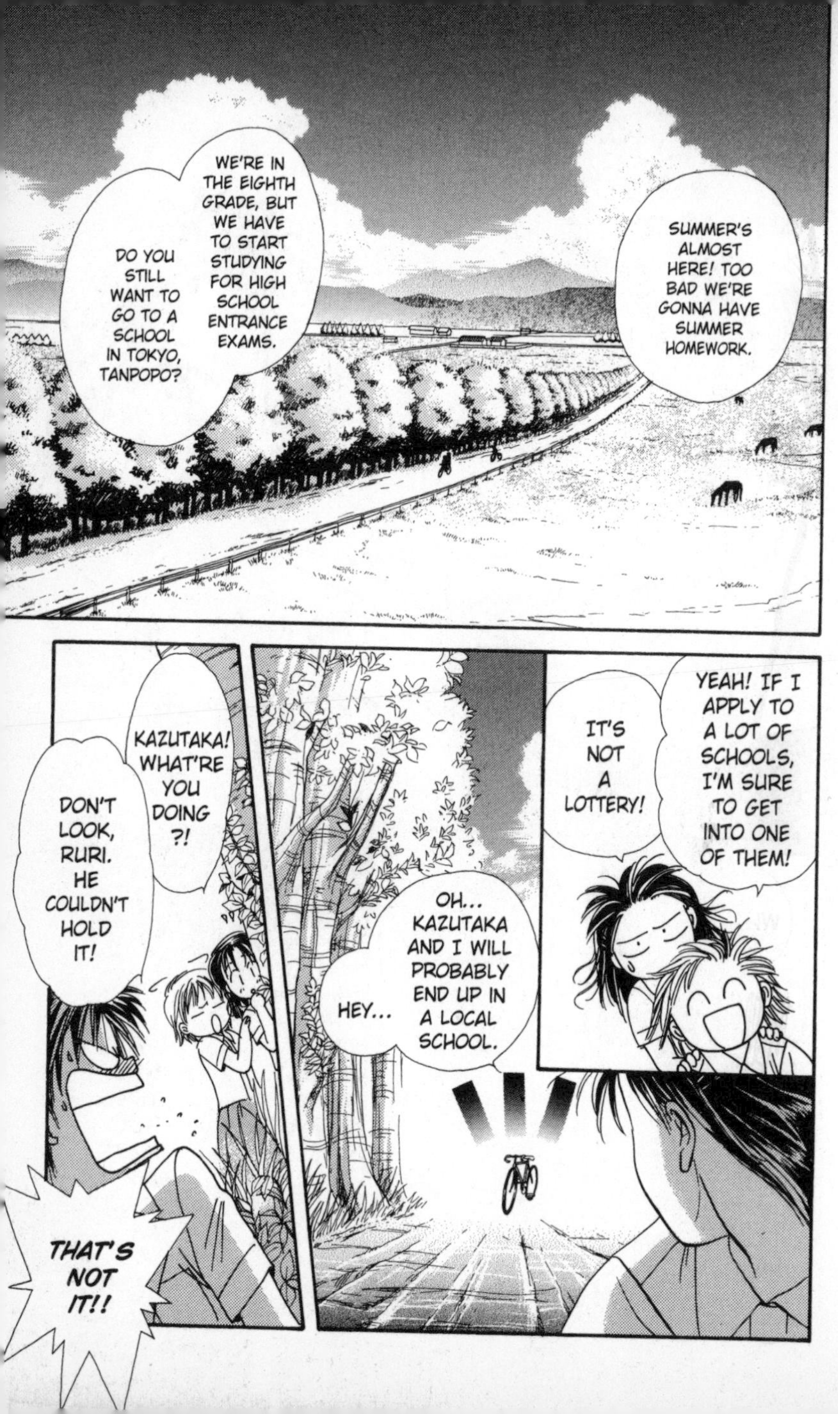
SUMMER'S ALMOST HERE! TOO BAD WE'RE GONNA HAVE SUMMER HOMEWORK.
WE'RE IN THE EIGHTH GRADE, BUT WE HAVE TO START STUDYING FOR HIGH SCHOOL ENTRANCE EXAMS.
DO YOU STILL WANT TO GO TO A SCHOOL IN TOKYO, TANPOPO?
YEAH! IF I APPLY TO A LOT OF SCHOOLS, I'M SURE TO GET INTO ONE OF THEM!
IT'S NOT A LOTTERY!
OH... KAZUTAKA AND I WILL PROBABLY END UP IN A LOCAL SCHOOL.
HEY...
KAZUTAKA! WHAT'RE YOU DOING?!
DON'T LOOK, RURI. HE COULDN'T HOLD IT!
THAT'S NOT IT!!

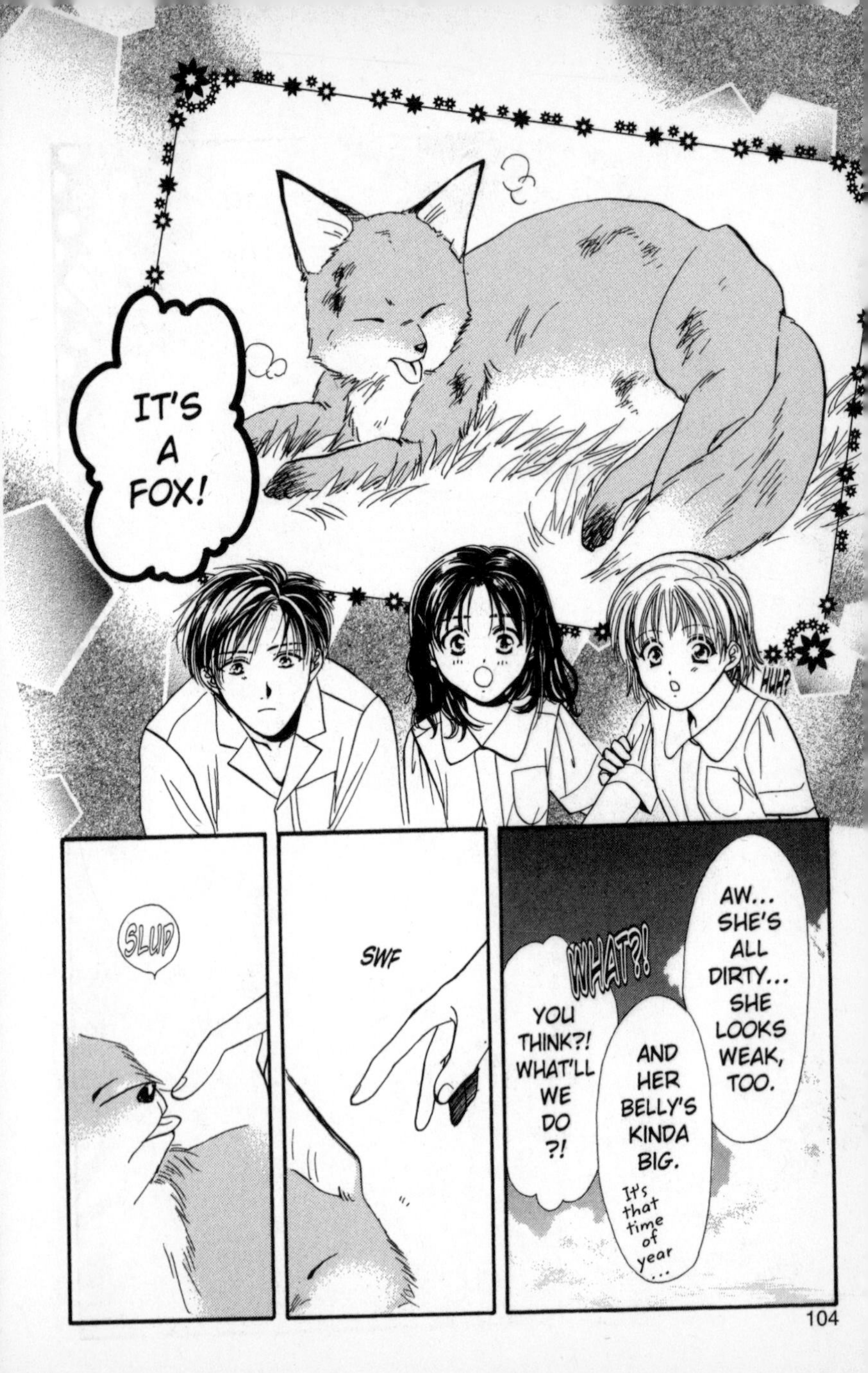
IT'S A FOX!
HUH?
AW... SHE'S ALL DIRTY... SHE LOOKS WEAK, TOO.
WHAT?!
YOU THINK?! WHAT'LL WE DO?!
AND HER BELLY'S KINDA BIG.
It's that time of year...
SWF
SLUP

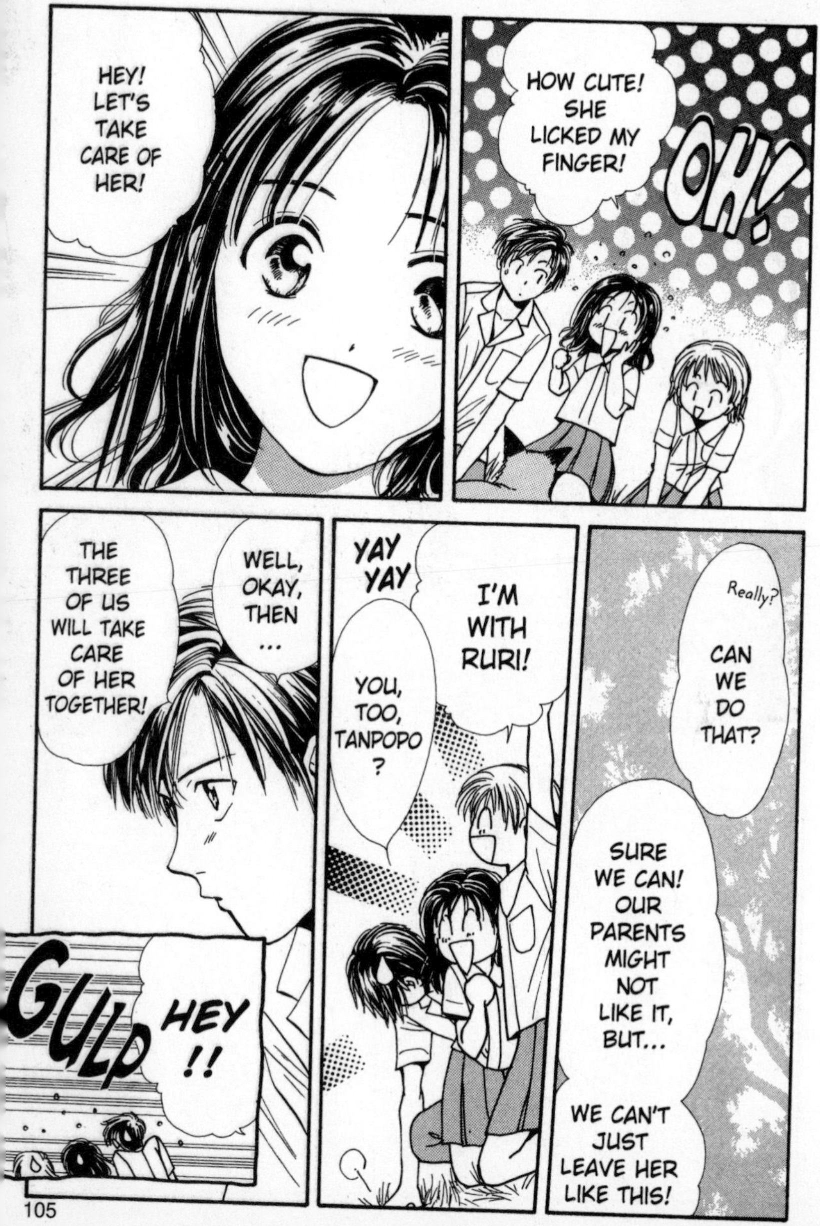
OH!
HOW CUTE! SHE LICKED MY FINGER!
HEY! LET'S TAKE CARE OF HER!
Really?
CAN WE DO THAT?
SURE WE CAN! OUR PARENTS MIGHT NOT LIKE IT, BUT...
WE CAN'T JUST LEAVE HER LIKE THIS!
YAY YAY
I'M WITH RURI!
YOU, TOO, TANPOPO?
WELL, OKAY, THEN ...
THE THREE OF US WILL TAKE CARE OF HER TOGETHER!
HEY!!
GULP

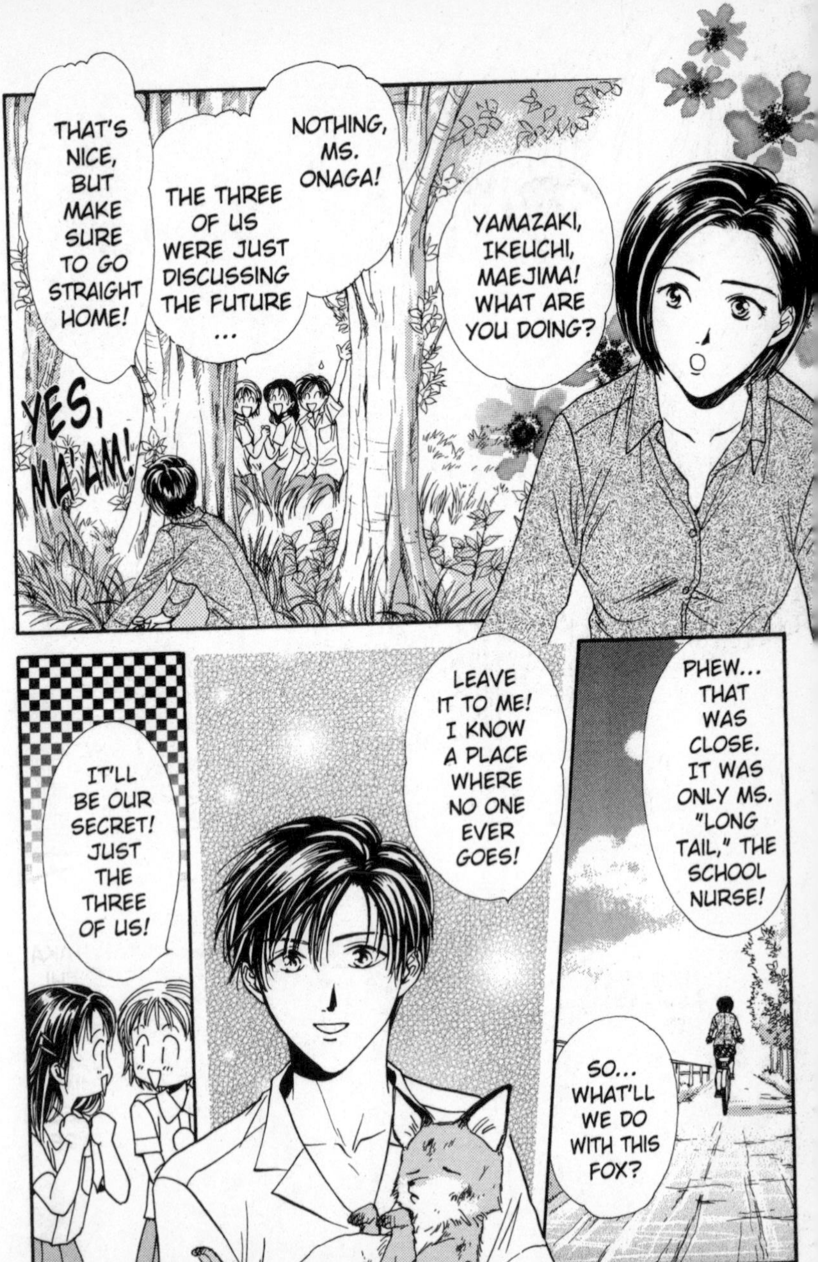
YAMAZAKI, IKEUCHI, MAEJIMA! WHAT ARE YOU DOING?
NOTHING, MS. ONAGA!
THE THREE OF US WERE JUST DISCUSSING THE FUTURE ...
THAT'S NICE, BUT MAKE SURE TO GO STRAIGHT HOME!
YES, MA'AM!
PHEW... THAT WAS CLOSE. IT WAS ONLY MS. "LONG TAIL," THE SCHOOL NURSE!
SO... WHAT'LL WE DO WITH THIS FOX?
LEAVE IT TO ME! I KNOW A PLACE WHERE NO ONE EVER GOES!
IT'LL BE OUR SECRET! JUST THE THREE OF US!

*ONAGA MEANS "LONG TAIL" IN JAPANESE.

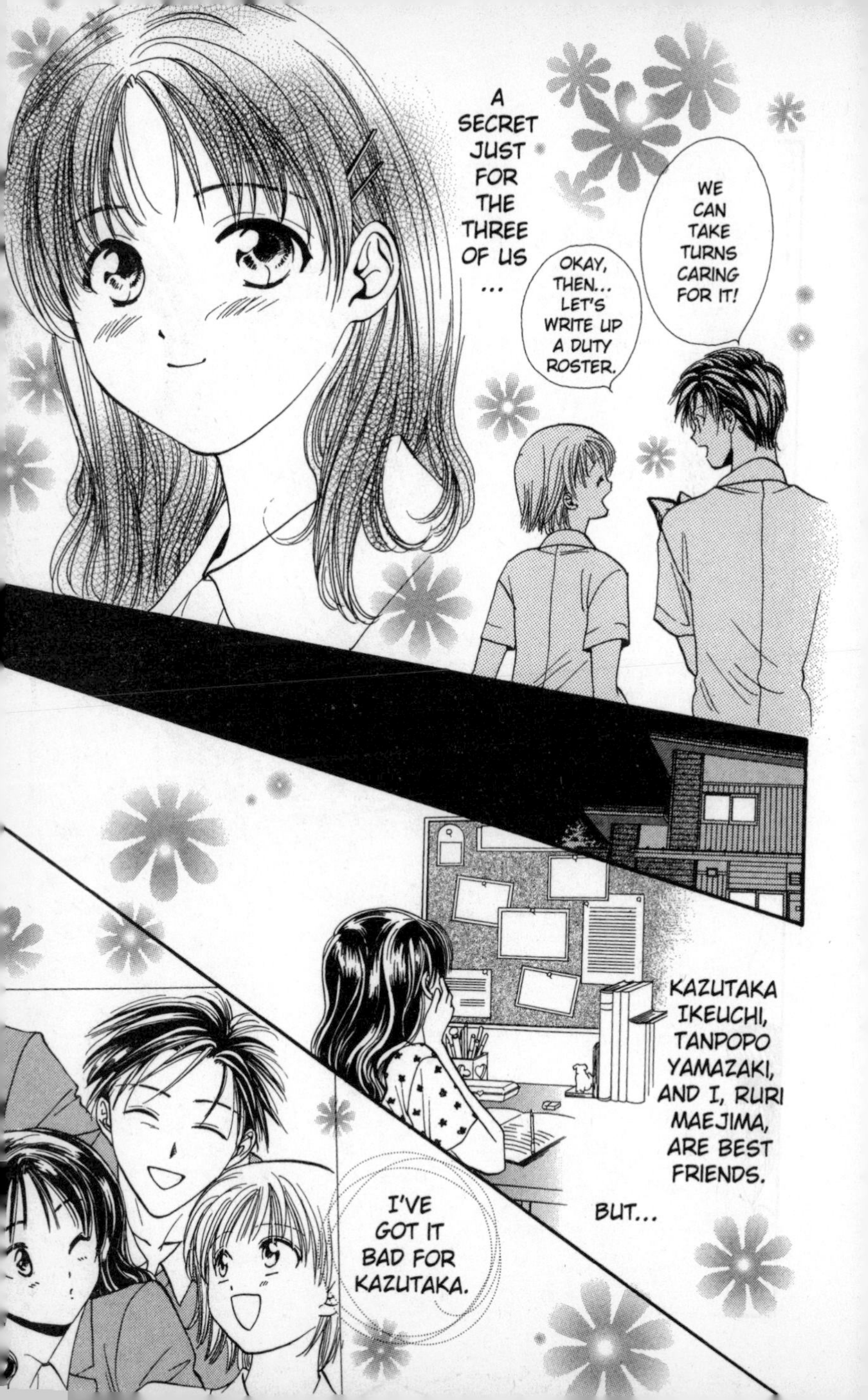
WE CAN TAKE TURNS CARING FOR IT!
OKAY, THEN... LET'S WRITE UP A DUTY ROSTER.
A SECRET JUST FOR THE THREE OF US ...
KAZUTAKA IKEUCHI, TANPOPO YAMAZAKI, AND I, RURI MAEJIMA, ARE BEST FRIENDS.
BUT...
I'VE GOT IT BAD FOR KAZUTAKA.

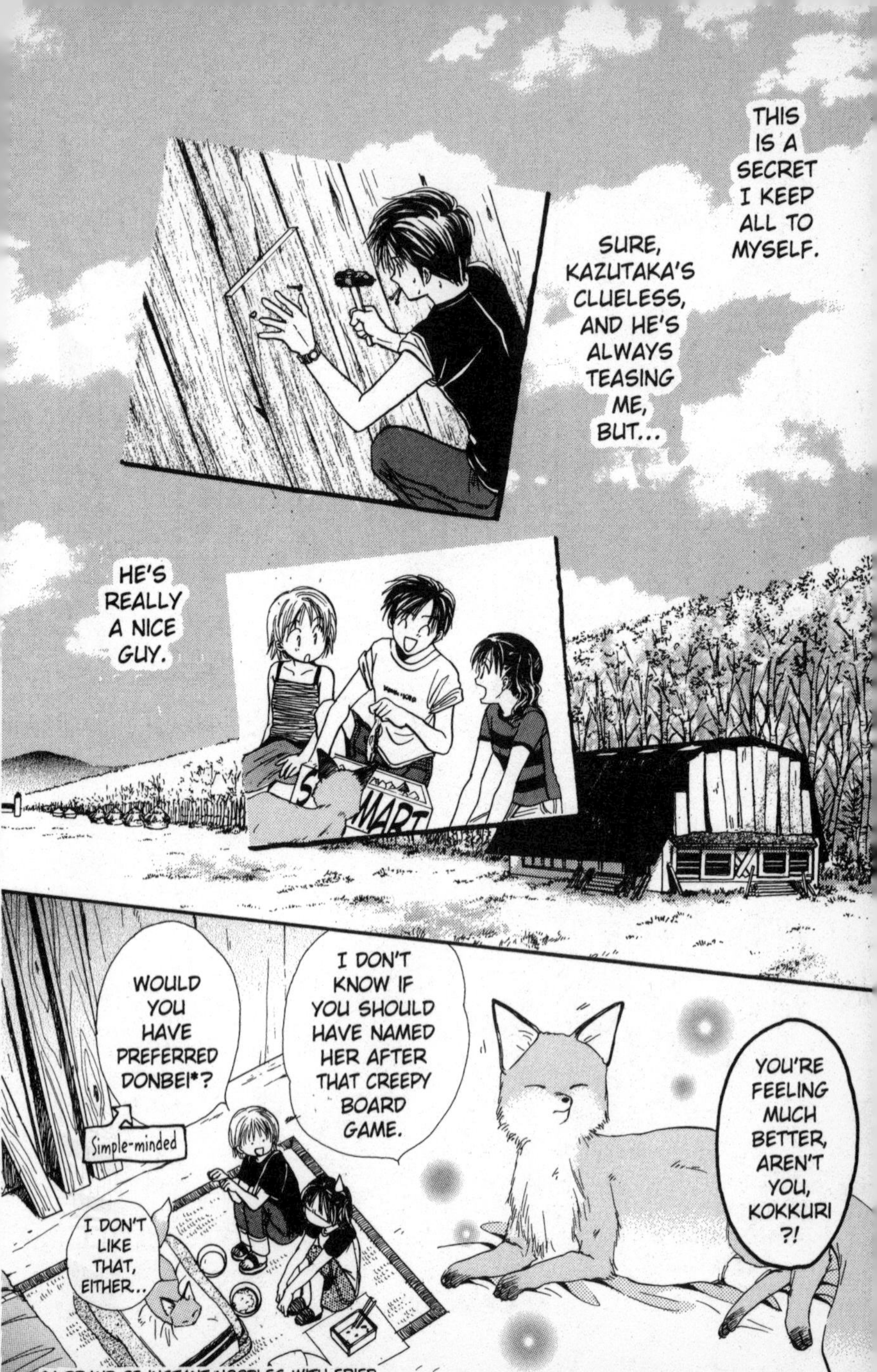
THIS IS A SECRET I KEEP ALL TO MYSELF.
SURE, KAZUTAKA'S CLUELESS, AND HE'S ALWAYS TEASING ME, BUT...
HE'S REALLY A NICE GUY.
YOU'RE FEELING MUCH BETTER, AREN'T YOU, KOKKURI ?!
I DON'T KNOW IF YOU SHOULD HAVE NAMED HER AFTER THAT CREEPY BOARD GAME.
WOULD YOU HAVE PREFERRED DONBEI*?
Simple-minded
I DON'T LIKE THAT, EITHER..

*A BRAND OF INSTANT NOODLES WITH FRIED BEAN CURD THAT FOXES ARE SAID TO LOVE.

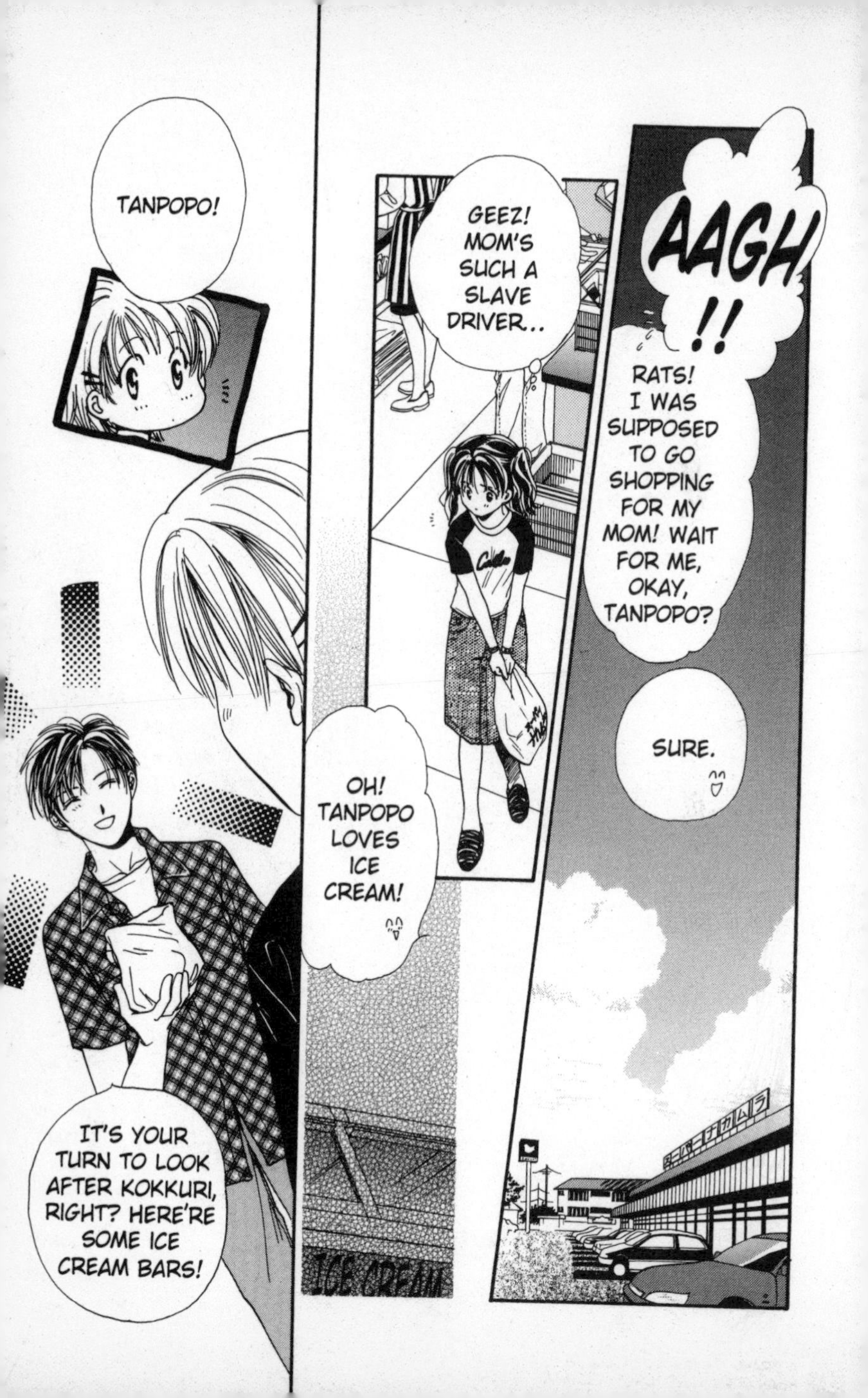
AAGH!!
RATS! I WAS SUPPOSED TO GO SHOPPING FOR MY MOM! WAIT FOR ME, OKAY, TANPOPO?
SURE.
GEEZ! MOM'S SUCH A SLAVE DRIVER..
OH! TANPOPO LOVES ICE CREAM!
ICE CREAM
TANPOPO!
IT'S YOUR TURN TO LOOK AFTER KOKKURI, RIGHT? HERE'RE SOME ICE CREAM BARS!

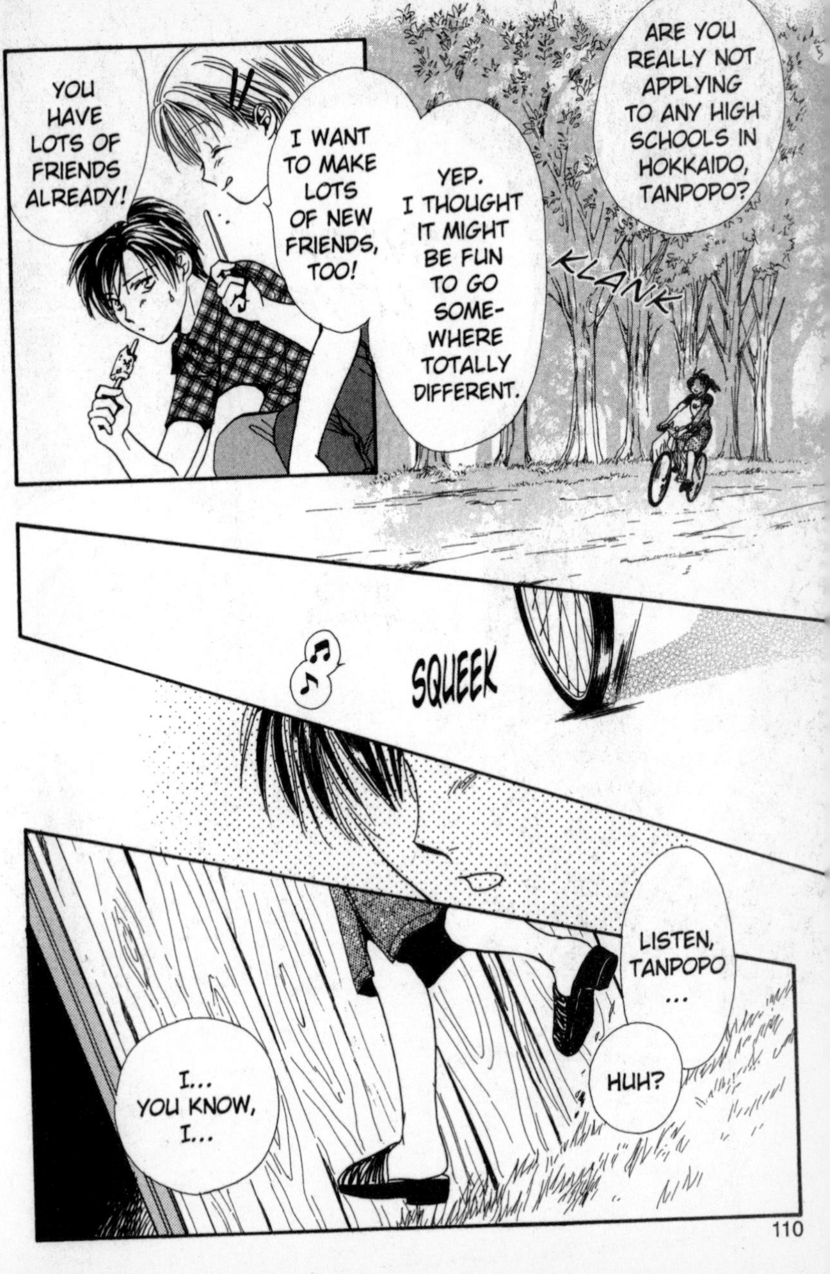
ARE YOU REALLY NOT APPLYING TO ANY HIGH SCHOOLS IN HOKKAIDO, TANPOPO?
KLANK
YEP. I THOUGHT IT MIGHT BE FUN TO GO SOME-WHERE TOTALLY DIFFERENT.
I WANT TO MAKE LOTS OF NEW FRIENDS, TOO!
YOU HAVE LOTS OF FRIENDS ALREADY!
SQUEEK
♪ ♪
LISTEN, TANPOPO ...
HUH?
I... YOU KNOW, I...

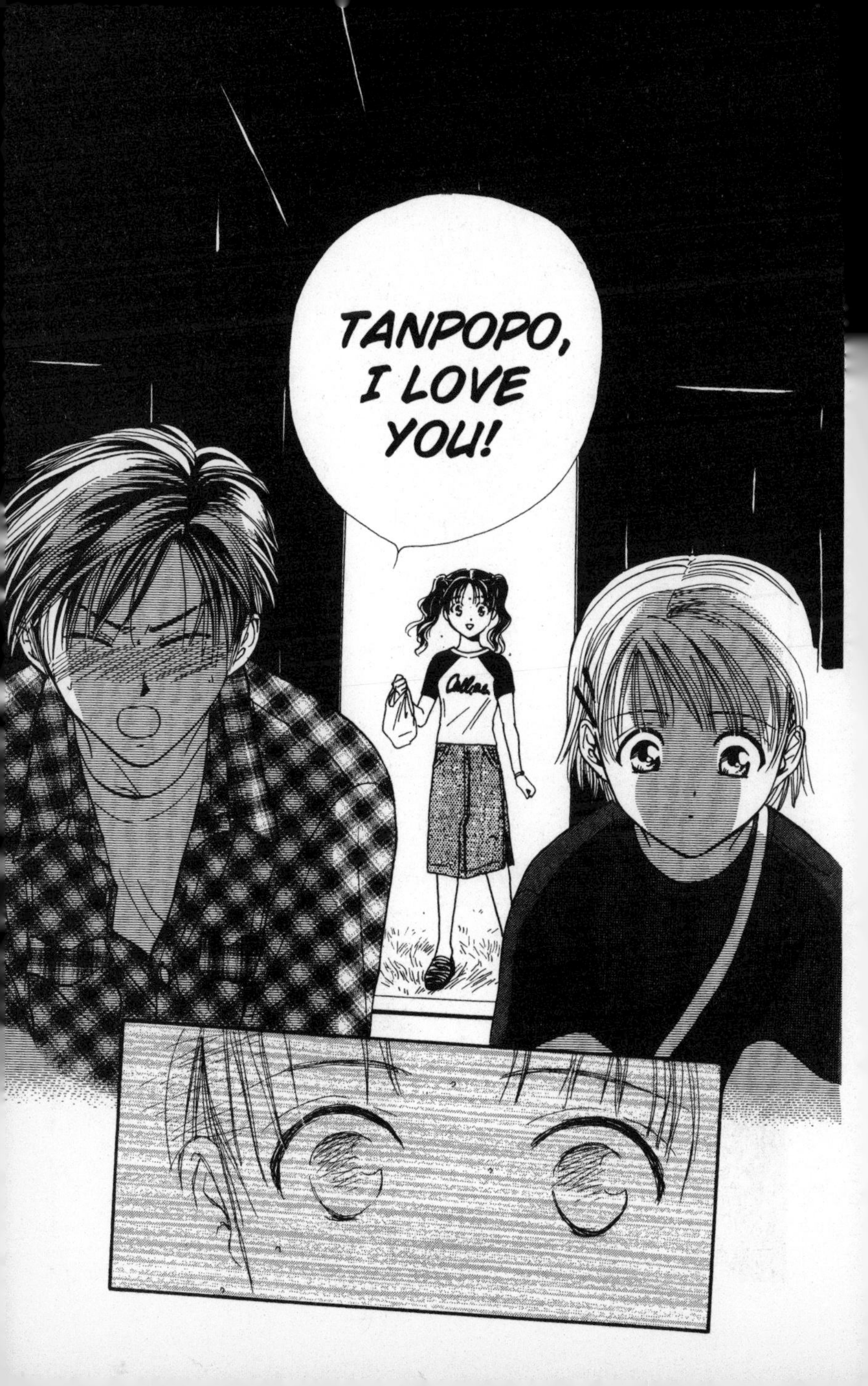
TANPOPO, I LOVE YOU!

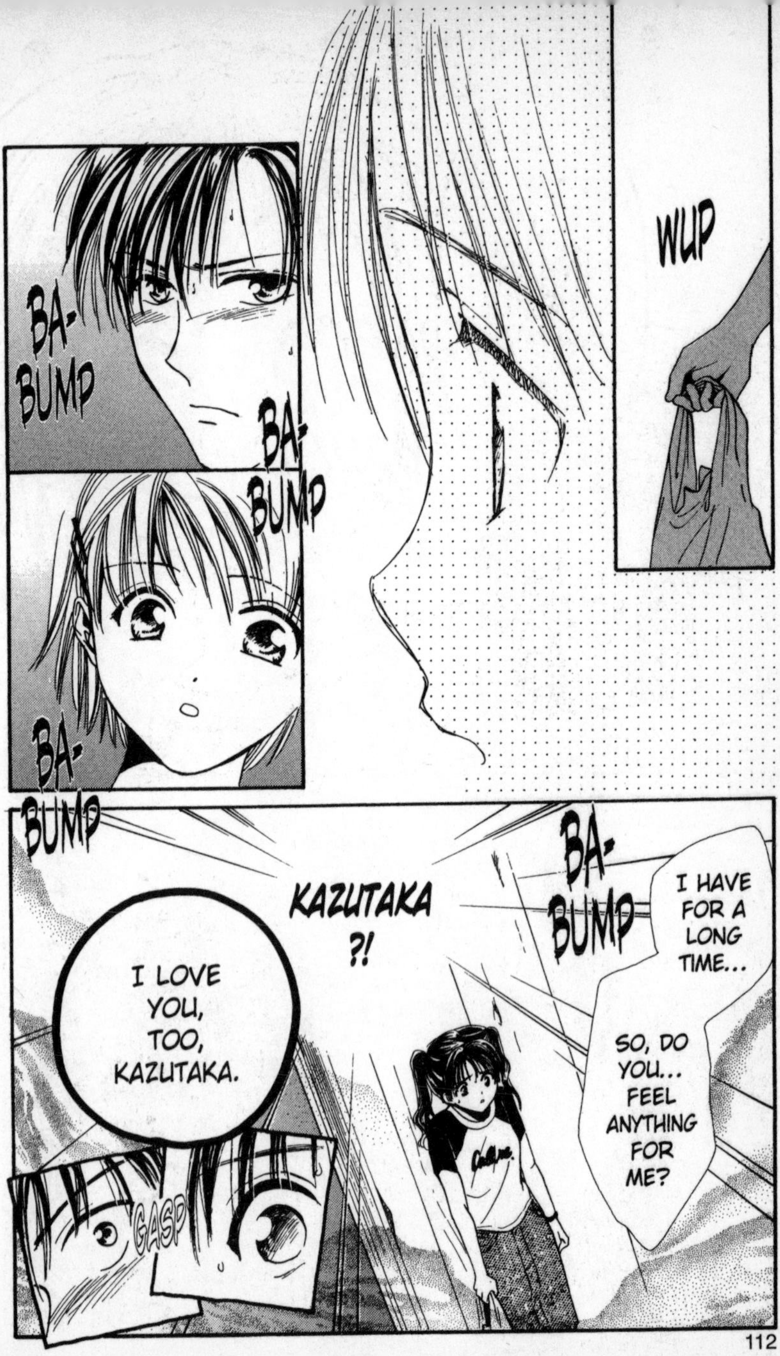
WUP
BA-BUMP
BA-BUMP
BA-BUMP
BA-BUMP
I HAVE FOR A LONG TIME...
SO, DO YOU... FEEL ANYTHING FOR ME?
KAZUTAKA ?!
I LOVE YOU, TOO, KAZUTAKA.
GASP

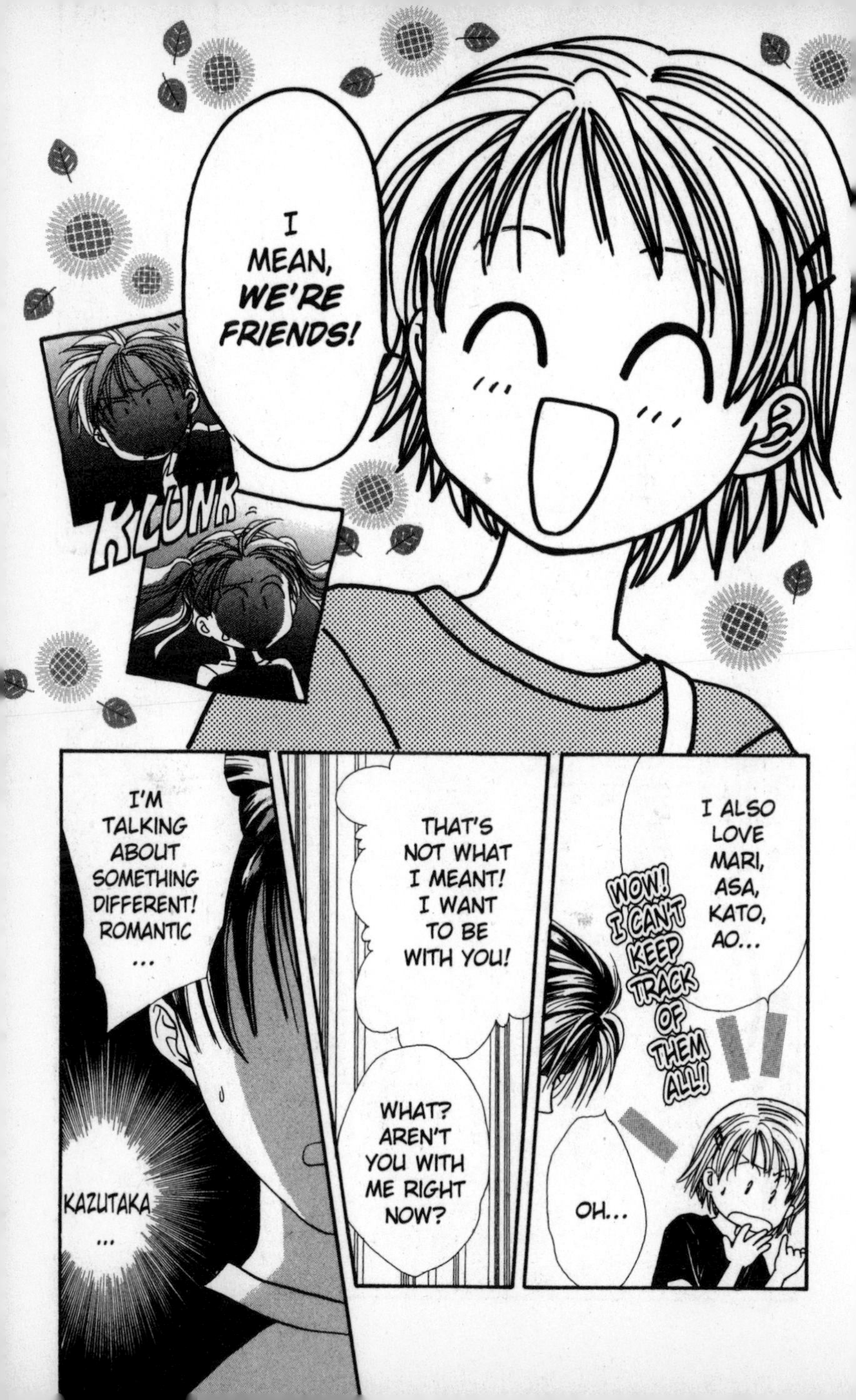
I MEAN, **WE'RE FRIENDS!**
KLUNK
I ALSO LOVE MARI, ASA, KATO, AO...
WOW! I CAN'T KEEP TRACK OF THEM ALL!
OH...
THAT'S NOT WHAT I MEANT! I WANT TO BE WITH YOU!
WHAT? AREN'T YOU WITH ME RIGHT NOW?
I'M TALKING ABOUT SOMETHING DIFFERENT! ROMANTIC ...
KAZUTAKA ...

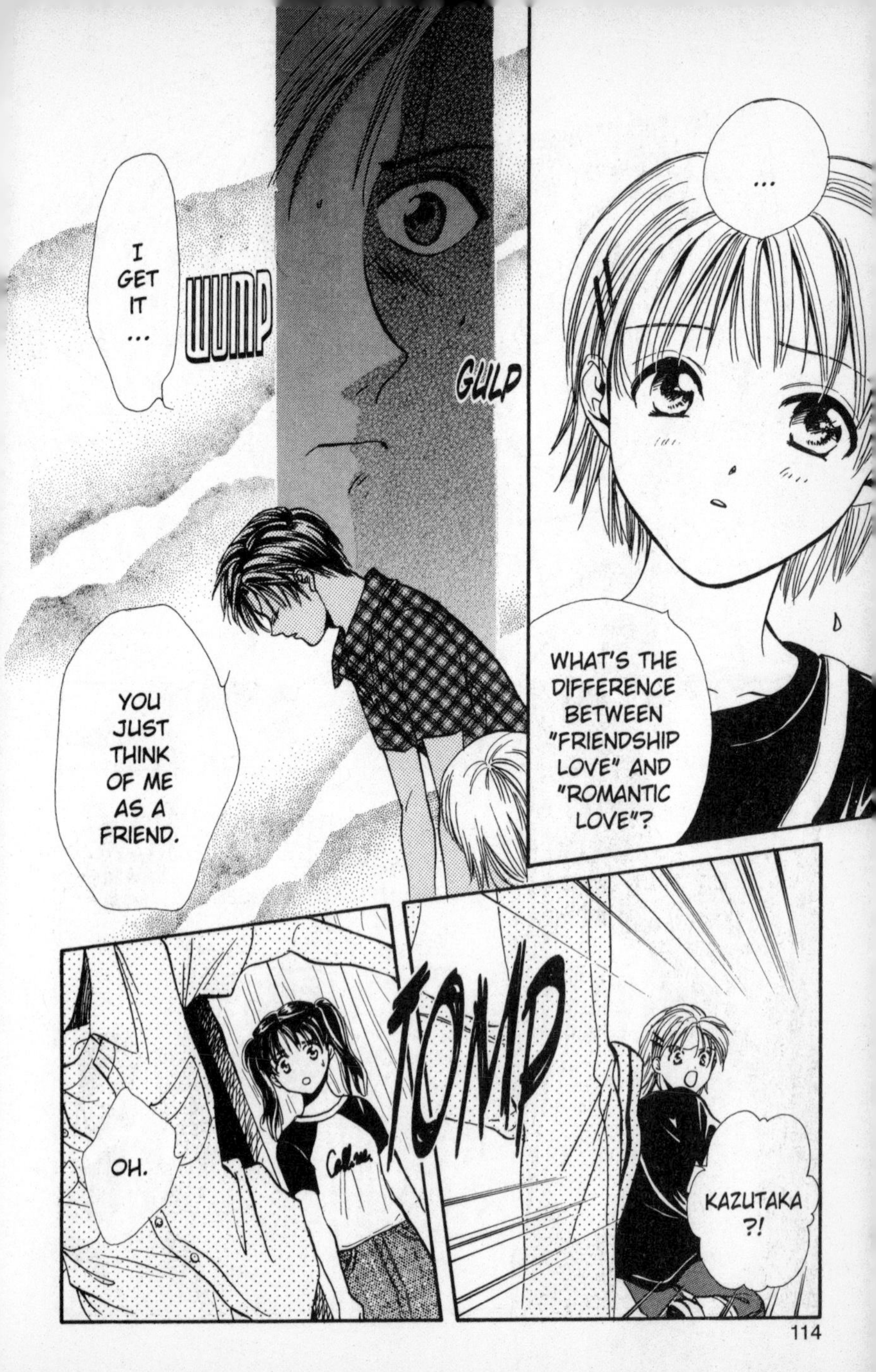
...
WHAT'S THE DIFFERENCE BETWEEN "FRIENDSHIP LOVE" AND "ROMANTIC LOVE"?
GULP
WUMP
I GET IT ...
YOU JUST THINK OF ME AS A FRIEND.
KAZUTAKA ?!
TOMP
OH.

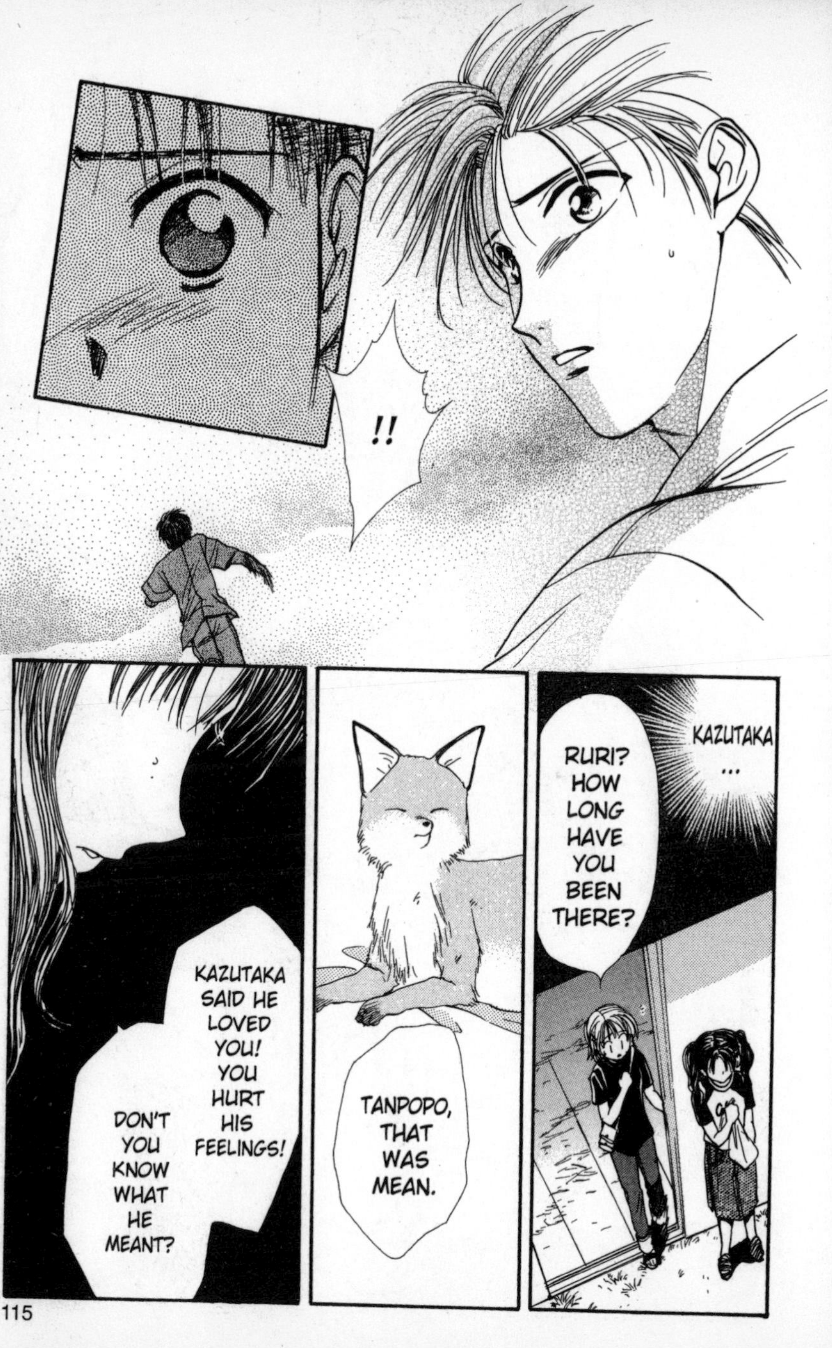
!!
KAZUTAKA ...
RURI? HOW LONG HAVE YOU BEEN THERE?
TANPOPO, THAT WAS MEAN.
KAZUTAKA SAID HE LOVED YOU! YOU HURT HIS FEELINGS!
DON'T YOU KNOW WHAT HE MEANT?

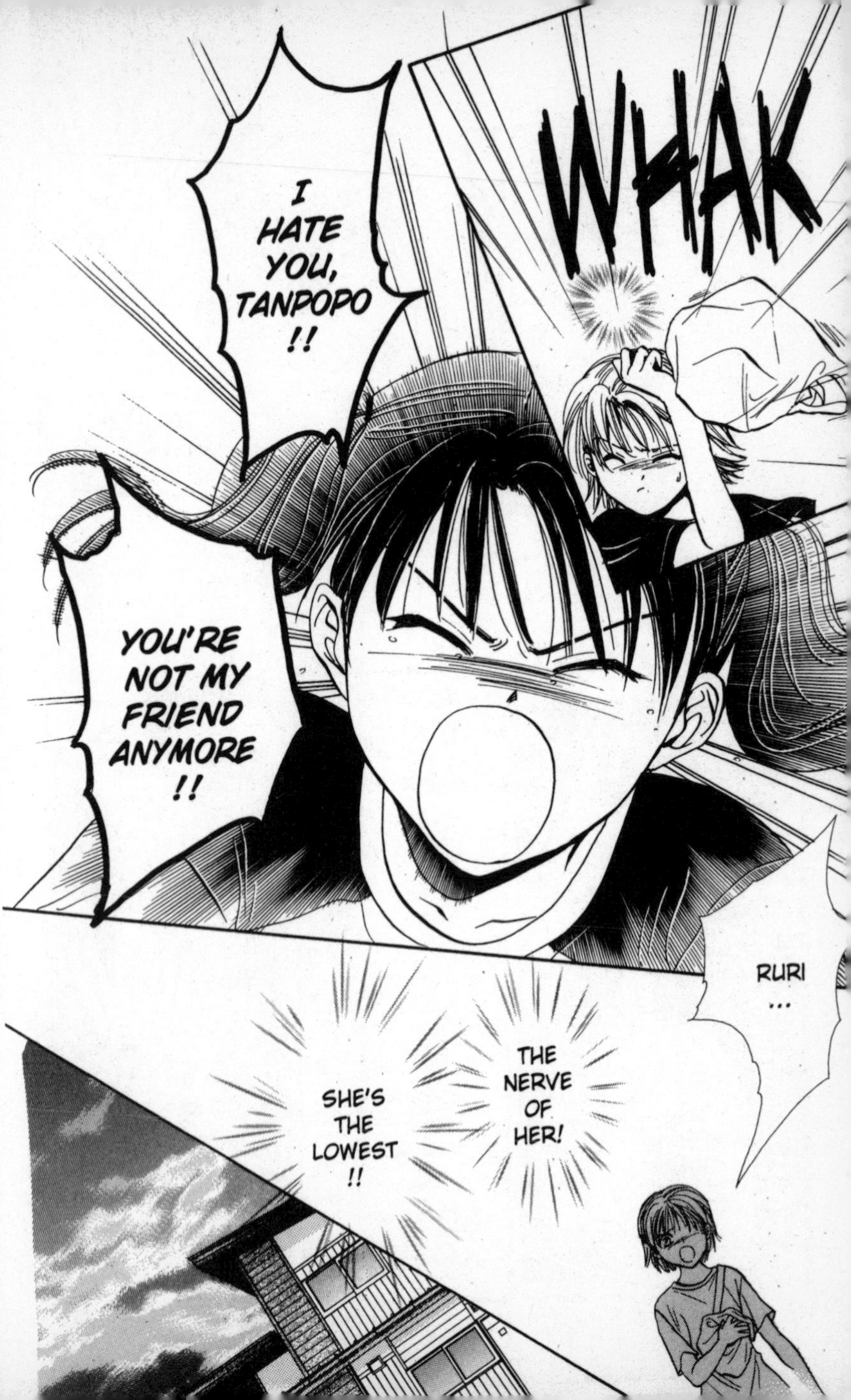
WHAK
I HATE YOU, TANPOPO !!
YOU'RE NOT MY FRIEND ANYMORE !!
RURI ...
THE NERVE OF HER!
SHE'S THE LOWEST !!

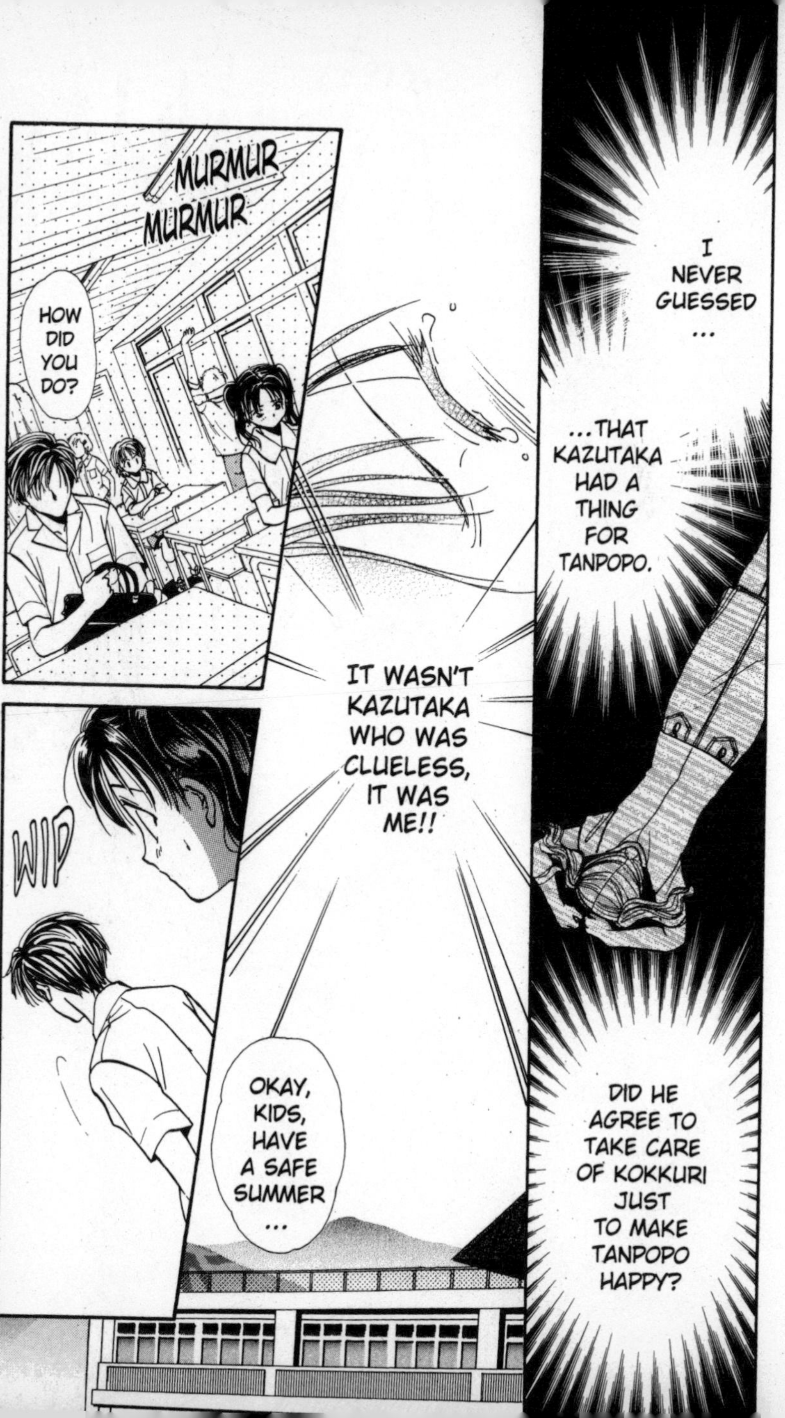
I NEVER GUESSED ...
...THAT KAZUTAKA HAD A THING FOR TANPOPO.
DID HE AGREE TO TAKE CARE OF KOKKURI JUST TO MAKE TANPOPO HAPPY?
IT WASN'T KAZUTAKA WHO WAS CLUELESS, IT WAS ME!!
MURMUR
MURMUR
HOW DID YOU DO?
WIP
OKAY, KIDS, HAVE A SAFE SUMMER ...

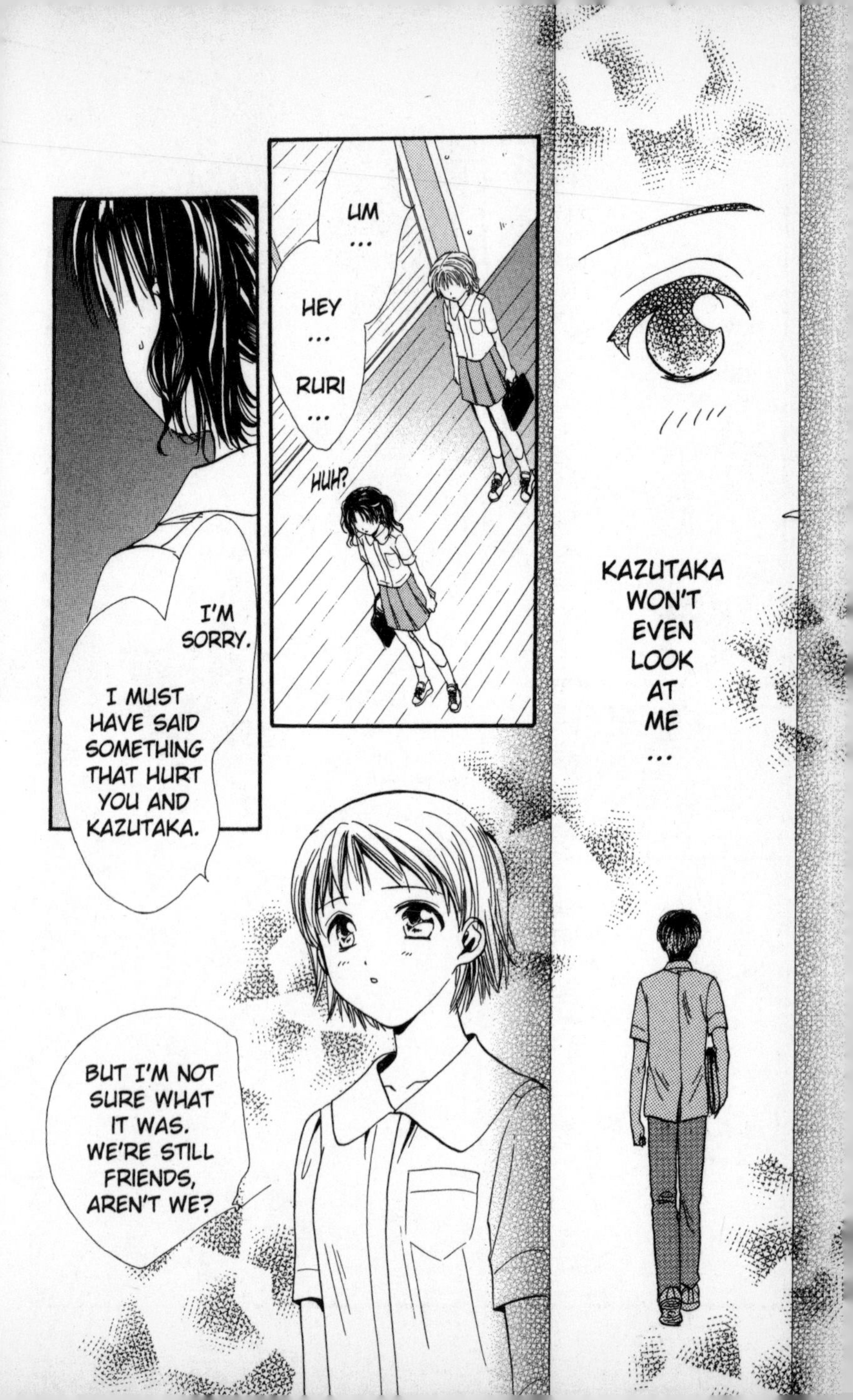
KAZUTAKA WON'T EVEN LOOK AT ME ...
UM ...
HEY ... RURI ...
HUH?
I'M SORRY.
I MUST HAVE SAID SOMETHING THAT HURT YOU AND KAZUTAKA.
BUT I'M NOT SURE WHAT IT WAS. WE'RE STILL FRIENDS, AREN'T WE?

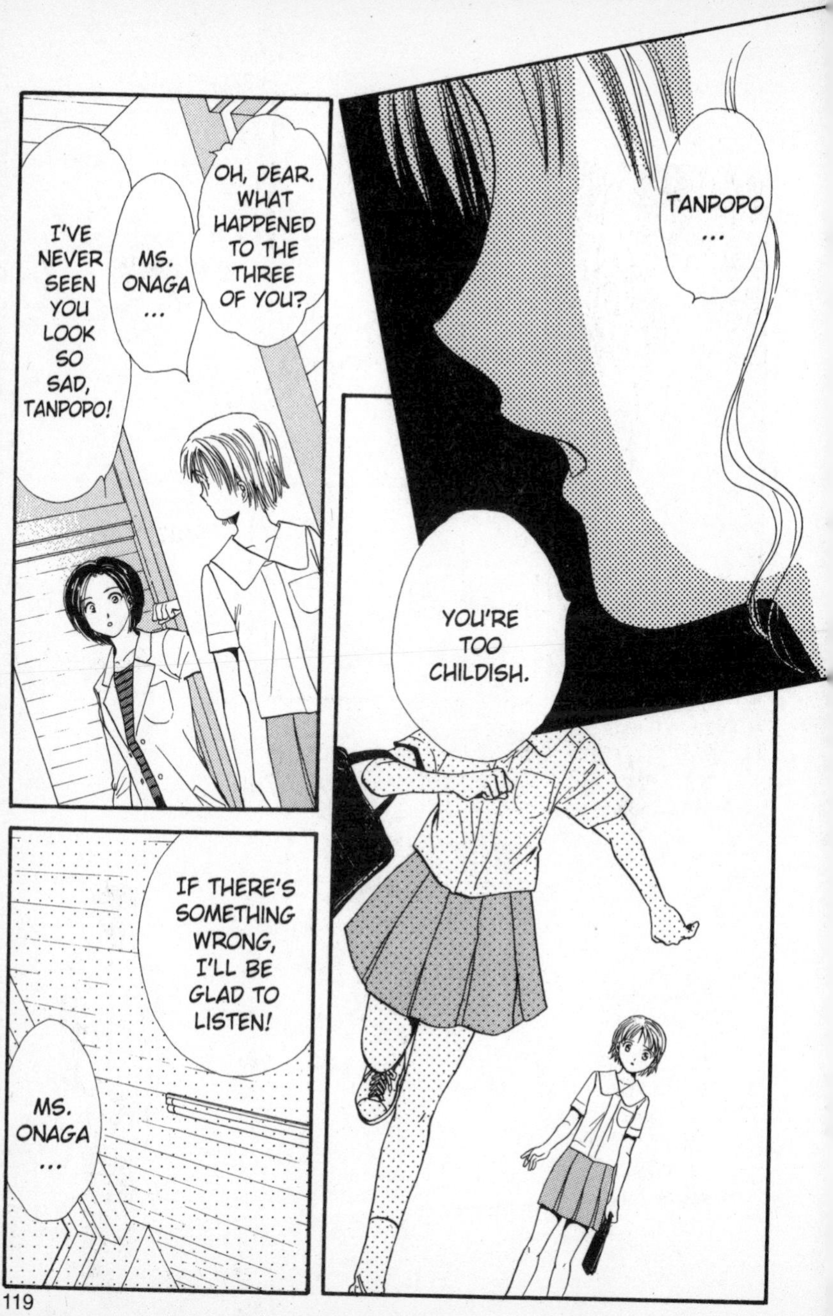
TANPOPO ...
YOU'RE TOO CHILDISH.
OH, DEAR. WHAT HAPPENED TO THE THREE OF YOU?
MS. ONAGA ...
I'VE NEVER SEEN YOU LOOK SO SAD, TANPOPO!
IF THERE'S SOMETHING WRONG, I'LL BE GLAD TO LISTEN!
MS. ONAGA ...

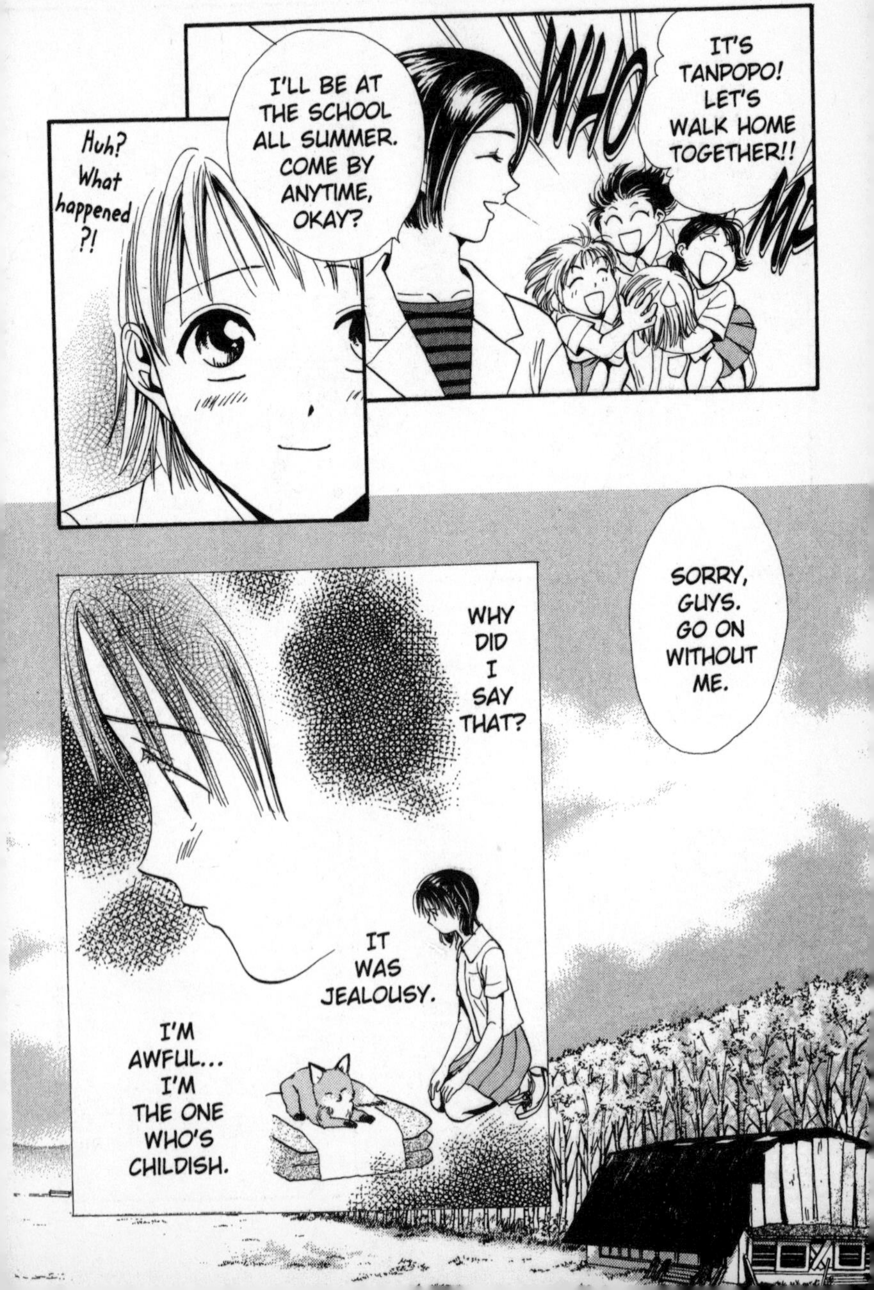
IT'S TANPOPO! LET'S WALK HOME TOGETHER!!
WHO
I'LL BE AT THE SCHOOL ALL SUMMER. COME BY ANYTIME, OKAY?
Huh? What happened?!
SORRY, GUYS. GO ON WITHOUT ME.
WHY DID I SAY THAT?
IT WAS JEALOUSY.
I'M AWFUL... I'M THE ONE WHO'S CHILDISH.

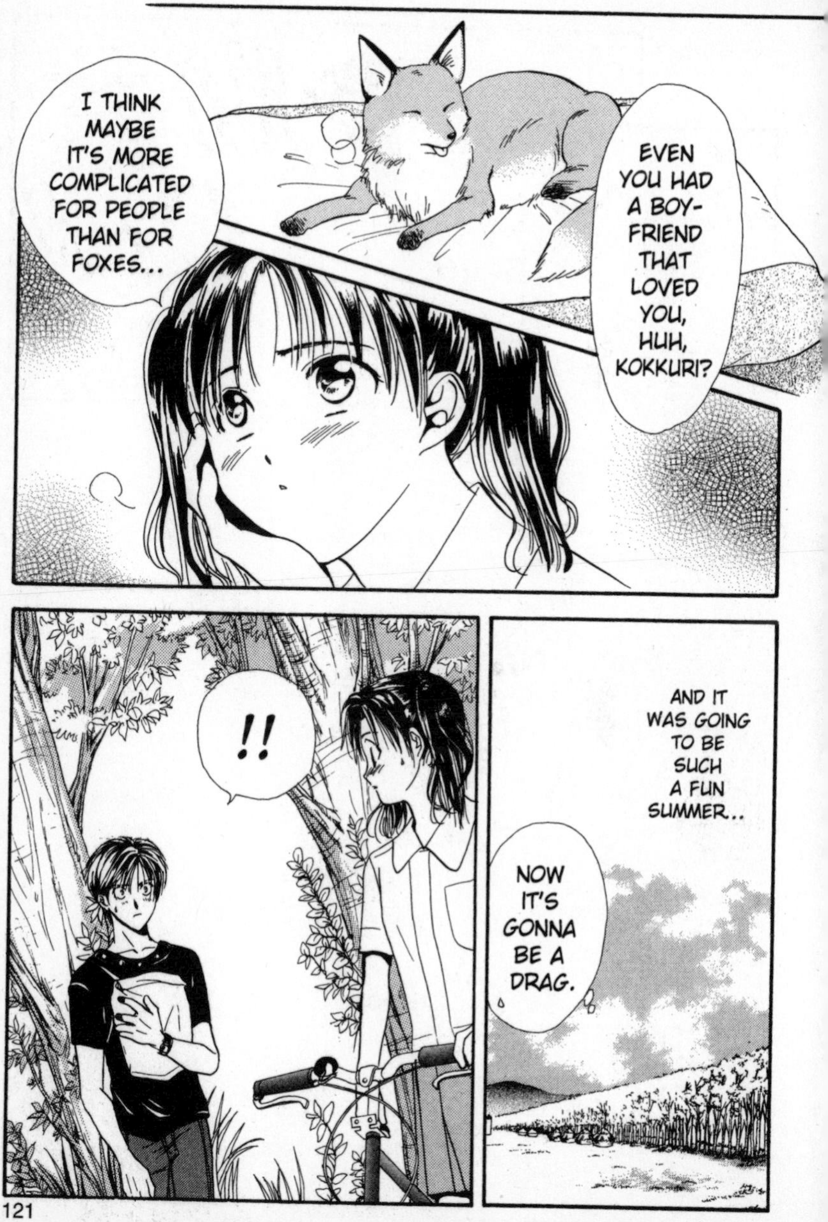
EVEN YOU HAD A BOY-FRIEND THAT LOVED YOU, HUH, KOKKURI?
I THINK MAYBE IT'S MORE COMPLICATED FOR PEOPLE THAN FOR FOXES...
AND IT WAS GOING TO BE SUCH A FUN SUMMER..
NOW IT'S GONNA BE A DRAG.
!!

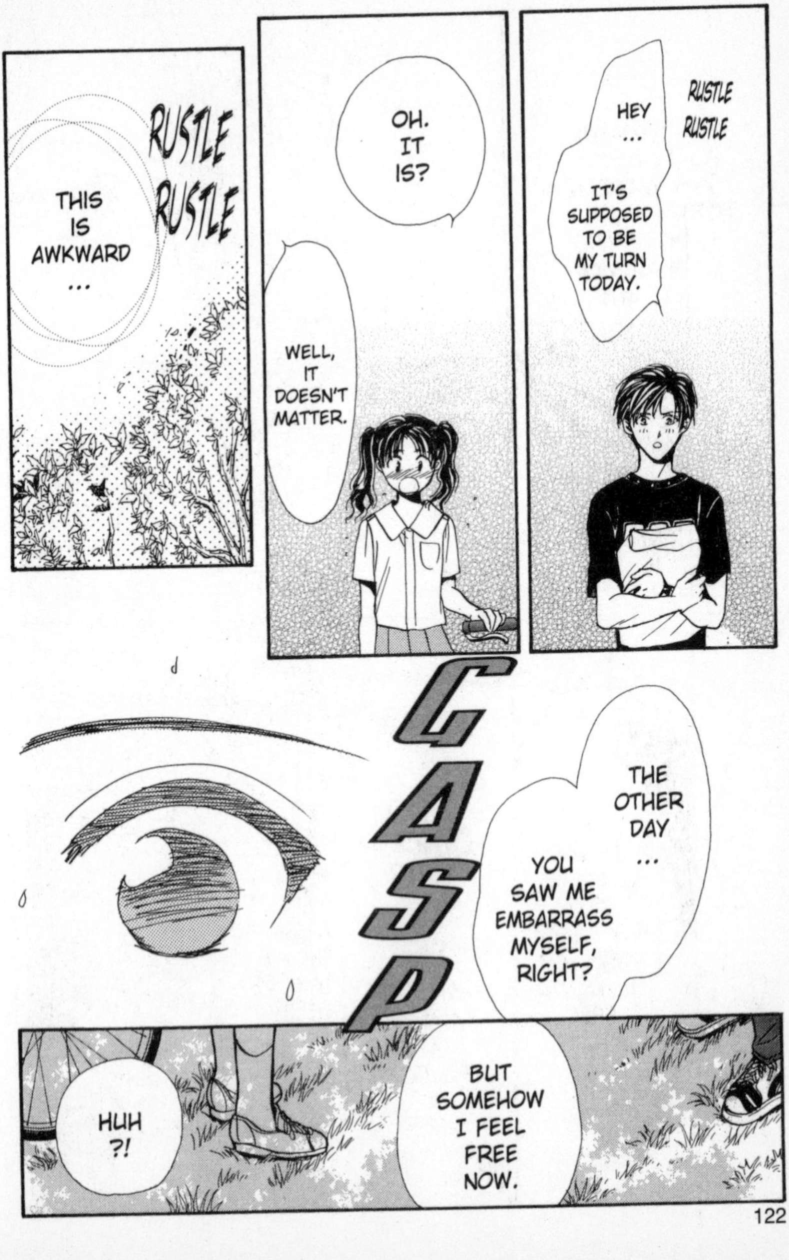
RUSTLE RUSTLE
HEY ...
IT'S SUPPOSED TO BE MY TURN TODAY.
OH. IT IS?
WELL, IT DOESN'T MATTER.
RUSTLE RUSTLE
THIS IS AWKWARD ...
THE OTHER DAY ...
YOU SAW ME EMBARRASS MYSELF, RIGHT?
GASP
BUT SOMEHOW I FEEL FREE NOW.
HUH ?!

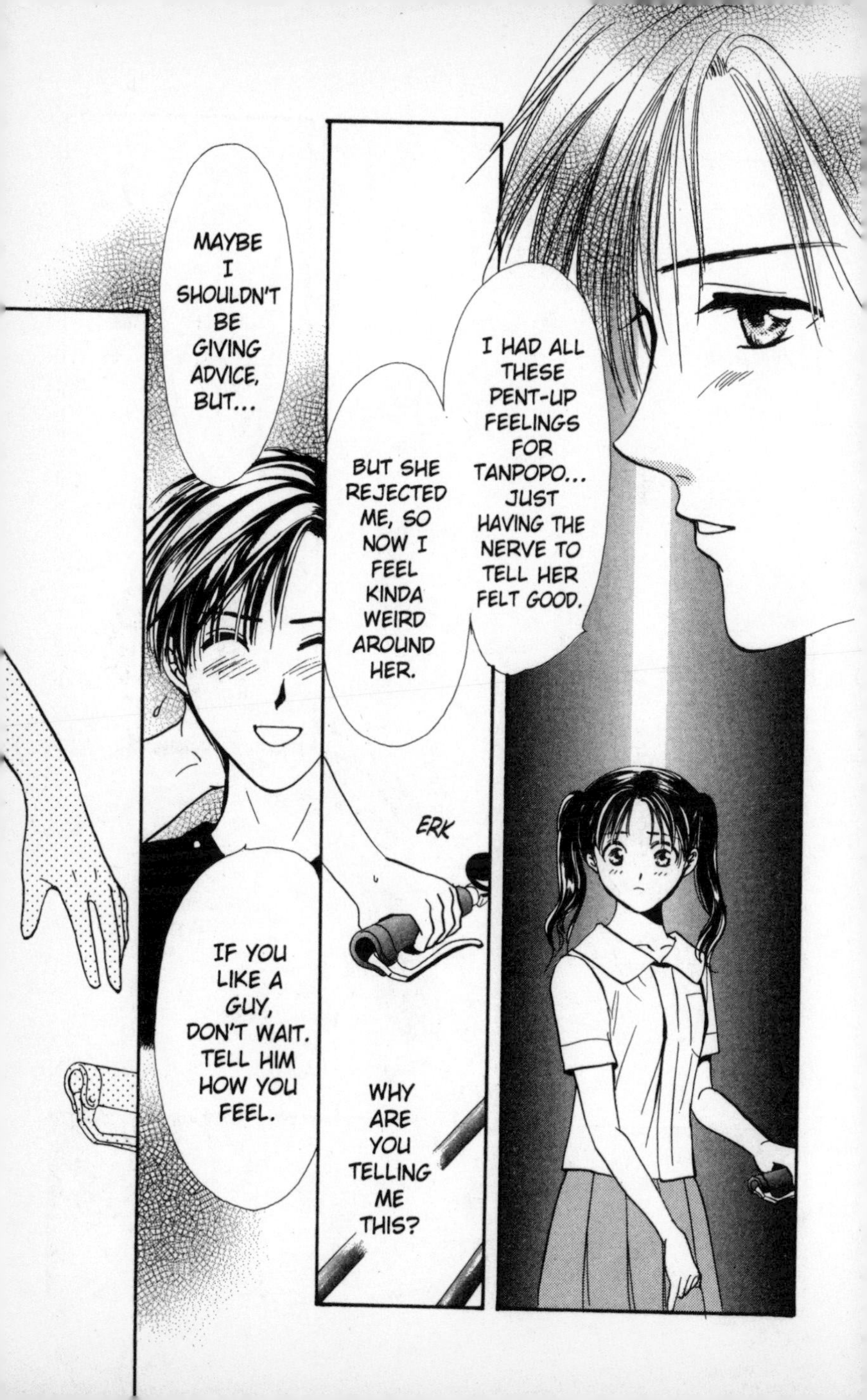
I HAD ALL THESE PENT-UP FEELINGS FOR TANPOPO... JUST HAVING THE NERVE TO TELL HER FELT GOOD.
BUT SHE REJECTED ME, SO NOW I FEEL KINDA WEIRD AROUND HER.
ERK
WHY ARE YOU TELLING ME THIS?
MAYBE I SHOULDN'T BE GIVING ADVICE, BUT...
IF YOU LIKE A GUY, DON'T WAIT. TELL HIM HOW YOU FEEL.

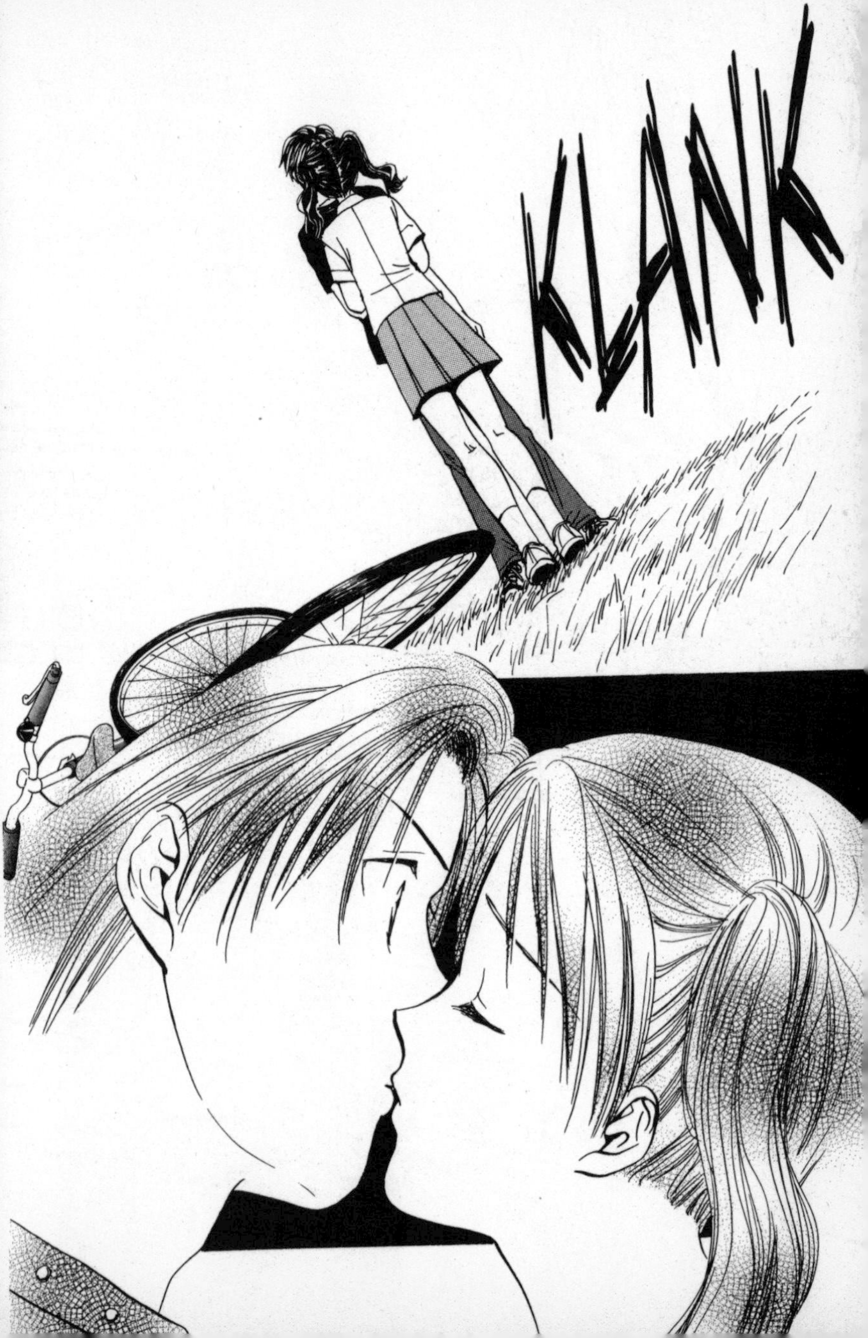
KLANK

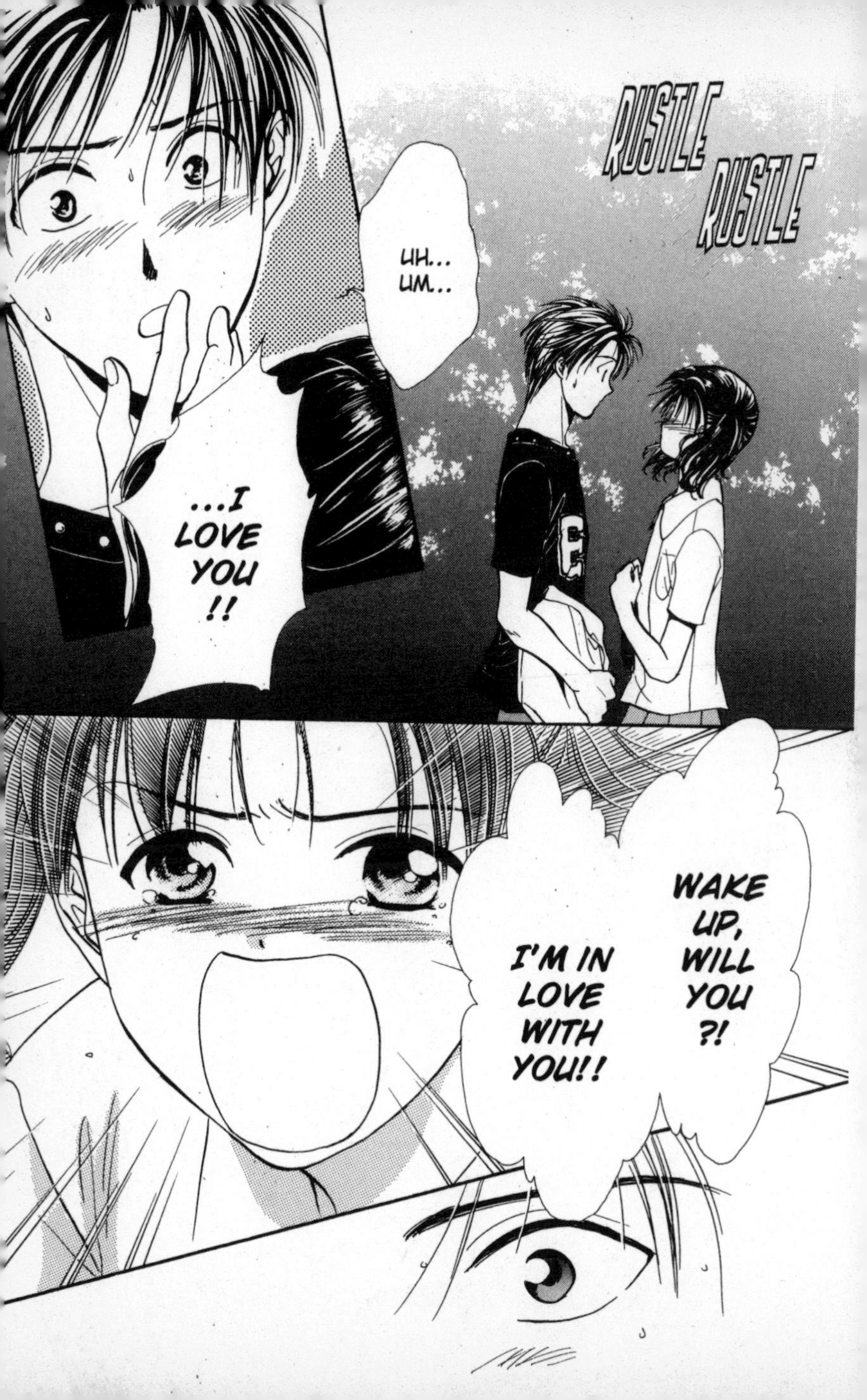
RUSTLE RUSTLE
UH... UM...
...I LOVE YOU !!
WAKE UP, WILL YOU ?!
I'M IN LOVE WITH YOU!!

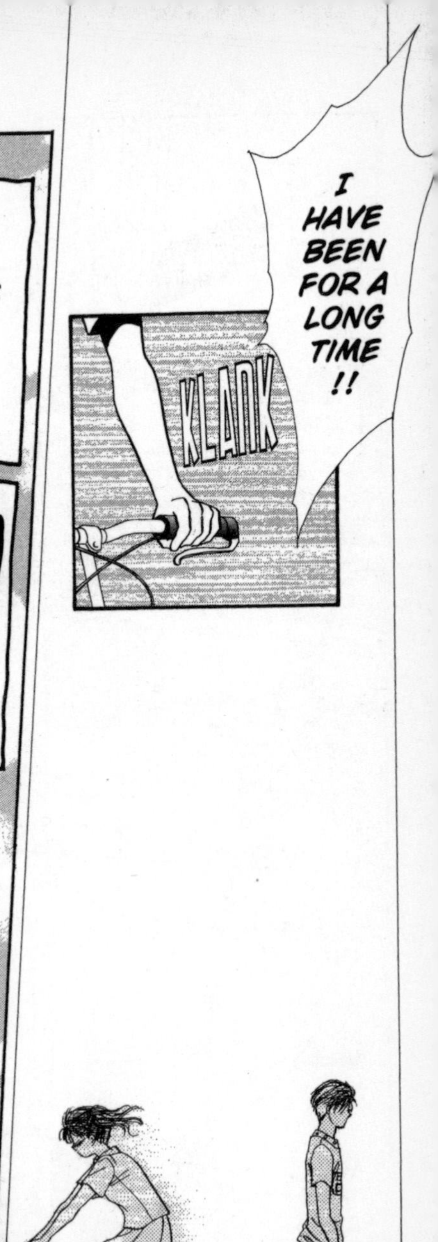
I HAVE BEEN FOR A LONG TIME!!
KLANK

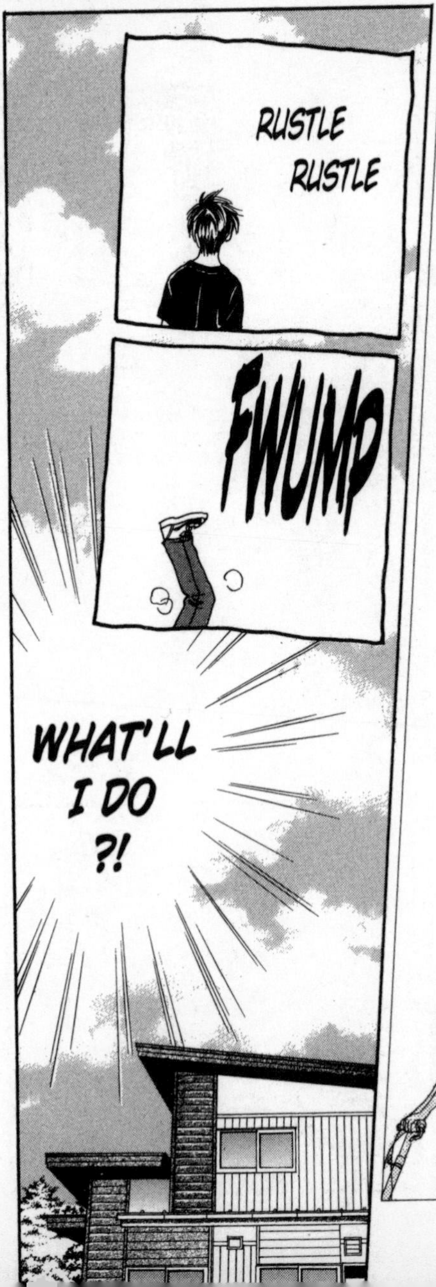
RUSTLE RUSTLE
FWUMP
WHAT'LL I DO ?!

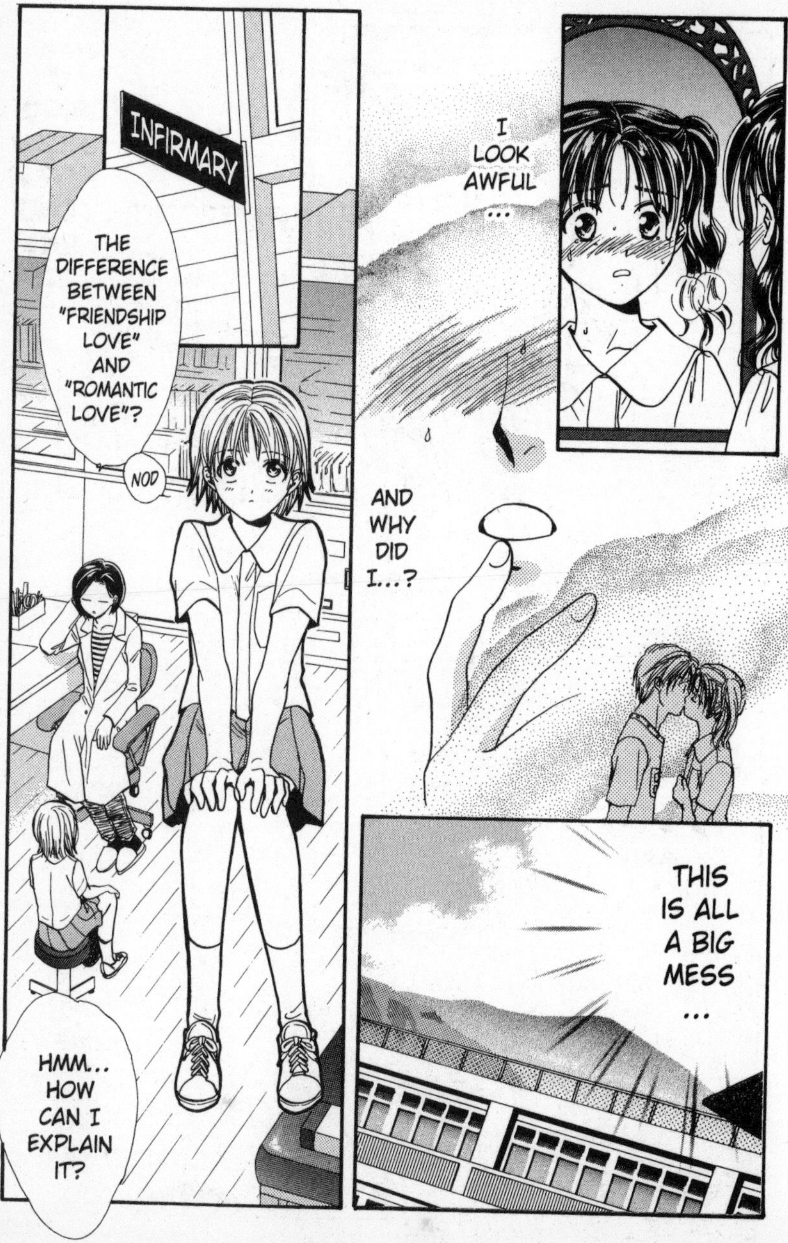
I LOOK AWFUL...
AND WHY DID I...?
THIS IS ALL A BIG MESS...
INFIRMARY
THE DIFFERENCE BETWEEN "FRIENDSHIP LOVE" AND "ROMANTIC LOVE"?
NOD
HMM... HOW CAN I EXPLAIN IT?

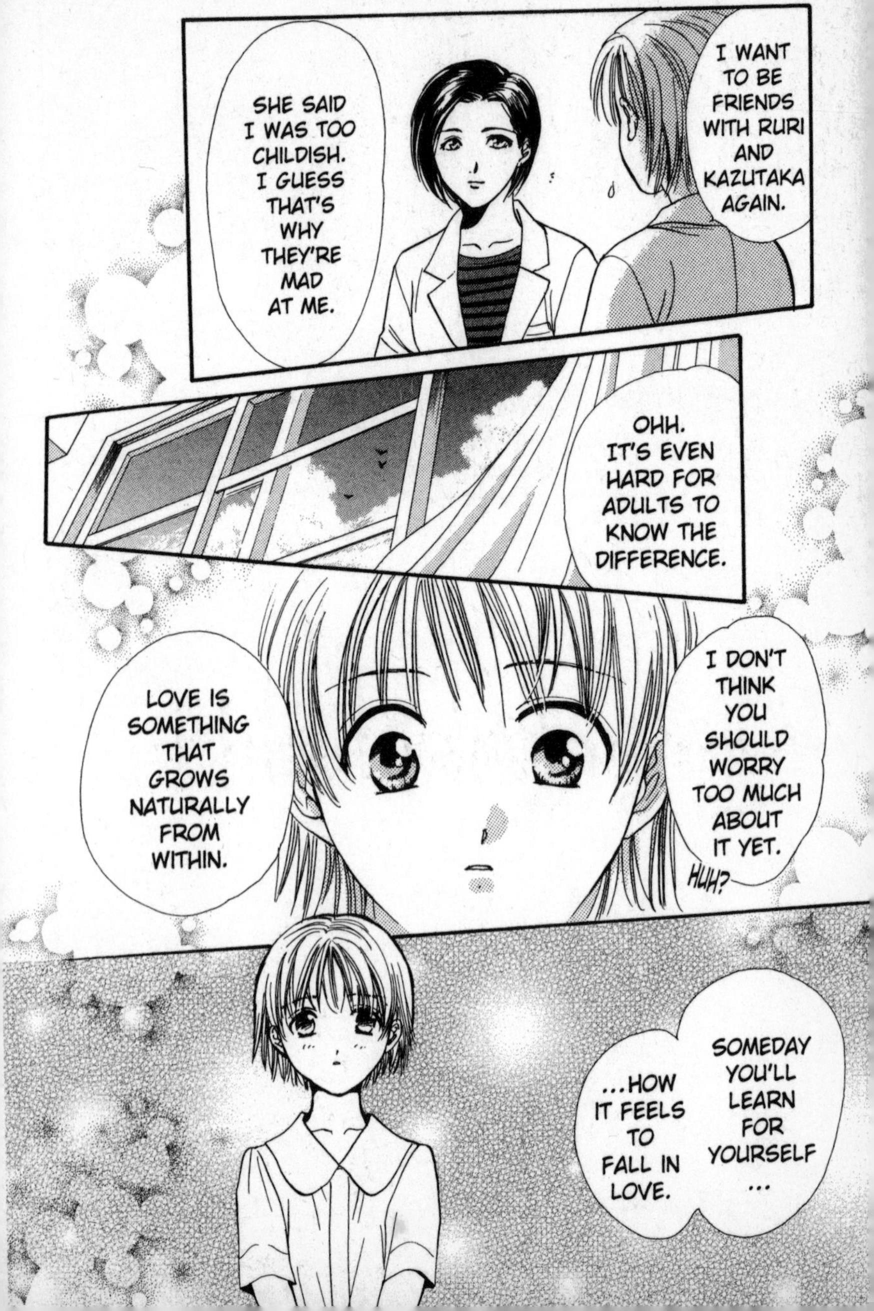
I WANT TO BE FRIENDS WITH RURI AND KAZUTAKA AGAIN.
SHE SAID I WAS TOO CHILDISH. I GUESS THAT'S WHY THEY'RE MAD AT ME.
OHH. IT'S EVEN HARD FOR ADULTS TO KNOW THE DIFFERENCE.
I DON'T THINK YOU SHOULD WORRY TOO MUCH ABOUT IT YET.
HUH?
LOVE IS SOMETHING THAT GROWS NATURALLY FROM WITHIN.
SOMEDAY YOU'LL LEARN FOR YOURSELF ...
...HOW IT FEELS TO FALL IN LOVE.

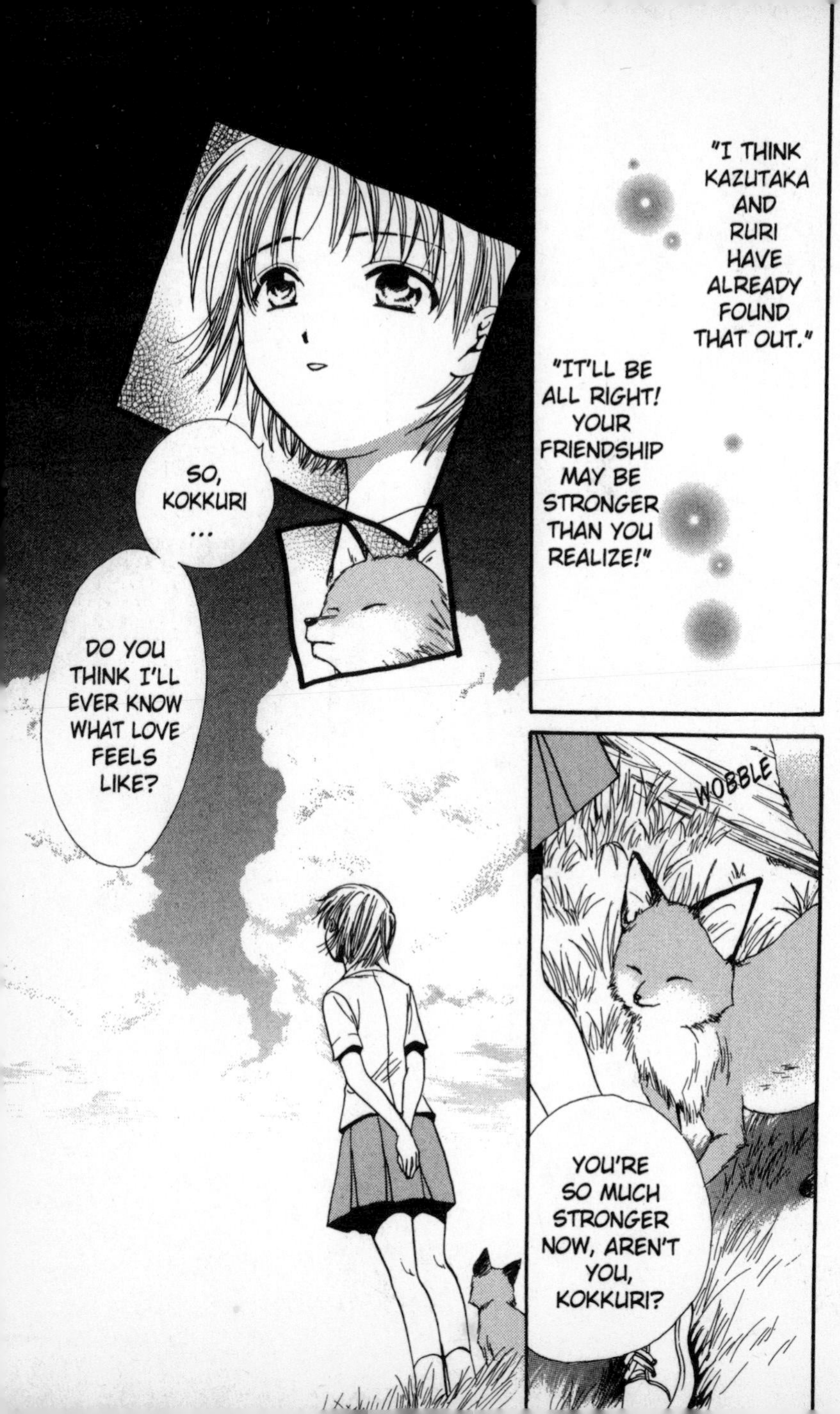
"I THINK KAZUTAKA AND RURI HAVE ALREADY FOUND THAT OUT."
"IT'LL BE ALL RIGHT! YOUR FRIENDSHIP MAY BE STRONGER THAN YOU REALIZE!"
WOBBLE
YOU'RE SO MUCH STRONGER NOW, AREN'T YOU, KOKKURI?
SO, KOKKURI ...
DO YOU THINK I'LL EVER KNOW WHAT LOVE FEELS LIKE?

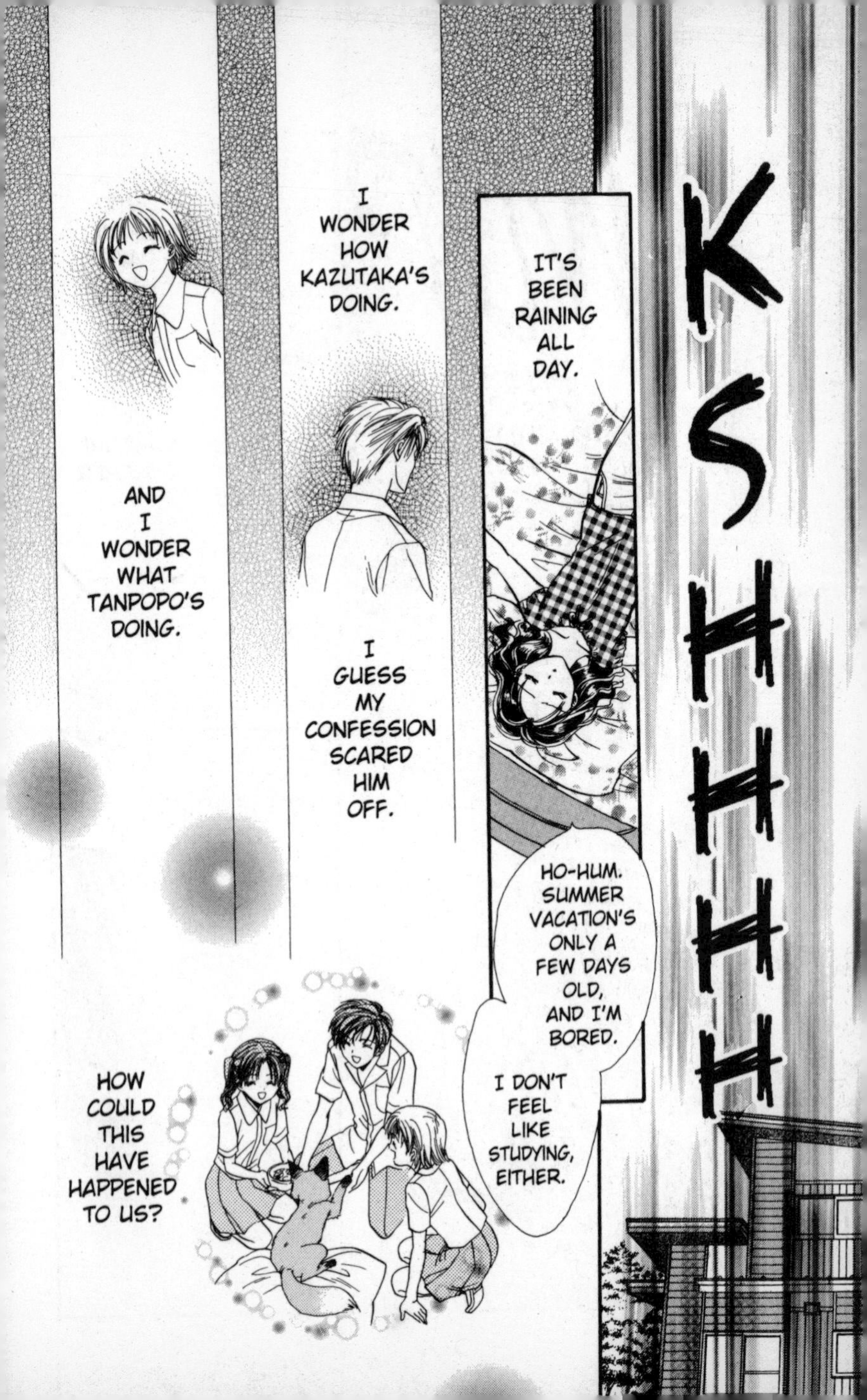
KSHHHHH
IT'S BEEN RAINING ALL DAY.
HO-HUM. SUMMER VACATION'S ONLY A FEW DAYS OLD, AND I'M BORED.
I DON'T FEEL LIKE STUDYING, EITHER.
I WONDER HOW KAZUTAKA'S DOING.
I GUESS MY CONFESSION SCARED HIM OFF.
AND I WONDER WHAT TANPOPO'S DOING.
HOW COULD THIS HAVE HAPPENED TO US?

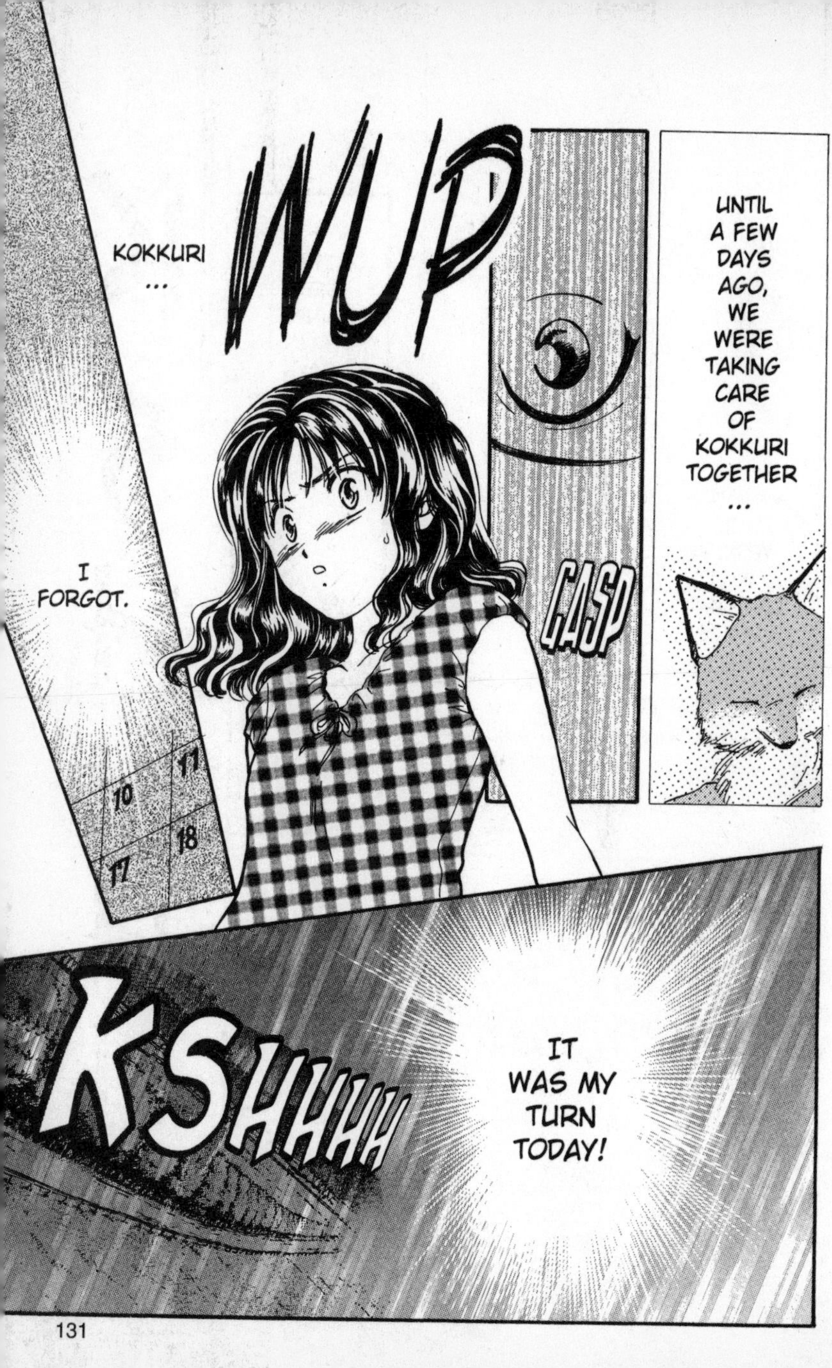
UNTIL A FEW DAYS AGO, WE WERE TAKING CARE OF KOKKURI TOGETHER ...
GASP
WUP
KOKKURI ...
I FORGOT.
11
10
18
17
KSHHHH
IT WAS MY TURN TODAY!

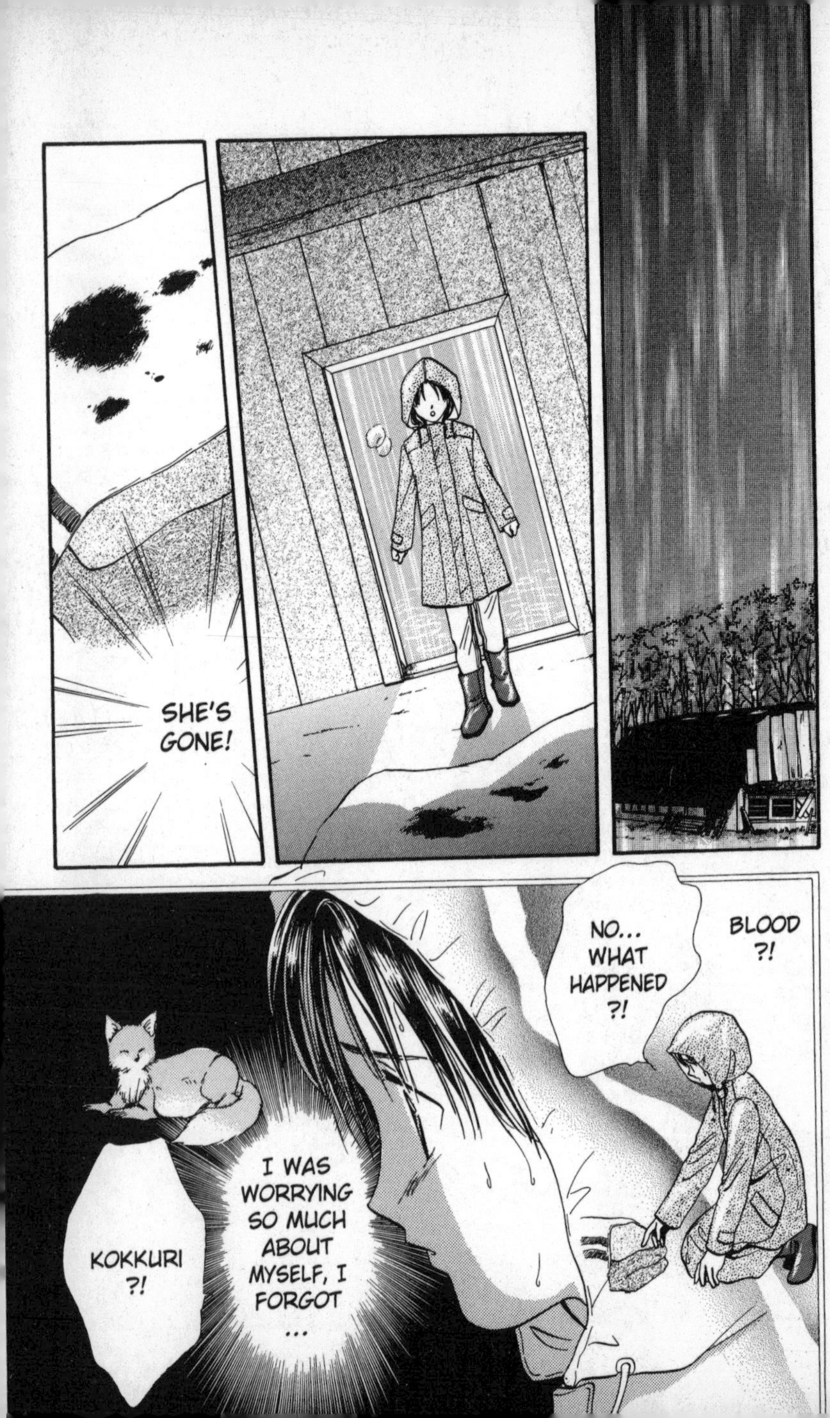
SHE'S GONE!
BLOOD ?!
NO... WHAT HAPPENED ?!
I WAS WORRYING SO MUCH ABOUT MYSELF, I FORGOT ...
KOKKURI ?!

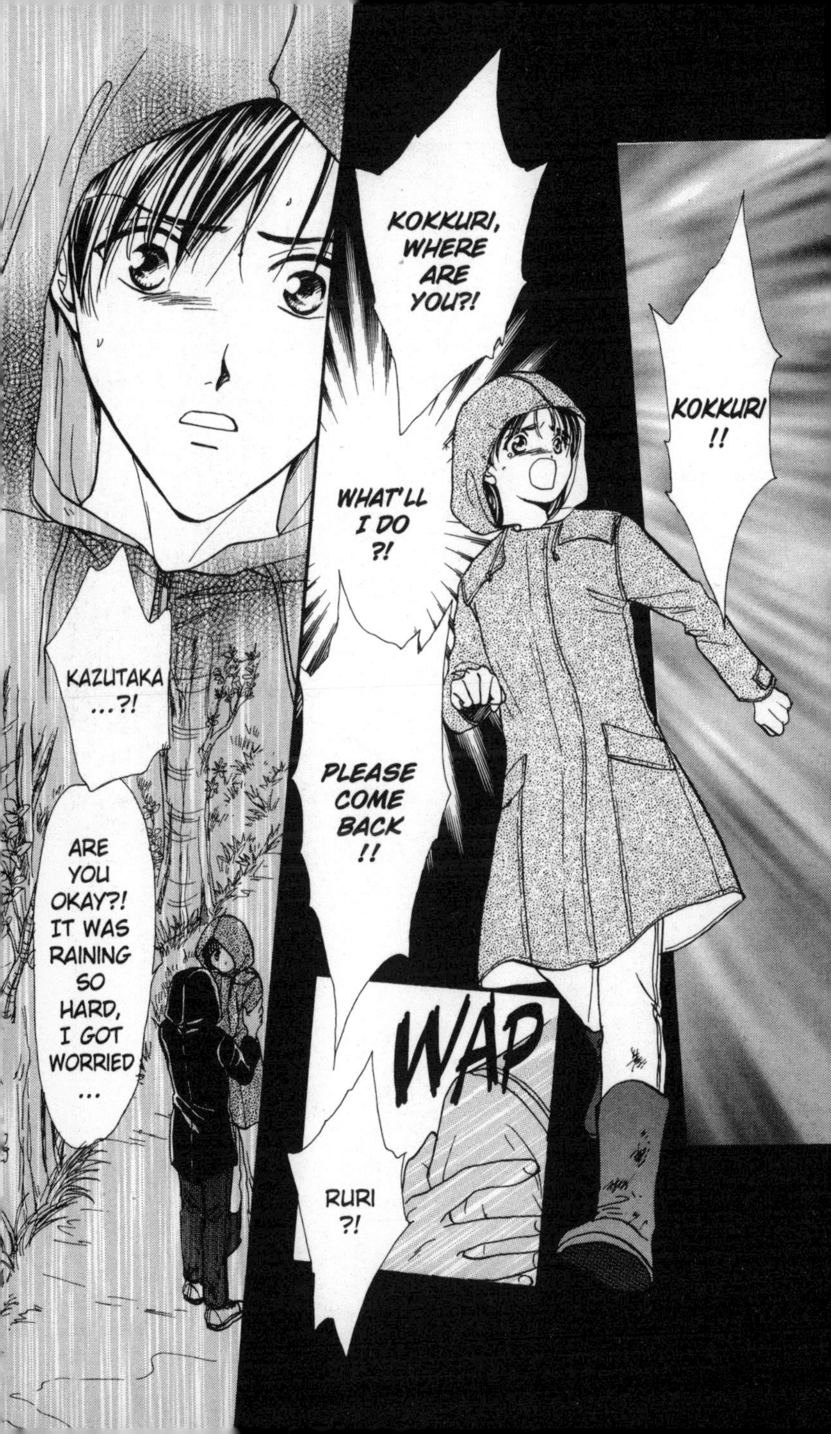
KOKKURI !!
KOKKURI, WHERE ARE YOU?!
WHAT'LL I DO ?!
PLEASE COME BACK !!
WAP
RURI ?!
KAZUTAKA ...?!
ARE YOU OKAY?! IT WAS RAINING SO HARD, I GOT WORRIED ...

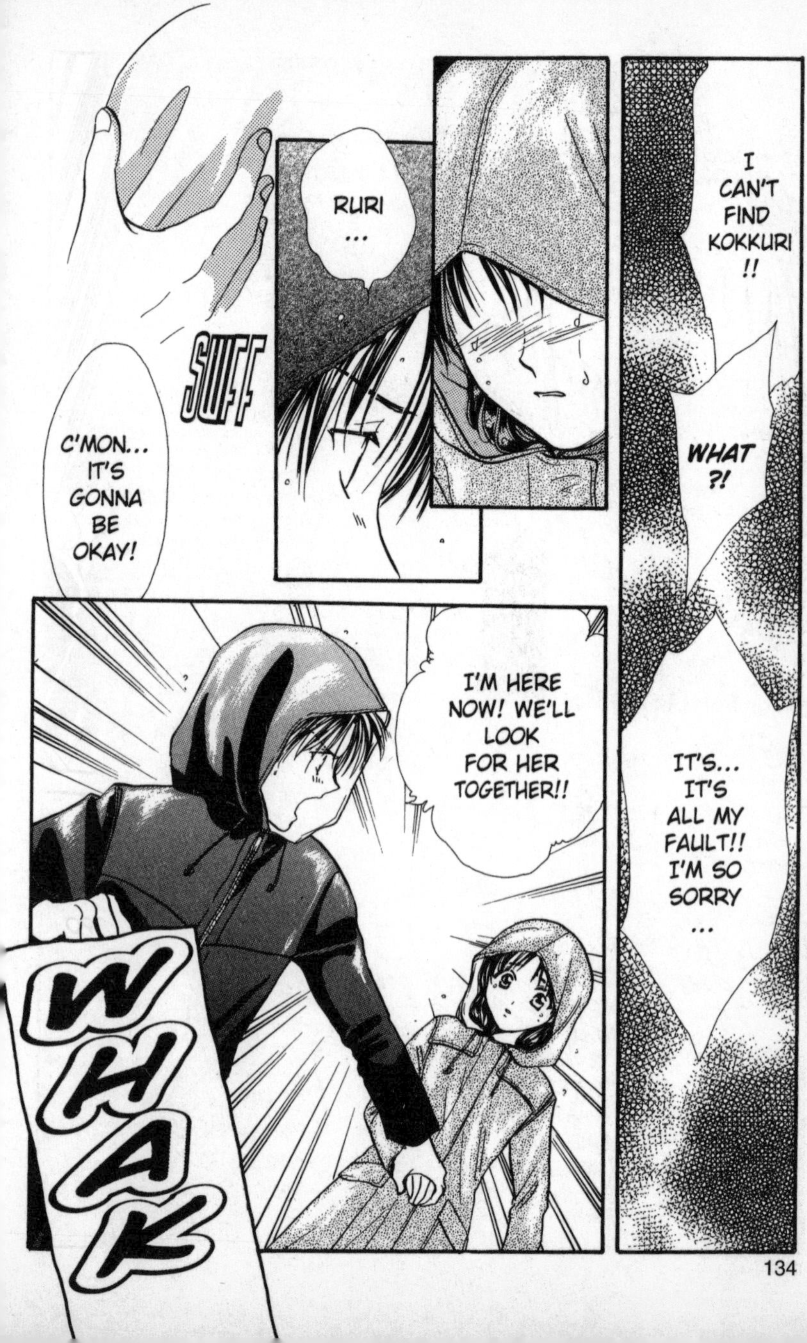
I CAN'T FIND KOKKURI !!
WHAT ?!
IT'S... IT'S ALL MY FAULT!! I'M SO SORRY ...
RURI ...
SUFF
C'MON... IT'S GONNA BE OKAY!
I'M HERE NOW! WE'LL LOOK FOR HER TOGETHER!!
WHAK

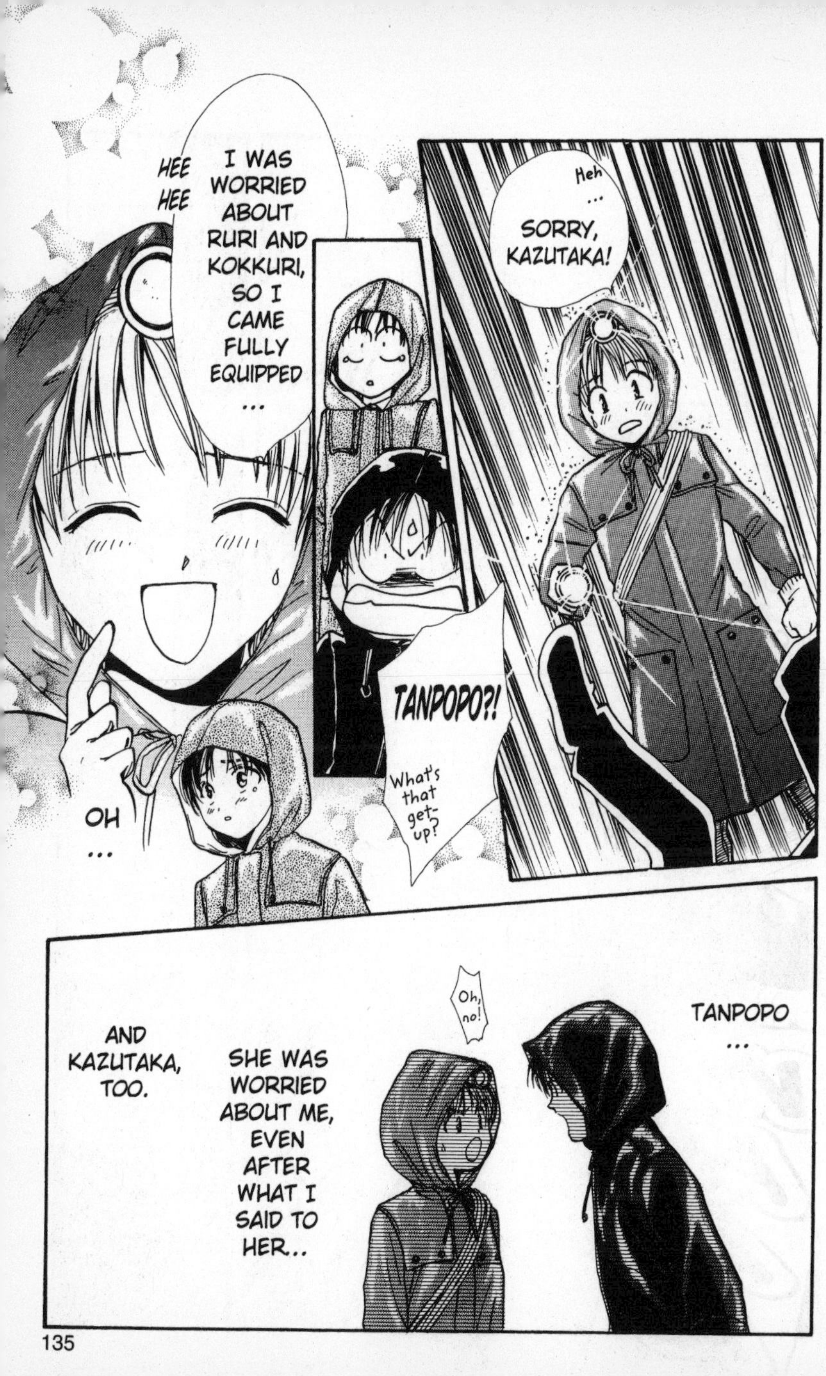
Heh ...
SORRY, KAZUTAKA!
TANPOPO?!
What's that get-up?
HEE HEE
I WAS WORRIED ABOUT RURI AND KOKKURI, SO I CAME FULLY EQUIPPED ...
OH ...
TANPOPO ...
Oh, no!
SHE WAS WORRIED ABOUT ME, EVEN AFTER WHAT I SAID TO HER...
AND KAZUTAKA, TOO.

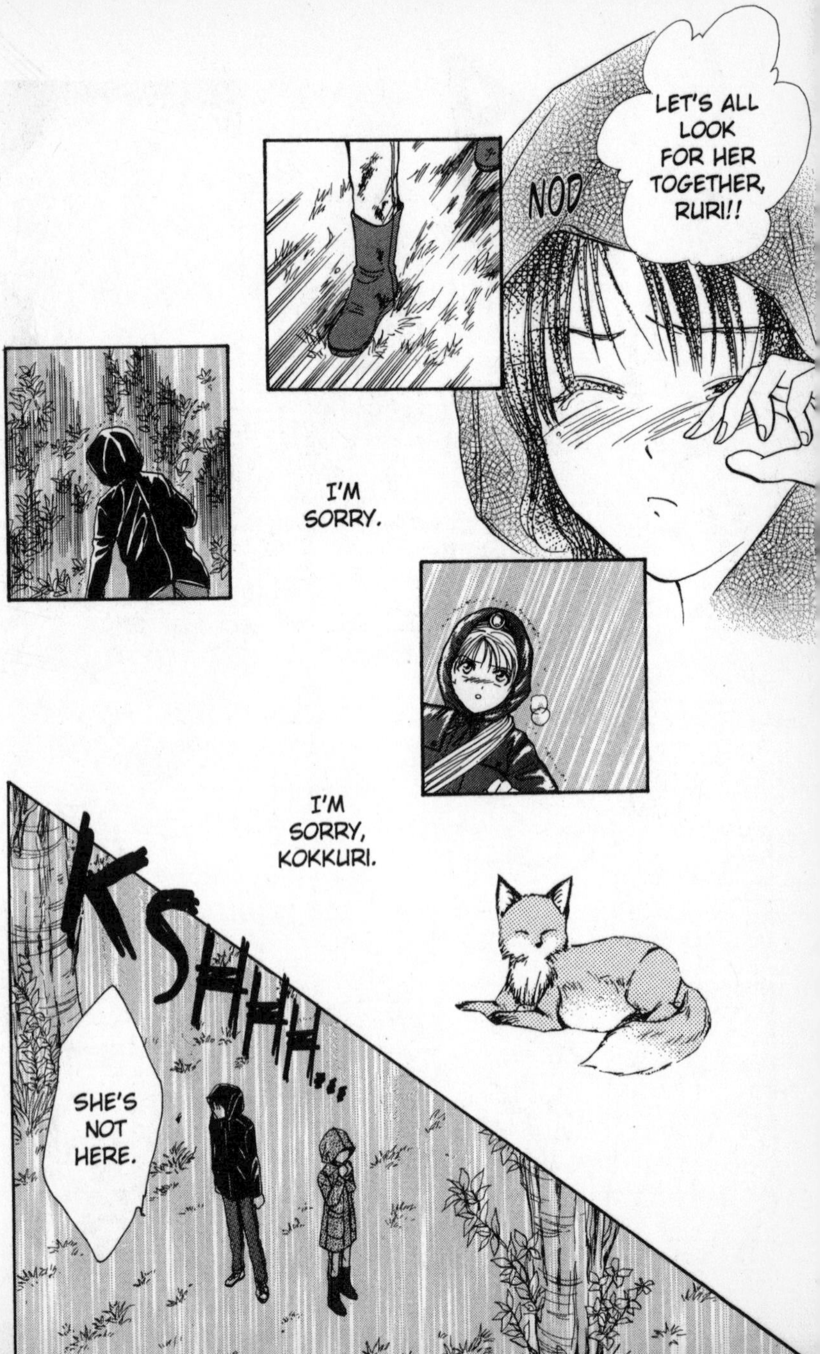
LET'S ALL LOOK FOR HER TOGETHER, RURI!!
NOD
I'M SORRY.
I'M SORRY, KOKKURI.
KSHHH...
SHE'S NOT HERE.

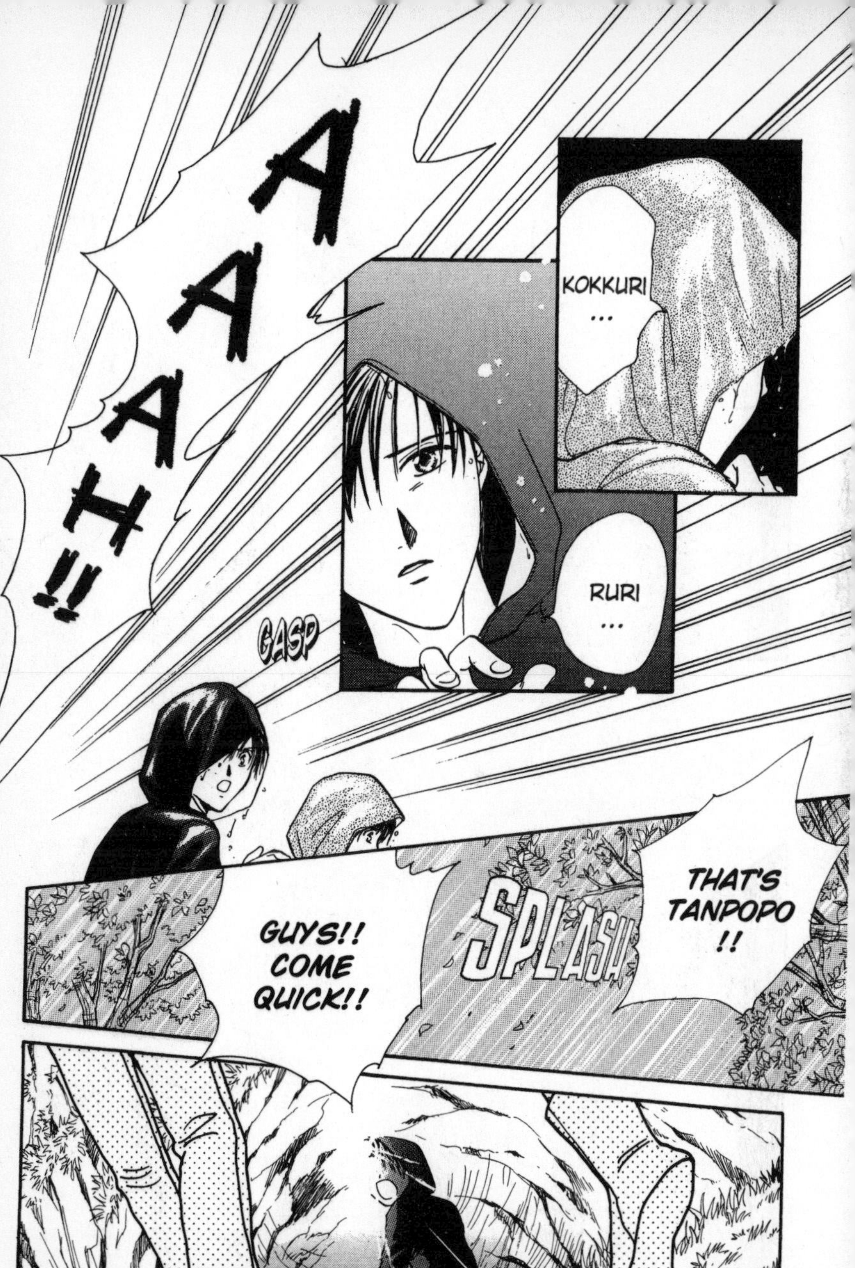

KOKKURI ...
RURI ...
GASP
AAAH!!
THAT'S TANPOPO !!
SPLASH
GUYS!! COME QUICK!!

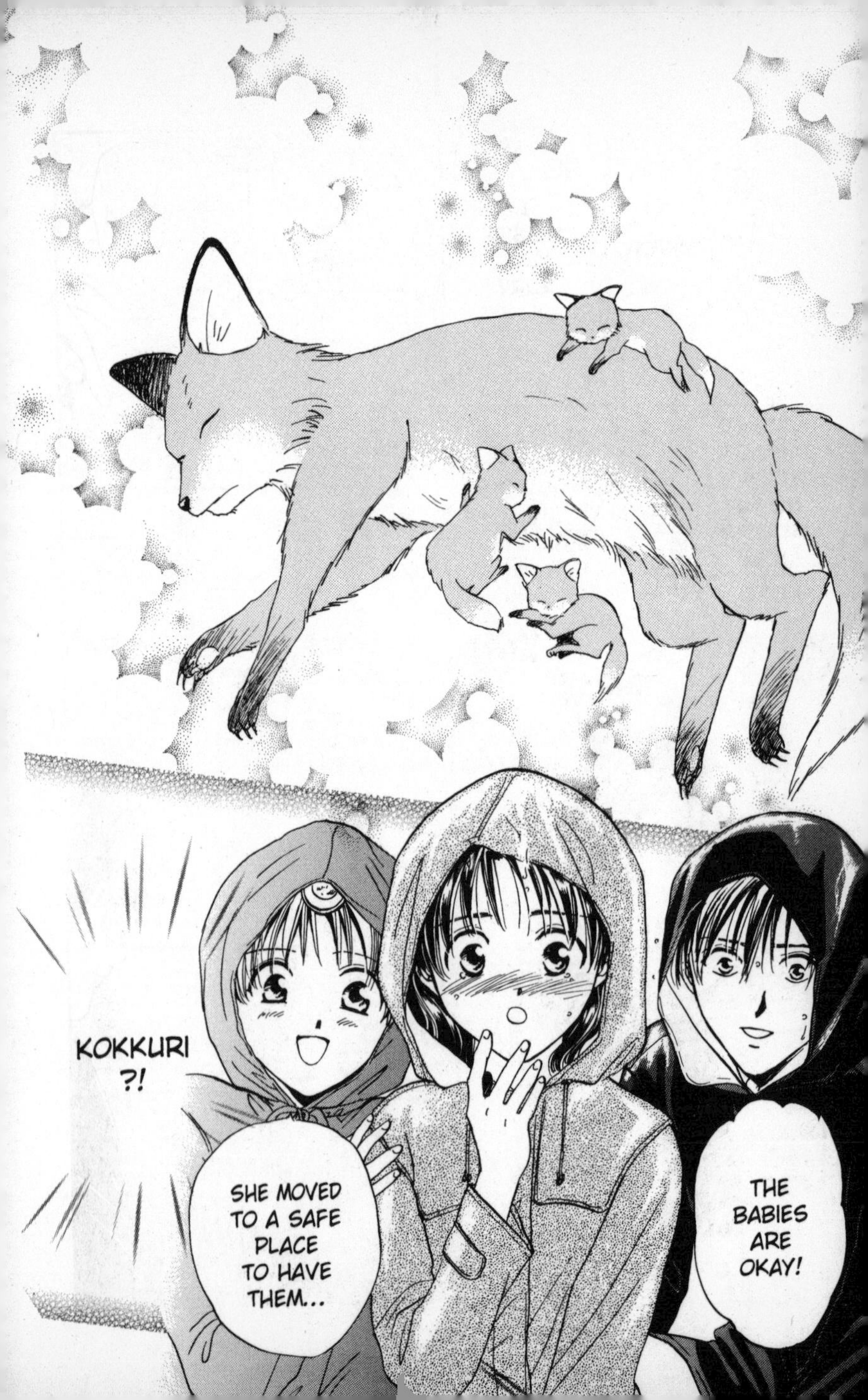
KOKKURI ?!
THE BABIES ARE OKAY!
SHE MOVED TO A SAFE PLACE TO HAVE THEM...

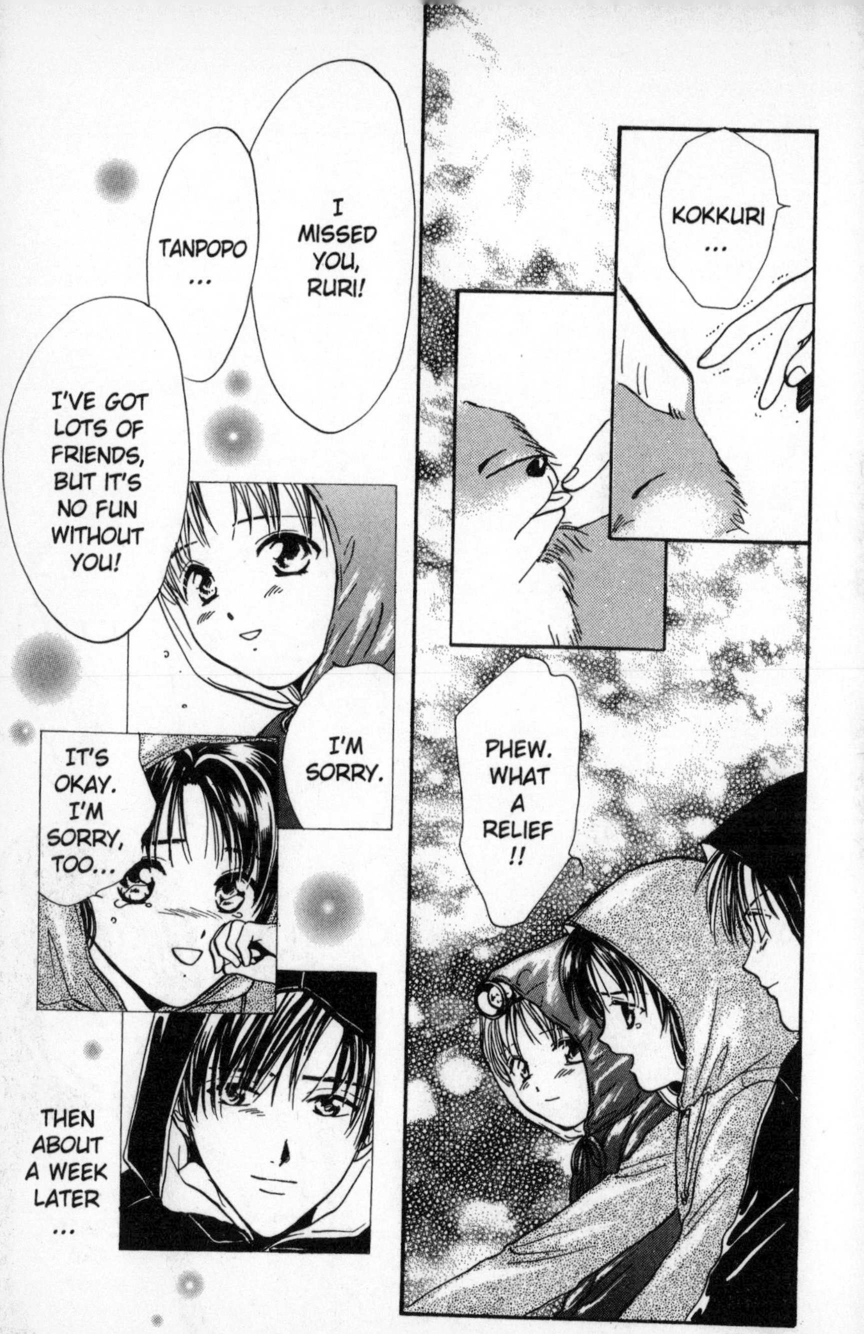
KOKKURI ...
PHEW. WHAT A RELIEF !!
I MISSED YOU, RURI!
TANPOPO ...
I'VE GOT LOTS OF FRIENDS, BUT IT'S NO FUN WITHOUT YOU!
I'M SORRY.
IT'S OKAY. I'M SORRY, TOO...
THEN ABOUT A WEEK LATER ...

KOKKURI
...

...NEVER GOT UP AGAIN.

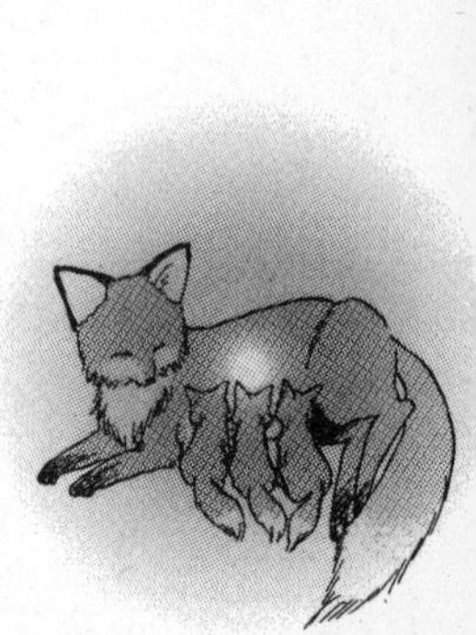

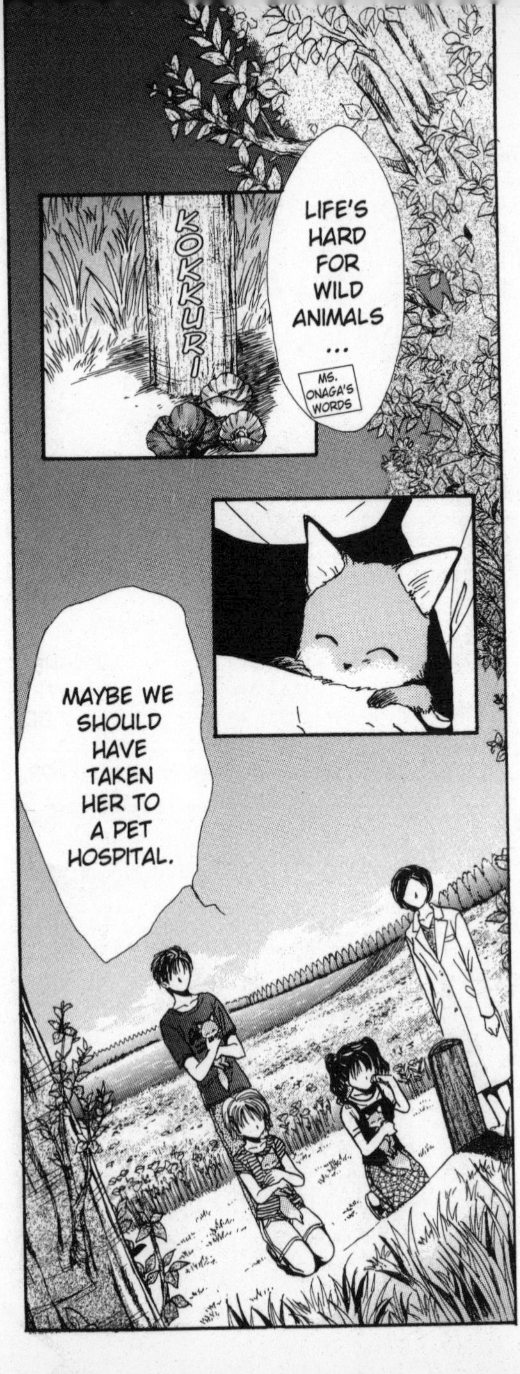
LIFE'S HARD FOR WILD ANIMALS ...
MS. ONAGA'S WORDS
KOKKURI
MAYBE WE SHOULD HAVE TAKEN HER TO A PET HOSPITAL.

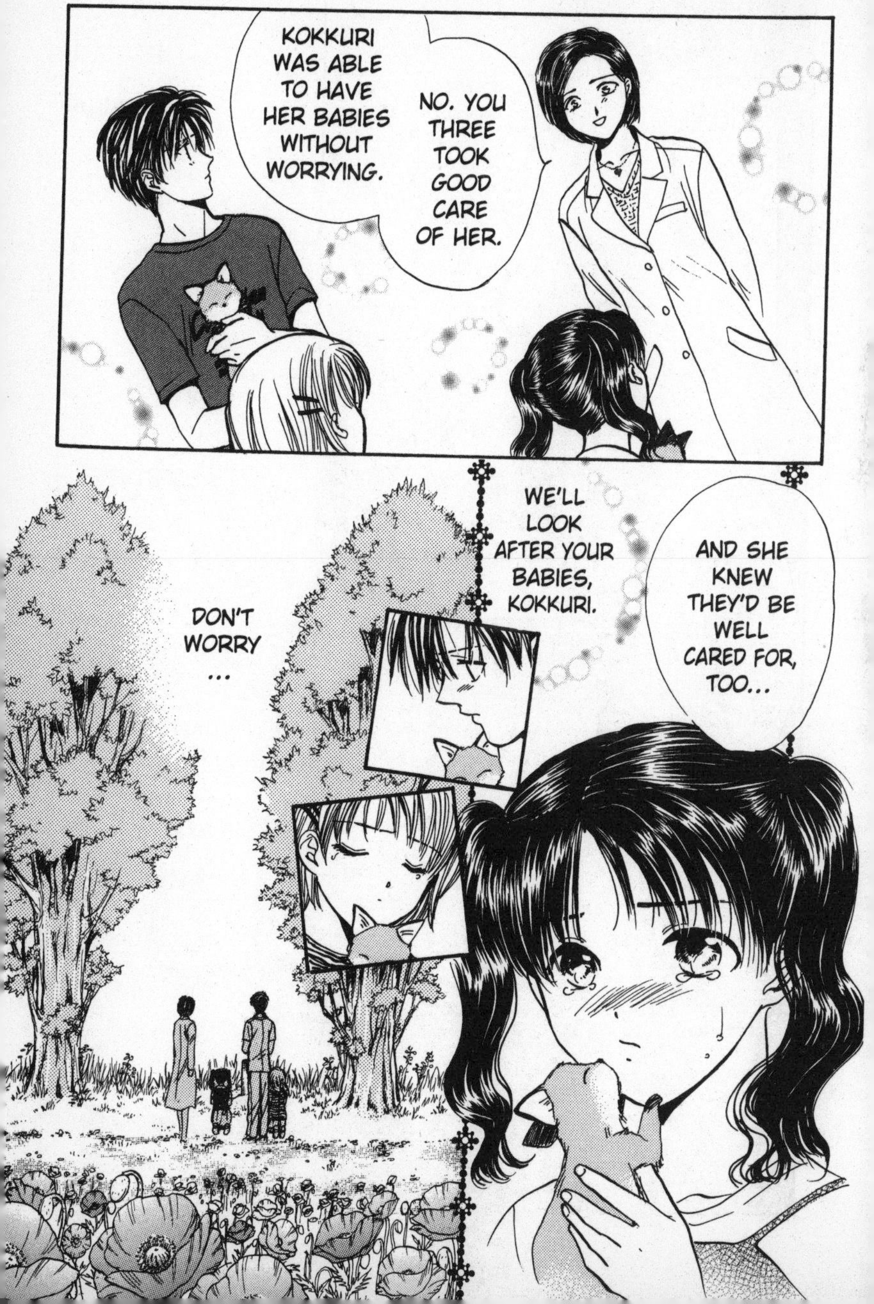
NO. YOU THREE TOOK GOOD CARE OF HER.
KOKKURI WAS ABLE TO HAVE HER BABIES WITHOUT WORRYING.
AND SHE KNEW THEY'D BE WELL CARED FOR, TOO...
WE'LL LOOK AFTER YOUR BABIES, KOKKURI.
DON'T WORRY ...

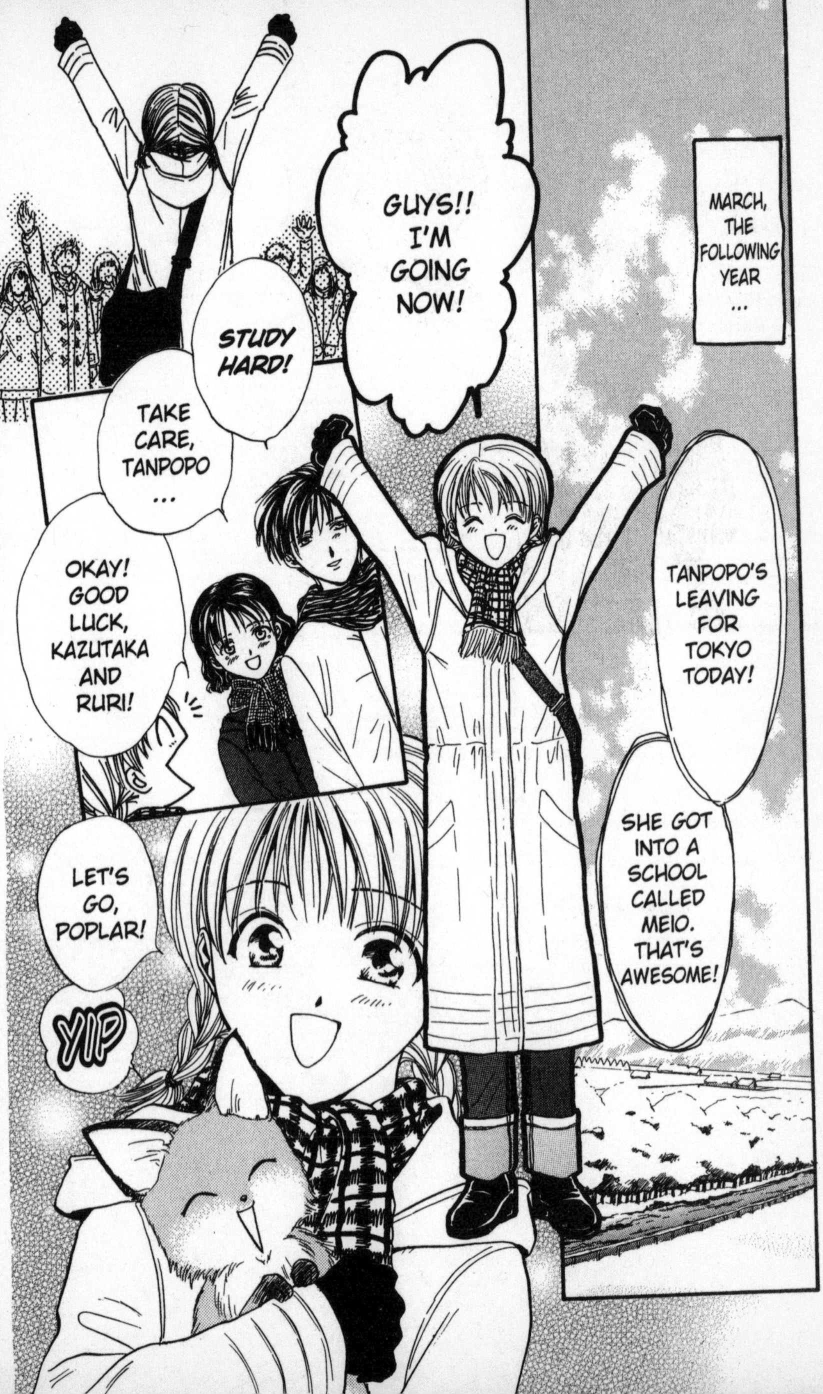
MARCH, THE FOLLOWING YEAR ...
TANPOPO'S LEAVING FOR TOKYO TODAY!
SHE GOT INTO A SCHOOL CALLED MEIO. THAT'S AWESOME!
GUYS!! I'M GOING NOW!
STUDY HARD!
TAKE CARE, TANPOPO ...
OKAY! GOOD LUCK, KAZUTAKA AND RURI!
LET'S GO, POPLAR!
YIP

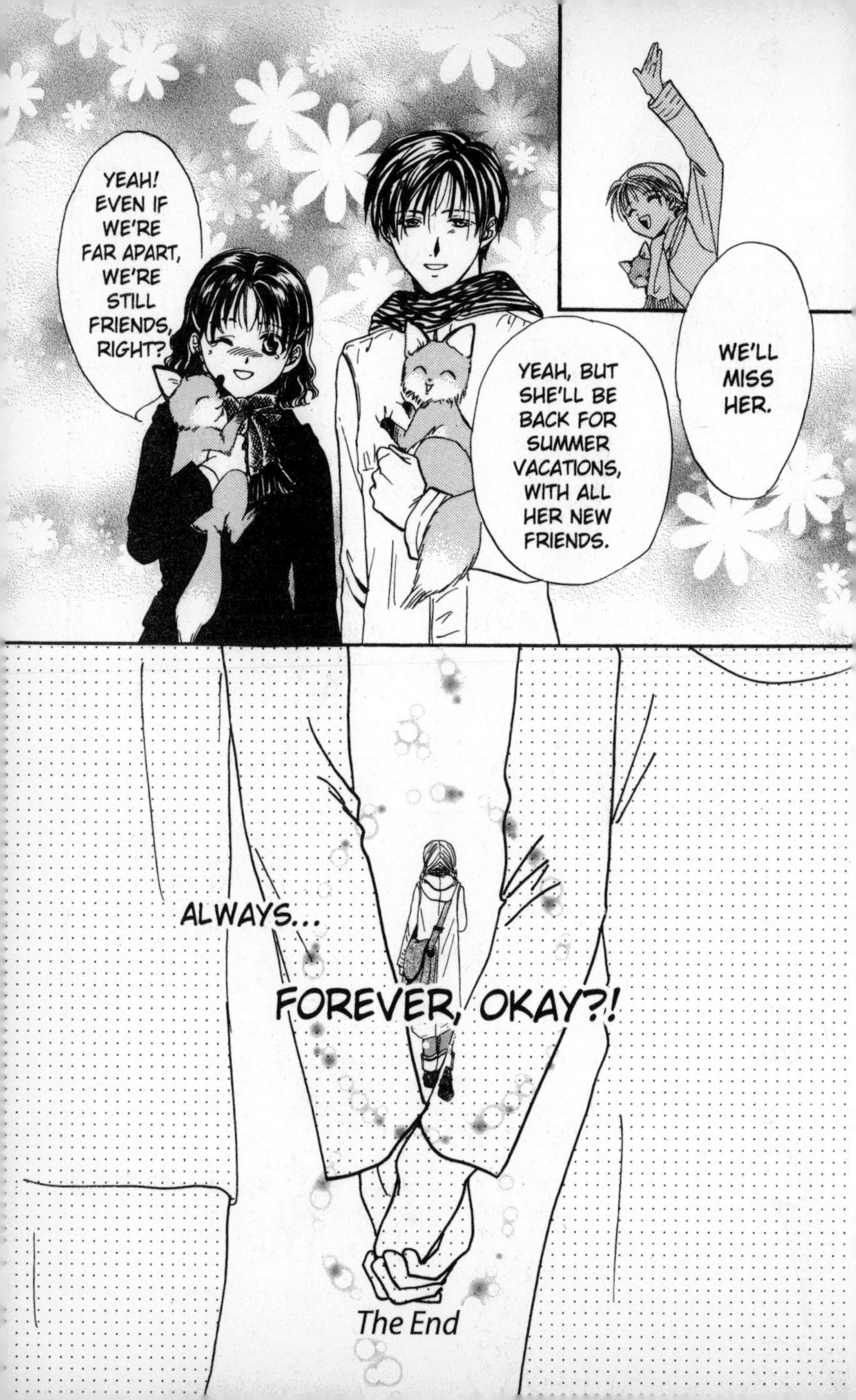
WE'LL MISS HER.
YEAH, BUT SHE'LL BE BACK FOR SUMMER VACATIONS, WITH ALL HER NEW FRIENDS.
YEAH! EVEN IF WE'RE FAR APART, WE'RE STILL FRIENDS, RIGHT?
ALWAYS...
FOREVER, OKAY?!
The End

YŪ WATASE'S GOAL FOR THE 21ST CENTURY...

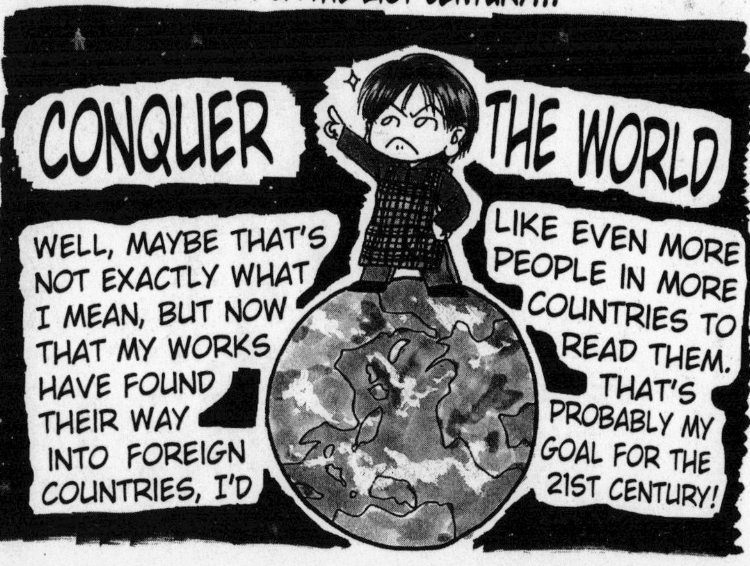
CONQUER
THE WORLD
WELL, MAYBE THAT'S NOT EXACTLY WHAT I MEAN, BUT NOW THAT MY WORKS HAVE FOUND THEIR WAY INTO FOREIGN COUNTRIES, I'D
LIKE EVEN MORE PEOPLE IN MORE COUNTRIES TO READ THEM. THAT'S PROBABLY MY GOAL FOR THE 21ST CENTURY!

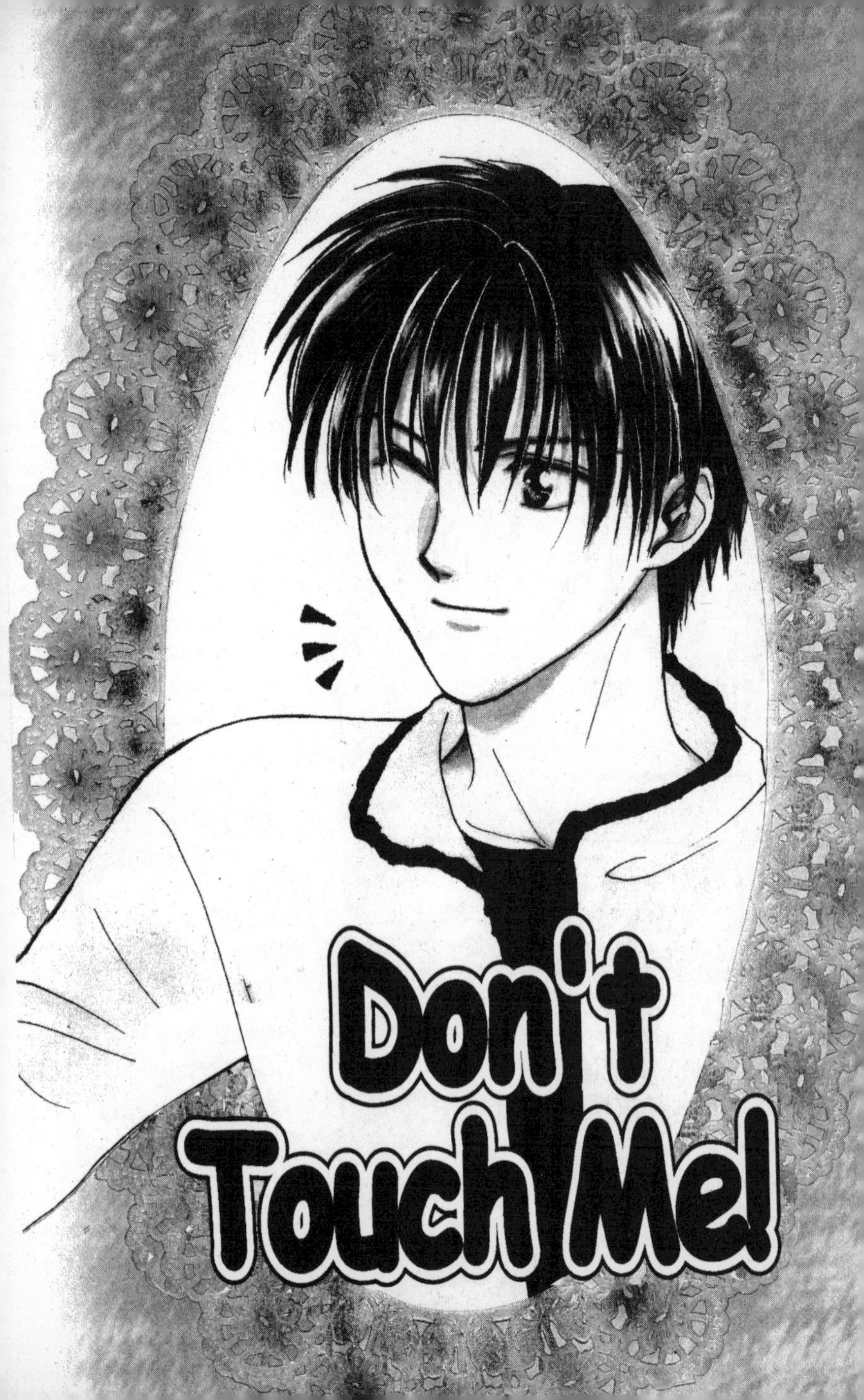
Don't
Touch Me!

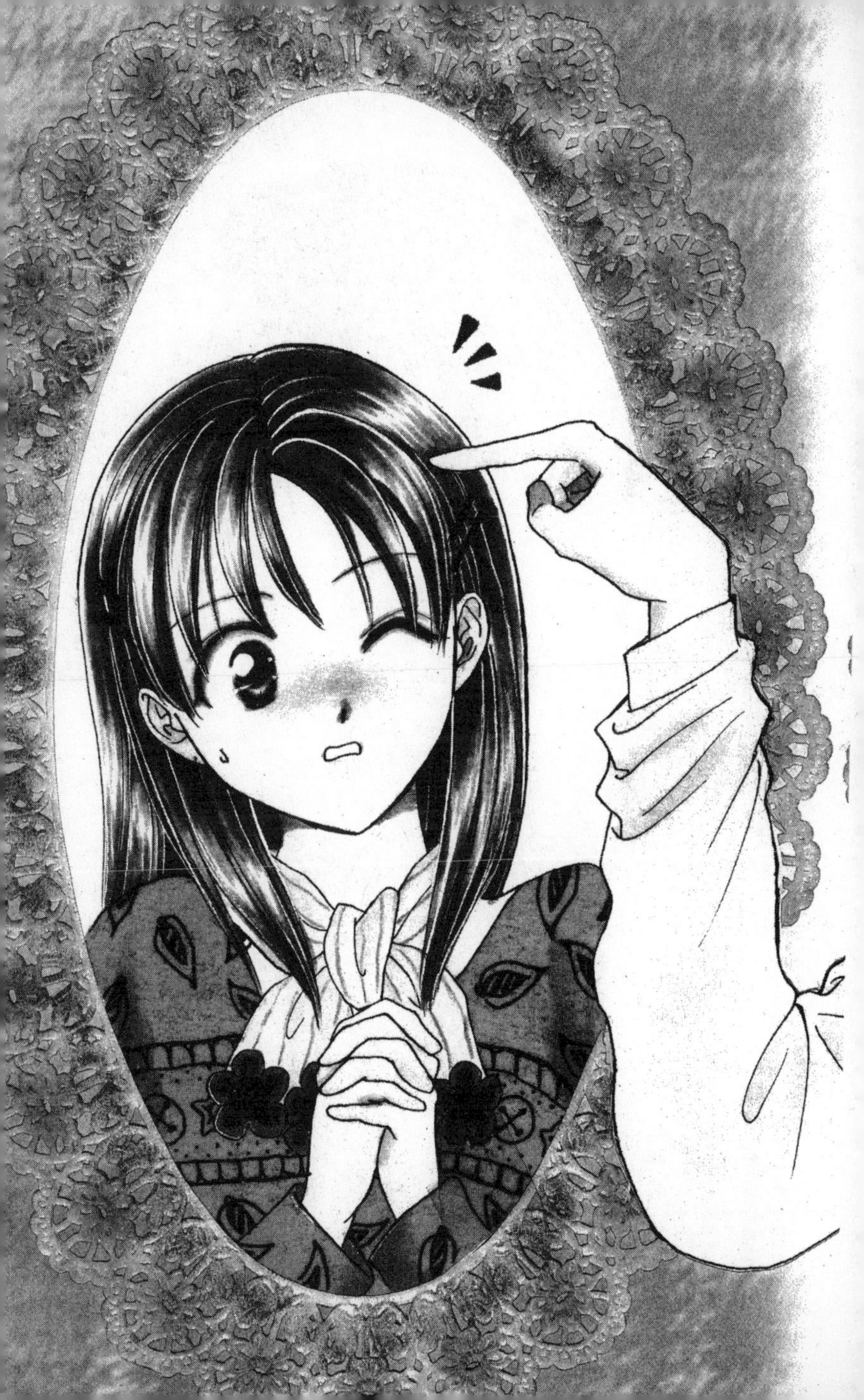

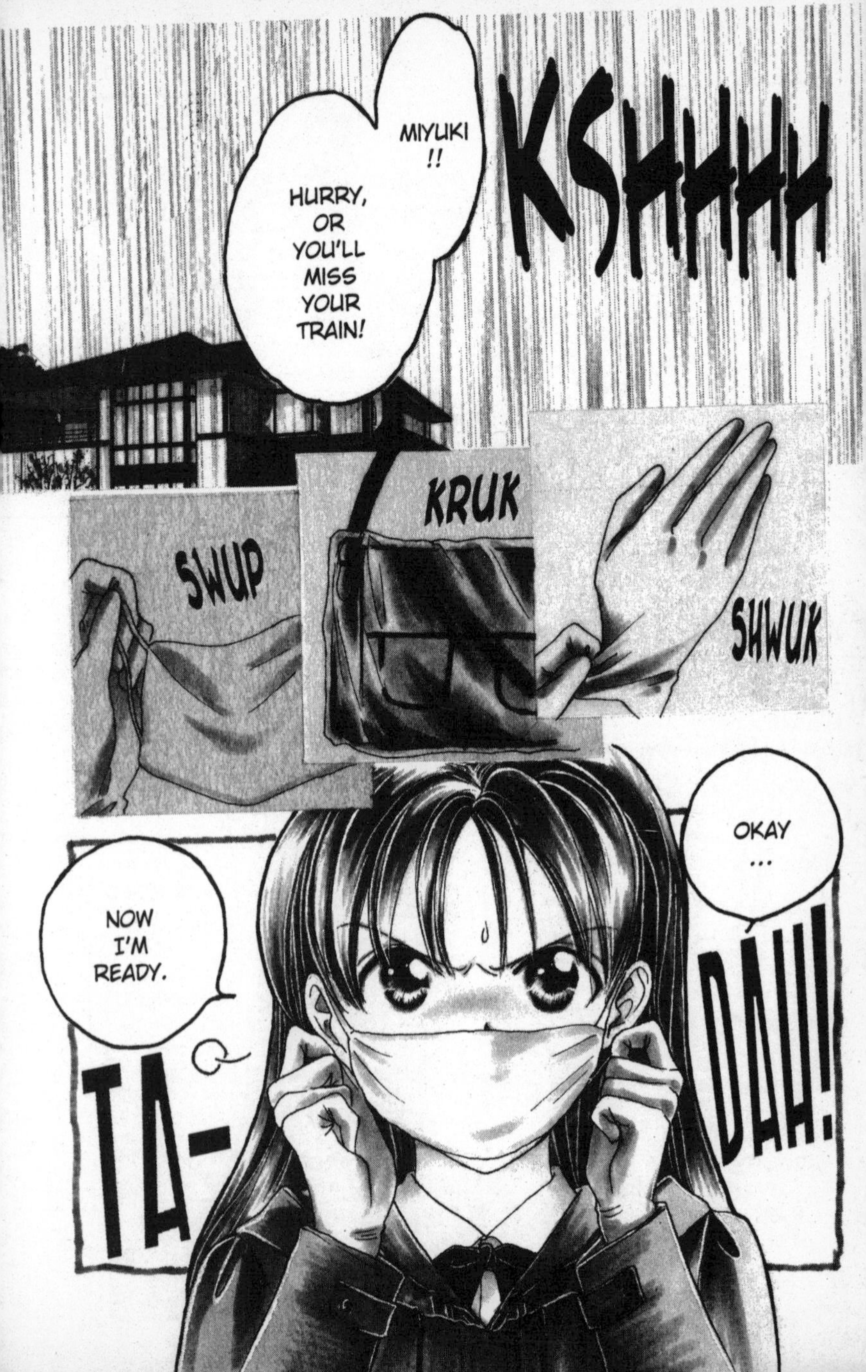
KSHHHH
MIYUKI !! HURRY, OR YOU'LL MISS YOUR TRAIN!
SHWUK
KRUK
SWUP
OKAY ...
TA-DAH!
NOW I'M READY.

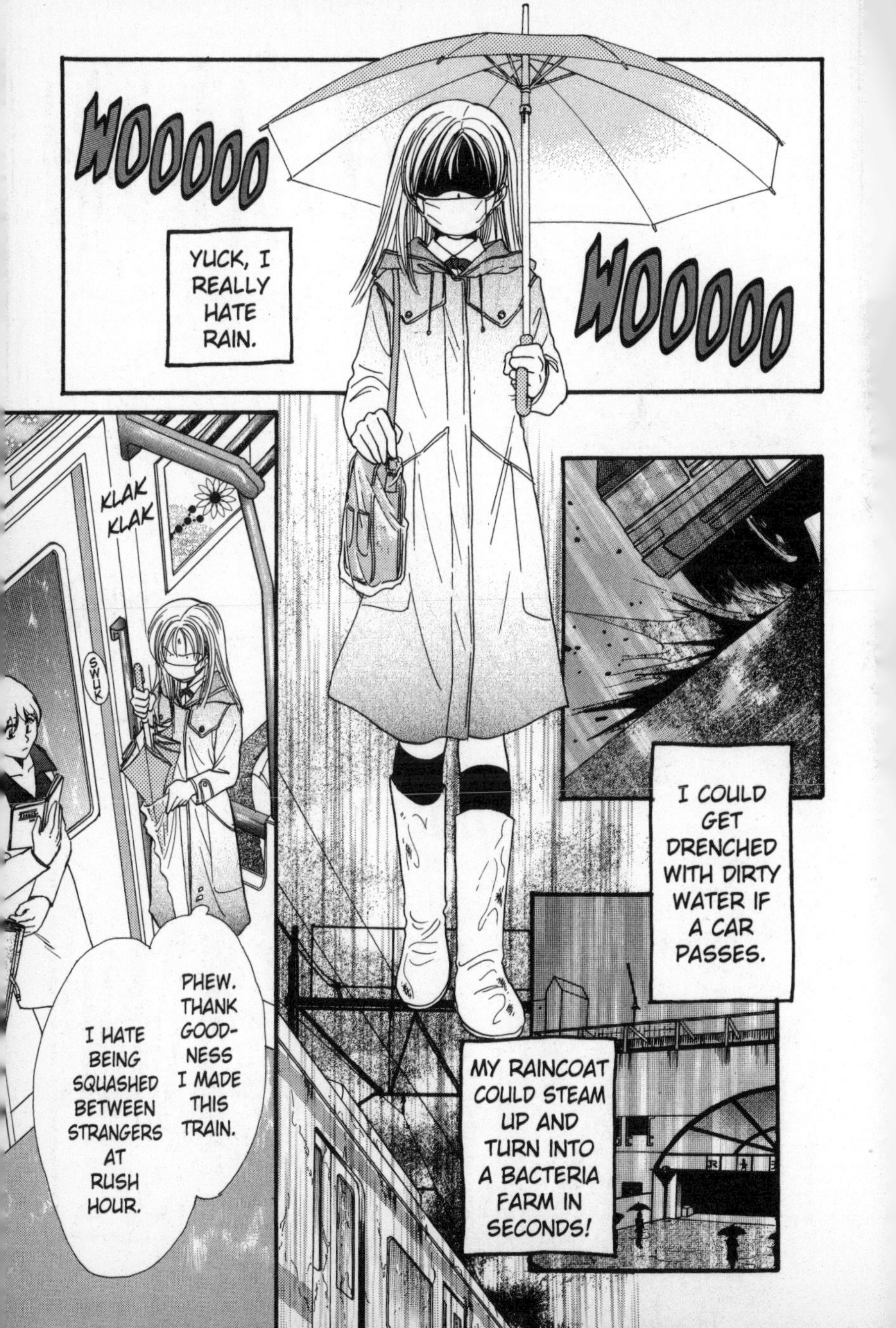
WOOOOO
WOOOOO
YUCK, I REALLY HATE RAIN.
I COULD GET DRENCHED WITH DIRTY WATER IF A CAR PASSES.
MY RAINCOAT COULD STEAM UP AND TURN INTO A BACTERIA FARM IN SECONDS!
KLAK KLAK
SWUK
PHEW. THANK GOOD-NESS I MADE THIS TRAIN.
I HATE BEING SQUASHED BETWEEN STRANGERS AT RUSH HOUR.

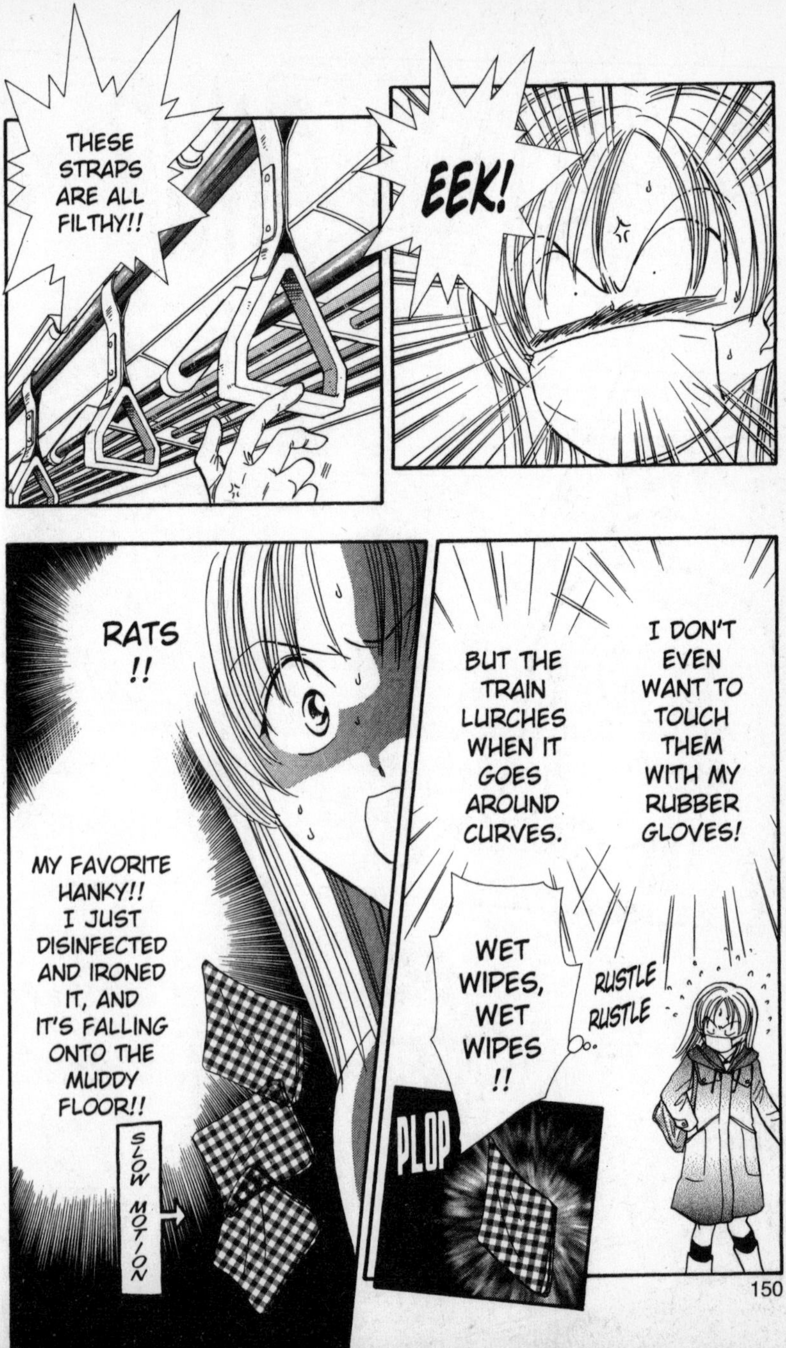
EEK!
THESE STRAPS ARE ALL FILTHY!!
I DON'T EVEN WANT TO TOUCH THEM WITH MY RUBBER GLOVES!
BUT THE TRAIN LURCHES WHEN IT GOES AROUND CURVES.
WET WIPES, WET WIPES !!
RUSTLE RUSTLE
PLOP
RATS !!
MY FAVORITE HANKY!! I JUST DISINFECTED AND IRONED IT, AND IT'S FALLING ONTO THE MUDDY FLOOR!!
SLOW MOTION

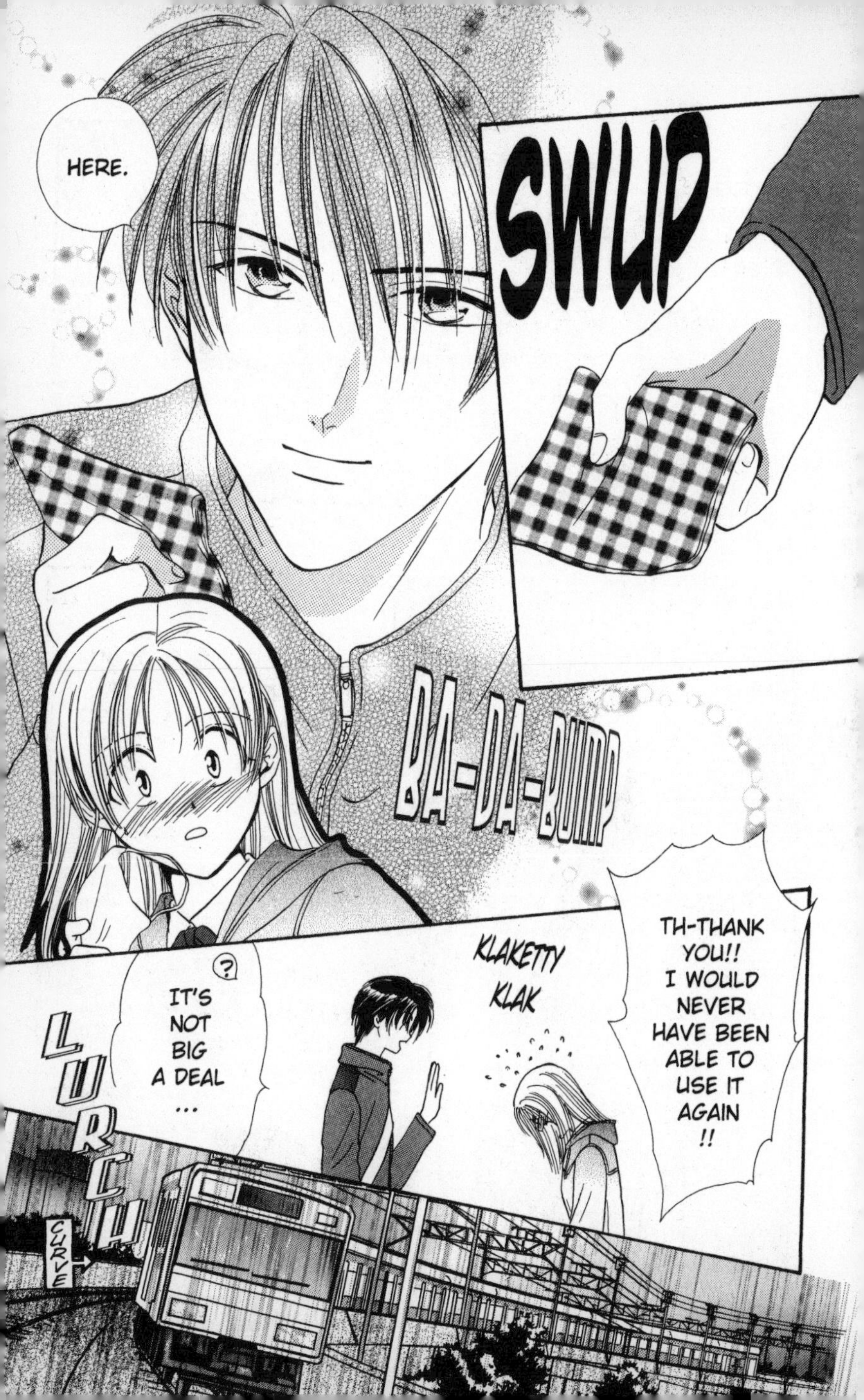
SWUP
HERE.
BA-DA-BUMP
TH-THANK YOU!! I WOULD NEVER HAVE BEEN ABLE TO USE IT AGAIN !!
KLAKETTY KLAK
?
IT'S NOT BIG A DEAL ...
LURCH
CURVE

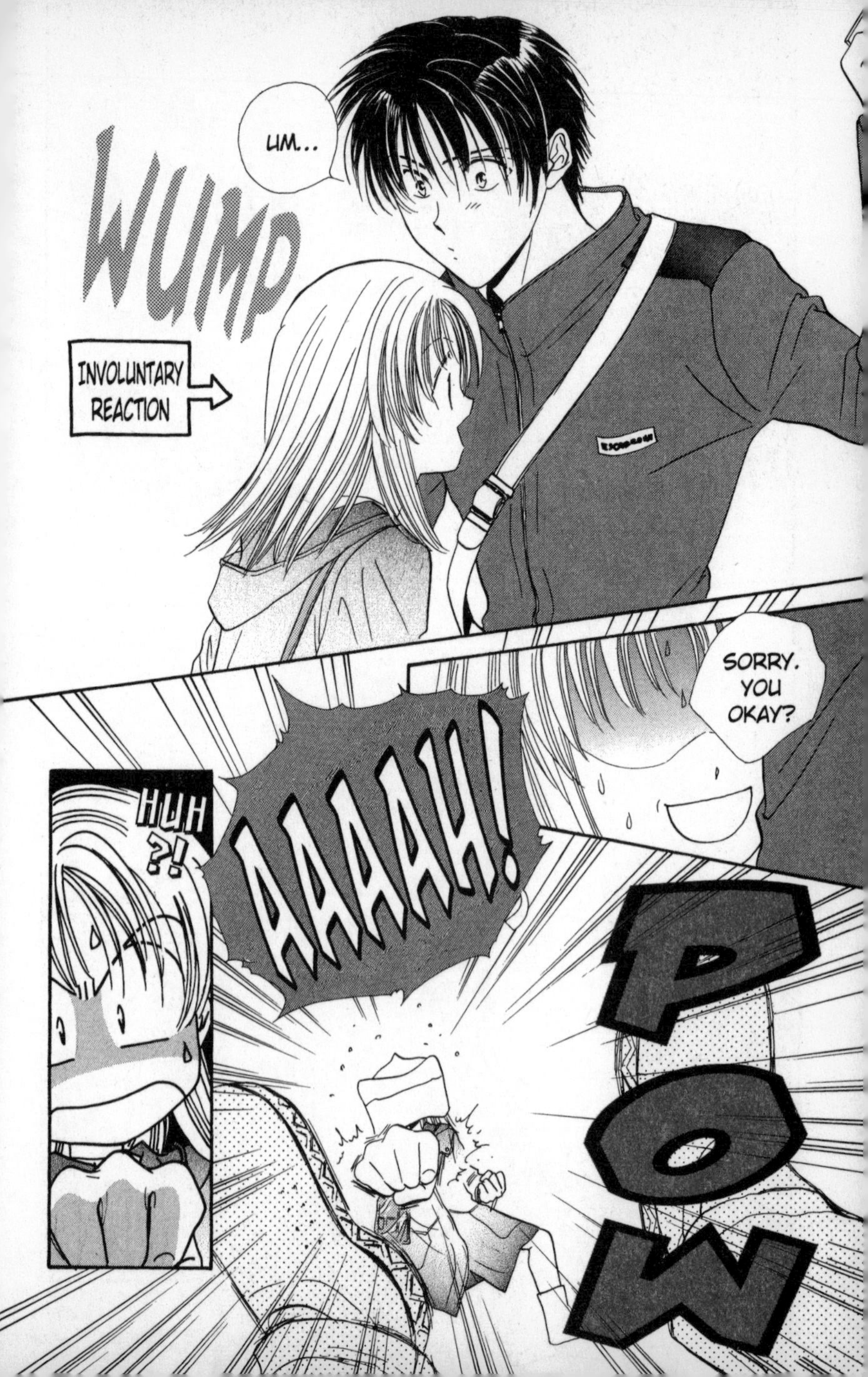
UM...
WUMP
INVOLUNTARY REACTION
SORRY. YOU OKAY?
AAAAH!
POW
HUH ?!

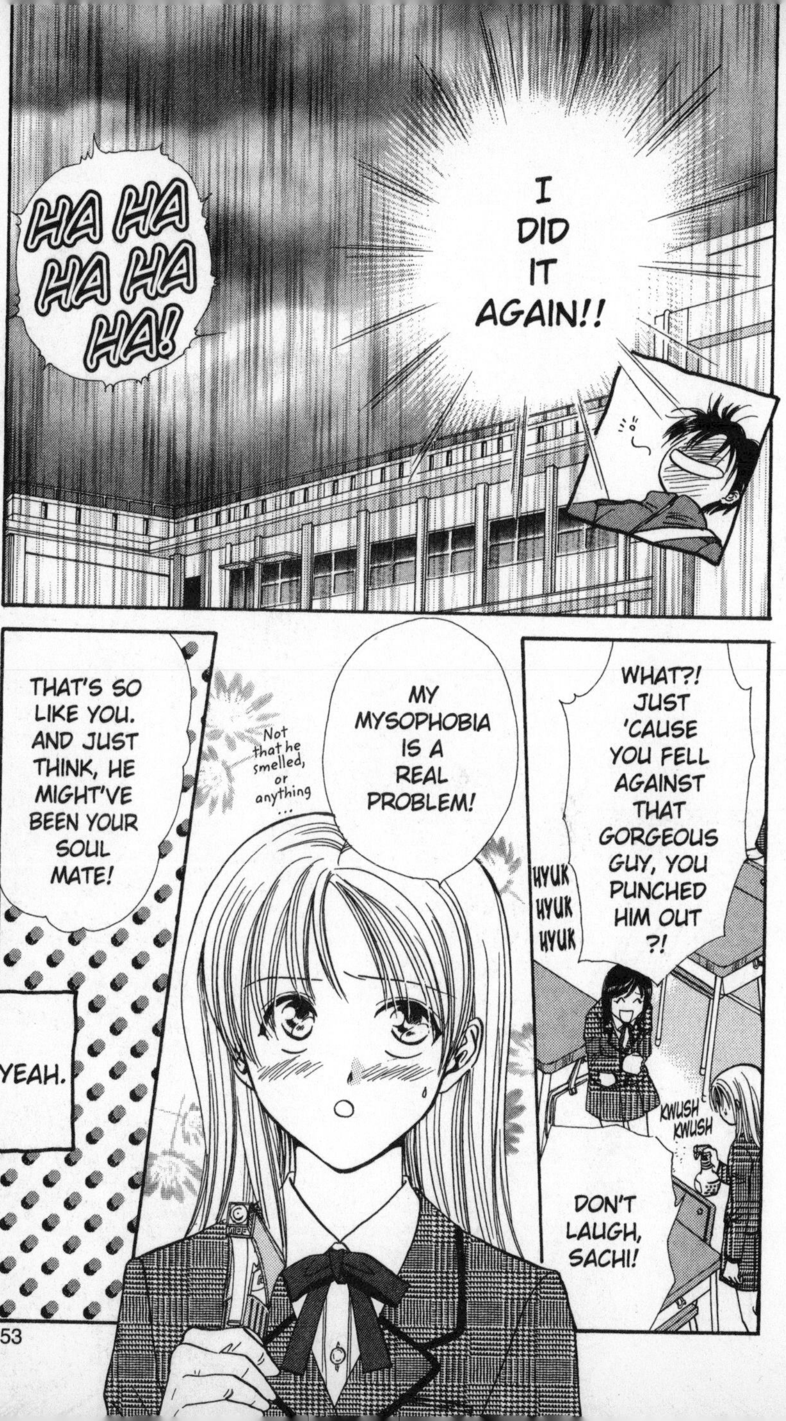

I DID IT AGAIN!!
HA HA HA HA HA!
WHAT?! JUST 'CAUSE YOU FELL AGAINST THAT GORGEOUS GUY, YOU PUNCHED HIM OUT ?!
HYUK HYUK HYUK
KWUSH KWUSH
DON'T LAUGH, SACHI!
MY MYSOPHOBIA IS A REAL PROBLEM!
Not that he smelled, or anything ...
THAT'S SO LIKE YOU. AND JUST THINK, HE MIGHT'VE BEEN YOUR SOUL MATE!
YEAH.

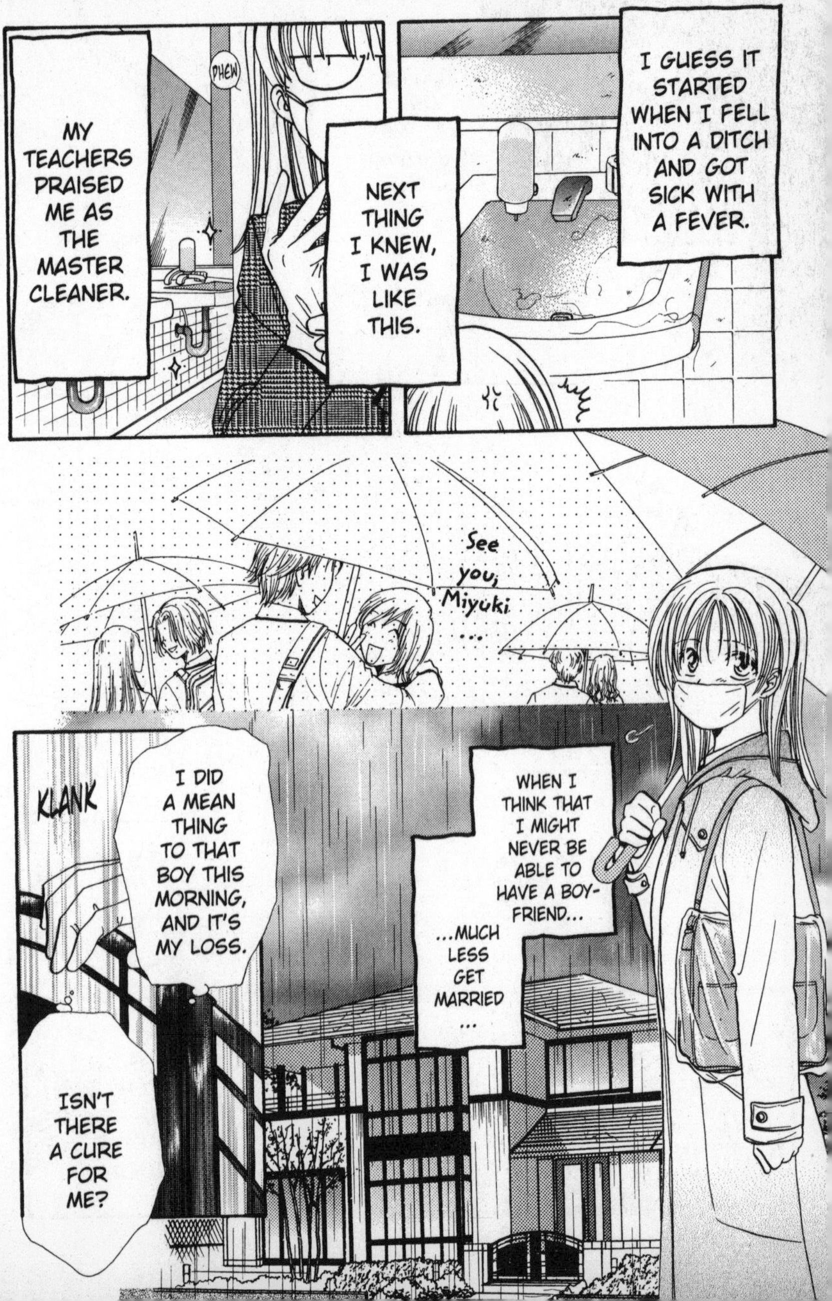
I GUESS IT STARTED WHEN I FELL INTO A DITCH AND GOT SICK WITH A FEVER.
PHEW
NEXT THING I KNEW, I WAS LIKE THIS.
MY TEACHERS PRAISED ME AS THE MASTER CLEANER.
See you, Miyuki...
WHEN I THINK THAT I MIGHT NEVER BE ABLE TO HAVE A BOY-FRIEND...
...MUCH LESS GET MARRIED...
KLANK
I DID A MEAN THING TO THAT BOY THIS MORNING, AND IT'S MY LOSS.
ISN'T THERE A CURE FOR ME?

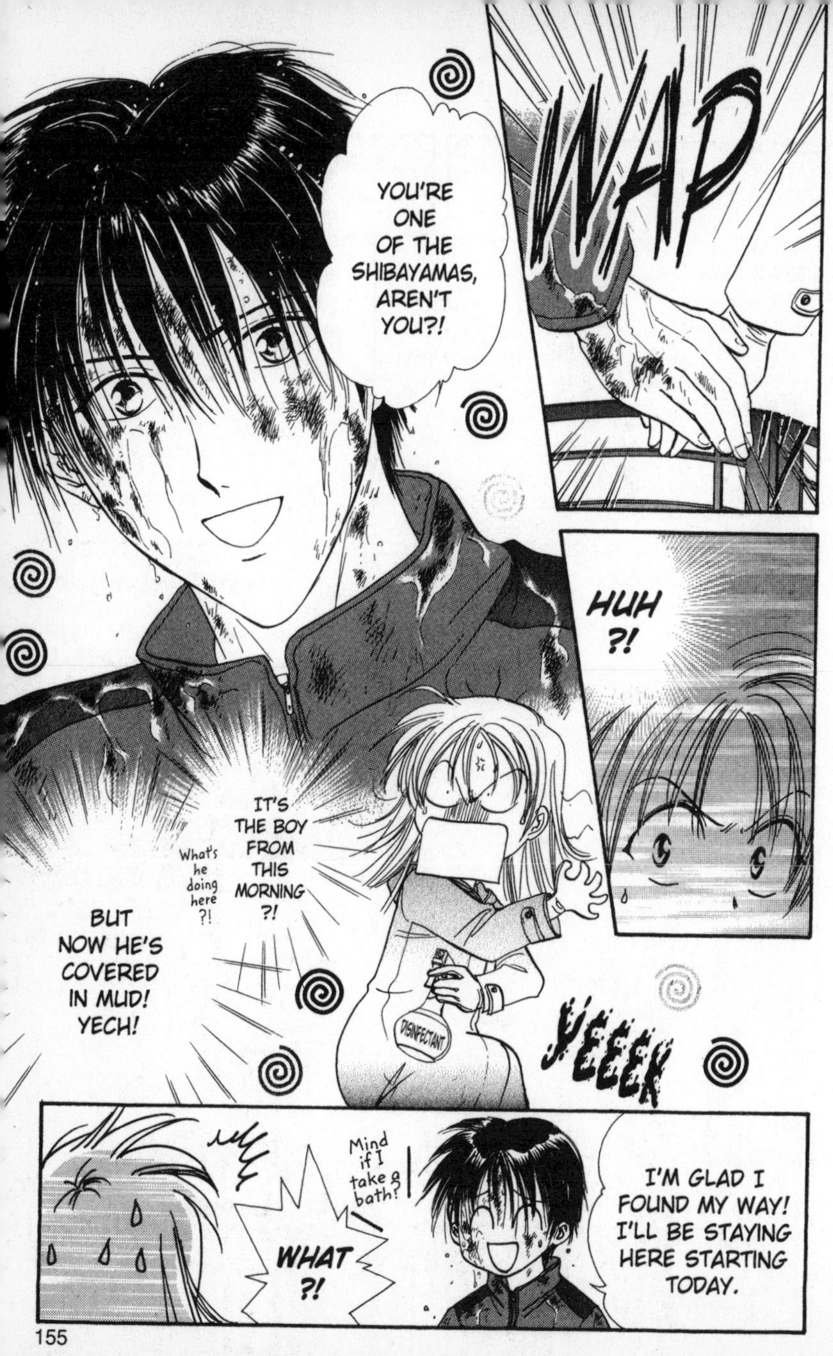
WAP
HUH ?!
YOU'RE ONE OF THE SHIBAYAMAS, AREN'T YOU?!
IT'S THE BOY FROM THIS MORNING ?!
What's he doing here ?!
BUT NOW HE'S COVERED IN MUD! YECH!
DISINFECTANT
YEEEK
I'M GLAD I FOUND MY WAY! I'LL BE STAYING HERE STARTING TODAY.
Mind if I take a bath?
WHAT ?!

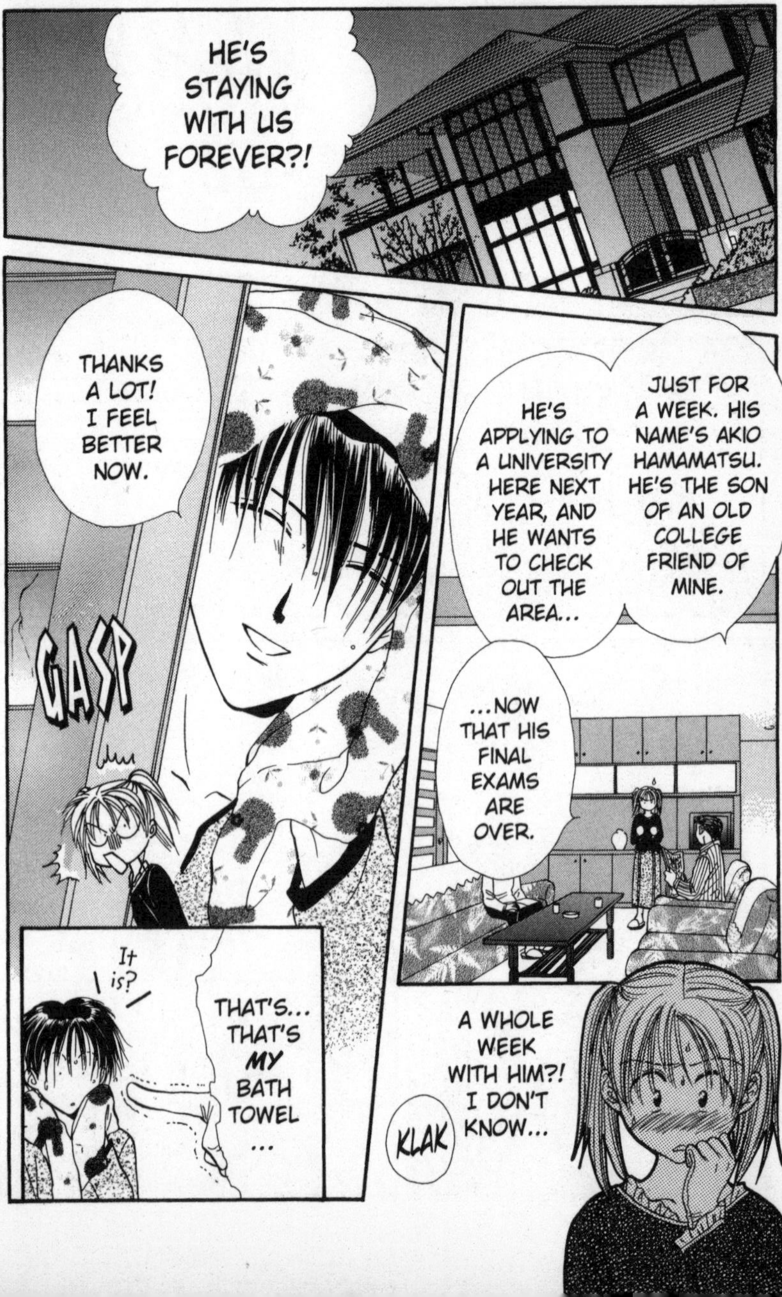
HE'S STAYING WITH US FOREVER?!
JUST FOR A WEEK. HIS NAME'S AKIO HAMAMATSU. HE'S THE SON OF AN OLD COLLEGE FRIEND OF MINE.
HE'S APPLYING TO A UNIVERSITY HERE NEXT YEAR, AND HE WANTS TO CHECK OUT THE AREA...
...NOW THAT HIS FINAL EXAMS ARE OVER.
A WHOLE WEEK WITH HIM?! I DON'T KNOW...
KLAK
THANKS A LOT! I FEEL BETTER NOW.
GASP
THAT'S... THAT'S *MY* BATH TOWEL ...
It is?

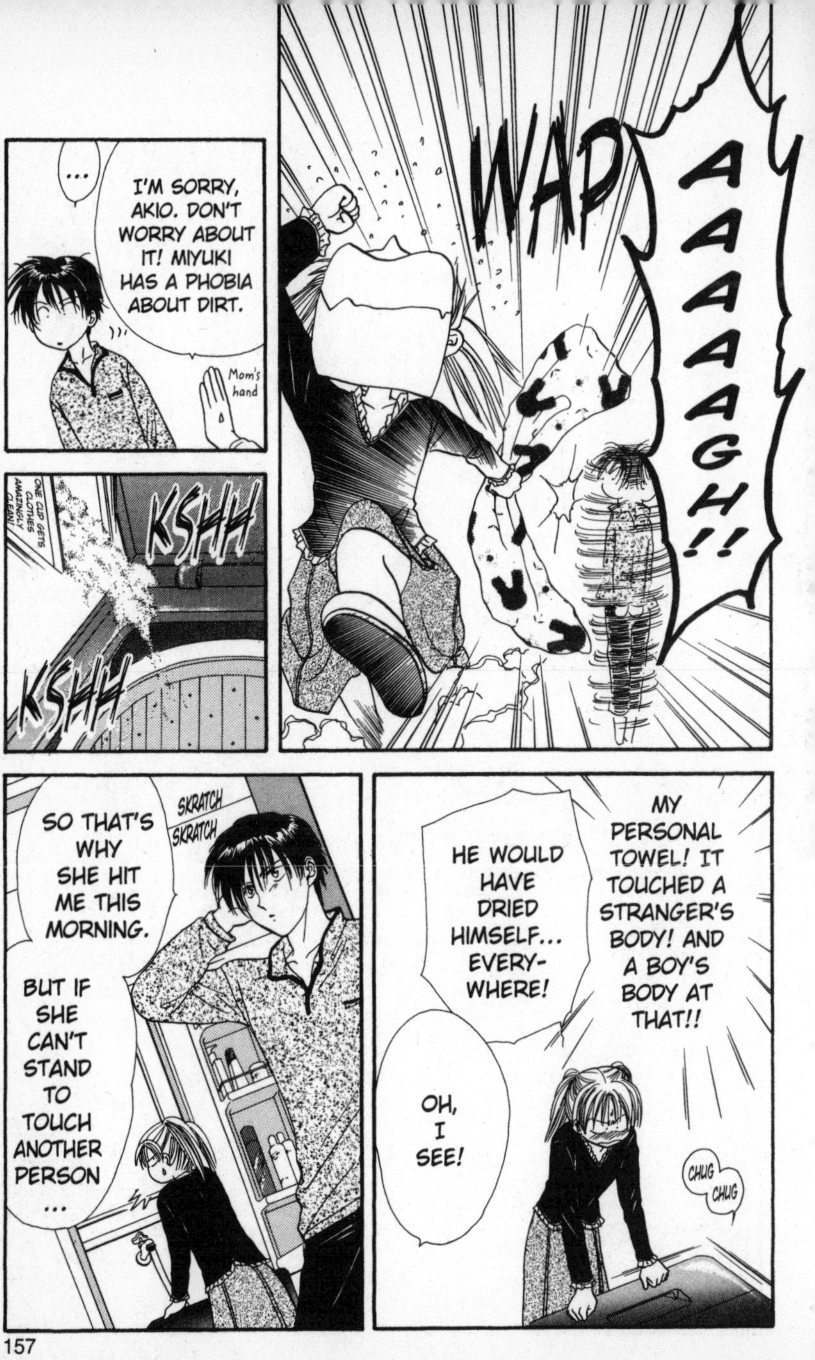
AAAAAAGH!!
WAP
...
I'M SORRY, AKIO. DON'T WORRY ABOUT IT! MIYUKI HAS A PHOBIA ABOUT DIRT.
Mom's hand
ONE CLIP GETS CLOTHES AMAZINGLY CLEAN!
KSHH
KSHH
MY PERSONAL TOWEL! IT TOUCHED A STRANGER'S BODY! AND A BOY'S BODY AT THAT!!
HE WOULD HAVE DRIED HIMSELF... EVERY-WHERE!
OH, I SEE!
CHUG CHUG
SKRATCH SKRATCH
SO THAT'S WHY SHE HIT ME THIS MORNING.
BUT IF SHE CAN'T STAND TO TOUCH ANOTHER PERSON ...

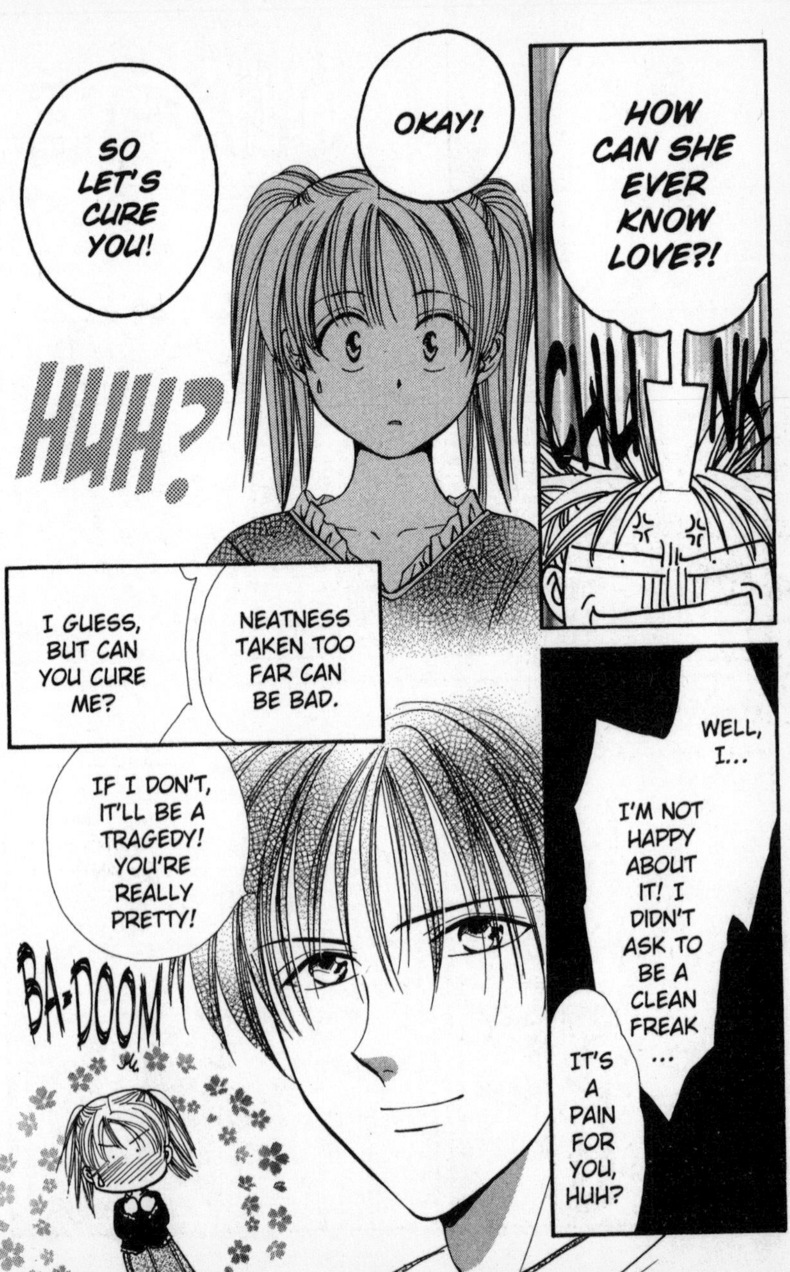

OKAY!
SO LET'S CURE YOU!
HUH?
HOW CAN SHE EVER KNOW LOVE?!
CHU NK
WELL, I...
I'M NOT HAPPY ABOUT IT! I DIDN'T ASK TO BE A CLEAN FREAK...
IT'S A PAIN FOR YOU, HUH?
NEATNESS TAKEN TOO FAR CAN BE BAD.
I GUESS, BUT CAN YOU CURE ME?
IF I DON'T, IT'LL BE A TRAGEDY! YOU'RE REALLY PRETTY!
BA-DOOM

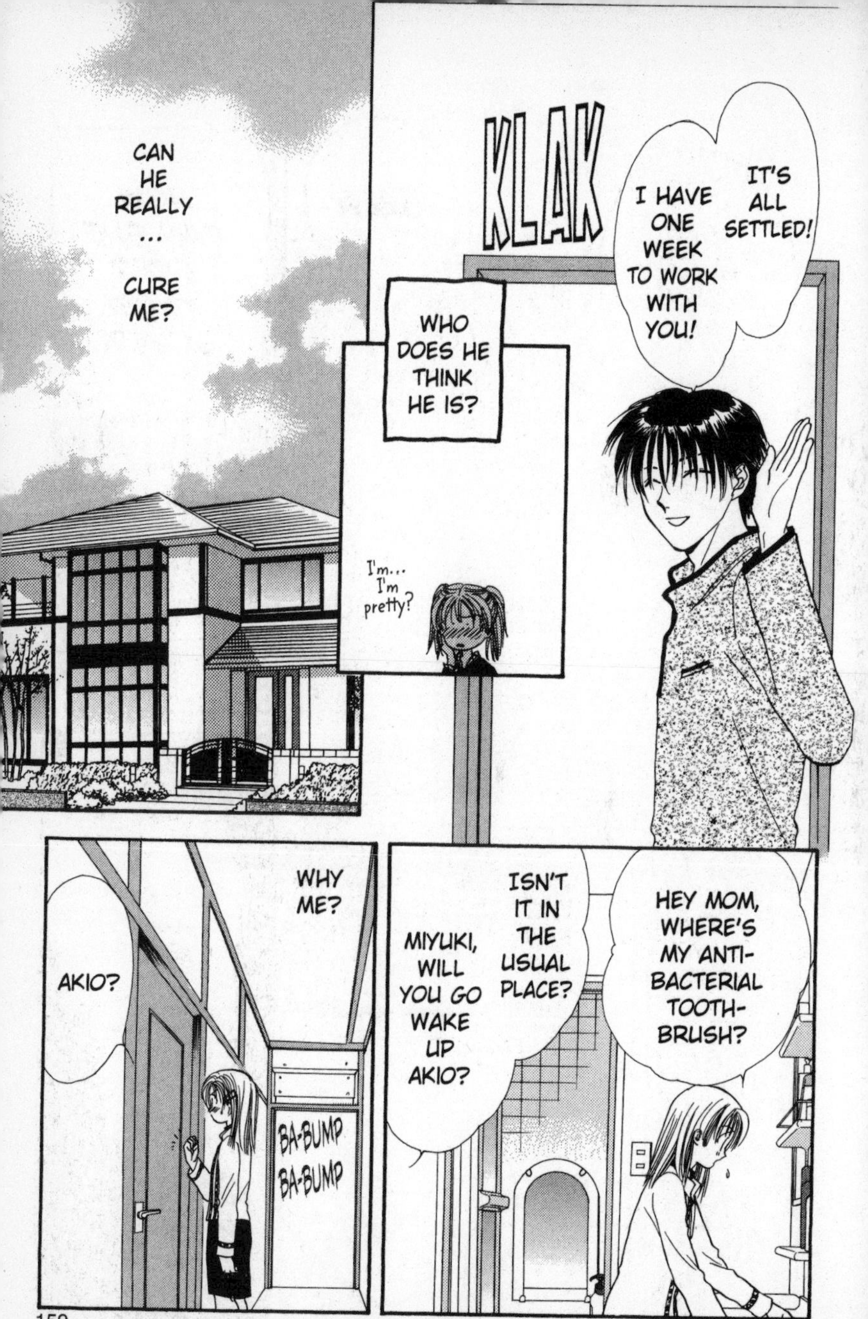
KLAK
IT'S ALL SETTLED!
I HAVE ONE WEEK TO WORK WITH YOU!
WHO DOES HE THINK HE IS?
I'm... I'm pretty?
CAN HE REALLY ... CURE ME?
HEY MOM, WHERE'S MY ANTI-BACTERIAL TOOTH-BRUSH?
ISN'T IT IN THE USUAL PLACE?
MIYUKI, WILL YOU GO WAKE UP AKIO?
WHY ME?
BA-BUMP BA-BUMP
AKIO?

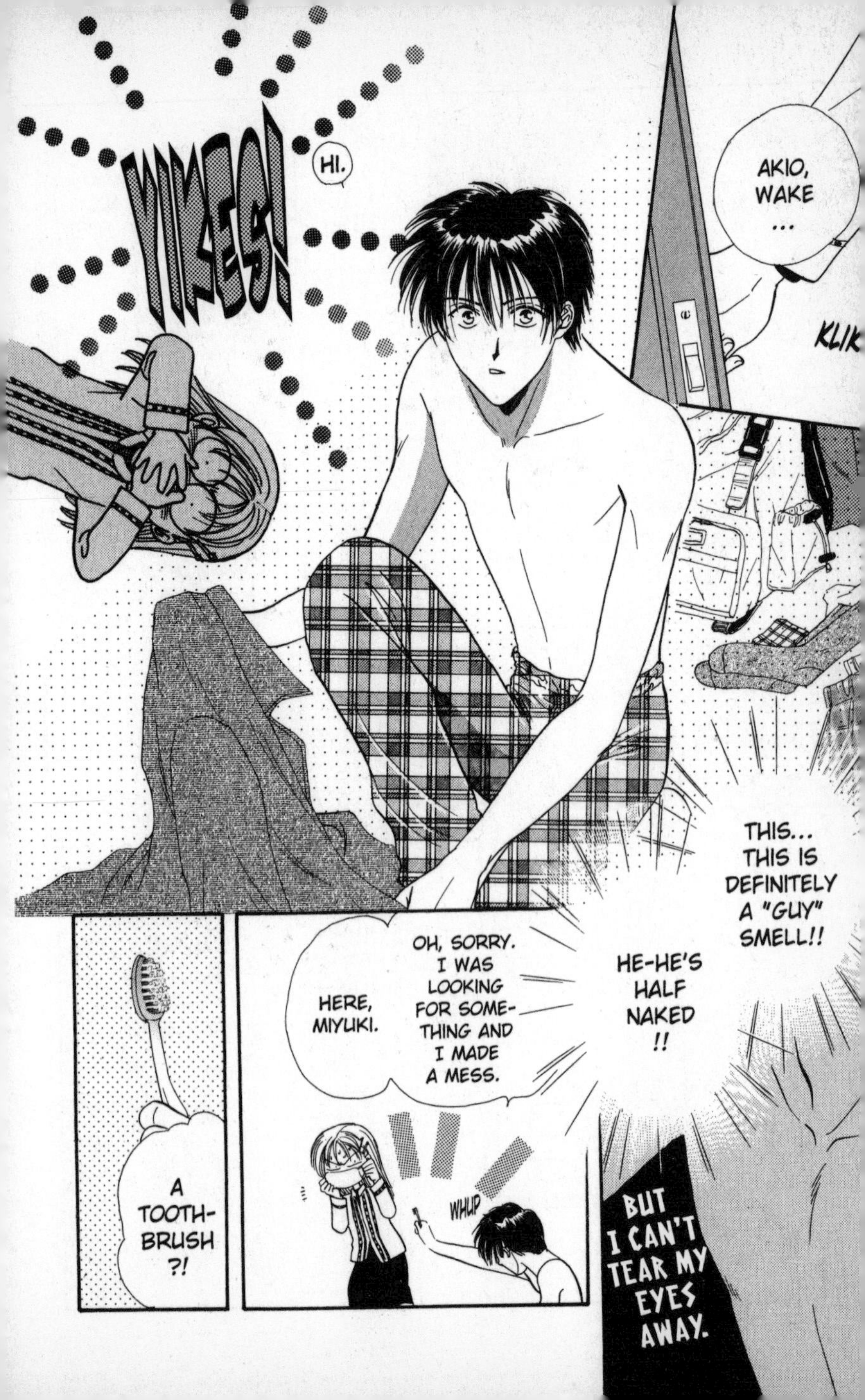

AKIO, WAKE ...
KLIK
YIKES!
HI.
THIS... THIS IS DEFINITELY A "GUY" SMELL!!
HE-HE'S HALF NAKED !!
BUT I CAN'T TEAR MY EYES AWAY.
OH, SORRY. I WAS LOOKING FOR SOME-THING AND I MADE A MESS.
HERE, MIYUKI.
WHUP
A TOOTH-BRUSH ?!

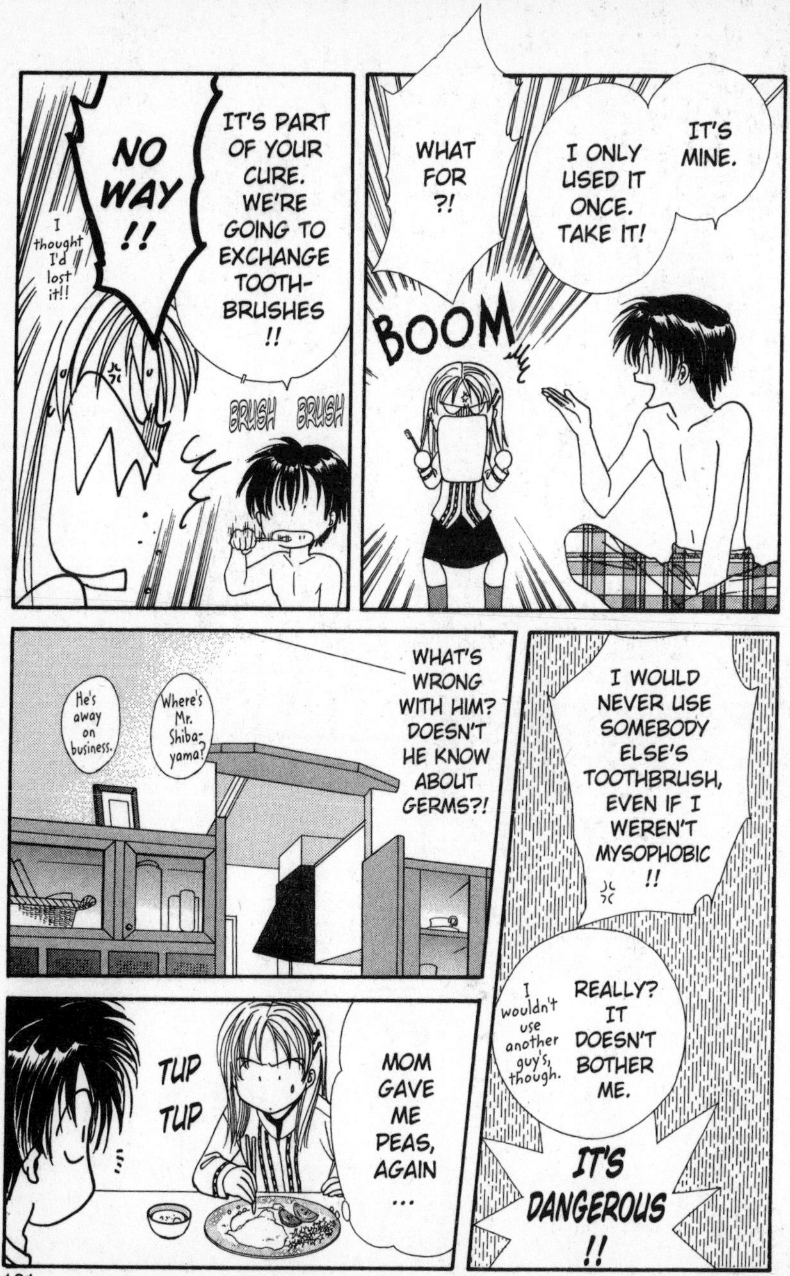
IT'S MINE.
I ONLY USED IT ONCE. TAKE IT!
WHAT FOR ?!
BOOM
IT'S PART OF YOUR CURE. WE'RE GOING TO EXCHANGE TOOTH-BRUSHES !!
NO WAY !!
I thought I'd lost it!!
BRUSH BRUSH
I WOULD NEVER USE SOMEBODY ELSE'S TOOTHBRUSH, EVEN IF I WEREN'T MYSOPHOBIC !!
REALLY? IT DOESN'T BOTHER ME.
I wouldn't use another guy's, though.
IT'S DANGEROUS !!
WHAT'S WRONG WITH HIM? DOESN'T HE KNOW ABOUT GERMS?!
Where's Mr. Shiba-yama?
He's away on business.
MOM GAVE ME PEAS, AGAIN ...
TUP TUP

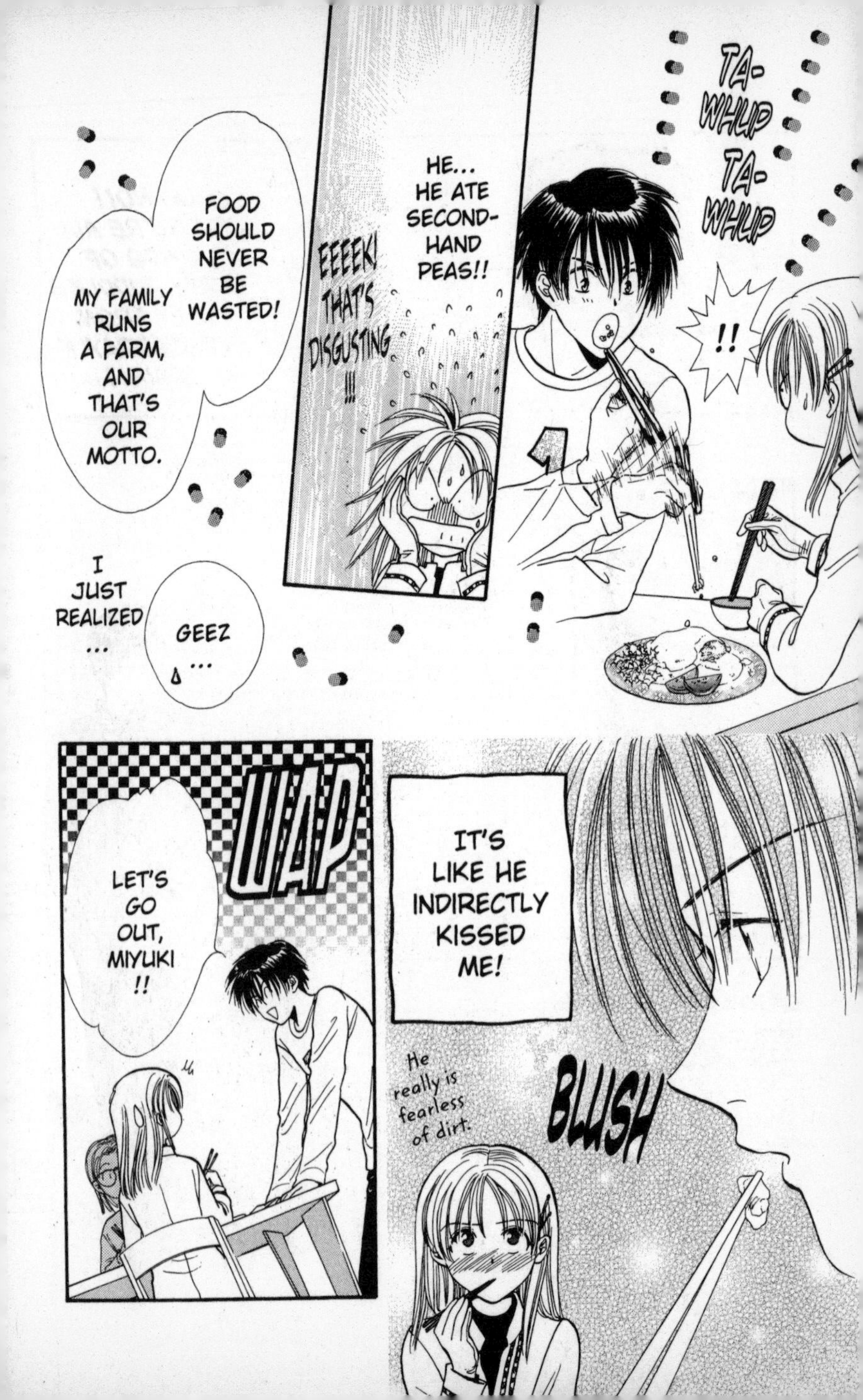
TA-WHUP TA-WHUP
!!
HE... HE ATE SECOND-HAND PEAS!!
EEEEK! THAT'S DISGUSTING!!!
FOOD SHOULD NEVER BE WASTED!
MY FAMILY RUNS A FARM, AND THAT'S OUR MOTTO.
GEEZ...
I JUST REALIZED...
IT'S LIKE HE INDIRECTLY KISSED ME!
BLUSH
He really is fearless of dirt.
WAP
LET'S GO OUT, MIYUKI!!

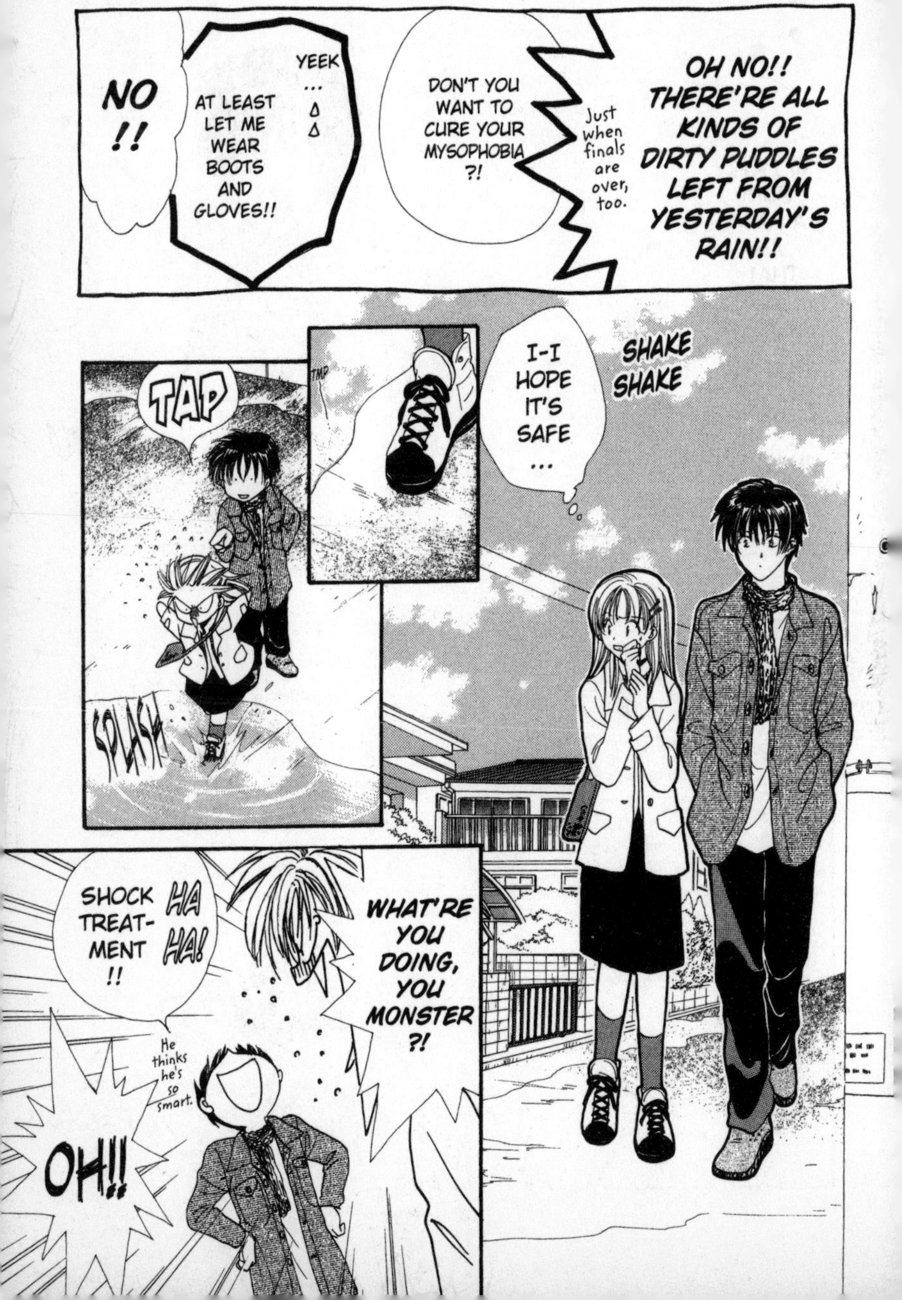
OH NO!! THERE'RE ALL KINDS OF DIRTY PUDDLES LEFT FROM YESTERDAY'S RAIN!!
Just when finals are over, too.
DON'T YOU WANT TO CURE YOUR MYSOPHOBIA ?!
YEEK ...
AT LEAST LET ME WEAR BOOTS AND GLOVES!!
NO !!
SHAKE SHAKE
I-I HOPE IT'S SAFE ...
TMP
TAP
SPLASH
WHAT'RE YOU DOING, YOU MONSTER ?!
HA HA!
SHOCK TREAT-MENT !!
He thinks he's so smart.
OH!!

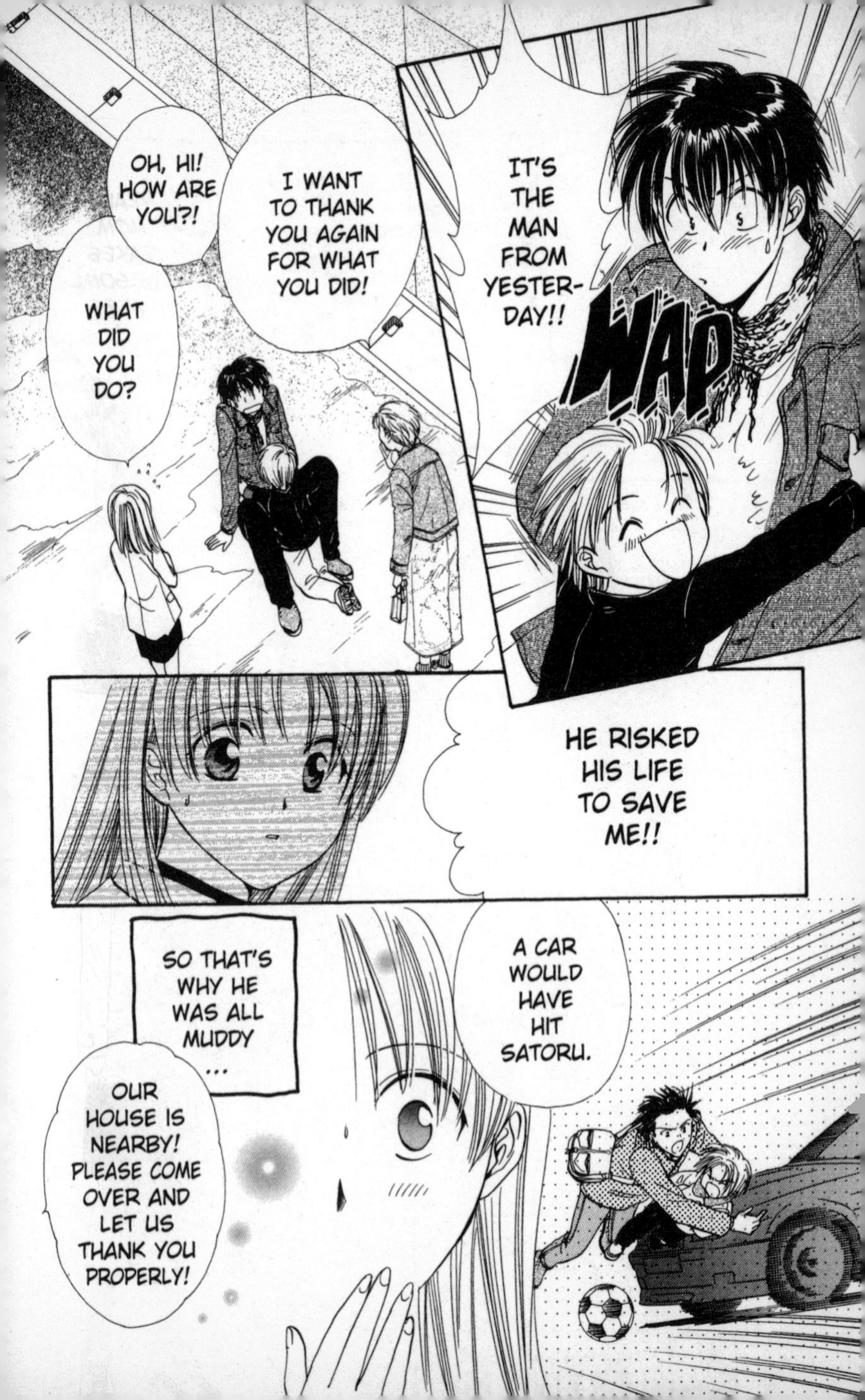
IT'S THE MAN FROM YESTERDAY!!
WAP
OH, HI! HOW ARE YOU?!
I WANT TO THANK YOU AGAIN FOR WHAT YOU DID!
WHAT DID YOU DO?
HE RISKED HIS LIFE TO SAVE ME!!
A CAR WOULD HAVE HIT SATORU.
SO THAT'S WHY HE WAS ALL MUDDY ...
OUR HOUSE IS NEARBY! PLEASE COME OVER AND LET US THANK YOU PROPERLY!

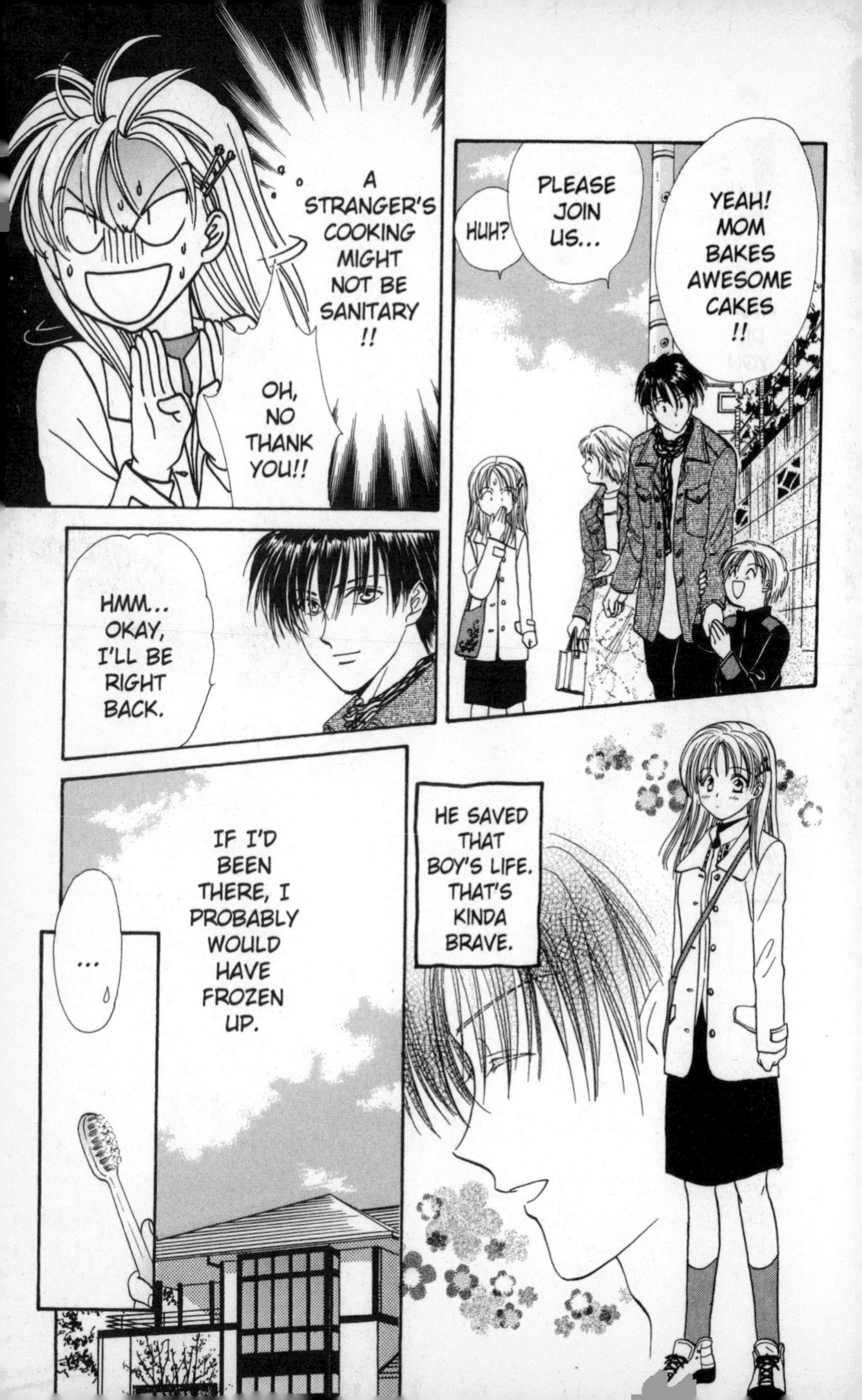
YEAH! MOM BAKES AWESOME CAKES !!
PLEASE JOIN US...
HUH?
A STRANGER'S COOKING MIGHT NOT BE SANITARY !!
OH, NO THANK YOU!!
HMM... OKAY, I'LL BE RIGHT BACK.
HE SAVED THAT BOY'S LIFE. THAT'S KINDA BRAVE.
IF I'D BEEN THERE, I PROBABLY WOULD HAVE FROZEN UP.
...

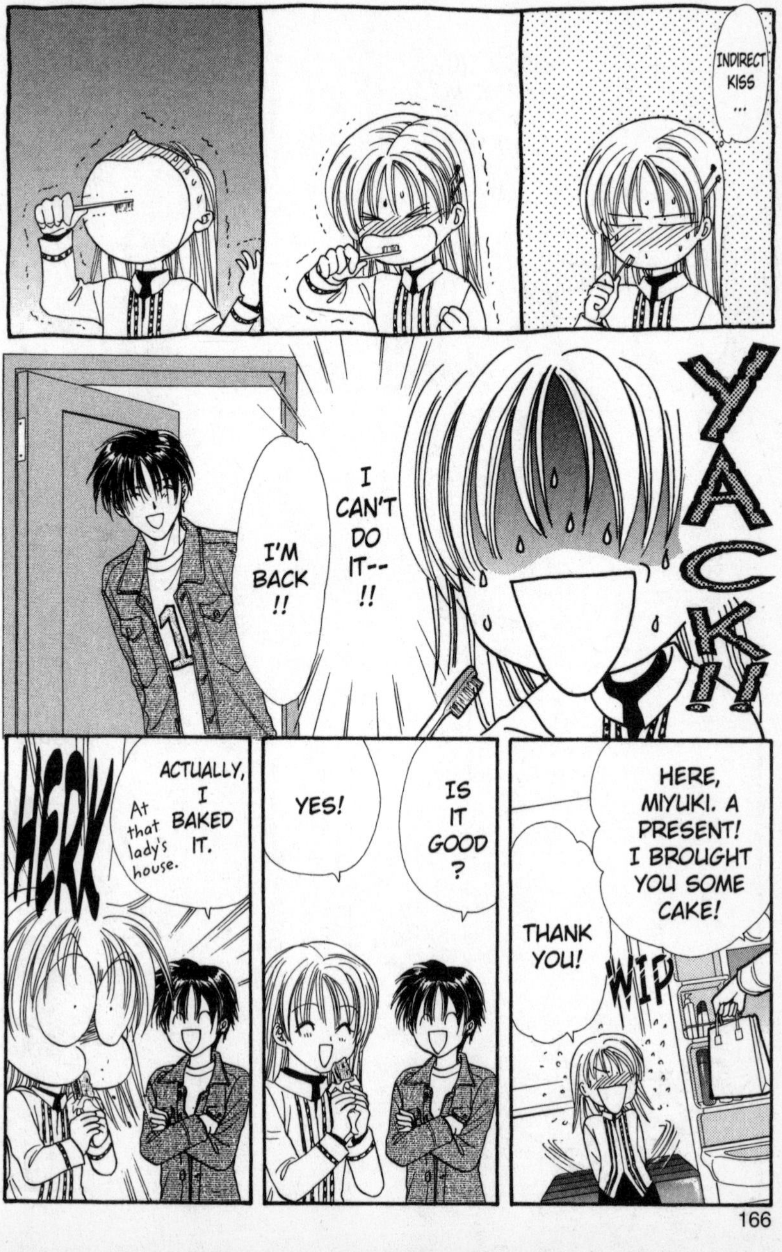
INDIRECT KISS ...
YACK!!
I CAN'T DO IT-- !!
I'M BACK !!
HERE, MIYUKI. A PRESENT! I BROUGHT YOU SOME CAKE!
WIP
THANK YOU!
IS IT GOOD ?
YES!
ACTUALLY, I BAKED IT.
At that lady's house.
HERK

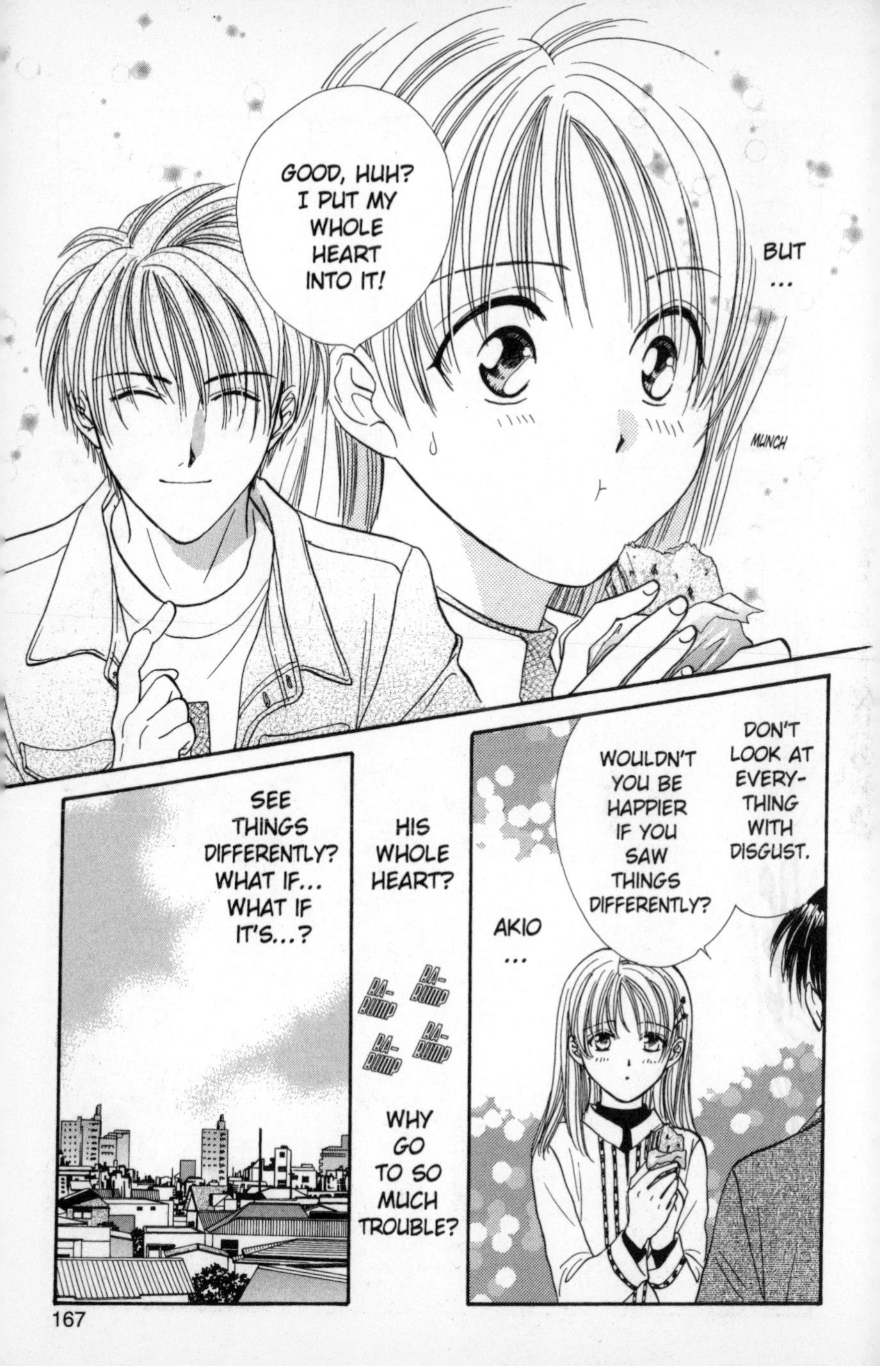
GOOD, HUH? I PUT MY WHOLE HEART INTO IT!
BUT ...
MUNCH
DON'T LOOK AT EVERY-THING WITH DISGUST.
WOULDN'T YOU BE HAPPIER IF YOU SAW THINGS DIFFERENTLY?
AKIO ...
HIS WHOLE HEART?
SEE THINGS DIFFERENTLY? WHAT IF... WHAT IF IT'S...?
BA-BUMP
BA-BUMP
BA-BUMP
BA-BUMP
WHY GO TO SO MUCH TROUBLE?

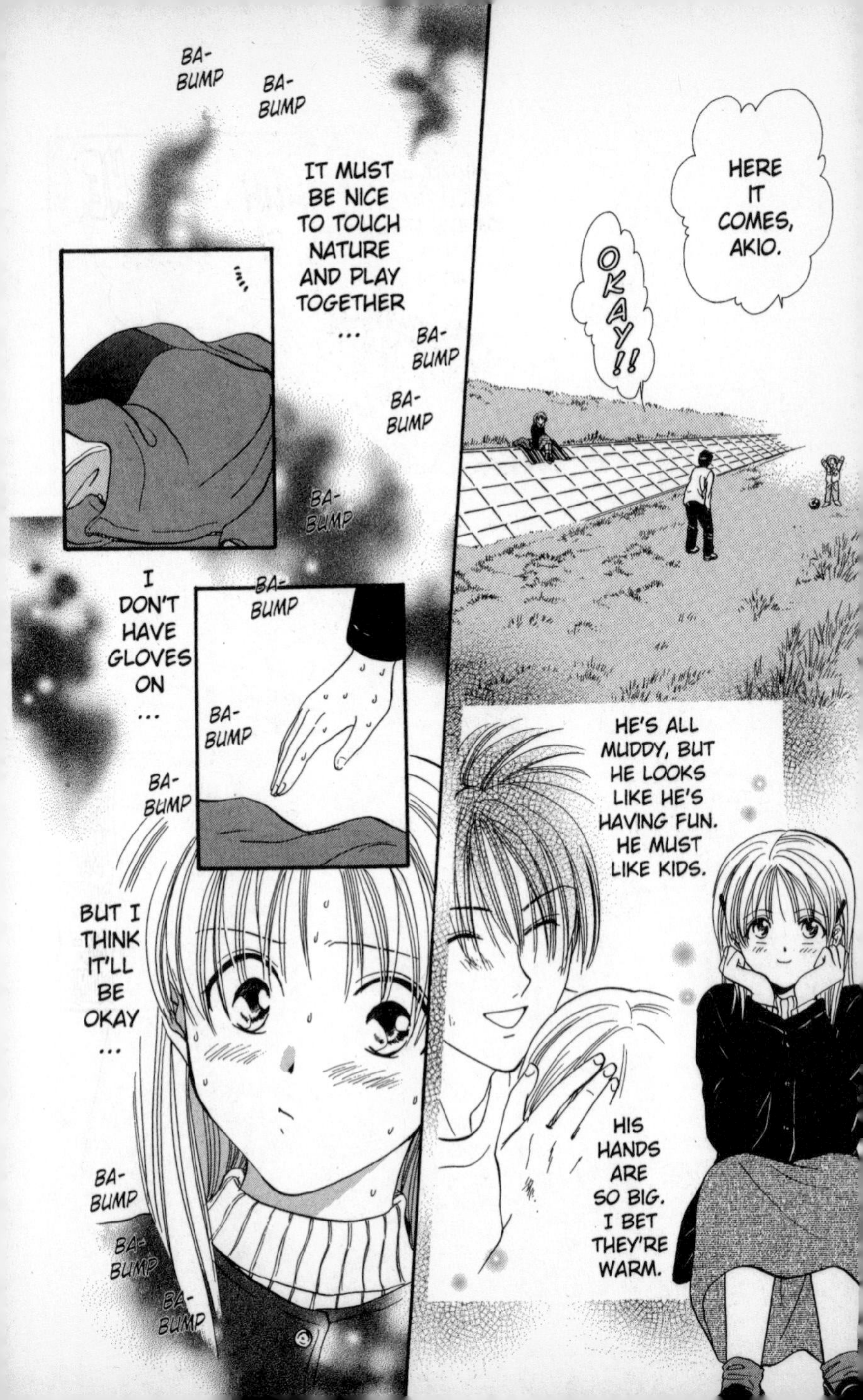

HERE IT COMES, AKIO.
OKAY!!
HE'S ALL MUDDY, BUT HE LOOKS LIKE HE'S HAVING FUN. HE MUST LIKE KIDS.
HIS HANDS ARE SO BIG. I BET THEY'RE WARM.
BA-BUMP
BA-BUMP
IT MUST BE NICE TO TOUCH NATURE AND PLAY TOGETHER...
BA-BUMP
BA-BUMP
...
BA-BUMP
I DON'T HAVE GLOVES ON...
BA-BUMP
BA-BUMP
BA-BUMP
BUT I THINK IT'LL BE OKAY...
BA-BUMP
BA-BUMP
BA-BUMP

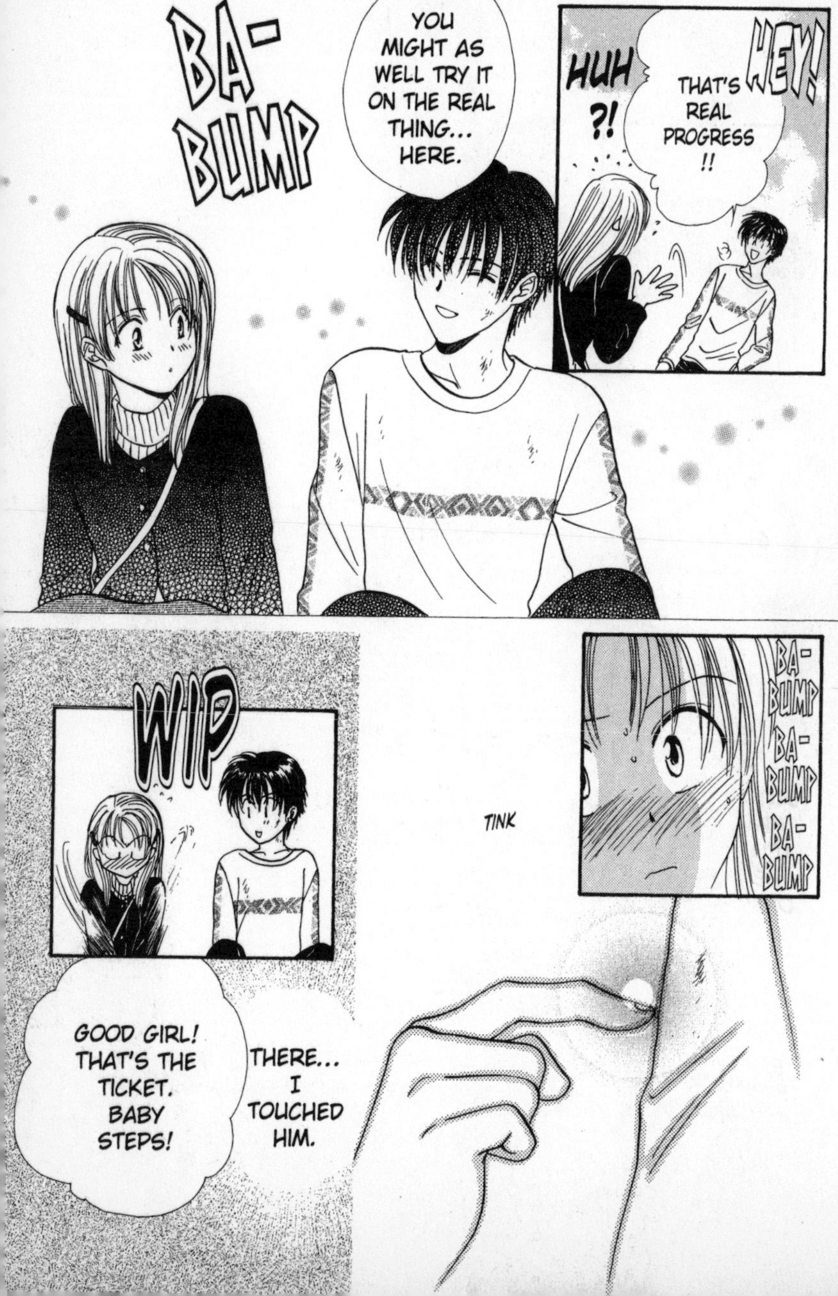
HEY!
HUH ?!
THAT'S REAL PROGRESS !!
YOU MIGHT AS WELL TRY IT ON THE REAL THING... HERE.
BA-BUMP
BA-BUMP BA-BUMP BA-BUMP
TINK
WIP
THERE... I TOUCHED HIM.
GOOD GIRL! THAT'S THE TICKET. BABY STEPS!

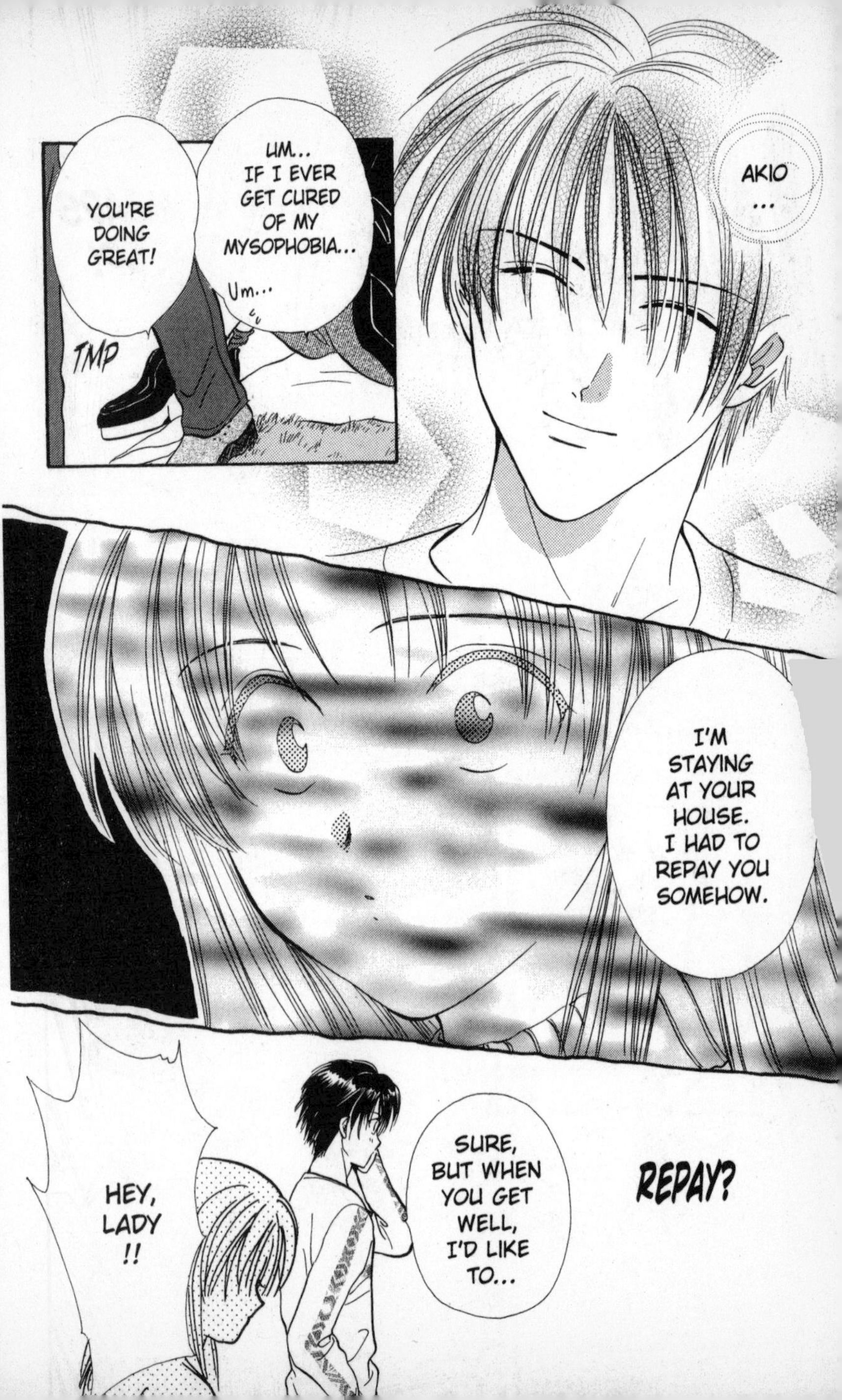
AKIO ...
UM... IF I EVER GET CURED OF MY MYSOPHOBIA...
Um...
YOU'RE DOING GREAT!
TMP
I'M STAYING AT YOUR HOUSE. I HAD TO REPAY YOU SOMEHOW.
REPAY?
SURE, BUT WHEN YOU GET WELL, I'D LIKE TO...
HEY, LADY !!

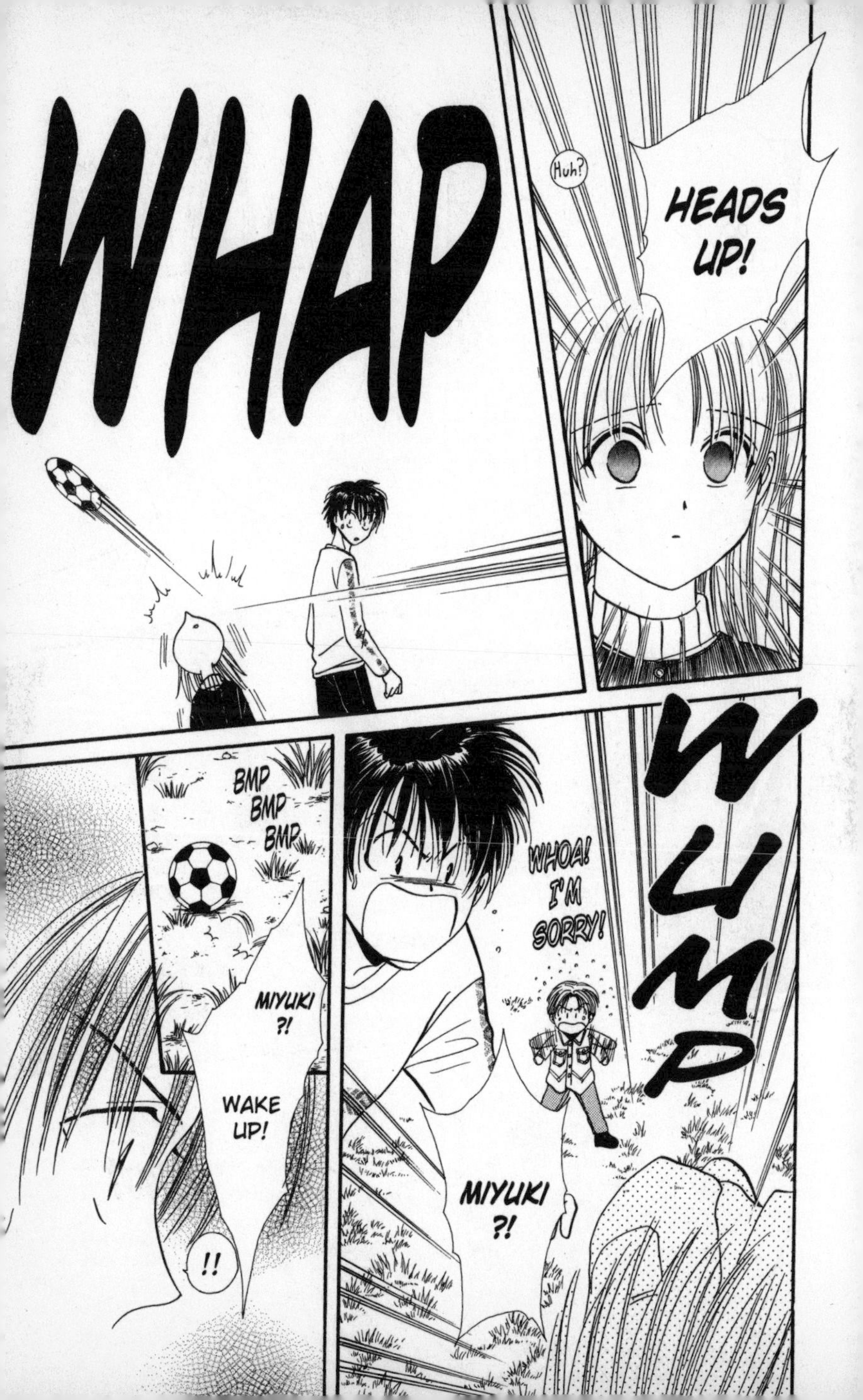
HEADS UP!
Huh?
WHAP
WUMP
WHOA! I'M SORRY!
MIYUKI ?!
BMP BMP BMP
MIYUKI ?!
WAKE UP!
!!

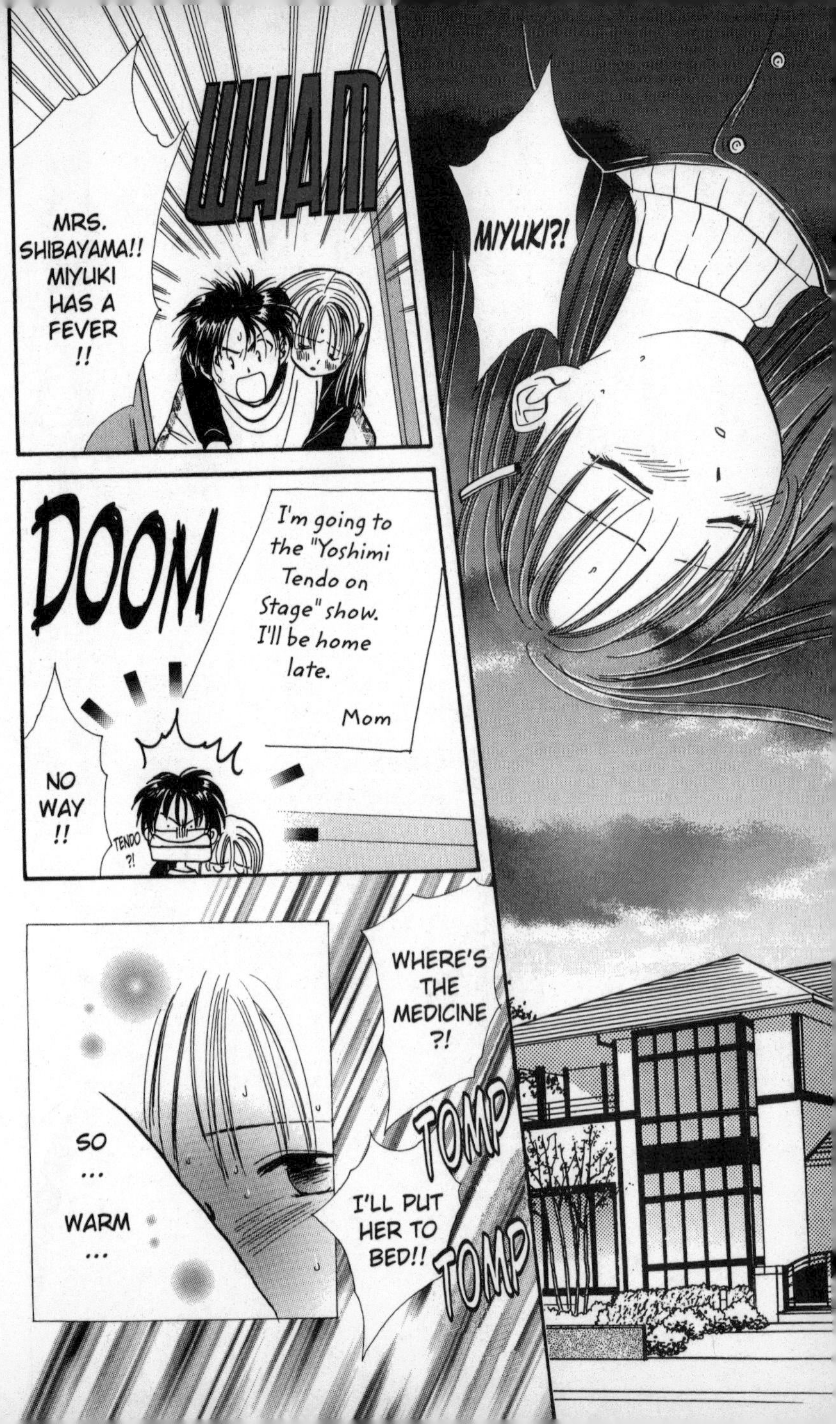
MIYUKI?!
WHAM
MRS. SHIBAYAMA!! MIYUKI HAS A FEVER!!
DOOM
I'm going to the "Yoshimi Tendo on Stage" show. I'll be home late. Mom
NO WAY!!
TENDO?!
WHERE'S THE MEDICINE?!
TOMP
I'LL PUT HER TO BED!!
TOMP
SO... WARM...

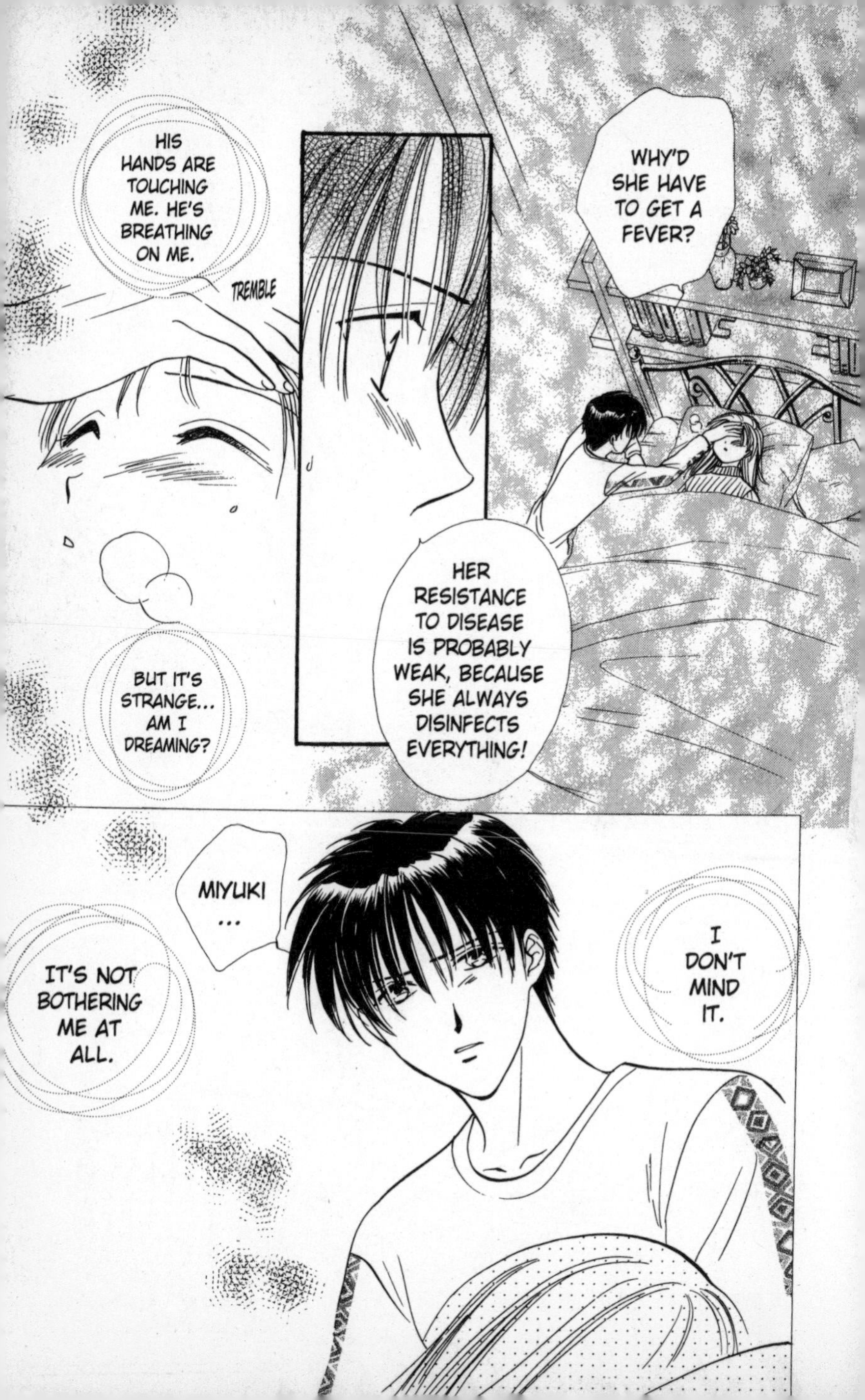

WHY'D SHE HAVE TO GET A FEVER?
HER RESISTANCE TO DISEASE IS PROBABLY WEAK, BECAUSE SHE ALWAYS DISINFECTS EVERYTHING!
HIS HANDS ARE TOUCHING ME. HE'S BREATHING ON ME.
TREMBLE
BUT IT'S STRANGE... AM I DREAMING?
I DON'T MIND IT.
MIYUKI ...
IT'S NOT BOTHERING ME AT ALL.

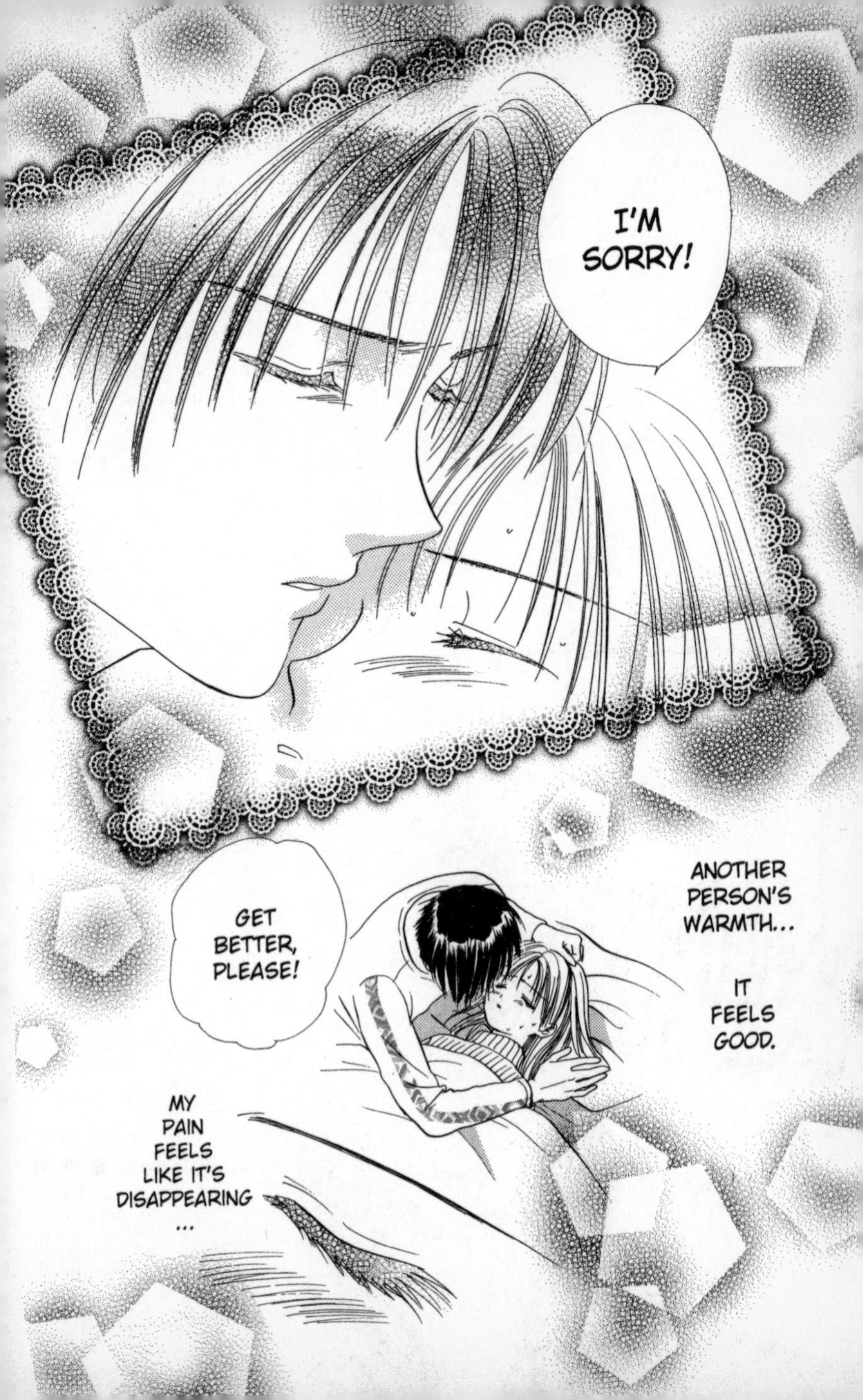
I'M SORRY!
ANOTHER PERSON'S WARMTH...
IT FEELS GOOD.
GET BETTER, PLEASE!
MY PAIN FEELS LIKE IT'S DISAPPEARING ...

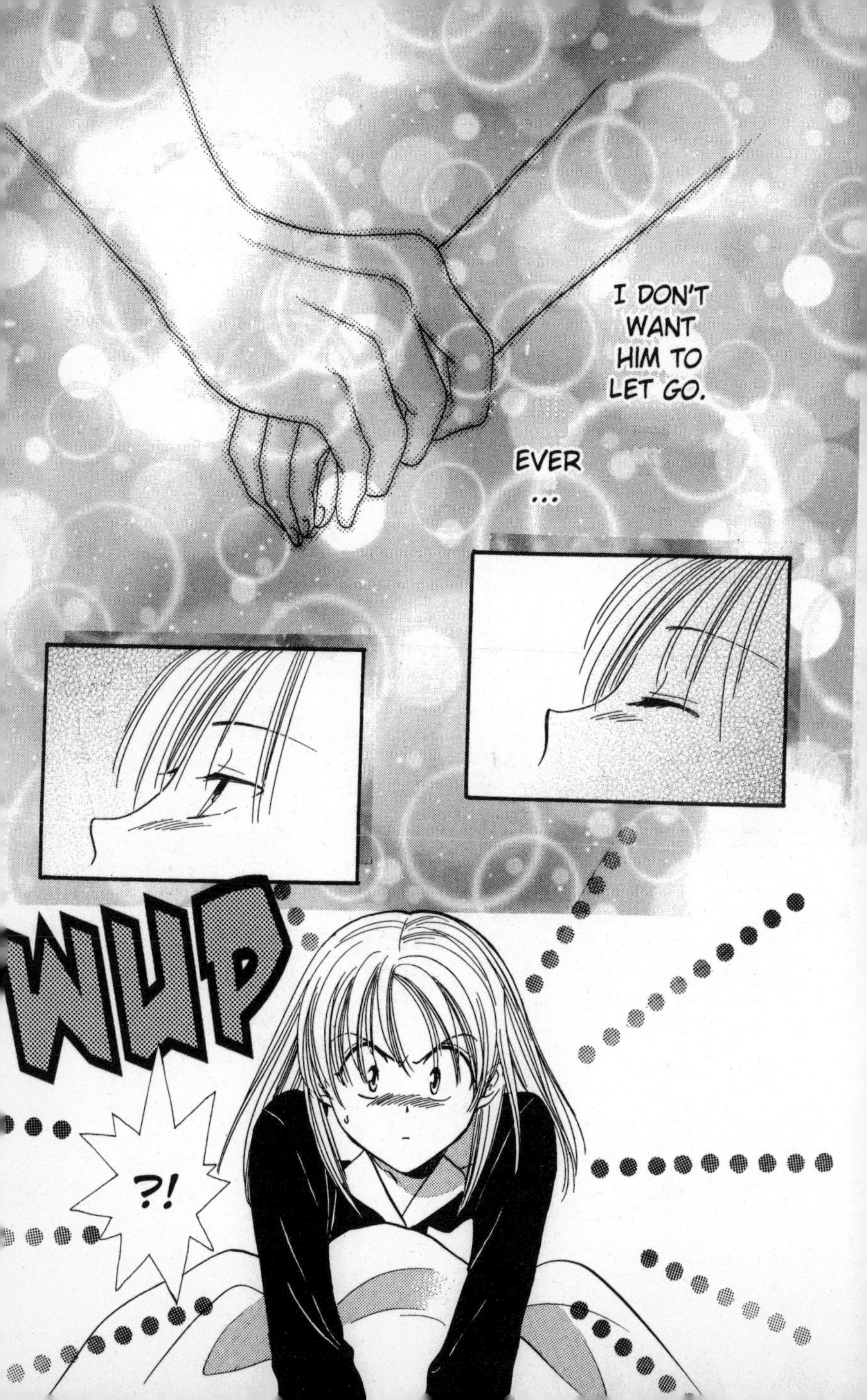
I DON'T WANT HIM TO LET GO.
EVER ...
WUP
?!

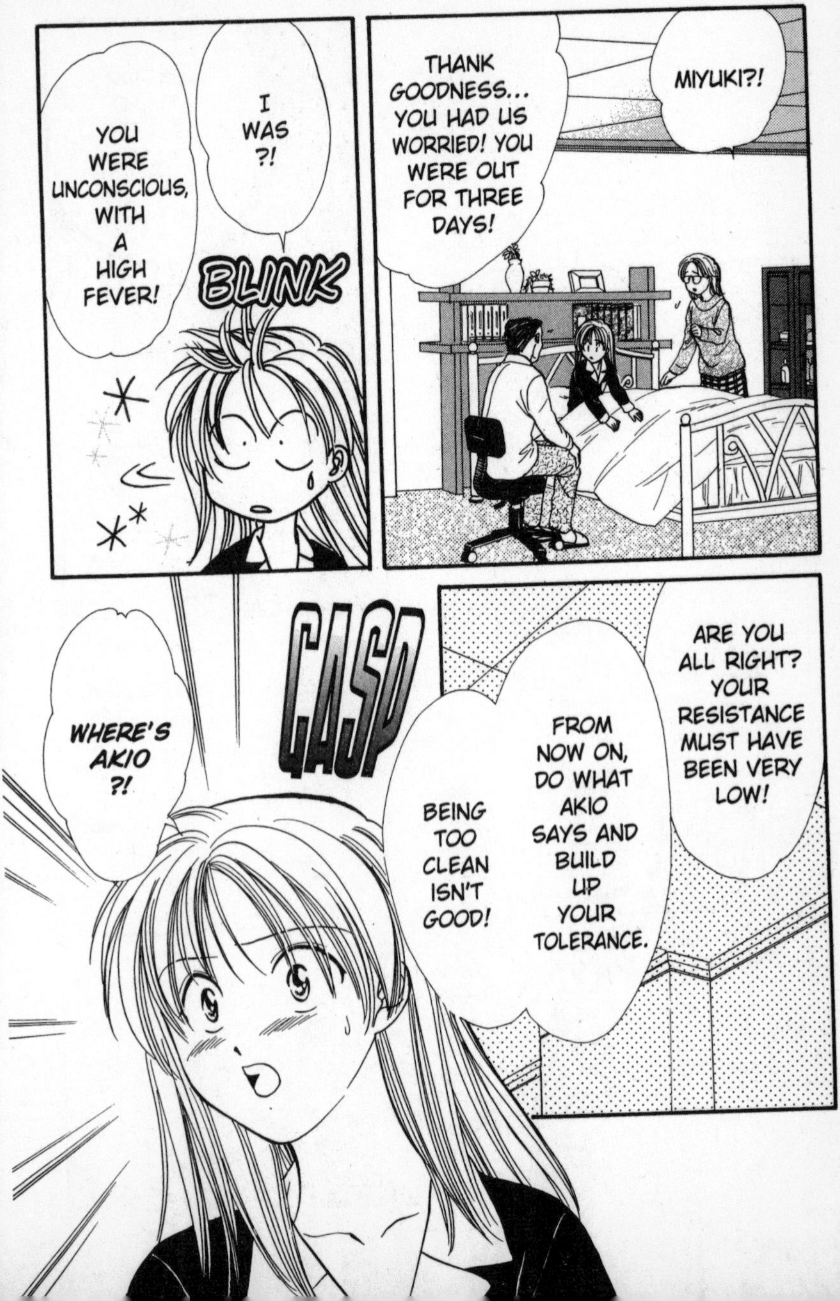
MIYUKI?!
THANK GOODNESS... YOU HAD US WORRIED! YOU WERE OUT FOR THREE DAYS!
I WAS?!
BLINK
YOU WERE UNCONSCIOUS, WITH A HIGH FEVER!
ARE YOU ALL RIGHT? YOUR RESISTANCE MUST HAVE BEEN VERY LOW!
FROM NOW ON, DO WHAT AKIO SAYS AND BUILD UP YOUR TOLERANCE.
BEING TOO CLEAN ISN'T GOOD!
GASP
WHERE'S AKIO?!

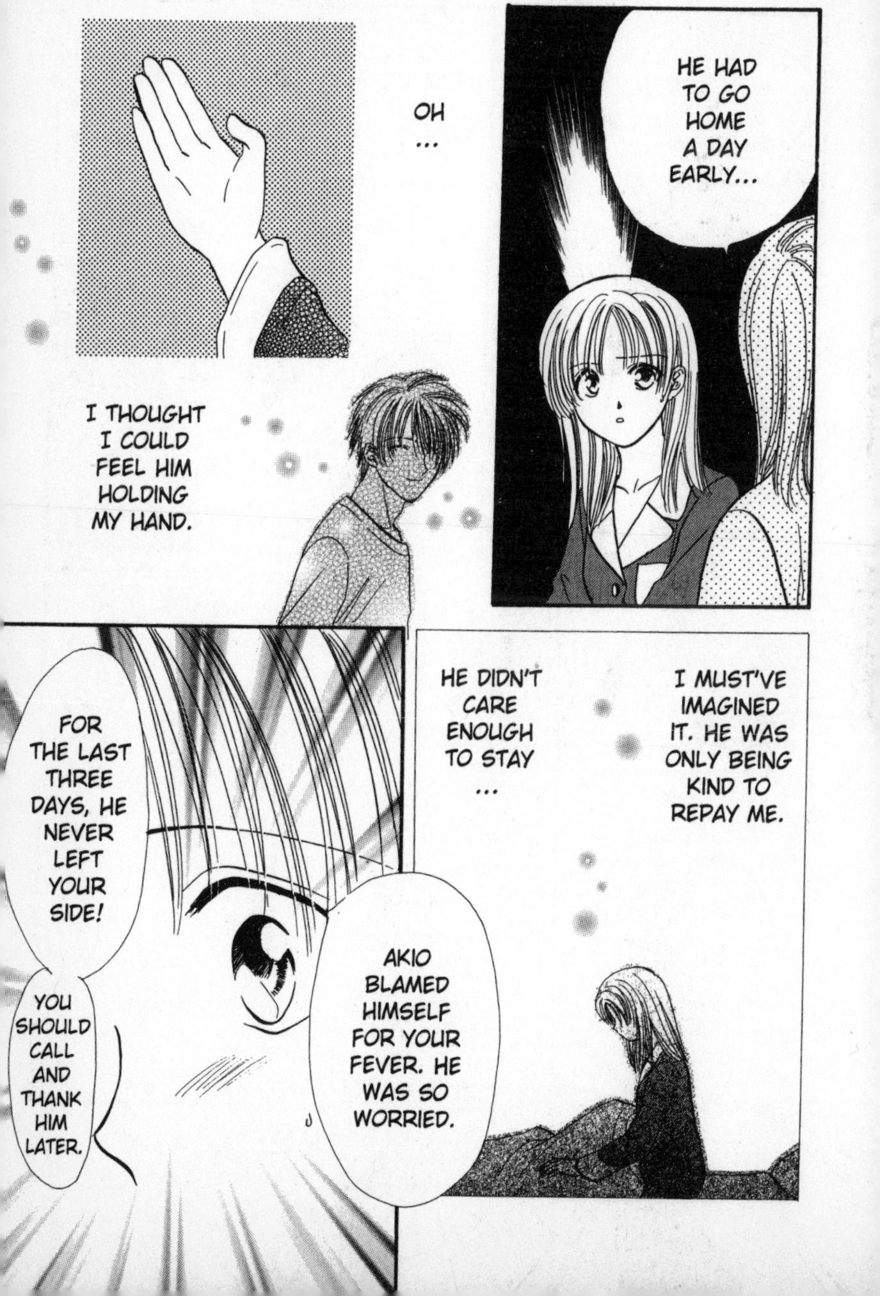
HE HAD TO GO HOME A DAY EARLY...
OH ...
I THOUGHT I COULD FEEL HIM HOLDING MY HAND.
I MUST'VE IMAGINED IT. HE WAS ONLY BEING KIND TO REPAY ME.
HE DIDN'T CARE ENOUGH TO STAY ...
FOR THE LAST THREE DAYS, HE NEVER LEFT YOUR SIDE!
AKIO BLAMED HIMSELF FOR YOUR FEVER. HE WAS SO WORRIED.
YOU SHOULD CALL AND THANK HIM LATER.

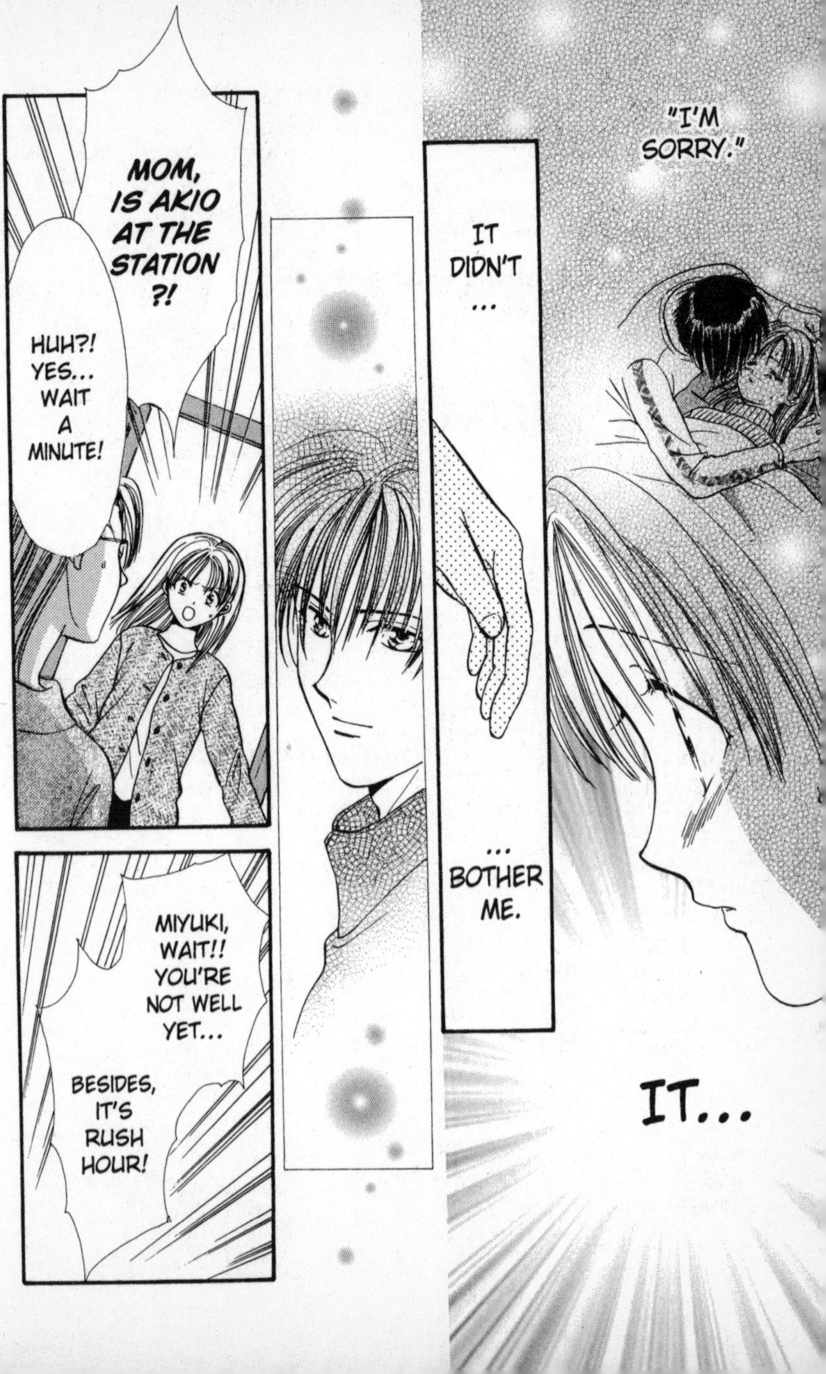
"I'M SORRY."
IT DIDN'T ...
... BOTHER ME.
IT...
MOM, IS AKIO AT THE STATION ?!
HUH?! YES... WAIT A MINUTE!
MIYUKI, WAIT!! YOU'RE NOT WELL YET...
BESIDES, IT'S RUSH HOUR!

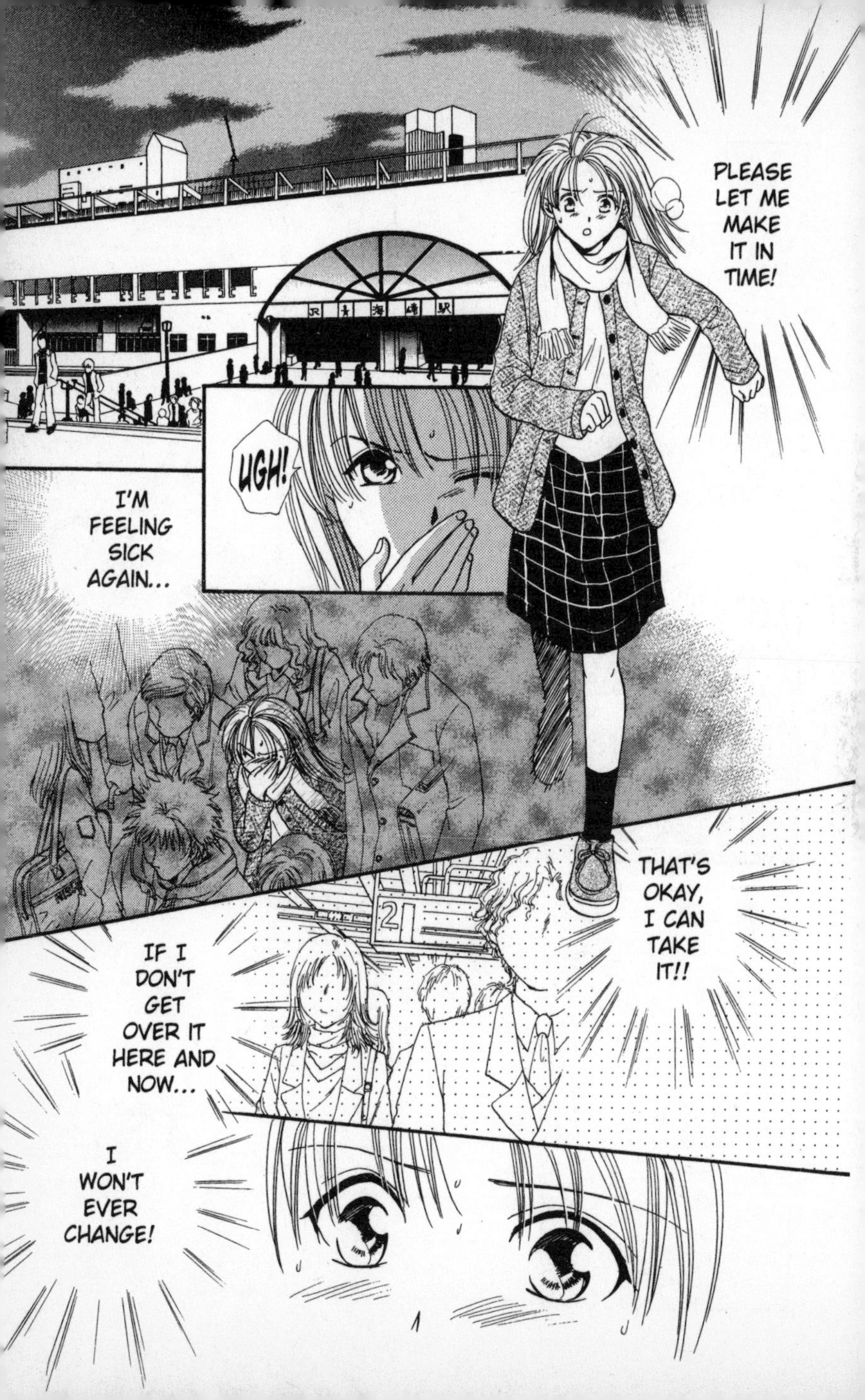
PLEASE LET ME MAKE IT IN TIME!
UGH!
I'M FEELING SICK AGAIN...
THAT'S OKAY, I CAN TAKE IT!!
IF I DON'T GET OVER IT HERE AND NOW...
I WON'T EVER CHANGE!

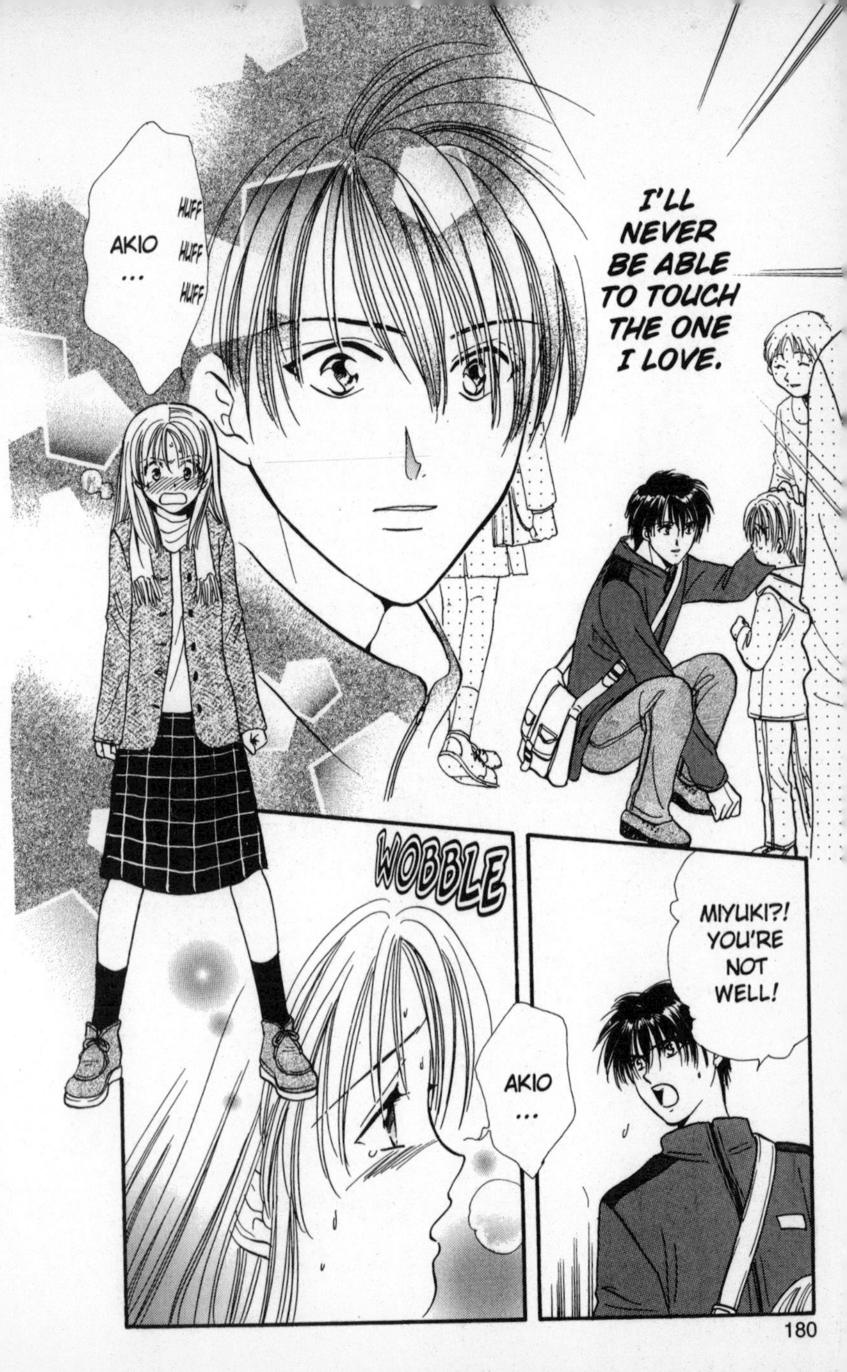
I'LL NEVER BE ABLE TO TOUCH THE ONE I LOVE.
HUFF
HUFF
HUFF
AKIO ...
MIYUKI?! YOU'RE NOT WELL!
WOBBLE
AKIO ...

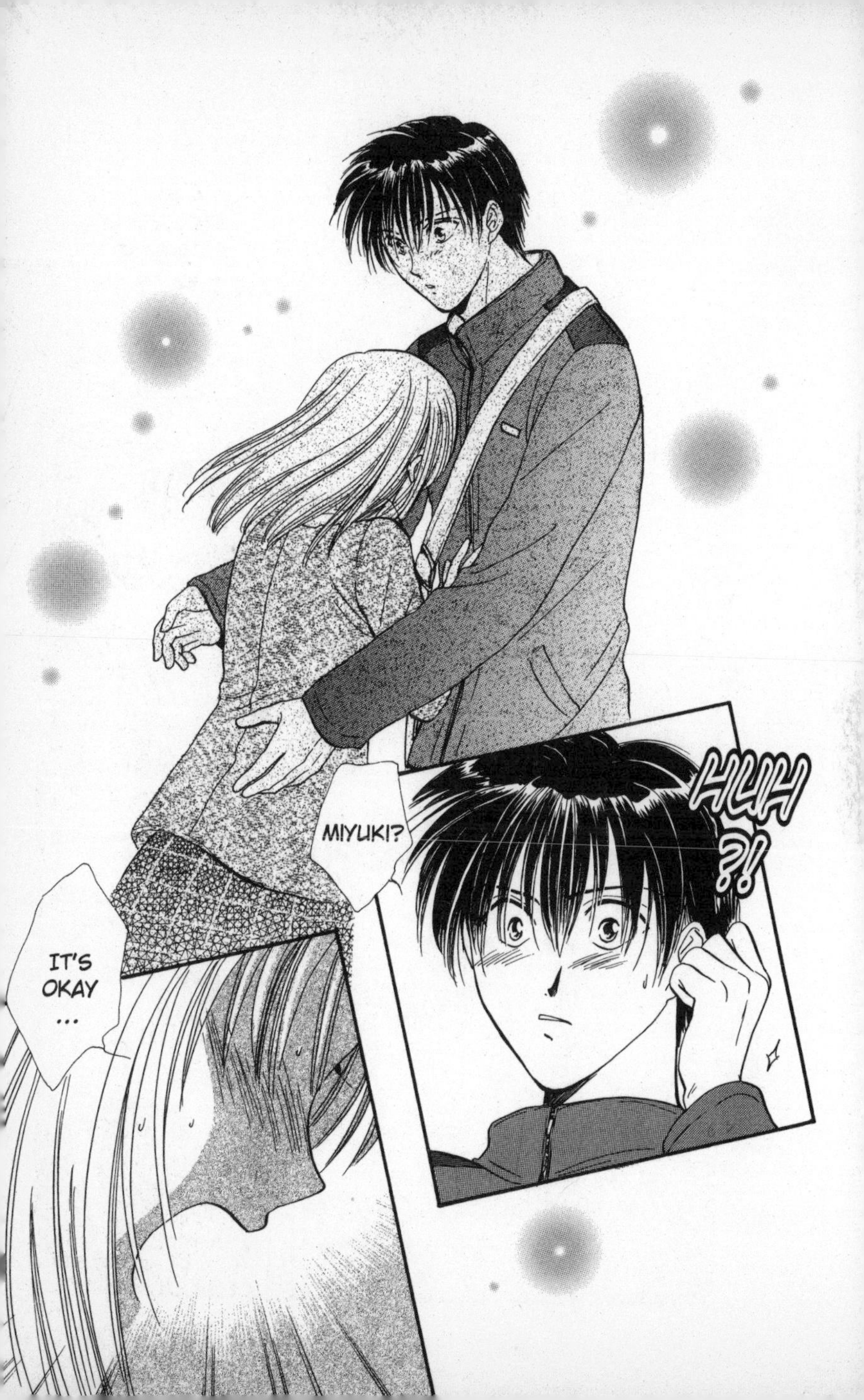
HUH ?!
MIYUKI?
IT'S OKAY ...

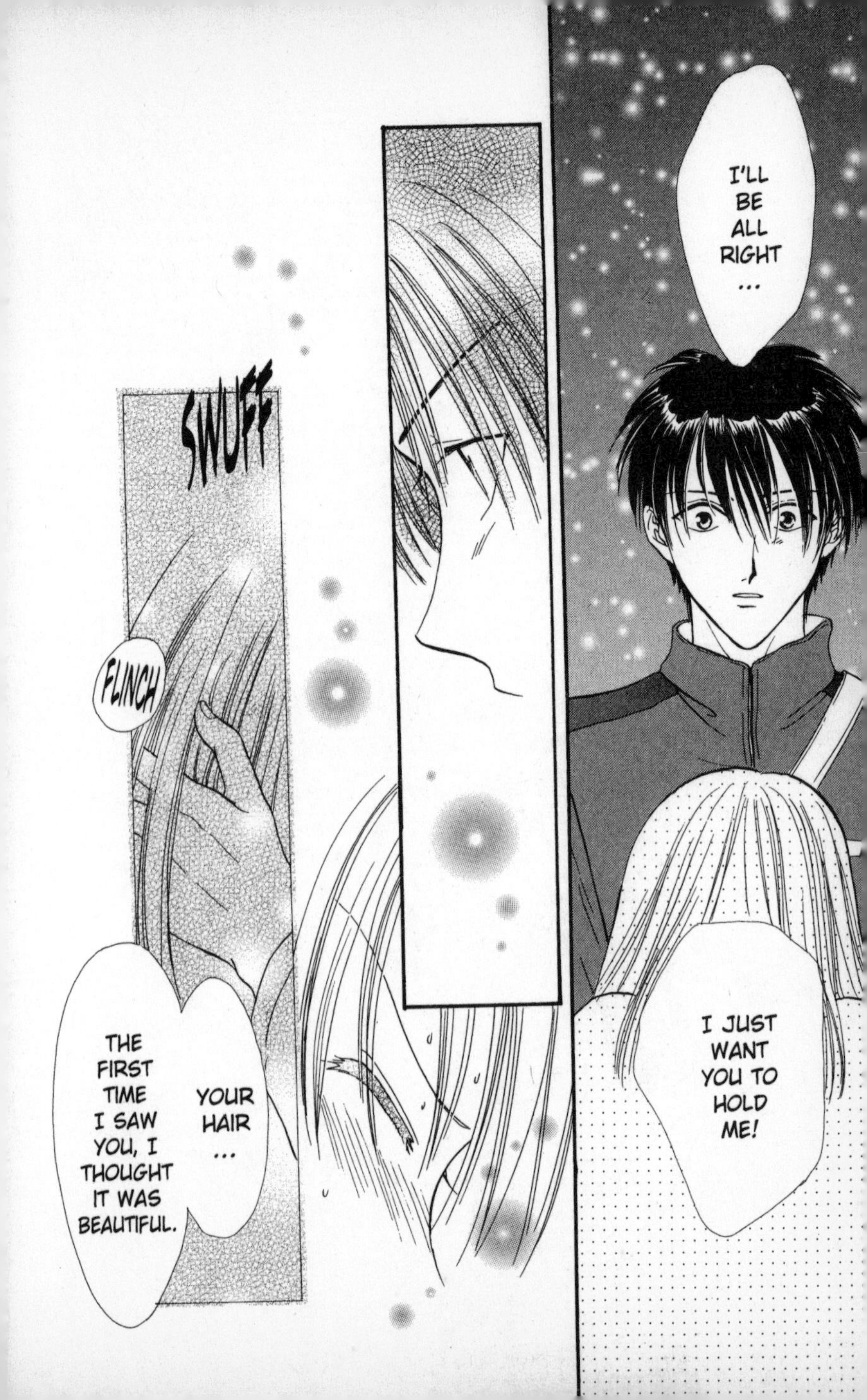
I'LL BE ALL RIGHT ...
I JUST WANT YOU TO HOLD ME!
SWUFF
FLINCH
YOUR HAIR ...
THE FIRST TIME I SAW YOU, I THOUGHT IT WAS BEAUTIFUL.

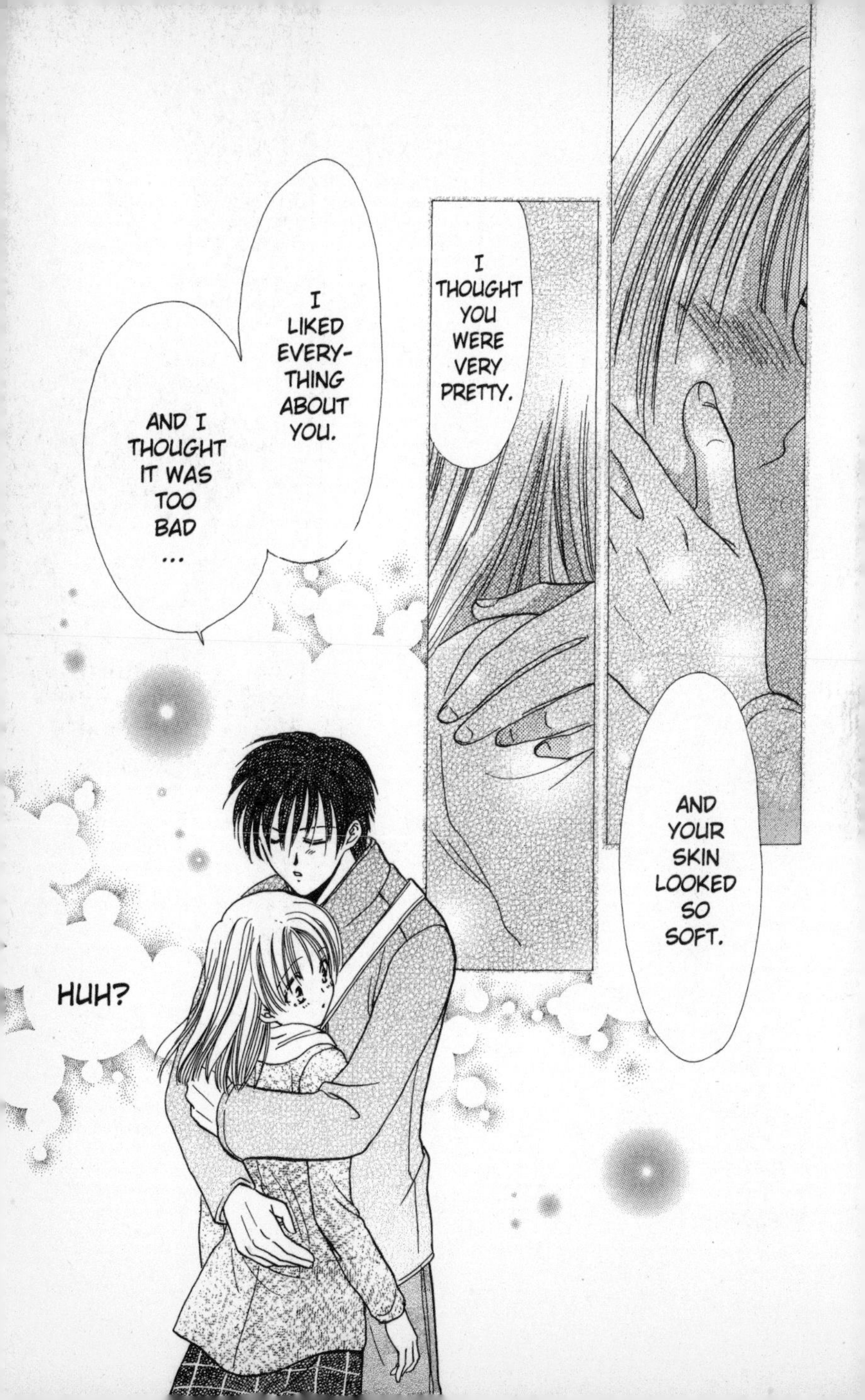
I THOUGHT YOU WERE VERY PRETTY.
AND YOUR SKIN LOOKED SO SOFT.
I LIKED EVERY-THING ABOUT YOU.
AND I THOUGHT IT WAS TOO BAD ...
HUH?

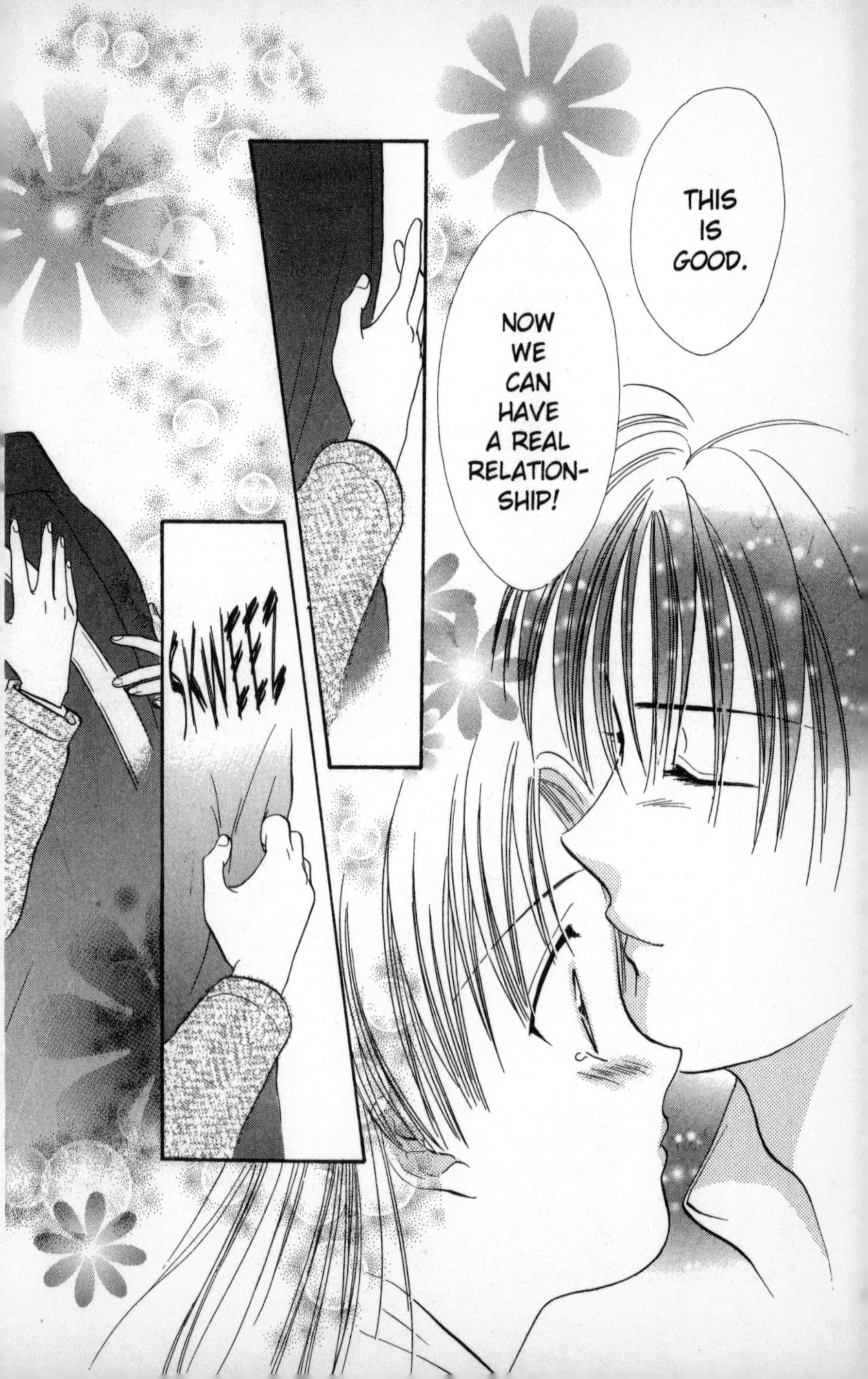
THIS IS GOOD.
NOW WE CAN HAVE A REAL RELATIONSHIP!
SKWEEZ

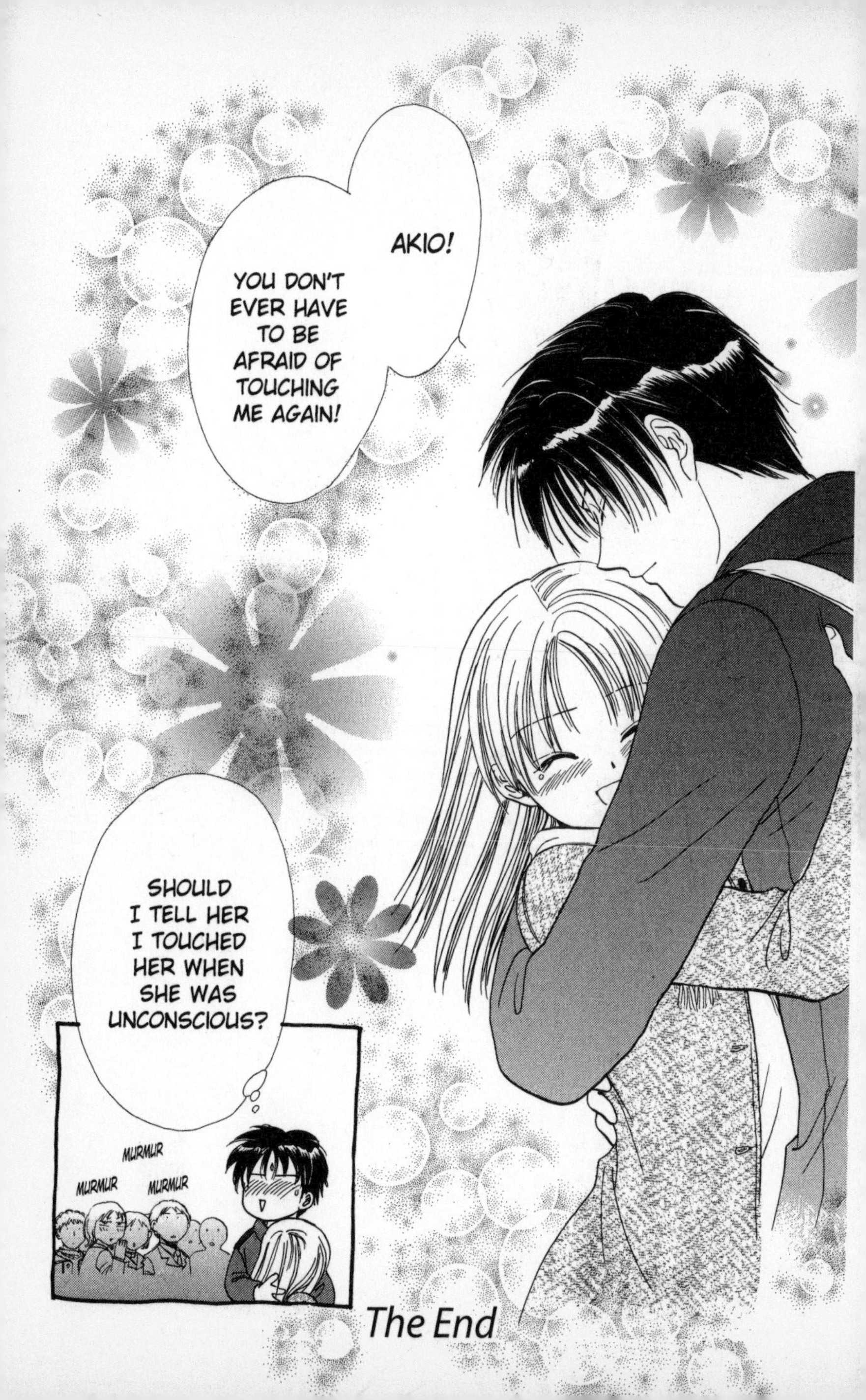
AKIO!
YOU DON'T EVER HAVE TO BE AFRAID OF TOUCHING ME AGAIN!
SHOULD I TELL HER I TOUCHED HER WHEN SHE WAS UNCONSCIOUS?
MURMUR
MURMUR
MURMUR
The End

Imadoki!
Nowadays
Vol. 5
Poppy

STORY AND ART BY Yuu Watase
English Adaptation/Lance Caselman
Translation/JN Productions, Inc.
Touch-up Art & Lettering/Walden Wong
Graphic Designer/Nozomi Akashi
Editor/Yuki Takagaki

Editor in Chief, Books/Alvin Lu
Editor in Chief, Magazines/Marc Weidenbaum
VP of Publishing Licensing/Rika Inouye
VP of Sales/Gonzalo Ferreyra
Sr. VP of Marketing/Liza Coppola
Publisher/Hyoe Narita

Printed in the U.S.A.

Published by VIZ Media, LLC
P.O. Box 77010 • San Francisco, CA 94107

Shôjo Edition
10 9 8 7 6 5 4
First printing, February 2005
Fourth printing, September 2007

www.viz.com

The Power of a Kiss

Soon after her first kiss, Yuri is pulled into a puddle and transported to an ancient Middle Eastern village. Surrounded by strange people speaking a language she can't understand, Yuri has no idea how to get back home and is soon embroiled in the politics and romance of the ancient Middle East. If a kiss helped get Yuri into this mess, can a kiss get her out?

RED RIVER

Start your graphic novel collection today!

ONLY $9.95!

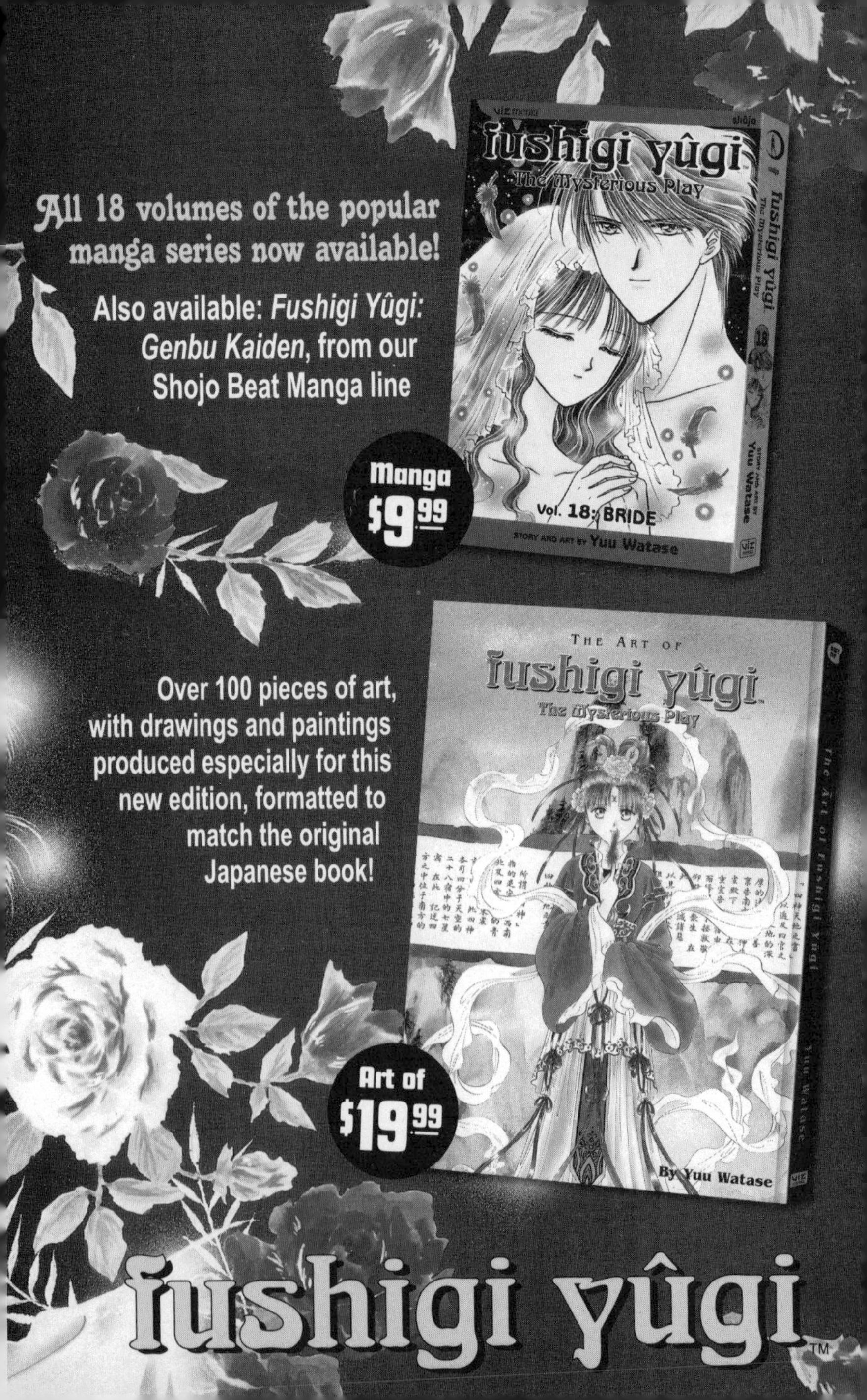

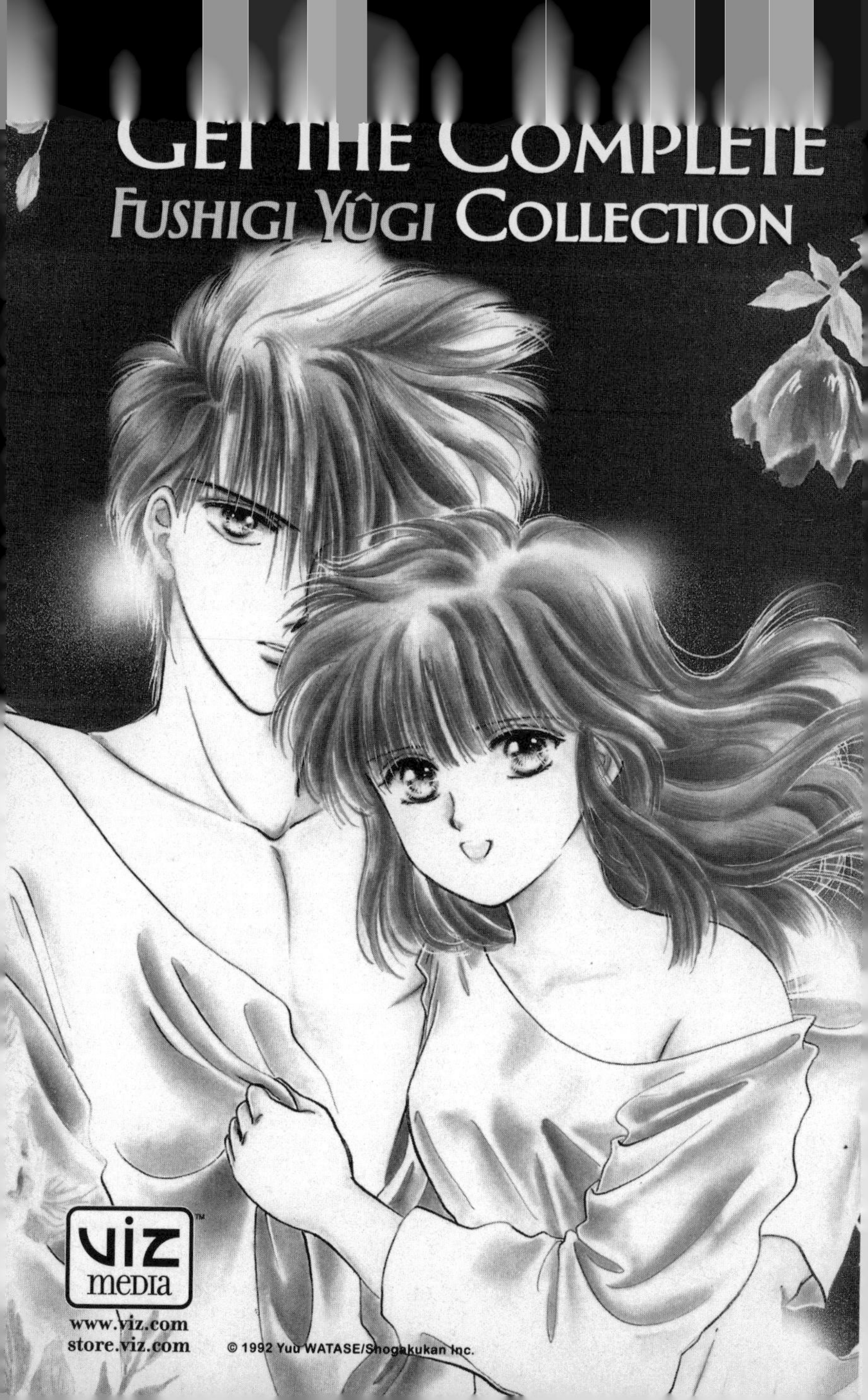
GET THE COMPLETE
FUSHIGI YÛGI COLLECTION
VIZ media™
www.viz.com
store.viz.com
© 1992 Yuu WATASE/Shogakukan Inc.

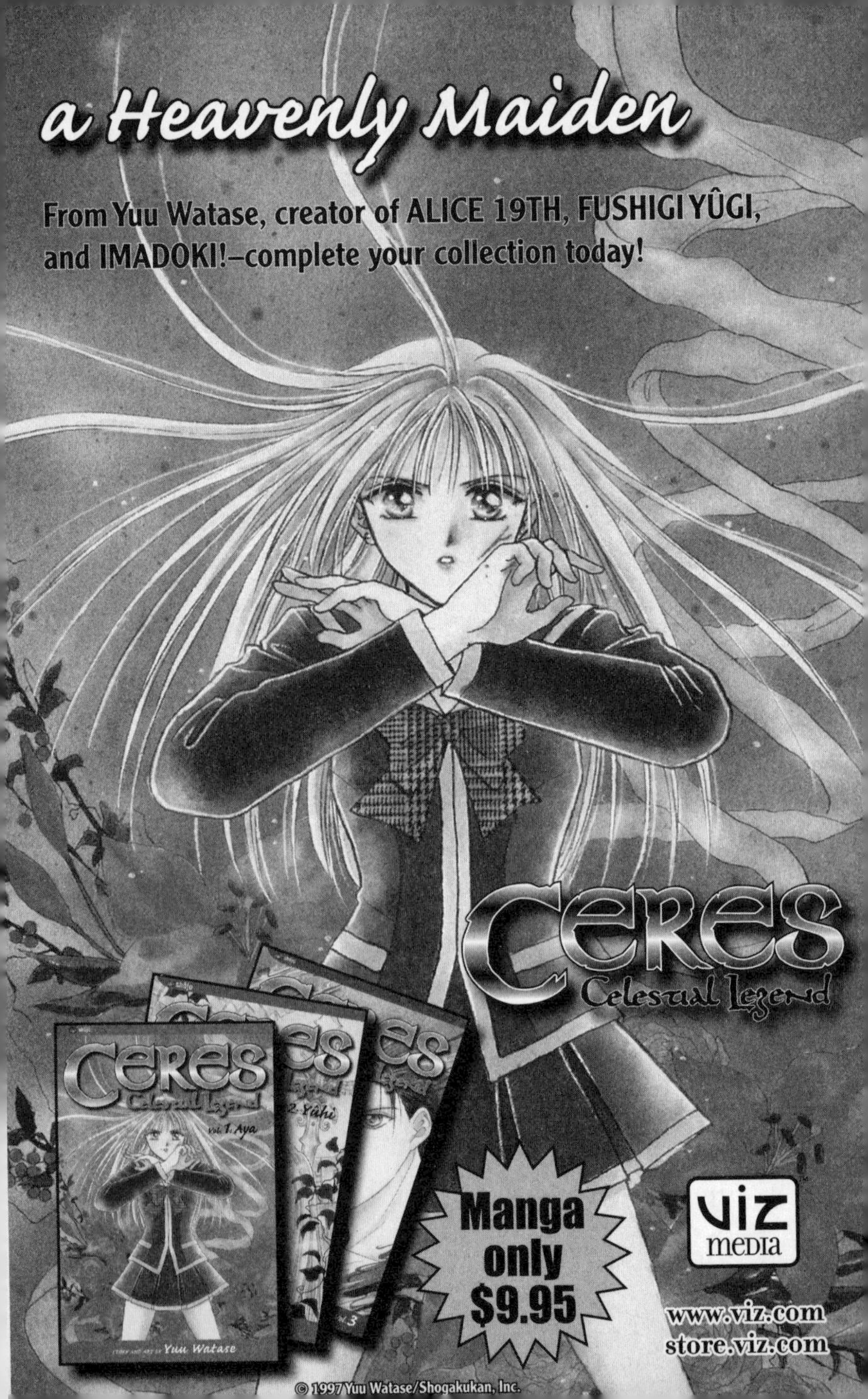
a Heavenly Maiden
From Yuu Watase, creator of ALICE 19TH, FUSHIGI YÛGI, and IMADOKI!–complete your collection today!
Ceres
Celestial Legend
Manga only $9.95
viz media
www.viz.com
store.viz.com
© 1997 Yuu Watase/Shogakukan, Inc.

Hell Hath No Fury Like

When an angel named Ceres is reincarnated in 16-year-old Aya Mikage, Aya becomes a liability to her family's survival. Not only does Ceres want revenge against the Mikage family for past wrongs, but her power is also about to manifest itself. Can Aya control Ceres' hold on her, or will her family mark her for death?

Complete anime series on two DVD box sets– 12 episodes per volume

only $49.98 each!

©Yuu Watase / Shogakukan • Bandai Visual • Studio Pierrot